It is conduct alone that shows whether
a man is good or bad, pure or impure.
RAMAYANA

The Heart Knows No Colour

Praba Moodley

KWELA BOOKS

Copyright © 2003 Prabashini Moodley c/o Kwela Books
40 Heerengracht, Cape Town 8001;
P.O. Box 6525, Roggebaai 8012
http://www.kwela.com

All rights reserved
No part of this book may be reproduced or transmitted in any form or
by any electronic or mechanical means, including photocopying and
recording, or by any other information storage or retrieval system,
without written permission from the publisher

Cover design by Andrew van der Merwe
Typography by Nazli Jacobs
Set in Erhardt
Printed and bound by Paarl Print
Oosterland Street, Paarl, South Africa

First edition, first printing 2003

ISBN 0-7957-0159-4

Dedicated to
Our forefathers

Who were courageous enough to
venture into the unknown and
determined enough to succeed.

For teaching us to be strong
and proud of
our culture and heritage.

ACKNOWLEDGEMENTS

Words will never be quite enough to express the immense
gratitude I feel towards

My parents,
Sathya and Kowsilla Naidoo,
for introducing me
to the wonderful world of books at a very early age.
My husband,
Ravi,
for giving me the space to put words to paper.
My sisters,
Neereshini and Thigeshri,
who continue to lend an ear . . .
My grandmother (Amma)
For always being strong and caring.

Cedric Samson for guiding me in the direction of Kwela Books,
Annari van der Merwe and her team at Kwela Books for
breaking boundaries and paving the way,
for asking me to trust them.
I did!
Henrietta Rose-Innes for her meticulous
editing, questions, and suggestions.
You were marvellous to work with!

To family and friends,
and Lynn Smith for her invaluable report.

Thank you all for your wonderful support.

PRABASHINI

PART ONE

CHAPTER ONE
1879

The young woman, spread-eagled on the wet, makeshift bed, perspired profusely. She moved her head from side to side, as if the movement alone could ward off the terrible pain.

"Don't be anxious," the older woman, draped in a simple red cotton sari, comforted her. "This will be over soon."

Another anguished cry escaped Ganga's parched lips. All she really wanted was for the pain to end and to bring her legs together, but Chumpa was holding her knees apart as she peered between them.

"Once you hold your little one in your arms, this will all seem worth it," Chumpa went on in a soothing tone. "Now, push as hard as you can."

Although Chumpa spoke encouragingly, she was concerned. Ganga had to deliver her baby soon: ten hours of labour at sea was not easy, and the young woman looked drained.

"Push, Ganga, push as hard as you can," she coaxed, as Ganga drew in a deep breath and pushed with all the strength she could muster. "I can see the baby's head. Please, just give me one more push," Chumpa begged.

As if sensing her urgency, Ganga responded and the baby slipped into Chumpa's waiting hands. Even before Chumpa could smack his slippery bottom he gave a healthy yell, which brought a smile to his mother's parched lips.

Quickly Chumpa cleaned both mother and son before settling the baby to suckle at his mother's tender breast. Chumpa knew that the young father was pacing anxiously outside the cabin door. She could hear the chatter of the other passengers who had gathered around Veerasamy Pillai to give him support.

"Congratulations, Veerasamy. You have a healthy son to carry your name," she announced as she allowed him into the hot, stuffy cabin. Chumpa's heart filled with joy at the look of love and pride in Veerasamy's eyes as he approached his wife. Ganga seemed to have drifted off to sleep, quite content for her son to suckle. Veerasamy stood spellbound at the sight before him.

"Go on," Chumpa nudged, "pick him up. He won't mind."

Veerasamy gave her an uncertain look, but encouraged, he reached over to pick up his son for the very first time. Ganga, sensing the baby's removal, opened her eyes. Her husband smiled at her tenderly. "He is so perfect." Slowly he sank to his knees and placed their son back in his wife's waiting arms.

Chumpa watched the love that radiated from the young parents, and silently wished them happiness and good fortune. Like her own family, they too were starting a new venture in a foreign land.

Sewcharran, Chumpa sighed, had never looked at her like that. After twenty years of marriage, Chumpa had long given up hope of ever seeing love in his eyes. Only lust. Yet she had remained a faithful wife, and had borne him eight children. Only four had survived. Over the years, Chumpa had learnt to become a typical, subservient Indian wife, dressed in the traditional cotton sari with a red dot on her forehead. She had learnt to tolerate her husband for the sake of peace and stability in her home. Now, much against her will, they were all on their way to Natal, in South Africa.

Looking at the young couple wrapped in the warm cloak of love, Chumpa prayed for a brighter future, not only for them, but for all the immigrants on board the ship which carried them from their motherland. She knew how much courage it took for them to leave their loved ones for the promise of a better life in a strange country.

"Chumpa," Ganga's tired but contented voice broke her reverie. "Look, my baby is fast asleep." The young mother was still awake, and gazing lovingly at her son.

Chumpa gave her a small smile. "Come," she tapped Veerasamy on his bony shoulder, "Ganga needs her rest. Go on and celebrate your son's arrival with your friends. You will have to name him according to his star and have his fortune read. There should be a yogi in Natal who can tell us what the future has in store for him," she reminded him as she ushered him out. Then she turned back to Ganga and the baby.

"He is so beautiful," Chumpa said, her voice was filled with years of motherly pride and longing.

Ganga lifted shining black eyes. "When you are a grandmother then you, too, will have a baby to spoil. You have such lovely children."

"Thank you," Chumpa said sadly. "I pray that they find the love and happiness that you and Veerasamy have."

"Why," Ganga's eyes opened with curiosity, "haven't you been happy?"

Chumpa gave her a melancholy smile. "Happy" was not a word she would use to describe her marriage. "I suppose I am one of those unfortunate women who do not have a fine, loving marriage, as you do."

"I am so sorry to hear that," Ganga's voice filled with compassion. "You are such a loving and gentle person!"

"Thank you for those lovely words . . . but . . ."

"It is so unfair," interrupted Ganga. "We should all be loved and appreciated. After all, Chumpa, look at what we have to go through, and you have borne your husband so many children!" Her voice dropped. "You must feel some sort of love towards your husband, and he must love you as well."

"My feelings for Sewcharran have nothing to do with my children," Chumpa replied, wondering why she was finally giving vent to her feelings to a young woman not much older than her eldest daughter. Perhaps it was Ganga's sincere concern and their shared experience of motherhood that eased conversation between them.

Slowly, she began in a voice that was barely a whisper: "I think it was during my first time with Sewcharran that I conceived." She shut her eyes. "I remember so clearly how hard I had to work in those early days as a daughter-in-law. I also learnt that my new husband was quick with his hands." Chumpa brought her hands up to her face, as though to shut off the horrible images that had suddenly flooded her mind, bringing back the past with such clarity. "He used to have the most dreadful fights with his brothers," she said softly, as though afraid he would hear and come charging in, after her again. "They could not even talk to me or look at me."

"See, he does love you," Ganga said.

"No," Chumpa shook her head. "It is not love that he feels, but ownership. That is one of the reasons he decided to leave India." She paced the tiny cabin, as though to escape the memories that haunted her. "I had one more month to go before my baby arrived, and I was dropping with fatigue. The day was unbearably hot, and I was so terribly uncomfortable. Sewcharran was not in the best of moods. His younger brother had been kind to me, helping me clear the fireplace and build the fire, and Sewcharran thought that . . ." Chumpa paused, her voice trembling with unshed tears. "I remember praying that a good meal would soothe him. I was so wrong!" Chumpa's laughter was filled with pain. "That night he wanted me. To show his brother that he owned me."

"How could he?" Ganga was aghast. "You were almost ready to deliver his child!"

"I told him that I was exhausted, and that it was not good for the baby, but you see, Ganga, he was drunk and too angry to listen." A shiver ran through Chumpa. "I only managed to increase his anger and he . . . beat me. All I can recall of that night was his rage." Tears rolled down Chumpa's cheeks as finally, after two decades of silence, she spoke of her past. "He punched and kicked me . . . on my swollen belly. Before I passed out I prayed that my baby was not harmed in any way." Wiping her eyes with the edge of her sari, Chumpa stared at Ganga's baby sorrowfully as she continued. "I don't remember . . . exactly what happened, but I was told that I went into labour. After many hours, floating in and out of consciousness, I gave birth to a baby girl. I never saw her." Chumpa heard Ganga's intake of breath. "His family . . . said she was born dead." Her voice dripped with bitterness. "They buried her quickly."

"Oh, Chumpa," Ganga's eyes filled with tears. "You have been through such hell . . ."

For a long moment Chumpa sat lost in memory, gazing at the baby. "Ah, come now," she sighed at last. "Today is a happy day. I am sorry to have put this on you. You must rest now. I will return later, to check on you and the little one." Chumpa attempted a smile of bravery as she tucked a lose bit of hair behind Ganga's ear.

Before Chumpa closed the door behind her, she took a quick look at the sleeping pair, and smiled. Her heart felt lighter.

The cool, gentle ocean breeze matched the peace within Chumpa. When she spotted her almost thirteen-year-old daughter her heart overflowed with pride. This child, with her heart-shaped face, dimpled chin and slender limbs, was growing up to be very graceful and beautiful.

"Sita!" she called out, and as the girl turned, Chumpa saw her face light up.

"Majee, how is Ganga and the baby? Veerasamy is so thrilled he has a son!"

"They are fine, Beti. He is a beautiful baby." Chumpa put her arm around her youngest daughter.

"You were wonderful, Ma." Sita hugged her mother. "I don't know how Ganga would have managed without you."

"Someone else would have helped." Chumpa replied in a matter-of-fact tone. "Soon we will be in a new land, Sita," she said, changing the subject.

Sita took hold of Chumpa's hands. "Majee, are you not a little bit frightened?"

Chumpa freed her hands from her daughter's tight grip. "My Beti," she replied as she cupped Sita's smooth face between her roughened palms, "I am terrified!" She smiled. "But I have my family with me, and together we will find the courage and strength to meet whatever awaits us." She placed a gentle kiss on Sita's forehead.

"Oh, Ma," Sita hugged her mother fiercely.

"You know what?" Chumpa forced brightness into her voice. "Seeing Ganga and her baby made me wish I were a grandmother."

"Ma!" Sita looked at her mother in surprise. "You are still too young to even think about being a grandmother. Wait at least until Geeta gets married," she grinned.

"And when you marry as well."

Sita pulled away from her instantly. "Ma, you know how I feel."

"Sita . . ."

"Majee," Sita turned to Chumpa stubbornly. "I am not going to let some man boss and bully me and turn me into his slave. I don't want to get married. I know that girls my age are already betrothed, but it's not for me!"

"Beti . . ." Chumpa's voice cracked with pain. But the look on her daughter's face told her that she was wasting her time.

Sita was such a high-spirited girl; she reminded Chumpa of herself – before she married Sewcharran, and he destroyed every shred of independence and gaiety she possessed. Geeta, on the other hand, was different. Three years older than Sita, she could not wait to marry and start a family of her own. She had agreed to marry a boy of her parents' choice, and Chumpa was training her well.

Chumpa had decided a long time ago that her daughters would marry into good homes, to husbands who would take care of them. She was determined that her daughters would turn out to be excellent wives and mothers – but so far, only Geeta seemed to be co-operating.

"Hurry up, hurry up, we don't have all day," a strange voice barked.

Small boats had been sent out to the ship to bring the immigrants ashore. After a couple of months of seasickness and bouts of terrible illness, which came with living on an overcrowded ship, relief was clearly written on their faces; in their haste to set foot on land, the newcomers virtually fell over one another.

On shore, confusion reigned, for many could not understand English. First, they had to undergo a medical examination and several tests. They were handed a strange liquid in bottles and told to bathe with it, to cleanse them from head to toe after months of travel. Chumpa felt like a cow on show as a white doctor peered into her ears and mouth, and a nurse checked her hair for lice.

Mr Kandasami, the appointed 'Coolie Agent', was given the task of explaining to the new arrivals what to expect and what was expected of them. He was to be of assistance to both the indentured labourers and their respective employers.

Sewcharran and Chumpa were assigned to the Campbell Sugar Estate in Verulam. "You will be earning ten shillings a month, Sewcharran Suklal, and your wife will earn five. You will also be given a place to stay and you will receive a sizeable ration every month from the Campbell Estate," Mr Kandasami explained to them in Hindi, although they had already been told the terms when they put their thumb-print to the recruitment papers in their home town.

"And what about my eldest boy?" Sewcharran pulled Gopi towards the Coolie Agent for inspection. "He is almost a man. Shouldn't he be earning ten shillings as well?" he demanded.

Taking in Gopi's tall but scrawny frame, Mr Kandasami replied in a stern voice. "I will have to speak to your Master and inform him of your boy." Then, in a much gentler tone, he added, "I am sure he could use another strong pair of hands."

Sewcharran did not miss the look of doubt. "My boy is strong," he insisted.

By the look on young Gopi's face and the sudden tenseness of his mother's body, Mr Kandasami realised that they were terrified of Sewcharran, and he felt pity for them. He hoped that life here would not bring disappointment and disillusionment to Chumpa and her children.

"You are contracted to Master Campbell for five years. After the five years expires you will receive a discharge certificate."

"What exactly are you saying?" Sewcharran interrupted tersely.

"Simply that during your five years on the Estate you cannot leave. However, once you have completed your contract," he explained patiently, "you can decide whether you want to carry on working for Master Campbell on the plantation or not. The decision is yours. If you choose to stay on he will give you a wage increase every year. If not, then you may seek your fortune elsewhere or return to India." Mr Kandasami smiled wistfully, wondering: will these people ever be able to rise above being mere indentured labourers?

Amidst the noise and chaos at the recruitment centre, Chumpa was surprised to learn that Ganga and Veerasamy Pillai were assigned to a plantation not far from the Campbell Estate.

"We will be working for Master Browne," Veerasamy supplied the information eagerly. "He has a sugar mill and I hope to work there, if I am lucky."

"Please come and visit us on your free day," invited Ganga.

"We will," Chumpa promised, as she gently rocked Veerasamy's son in her arms.

Master Campbell was a tall and powerfully built man who preferred to collect his labourers personally. His black pants were tucked into hardworking black boots, and Chumpa admired the snow-white shirt he wore. Suddenly she felt very self-conscious. How strange they all must look to this man! She in an old, faded cotton sari with rings in her nose and two gold bangles on each arm; Sewcharran in his old shirt, with a dhoti wrapped around his hips and thighs. Her sons were dressed in similar attire, and her daughters in long skirts and blouses that covered them fully. Under their long blouses they too wore gold bangles.

Chumpa clutched her little bundle of clothes to her. As Master Campbell neared them she moved closer to her family, as though to protect them from this imposing stranger.

Then he smiled, and Chumpa felt something move inside her. She liked the way his thick reddish-brown moustache curled, and saw the compassion in his eyes. Suddenly, she realised that it was going to be all right.

Master Campbell listened very carefully to Mr Kandasami before nodding and turning to the Suklals, giving them his full attention.

Mr Kandasami explained that Master Campbell had agreed to employ them all, as he did not like splitting up a family, and that they need not worry. There was plenty of work for everyone in his estate.

So the Suklals, with their small bundles of clothes, their precious seeds to start a small herb garden and few pieces of valuable jewellery, followed their new Master to begin life on his sugar-cane plantation.

The air was hot and stifling and did nothing to eliminate the smells of unwashed people that hung thick and heavy around them. The yelling, and the laughter, and the crying of people lost was clamorous and confusing, and it sank deep into Chumpa's memory, like a drop of bright red blood against a snow-white piece of Indian cotton.

CHAPTER TWO

1882

"It is simply unbelievable that we are here for three years, now," remarked Chumpa as she looked at her family. They were seated cross-legged on grass mats in a circle as she served them their evening meal of fish curry and mielie rice – a rare treat.

Gopi was nineteen today, and his sister Geeta exactly a year younger. Sita was just sixteen and Bharath had another three months to go before turning fourteen. To Chumpa, they would always remain her babies, no matter how tall her sons grew or how much her daughters blossomed into young women. She served Sewcharran the first helping before moving on to Gopi. She placed a little extra on his tin plate, as a special birthday treat. Besides, she decided he needed fattening up. Chumpa ensured her children had their small plates filled before helping herself to the tiny portion left in the pot. There were too many nights when they went to bed on hungry stomachs.

"So what?" Sewcharran's retort caused his children and Chumpa to look up, startled at the vehemence in his voice. "We work like animals here. We have to be up before the sun rises in the east, and toil in these stupid fields until after the sun sets in the west, and they even expect us to work on a Sunday, without any extra pay!"

"Really, father, all you do is complain – and yet you are the one who insisted that we come to this place."

Sita's reminder brought a bellow of anger from Sewcharran: "Don't you 'father' me, girl!" he yelled, eyes round and bulging with rage. "Just because you are fortunate enough to work in the Big House, don't think that you can come home and use those fancy English terms on me. You will call me Pithaji, like you always have!" he wagged a thick and blistered finger at her.

Sita opened her mouth to reply, but a nudge from her mother and the sudden silence in the room warned her to refrain from talking back. She read the danger signal in Chumpa's eyes before bowing her head wordlessly. Her father's outburst had stolen her appetite.

Sleep did not come easily that night to either of the Suklal girls. The muggy Natal night made them feel sweaty and restless, and the buzzing of mosquitoes was an irritation they could well do without. Outside, they could hear the tempting whispers of the surf in the distance. It was one of those nights when a walk on the sand would have been a magical treat.

Sita still felt the anger in her at her father's words, but in her heart she knew he was right. She was fortunate to be working at the Big House while the rest of her family slaved in the fields all day long.

The excitement of her pending marriage kept Geeta awake. "Sita," whispered Geeta, after Sita turned on her side for the umpteenth time. "Are you awake?"

"Who could sleep in this heat, and with mosquitoes for company?" Sita slapped one that stung her arm.

"I know." Ignoring the irritation in her sister's voice, Geeta continued in an excited whisper: "But imagine, Sita, two more months to go before I become Anoop's wife. I can't wait for my wedding night. Can you?"

"What, wait for your wedding night?" Sita suddenly found her sister's question hilarious, and giggled.

"No, silly." Geeta poked her in her ribs. "*Your* wedding night."

"Whatever for? I don't want to be married and you know that!"

"How can you say that? You have to marry."

"Where does it say that I have to marry?" Sita retorted in a hot whisper.

"Sita Suklal, you really should watch your tongue," Geeta scolded, adopting a stern older-sister tone. "Pithaji is right. Since you started at the Big House . . . you have changed."

"And why shouldn't I?" demanded Sita rebelliously. "I only want to improve myself. I do not want to marry someone I do not love, and have his children. Besides," she smiled, her voice taking on a teasing tone, "I have not met a man here who meets my needs as yet."

"Oh, and what needs are those?" Geeta's eyes narrowed shrewdly, and in the moonlight which streamed through the small window, she reminded Sita once more of their father.

Sita evaded Geeta's question. "And Albert says that I must be very intelligent to speak English so well," she ended in a whisper, and then wished she had kept her mouth shut. The last thing she needed now was probing questions from her sister.

Geeta continued to scrutinise her with narrowed eyes, and then remarked rather casually: "Albert . . . huh, isn't he Madam Elizabeth's brother?"

Sita nodded. "Apparently he is here to learn about managing the estate."

"What is he like?" Geeta inquired. She hardly came into contact with the people from the Big House, and she envied Sita.

"Like a normal man with two legs," Sita retorted.

"Oh, come on!"

"Well . . . let me see . . ." Sita closed her eyes and the image of Albert Sheldon filled her mind and her heart. "He is tall and slender. Unlike Master Campbell with his strong muscles. No," she decided, "he is more like Gopi Bhai, although he may be slightly older."

"Go on," Geeta prompted when Sita paused, lost in her memories.

Sita turned on her tummy, and the faraway look in her brown almond-shaped eyes gave Geeta reason to frown. "His hair is slightly curly and dark brown and his eyes are slightly lighter than mine. I think he has the lightest, most beautiful brown eyes I have ever seen."

"Sita! You should not be saying such things," Geeta chastised, her face turning bright red with embarrassment. Sometimes Sita could really say the most outrageous things. "It is not proper for an Indian girl to look at a white man with teasing eyes. You are asking for trouble."

"Oh, don't be such a stuck-up. I don't look at him with teasing eyes,"

Sita retaliated. "You asked what he is like and all I did was tell you." Sita wondered why Geeta was getting so upset.

"But . . . you just told me that he actually *spoke* to you," Geeta reminded her.

"No," declared Sita emphatically, "all he said was that I speak very well for an Indian."

"Still, that doesn't explain how you met him," Geeta persisted, as she shifted into a more comfortable position.

"All right." Sita gave up trying to be evasive. "I'll tell you." She knew from Geeta's determined look that she would not be able to get a wink of sleep if she did not tell her everything, or very nearly everything. "I was returning home and somehow I lost my earring and was looking for it when he came across me. It is the truth," Sita defended herself, hearing Geeta's gasp of disbelief. "Please don't tell Majee that I have lost the earring. She would be most upset." Sita paused dramatically, knowing that her sister would promise, for curiosity often got the better of her.

"I won't tell, I promise. Now go on."

"You should have listened to him, Geeta," Sita giggled mischievously. "He was trying to speak to me in Hindi and it was terrible."

"You're having me on!" Geeta joined her laughter. "And what did you say?" she managed, between giggles.

"I replied in my haughtiest English voice: 'I have lost my earring', and for a second he just stared at me as though I were unreal, before bursting into laughter. When I asked him what was so funny he replied that the joke was on him, and that I spoke better English than most 'coolies' he meets. I then looked him in the eye and said, 'I prefer to be called an Indian.'"

"What did he say to that?" Geeta smothered her laugh. She could just imagine her little sister appearing English and haughty.

"He just laughed harder and added that I was cheeky as well."

"Well, he is not far off in his observations. Does he know who you are?"

"No . . . I don't think so."

"Just make sure that you don't say or do anything that will hurt Majee or bring shame to this family," warned Geeta seriously. "You know how important respect is to her. Besides, Pithaji will kill you."

"What are you implying?" Sita turned to Geeta, eyes round with confusion.

"You know, in here." Geeta pointed to her heart, with all the wisdom of an older sister who was about to be married.

"Huh, you are just imagining things," Sita whispered heatedly before turning her back to Geeta, irritated that her sister knew her so well, and vowing never to discuss anything personal with her again.

"Well, it probably runs in the blood," Geeta added, before turning away from Sita as well.

Finally, Sita managed to fall asleep, with the image of Albert Sheldon burnt in her memory. He was so strong and healthy, and the hot Natal sun lent him a nice brown colour that made him look almost like a fair-skinned Indian. Not like the Indians, Sita decided, who worked in the fields. No, they were sunburnt due to the many hours they toiled in the harsh South African climate.

Albert, Sita decided, looked like a fair-skinned Gujurati businessman. She admired his gentle manner of speaking, and when she heard his soft, clear laugh her skin tingled and her cheeks burned.

Chumpa, who had let her family stay in bed a little longer than usual as it was Sunday and they actually had the day off, decided that it was time for them to get up. She had not seen the Pillais for a couple of months now. Ganga was due to have her third child, and Chumpa had promised to be there to help with the birth. "If we don't hurry we are going to be late." She smacked Bharath playfully on his head as he groaned and tried to snuggle up to Gopi.

"Late for what?" Gopi groaned, sleepily.

"Don't ask questions. Just get up," Chumpa ordered as she sorted their clothing. Chumpa made sure that her children were always neatly dressed, no matter how old their clothes were or how many times she patched them up.

"Time to visit Veerasamy, I see," observed Gopi, as he watched his mother pack her small bamboo basket with fresh herbs that she had grown in their tiny back garden.

"You know how Veerasamy likes these herbs," she replied. Chumpa had been so happy when Gopi had befriended Veerasamy. Their friendship made visiting the young couple so much more enjoyable. Sewcharran, on the other hand, preferred to stay at home and get drunk on cane spirit. Chumpa decided that it was best to leave him alone so that he could sleep off his liquor, and then there would be no arguments.

This morning was no different from the few other free Sundays that they'd had, except that Sita had to report to the Big House.

"Majee, Madam Elizabeth has asked me to help with the children. They have been invited to tea with the Brownes . . ."

"Why didn't you say so earlier?" Chumpa scolded. "You know I don't like leaving one of you behind."

"Ma, I can take care of myself. Besides, I'll be busy. I don't want to spoil your only free day." She smiled sweetly at Chumpa and gave her a quick hug.

"Sita is right, Majee. Besides, Ganga is expecting us," Geeta added, wanting to leave as soon as possible. She was going to see Anoop as well, and could not wait.

"All right," Chumpa conceded, and Sita waved goodbye to them before hurriedly wrapping into a small bundle a pretty yellow blouse and matching skirt she liked to wear on her days off. She also packed an old but clean set of underwear and the treasured, rose-scented soap Madam Elizabeth had given her.

Even after three years, the sight of the big white house never failed to send a thrill through her. Indar, an indentured labourer who had green fingers and loved taking care of the Campbell's massive garden, kept the sprawling lawns immaculate. The roses bloomed bright and colourful and filled the garden with intoxicating scents. Elizabeth often said she wanted her garden to remind her of her home in England, even though the climate was so different. The interior of the house was just as impressive: dark wood and beautiful carpets covered the floors and sunlight filtered through lace, making the house bright and airy. At night the heavy red velvet curtains were drawn, bathing the house in darkness and privacy.

Sumi, who had arrived as a young girl with an earlier batch of labourers in the sixties, maintained the house with the pride of an owner. She had spent almost two decades with the Campbells, and loved to show off her culinary skills for the family. Sumi, famous for her curries, was utterly devoted to her employers.

Sita was employed as Sumi's helper, together with a young African girl, Mbali.

Although Sita helped with the cleaning of the Big House, her main task was to take care of the two Campbell children. Elizabeth Campbell discovered quite by chance that Sita had a way with her children when she found her carrying the crying, two-year-old Richard in her arms and rocking him to sleep, singing a gentle lullaby in a language sweet and different. It was this special rapport with the children that Elizabeth found so appealing. She insisted Sita learn English, and allowed her a couple of afternoons off to take some reading and writing lessons from the children's governess. Sita was a quick learner, and her grasp of English made life at the Big House much less complicated. Sita also utilised the lessons to her advantage. She taught her family to read, write and speak English.

Dressing the children proved a tiresome task for Sita. It was a humid afternoon and they were beginning to feel confined in their elegant clothes.

"Are you also invited to the party?" asked Charlotte. She was a typical eight-year-old: full of questions, demanding answers.

"No."

"Why not?" she asked right back. Charlotte was a pretty child with lovely red hair, which fell in ringlets down her back, and which she fiddled with. When she did not get her way she loved to pout – a habit Sita was trying to get her to break.

"Because this party is just for you," she explained carefully. "I am not invited."

"Well, I am inviting you," piped Richard, now almost five. He simply loved giving orders.

"Oh, little Richard," Sita sighed, as she went down on her knees to straighten his bow tie. "When you are older and have a party and invite me, I will come."

"But I want you to come with us, now!" He stamped his small foot and wailed.

"What on earth is going on in here?" Elizabeth Campbell entered the nursery. She looked very cool and elegant in a peach muslin gown, and wore her dark brown hair in a neat chignon. For a petite lady she carried herself with an air of regality. Sita admired her femininity and elegance; without realising it, she used Madam Elizabeth as a role model.

At the sight of his mother, Richard began to wail. "Mama, I want Sita to come with us."

Elizabeth looked at his little red face and shook her head. How could she take an Indian girl to high tea? As much as she liked Sita, she could not expect her hostess to welcome the girl.

"Sweetheart," she began, "Sita has been working very hard and this is her day off. Today, she has come to help as a special favour to Mama," she explained softly but firmly, wiping away his tears. "Tell you what," she decided, seeing his crestfallen expression and the tears that threatened to spill from Charlotte's green eyes, "Tomorrow we will have our very own tea party, and Sita, you are invited as our very special guest."

The children turned to Sita eagerly.

"Thank you. I am honour," she said.

"It is, 'I am honoured', Sita," Elizabeth corrected her.

"Yes, Madam."

After bidding them goodbye and lending Sumi a hand in the kitchen with the evening meal, Sita picked up her bundle and made her way across the plantation. Chewing on a piece of sugar cane and enjoying the sweet juice, she headed directly for the little stream that bordered the estate.

It was on one such a free Sunday afternoon that she had discovered, amidst the high grass which grew along the stream, the most beautiful natural pool, overgrown and unused. She cleared a path to the pool and kept the surrounding area free of weeds. This little haven was her special secret place. Often she went there to bathe. Water was rationed and they had to take care of what little they received, and so she made the best of the pool. Sita was aware of how selfish she was to keep it a secret, but it brought her such pleasure she could not bear to share it with anyone.

The huge wattle trees hid her little pool, giving her a sense of safety and freedom. Humming to herself, she stripped away her clothes, and standing naked as the day she was born, she rose on her toes and stretched her arms above her head, before drawing in a deep breath and diving into the pool. The cold water hit her hard and she came up gasping for air. A tinkle of laughter escaped through her full lips as she floated on her back for a while, before reaching for the rose-scented soap. Slowly, lazily, Sita lathered her long, black hair and her slim body. All the while she sang to herself in her warm, husky voice.

It was the voice that drew and held his attention, causing him to stop and listen. The words were unusual and yet so melodious. He felt himself drawn towards that husky sound, which he found sweet and hypnotic. He dismounted from his horse and cautiously made his way towards the voice, holding the reins in his hand.

The sight that met his eyes made him catch his breath. Guiltily, he stepped behind the wattle tree and looked away. No gentleman would ever spy on an unsuspecting female, he told himself. And yet the urge to look captured him, and he found himself turning to gaze at her.

He had never seen a more beautiful sight than the one before him. The girl stooped to cup water in her hands. Mesmerised, he watched as she brought it up to wash away the rich lather to reveal full, firm breasts. He drank in her warm, honey-toned skin and wondered at its golden hue: most Indians, even the women, were darker.

She was mysterious and lovely; he longed to reach out and touch her, to make sure she was real. His longing to run his hands down her smooth, satiny skin and make her come alive beneath his touch alarmed him. He wiped his sweaty palms on the front of his trousers. His heart was beating so fiercely he was sure she could hear it. He had never felt like this before, never in his twenty-two years.

Her eyes, he noticed from where he was hidden, were most unusual. They were slanted upwards, and her lashes were long and curly against her cheeks. She looked familiar . . . and then he remembered where he had met her. She was the young girl who had lost an earring, and who had surprised him with her ability to speak English. She had impressed him then; now she fascinated him.

Emerging from the pool, she moved with unconscious grace. He wanted to reach out and span her slender waist with his hands and draw her gently rounded hips to him. As his eyes moved lower he tensed, fighting down his desire. Her thighs were firm and her legs shapely, with dainty ankles he knew many an English lass would die for. Silently, holding his breath, he watched as she bent to pick up an old, clean cloth and very slowly, as though savouring the sensation, wipe herself dry.

Burning with desire, he knew that he could not stand to watch her a minute longer and turned, a bit too sharply, towards his horse. Thunder snorted loudly in protest at his master's sudden action.

Sita's heart lurched with fear as she swung around. Her brown eyes widened in terror when they clashed with that of the white man's. Her heart pounded, as rapid as a drum-beat, as he stepped forward.

Opening her mouth to scream was a futile effort, she discovered. Instead she felt herself go limp, and darkness surrounded her. Her last thought was for him not to hurt her.

"Damn!" Albert Sheldon swore as he rushed forward to catch her a split second before she hit the ground. Gently, as though she was made of porcelain, he gathered her in his arms and placed her on the ground. Quickly he covered her with the cloth she had used to dry herself, before turning to dip his handkerchief into the pool where minutes ago he had watched her bathe.

Tenderly he wiped her forehead and patted her smooth cheek. "Come on, sweetheart," he coaxed, "open your beautiful eyes for me."

For a couple of seconds she lay still, and then, very slowly, her lids fluttered like the wings of a captured butterfly.

"Are you all right?" Albert asked, his voice thick with concern.

Sita opened her mouth to respond, and still no words came out. A shiver ran through her as she stared at him; then suddenly she realised that she was lying naked on the ground, with just a cloth barely covering her.

"My clothes . . ." she stammered in English, mortified; but Albert made no move to help her. Instead his eyes travelled over her body, slowly and lazily. No man had ever looked at her like that.

"I am sorry," he apologised, without taking his eyes off her. "I did not mean to frighten you. It is just that you are so very beautiful," he whispered, his English accent becoming more pronounced. He ran a finger down her cheek.

Sita's cheek was aflame and she lowered her lashes quickly, not wanting him to see her shyness.

"Please get dressed, and I will walk you to where you live."

"No!" Sita suddenly came alive. How could he even suggest such a thing? If her father caught her walking home with a white man, he would surely kill her. "Please go . . . leave me alone," she begged, her eyes round with unspoken fear.

Albert found her accent charming, her voice velvety soft. His eyes were drawn to her full lips, and he wondered if they felt and tasted as soft and sweet as they looked. He adored the cleft on her chin.

Sita read the look in his eyes, and suddenly she was too scared to even move. Slowly, as though giving her a chance to pull away from him, he cupped her face very gently in his palms and lowered his lips to hers, hesitating for just a fraction of a second. Instinctively, Albert knew that she had never been kissed before, and a thrill ran through him when he felt her tremble in his arms. Slowly, he moved his lips over hers and gently parted them with his tongue. She tasted of sugar cane.

Sita's lids felt heavy, and as he deepened the kiss her lids closed and her limbs went slack. She did not have the strength to push him away. Her body felt alive and yet drugged at the same time, and feelings she never knew existed, engulfed her.

As though in a dream, she lifted her arms and brought them across his back – unthinkingly bringing them closer together. Her fingertips burned with the heat of his body.

Her response delighted and aroused him. His lips slid across her baby-smooth cheeks and down towards her neck, which she lifted with the grace of a swan to allow him to explore her loveliness. A little moan of pleasure escaped from Sita, and Albert felt himself respond.

His mouth moved further down her neck to the swell of her soft breast, and when he captured one hardened nipple between his lips she instinctively moved towards him.

Albert marvelled at her radiant beauty, and realised that if he were not careful she would steal his heart. He did not even know her name! The sudden realisation made him pull away from her. Sita's eyes flew open instantly and she looked at him in confusion.

"Get dressed," he ordered, his voice gruff with unspoken passion as he turned away. He did not want her to see just how much she had affected him.

Sita did not wait for him to say another word. With hands that trembled she quickly pulled on her clothes.

Albert waited until she had finished dressing before turning to look at her. God, but she looked beautiful, he thought, swallowing a silent moan – for he wanted to take her in his arms again. But he pulled himself together.

"What is your name?" The gruffness remained in his voice, and he put his hands behind his back to avoid touching her.

Sita stared at her toes. She could not bring herself to look at him. Swallowing hard, she whispered, "Sita . . . Suklal."

Albert noticed that she did not add the customary "Sir", and he wanted to laugh. Had he really expected her to call him "Sir" after what they had experienced?

"Look at me." He spoke gently. Giving in to the desire to touch her, he lifted her chin, and was surprised to see the tears that shone so brightly in her eyes. She blinked, and one perfect drop fell onto his hand. His heart swelled with the newness of love for her. "Where are you from, Sita?"

"I live on the estate, but I work at the Big House." Sita glanced in the direction she had come from.

"And I have never seen you there," he remarked, amazed that they had missed each other.

Sita wanted to reach out and touch the crinkles around his eyes.

"My name is Albert Sheldon," he introduced himself. "I am from England . . ."

"I must go," she stammered after a few seconds of silence.

As she stooped to pick up her clothes he bent to help, and their fingers met. Sita pulled away, as though his touch scorched her; then she turned to flee.

Albert watched mesmerised as she grew smaller and smaller in the distance. Her sweet scent had left him intoxicated: he knew he would never smell another rose or taste sugar cane again without thinking of her.

CHAPTER THREE

Sita was breathless by the time she reached home. She stood outside, taking in great gulps of air, not daring to enter until she felt more composed. She wondered if her family would be able to tell that she had somehow changed. Did she look any different? Sita stared at the tiny wattle and daub cottage: how different it was from the magnificent house she worked in during the day!

When her family first arrived at the plantation, they had been allocated rooms in a long building called a barracks, erected solely for the labourers. It was cramped and unhygienic and the Suklals, like the other labourers on the plantation, hated it. When one family of indentured labourers decided to return to India after serving their five-year period, a cottage they had built became available and Sita plucked up the courage to ask Madam Elizabeth if her family could move into it. Permission was granted.

The Suklals were thrilled, although they were aware of the envious talk that went around – that they were favoured because their daughter worked at the Big House. But they ignored the gossip and it died down eventually.

Chumpa turned the little cottage into a comfortable home for her family. After a thorough cleaning, grass mats were placed on the hard floor for them to sit and sleep on. A little part of the cottage was set aside to serve as a kitchen, and Chumpa's sons made a small fireplace for her, so that she could cook their meals and boil water for their weekly baths. Geeta and Sita shared a room with Gopi and Bharath, and Chumpa hung a huge grass mat to divide the room in two, allowing her children some privacy.

Sita swallowed hard as she took in the shabby appearance of her home. Did Albert know that she slept on the hard floor while he had the luxury of a soft bed, a bed she made every morning? They were worlds apart, and the thought brought tears to her eyes and an ache to her young heart.

"What is the matter with you, Sita Suklal?" she admonished herself. "You cannot even think of him. He is not for you at all." Besides, she had already decided that she would never become involved with a man – any man. She was never going to marry.

But she had felt so wonderful and safe in Albert's arms . . . He had held her as though she were the most precious thing on God's green earth. He had not seen the colour of her skin: all he had seen was that she was everything he wanted. A tingle of sudden delight shot through her.

"Sita, don't just stand there. Come on in, Beti," her mother called, and Sita gathered her skirt and ran to her mother. She hugged Chumpa, wanting to spread some of her sudden happiness and good humour.

"Why, Beti, you look so flushed and excited." Chumpa felt her daughter's hot cheeks and saw the sparkle in her eyes. "How was your day?"

"Wonderful," Sita twirled around the tiny room, skirt flying to reveal her slim ankles. "The children wanted me to accompany them to the Brownes. Just imagine, Majee, me at high tea with the English!" she laughed gaily, her earlier feelings of confusion and sadness dissipating.

"Stop imagining," Chumpa scolded, "and listen to me. I met Geeta's future in-laws today and they wanted to know if you were proposed."

Sita's heart lurched, and she stopped twirling immediately to stare at her mother suspiciously. "I hope you told them that I am not interested in a marriage proposal."

Chumpa turned away from her. "I told them that you are not proposed . . ."

Sita's arms went around her and she smothered her mother in quick kisses. "Ma, you are wonderful!"

"Not so fast, little one," Chumpa stepped aside. "They were very pleased because someone has seen you and is very interested."

"What?"

"You heard me," Chumpa replied. Her eyes shone with pride as she smiled at Sita.

Tears of anger filled Sita's eyes as she turned to her mother. "Please, Ma, I am not going to say yes to a marriage proposal just because some boy's parents decided they like the way I look and think I will make a suitable wife!"

"Sita . . . you are no longer a young girl," Chumpa began, and instantly Sita read the message in her voice. Chumpa was going to use her old arguments: that all men were not the same and that she must give it a chance. In a way, she had discovered that her mother was right. All men were not the same. Albert was wonderful, kind, gentle and loving. But the others . . .

Anger and pain made Sita's voice tremble. "Pithaji asked for your hand in marriage – and look at how . . ." The change in Chumpa's expression from happiness to shock stunned Sita for a few seconds into silence before she continued. "I don't want to end up in a loveless marriage like you, Ma. No!" she suddenly stamped her foot. "This is South Africa, not India," she declared, "and *I* will decide who to marry!" A tiny voice told Chumpa that her daughter was right.

"What the hell is going on in here?"

Both Sita and Chumpa jumped in surprise. They had been so caught up in their argument that they had not even noticed Sewcharran enter the kitchen. Both mother and daughter stared at him – Sita a little defiantly, and Chumpa with caution.

"What is this nonsense I hear about you choosing the boy you are going to marry?" he demanded, stepping in front of them.

"It is nothing," Chumpa replied for Sita, moving a step closer to her daughter.

"I have ears. I don't want her feeding you with this English nonsense." His eyes darted to Sita. "I have been approached by the Harilakens for your hand in marriage to their son, Hemith, and I told the father that I will discuss the matter after Geeta's wedding."

"Well, you can tell him that the answer is no, Taj." Sita looked at him with a glint in her almond-shaped eyes and her small hands on her hips.

"Actually, I have decided that you and Hemith Harilaken make a good couple," said Sewcharran. "Both of you have very light skin and both think that you are a cut above the rest of us," he added nastily.

"No . . . no!" Sita stamped her foot again. Her father always managed to somehow bring out the very worst in her.

"Sita, calm down!" Chumpa's voice carried a warning note that reached Sita, but not before she felt her cheek sting. Her father had not hesitated to silence her with a slap.

"I will inform the Harilakens that I have discussed the issue with my family and we agreed that the match is most suitable." He gave Sita a penetrating stare. "And I don't want another word out of you." With those words, Sewcharran Suklal walked away from mother and daughter.

Chumpa read the anguish in her daughter's eyes before Sita turned to flee from the kitchen. It tore at her heart, for Chumpa had felt that same fear and anger, twenty years before.

She remembered the first time she had laid eyes on Sewcharran. Chumpa had lived in a tiny village near Sandila in Uttar Pradesh, where everyone knew one another well. A group of young maidens had often gathered at the local stream to do their family washing. They gossiped and giggled at new-found secrets, and for Chumpa it was the most delightful and carefree time of her life. It was at one such meeting that Sewcharran Suklal had come across her.

He was passing through the village when he stopped for a drink of water, and caught sight of the giggling maidens. His roving eye had fallen on one particular girl, Chumpa. At fifteen she was ripe and more than ready for marriage. He later told her, with a lecherous sneer, that he had liked the way her wet clothes had clung to her small yet shapely body. The mere sight of her softly rounded form and the sound of her throaty laughter had aroused him intensely.

Chumpa's laughter died when she felt the stranger's eyes on her. When she raised her almost black, almond-shaped eyes, fringed with long curly lashes, she felt something akin to fear enter her heart. Chumpa was old enough to understand desire and lust in a man's eye, and what she saw made her turn away in embarrassment.

Sewcharran and his family made inquiries about her family before approaching them for her hand in marriage. His parents had decided that it was time for their wayward son to take a wife. Although Chumpa's parents were delighted, they did not want to appear desperate to have their daughter married off. So they, too, made a few discreet inquiries, and when they were satisfied they accepted the offer. So Chumpa, with fear in her heart, found herself married to Sewcharran Suklal.

Sewcharran was eager to sample the delights of wedded bliss; he showed no consideration towards Chumpa's inexperience and innocence. Chumpa's wedding night turned into a nightmare. She could still remember how the tears had flowed and dried on her burning cheeks. She could still feel the sharp pain his invasion of her body had caused, and the bitter hurt that entered her heart when she realised that she could never bring herself to love the snoring, lustful man who slept beside her.

How could she wish the same fate on their lovely daughter?

The ache in Sita's heart was more painful than the sting on her cheek. That night she tossed and turned. Thoughts of Albert Sheldon filled her mind and made her body ache with a strange longing; and then the angry words of her father washed away any pleasure that memory gave her. All she could do was wait and see how far her father would go with this marriage proposal.

Geeta, much to Sita's annoyance, supported the match. Sita looked at her sister snoring gently beside her, and wondered how they could be so different.

The next morning, Sita made her way to the Big House with a heavy heart.

Albert Sheldon sat with his sister at the breakfast table – something he had never done before. Usually he rose early with his brother-in-law to be served breakfast by Sumi, and always ate a packed lunch out in the plantation. He had supper with the whole family, but by then Sita had already left for the day, so he had not seen her in the house.

"Good morning, Sita."

"Good morning, Madam." Sita returned the greeting, keeping her eyes downcast as she moved around the table, avoiding Albert's bemused look. Quickly she placed the hot plate of freshly baked bread-rolls on the table and hurried out, but not before she caught Albert's remark to his sister.

"She is quite lovely."

"Ah," smiled Elizabeth, "so you have noticed."

With her heart pounding crazily, and a silly smile on her lips, she made her way to the kitchen. Had she heard the rest of the conversation, she would have wept.

"Sita's mother stopped by early this morning, asking to speak to me. Fortunately I was up, to check on my roses," Elizabeth reported as she smeared butter onto a hot roll.

"Why?" Albert asked anxiously, wondering if Sita had told her mother something about him.

"Apparently Sita is refusing to think about a marriage proposal she has received. Her mother wants me to talk some sense into the girl."

"Why you?" Albert breathed a sigh of relief as he passed his sister a cup of coffee. "I mean how old is she anyway?"

"Sixteen. Most Indian girls her age are married and have started families. Her mother feels that Sita has adopted many of our habits and has rejected the offer without thought."

"So what will you do?" Albert sipped his coffee, curious to know how his sister would handle this.

"My dear brother," Elizabeth replied. "She will have to do as her parents ask. With these people their parents arrange everything. Sita can consider herself fortunate that her parents have discussed this issue with her first." Elizabeth bit into her roll. "Sometimes, the couple never set eyes on each other until their wedding night."

"How barbaric," Albert almost choked on his coffee.

"Family honour and respect means a great deal to these simple people." She had met many Indians since the period of indenture began, and she had found herself learning their culture and customs. Although it was all strange to her, she admired this proud group of people who wanted to keep their lives and identity intact, while adjusting to a new land.

"Are you going to speak to Sita?" Albert asked, trying hard to disguise the concern in his voice.

"Yes, but I cannot and will not force her to do something she does not want!"

"Well," Albert smiled at his sister casually, as he wiped his mouth with a napkin. "It will be interesting to see how this all works out."

Geeta's wedding day dawned, and the little cottage was filled with guests, who had been given a free Sunday. Although the Indians were poor, they loved social gatherings and thrived on happy events like weddings and births. They all rallied around to help make any occasion a joyous and special one with music and songs and dancing.

Geeta wore a pretty red, green and white silk sari, which helped hide her plumpness, and her nose ring and earrings enhanced her features. Chumpa draped the sari over Geeta's head as a veil, so that her face was hidden from the bridegroom.

The sun shone brightly as Anoop Balraj lifted the veil to run the red powder from Geeta's forehead to the centre of her head, and to place a red dot on her forehead, making her his wife.

Geeta's smile was triumphant as she received good wishes from her guests, with Anoop at her side. The simple meal which the women prepared and served was eagerly eaten: many would go home with a full belly that night.

When the time came for the bride to bid her family goodbye, many tears were shed, but Geeta was leaving with a happy heart. After all, marriage and children and a home of her own were just a few of the things she was looking forward too. The new Mrs Balraj had very definite plans for her future. Sita missed her sister very much. She missed their secret talks at night, their giggles in the dark and even their little fights.

Geeta was radiant when she visited, which was not often, although she still worked on the Campbell Estate. She could only visit when her husband allowed her to, and he would also accompany her on these visits. Although this annoyed her and was not what she had expected, she smiled and pretended that she did not mind. One consolation, though, was that Anoop got on well with her family, and that included her father.

"Majee," Geeta asked on one such visit. "Hemith's parents want to know if you and Taj have reached a decision."

"What decision?" Chumpa asked, feigning ignorance.

"Ma, you know! About Sita."

"That . . ." Chumpa played for time. After Geeta's wedding she had deliberately avoided the topic, and so had Sita and Sewcharran. She prayed, for her daughter's sake, that Sewcharran had forgotten all about it.

"Ma, you know that Hemith is a nice boy." Geeta did not stop. "He works in the mill. He is quite educated, you know. Because he can read and write a little English, he helps with the mill records when they need him. Sita is so lucky someone like him is interested in her," she added with a touch of envy.

Anoop seemed content to work in the mill, milling the cane so the juices ran out into huge containers – a dangerous and exhausting job. But Geeta had plans for them. They had another year to go before they earned their discharge certificates, and she was saving every spare penny. She was secretly proud of her small but growing nest egg.

Realising that she was not going to get anything out of her mother, Geeta changed the topic. "Anyway, Majee," Geeta's eyes sparkled, "I have something to share. Call everyone together."

As the family gathered together in Chumpa's small kitchen, Anoop looked at his wife in surprise.

"We have really wonderful news," Geeta said, smiling coyly at Anoop.

Anoop's small black eyes narrowed for an instant, and Geeta read and ignored this sign of annoyance. She knew that he had wanted to inform his parents first – and now she was beating him to it. Geeta nudged him: if he failed to make the announcement then she would do it for him, Geeta decided.

Anoop cleared his throat. "We are going to have a baby," he declared, and suddenly he realised that it wasn't so bad after all. It didn't really matter who received the news first. Anoop felt proud and excited – but he did not miss Geeta's triumphant grin. She had won her first battle, and so, without him realising it, set the tone of their marriage.

"Hare Bhagavan. Thank you, thank you," Chumpa clasped her hands together in prayer before she hugged and kissed her daughter. Sewcharran shook Anoop's hand with genuine goodwill.

Sita kissed Geeta and wished her well, but she saw the smug look in her eyes.

"Hope it's a boy," Gopi smiled as he gave Anoop a playful punch. Despite the morning sickness and her sudden urges for food – which she demanded from every person she saw fit to ask – Geeta still worked hard in the cane fields. Her job, like most of the other women on the estate, was to put the cane into bundles, ready to be carted off to the mills for crushing. This was back-breaking work, and being pregnant did not make it any easier.

The family listened to Geeta's constant commentary about the baby they were so looking forward to, and spoilt her terribly, while she grew round, fat and extremely demanding.

While Geeta grew bigger with each passing day, Sita felt the sadness in herself expand as well. She had not had another encounter with Albert Sheldon, and their efforts to avoid each other seemed mutual.

However, the topic of her proposal could never be successfully avoided. Chumpa, under pressure from her husband, told her that the Harilakens wanted permission for their son to court her.

"No... Majee!" Sita moaned. Her mouth went dry with dread. "Please tell him that you and Taj are not ready. Tell him anything!" she cried in desperation.

"Beti," Chumpa grabbed hold of her hands, " you are not getting any younger and it is time for you to settle down and start a family, like Geeta. Look how happy she is," Chumpa cajoled, as Sita tried to free her hands from her hold. "I don't want to see you end up an old maid serving the Campbells for the rest of your life. You are far too beautiful... and too full of love."

"Majee, leave me alone! I always thought you were on my side, but I can see now how wrong I was. You are on *his*!" she sobbed bitterly, wrenching her hands from her mother's grip.

Sobbing uncontrollably, she sank to her knees next to her secret pool, and buried her face in her hands.

"What is wrong, Sita?"

Almost choking in surprise, Sita lifted her head. Albert Sheldon was kneeling beside her, with a look of genuine concern on his tanned face and tenderness in his eyes. Did he always have to look at her like that? Her heart started its wild dance all over again.

"Nothing... that you would understand," she hiccuped, turning her wet, tearstained face away.

"Tell me," he invited softly, taking her face in his hands and wiping her tears away, again with such unexpected gentleness.

But how could she confide in him? What would she tell him anyway?

"Let me guess," Albert's voice was light and teasing, but it held a thread of pain. "Your parents want to arrange a marriage for you."

"How . . . did you . . . guess?" Sita stammered, looking at him in disbelief through her curly wet lashes

"Luck," he replied, trying to keep the pain out of his voice. "From what I can see, you are definitely not happy."

Sita nodded. "Why should I marry someone I don't love?" she cried, in a fresh flood of tears."Is there someone you do love?" Albert inquired. Sita blushed and looked away.

"Please look at me, Sita," he requested gently, tilting her chin and forcing her to meet his eyes. The expression in her wide, terrified eyes felt like a kick in his stomach.

Sita heard his cry of pain before she felt him capture her lips in a kiss of great desperation.

"I love you," he whispered hoarsely in her ear as he slid his arms around her, drawing her closer. It amazed him how the scent of fresh roses always surrounded him when she was near.

"And . . . I love . . . you," she confessed, in a voice that trembled. "I . . . don't want to . . . but I can't help myself."

Albert's heart tightened. He kissed away her tears before gathering her close to him again. They fitted perfectly together, he thought, as he ran his fingers through her long, silky hair.

"We have been deliberately avoiding each other," he said.

The intensity of his look quickened Sita's breath and as he gently placed her on her back. Sita closed her eyes, wanting to shut out the look of love and passion she read in his eyes. But the image burned in her mind.

His body felt hot and vibrant to her touch and Sita responded with kiss for kiss, caress for caress. Suddenly terrified, she pushed him away, dragging her swollen lips from his.

"Stop this," she cried out, pressing her fingers to her tingling lips.

"Why?" Albert's eyes registered confusion as he took in her trembling form. "Did I hurt you?" he asked, sitting up beside her.

"No," she shook her head as she moved away from him. Putting distance between them seemed the safest thing to do. "But I will be hurt if we carry on." Fresh tears gathered in her eyes, but she hastily brushed them away and stood up, looking at him with determination.

Even with red, swollen eyes she looked so appealing. Shaking his head to keep himself focused, he heard her continue.

"If my father discovers us like this he will surely kill me," she explained, appealing for him to understand. "My older sister is married to a nice Indian boy and they are going to have a baby soon. She has made my parents . . . very proud . . ."

She started crying again.

"And so you have to marry someone of their choice," Albert stated, his voice bitter, for he could not understand why this had to happen.

"What can I do?" she pleaded, looking at him as though he could provide her with an answer.

"Stall them," he suggested after a few minutes. Sita's eyes widened. "Maybe they will get tired of waiting for an answer," he added hopefully.

"I can't do that!"

"Yes, you can," he insisted. "I will be inheriting some money on my twenty-fifth birthday and then we can be married. "

"You are . . . crazy!" Sita spluttered, wanting to laugh as hysteria rose in her. "Whoever heard of an . . . an . . . Indian marrying a White! I will be treated as an outcast, and so will you."

"No," Albert grabbed her by her arms, "we won't be. Not when they see how much we love each other," he implored. "We just need more time."

Sita loved him all the more. Were this situation not so absurd, she really would marry him. "How long?" Sita asked, wanting desperately to believe that he had a solution.

"I will be twenty-three in another two months."

Sita looked at him with round, worried eyes. "It is impossible," she cried. "I have to give my parents an answer soon."

How on earth would she get her parents to wait?

Three days later, Chumpa brought up the subject once more. Since her father was nowhere to be seen or heard, Sita confidently informed her mother that she had no intention of tying herself to a man at sixteen.

"After all, Geeta is married and you will be grandparents soon. So I can't see why this has to be done so soon." She smiled beguilingly at Chumpa. "Perhaps in a year or two. If Hemith really wants to marry me, then he will abide by my wishes."

Taken aback by Sita's sudden willingness to discuss this issue without the normal tears and tantrums, Chumpa replied, "Well, the least we can do is tell his parents that you have agreed to let him court you."

"As long as I don't have to marry him soon."

CHAPTER FOUR

Sita dared not tell her mother of her special love; and she was terrified of her father's reaction should he discover her feelings for a man whose colour he detested. So Sita decided to keep her secret until it was necessary for her and Albert to disclose their love for each other.

Chumpa had agreed to speak to the Harilakens, without Sewcharran's knowledge, to inform them that Sita had agreed to the courtship, but that she was in no hurry to get married just yet. Sita felt safe, for the moment.

With Albert helping Master Campbell and Sita busy at the Big House, they rarely had time to see each other. They devised a system of leaving each other little love notes, which they read and then destroyed immediately. One morning Albert left a note informing Sita that he had to see her urgently at their secret place. They arranged to meet that Sunday afternoon. Sita had to help Sumi that morning, so she had a perfect excuse to go to the Big House, which did not involve lying to her mother.

Albert was waiting for her at the pool.

"I have something important to tell you," he said, drawing her into his arms. She sensed an urgency in him.

"What is it?" she asked, placing her palm against his cheek, her honey-brown eyes wide with concern.

"I have to leave soon," he told her. "My father is terribly ill and I am needed at home."

"I am so sorry to hear that," she cried. "When do you leave?"

"Almost immediately, but I cannot bear to be parted from you." Albert hugged her fiercely. "I want you to promise me that you will wait for me to return."

"Albert . . ." The tears which she had been holding back so bravely flowed now, as the implication of his words invaded her heart.

"Sweetheart." Albert cupped her face with his gentle hands, a gesture that was becoming familiar to Sita, as he slowly kissed away her tears. "I will be back, and then we will be together, forever. Please, promise me that."

And although she knew how impossible it really was, Sita's heart ruled her head, and in a voice that trembled she replied, "I promise." He wrapped her once more in his arms and they clung to each other. "I am so scared, Albert." Sita whispered tremulously, her face hidden in Albert's chest, dampening his soft cotton shirt with her tears.

"Everything will be all right." He drew her away from the safety of his arms and looked deeply into her sad eyes. Slowly he lifted her hand to his lips and placed a tender kiss on her palm.

Lifting herself onto the tips of her toes, she pulled Albert's lips down to meet hers, and gave him the softest, lightest butterfly kiss he had ever experienced. Albert had difficulty swallowing the groan of passion that Sita's simple, sweet kiss had wrung from him.

But Sita wanted something more, to keep her sane during his time away from her. Tentatively, she opened her lips and touched his lips with the tip of her tongue, as she slid her fingers through his hair and brought him closer. So close she could feel his heart beating and the hardness of his growing arousal against her, and this time she felt no fear.

"You don't know what you are doing to me," he groaned against her lips. Then he took over from her lead. He drank from her hungrily, sliding his lips across the silky expanse of her throat and then upwards again to her cheeks, revelling in their softness. Albert tasted the tears that flowed down her cheeks and his heart ached for the pain he was causing her.

"Please don't cry. Not now, my love," he whispered. And when Sita attempted a brave smile through her tears he knew his heart belonged to her, forever.

Slowly, Sita's slender fingers moved towards the buttons on his shirt; she opened them to slip her palms across his tanned, hair-roughened chest.

"Please love me," Sita whispered desperately.

At their first passionate encounter, Albert had made sure not to reach the point of no turning back; but this time he wanted her as much as she desired him, and Albert was not going to refuse what she so lovingly, generously offered. At least he would go back knowing she loved him and would be waiting for his return.

Both were desperate for memories of each other to survive their time apart. Sita did not object when Albert peeled away her clothes and, caught up in her need for him, gasped as their heated bodies met.

But Albert was in no hurry. "Slowly," he whispered, as his warm, moist tongue caught her hardened nipple. Gently, not wanting to frighten her, Albert guided her free hand to his already swollen and throbbing hardness.

"I love you," he whispered in her ear, and delicious tingles travelled throughout her body. Albert's gentle yet passionate kisses brought her to the height of desire, and a purr of pure pleasure escaped through her swollen lips as she moved beneath him.

"I will always love you," Albert promised, taking in the sincere look of love and trust in Sita's soft eyes. Gently, he parted her slender thighs with his to slide gently into her.

Sita was wet and ready for him, but he did not miss her gasp of pain as she gave herself to him completely. He moved slowly inside her, careful not to hurt her any more, and she met his movements perfectly. Instinctively, she wrapped her slender legs around his waist, and they moved as one.

Fresh tears flowed from Sita's eyes. She had never felt anything more pure and beautiful. Her heart was bursting with love for this tender and loving man, who was making sweet, passionate love to her as though she were the most precious thing on earth and if he had to take his eyes off her, she would surely disappear.

When he made his final thrust she responded by lifting up her hips to help him, and with a deep groan he felt himself explode within her silken warmth.

Quietly, they lay in each other's arms, and with the sun's soft caress on them the young lovers dozed off.

Albert woke with a start, his arm numb, to find Sita curled against him. He looked at her tenderly for a few moments and gently smoothed her hair across her forehead. So young and innocent, he thought, dropping a kiss on her forehead before shaking her awake.

"Sweetheart, it is time for you to go home," he whispered. Sleepily, she opened her eyes, gave him a soft, seductive smile and wrapped her arms around him once again. Gently, knowing that if he delayed her any further she would get into trouble, he unwound himself from her loving arms. Silently, Albert helped her dress, and when they both were ready he pulled her into his arms once more.

Sita's heart contracted with pain as she watched Albert. He reached up to remove from around his neck a slim gold chain his mother had given to him before she died.

"This is for you to remember me and what we have shared together," Albert cupped her face in his palms, running his thumbs across her smooth cheeks, "and my promise to you is that I will return to make you my wife."

Startled, Sita stepped back, away from him. "Albert . . . I cannot accept this."

"I don't want any arguments," Albert stated firmly as he placed the necklace around her neck.

"You don't understand." She explained, removing it. "My mother would want to know where I got it from, and besides, it looks far too expensive."

Albert took it from her. "Well, then you don't have to wear it around your neck." He lifted her blouse and fastened the clasp around her slim waist. "There, it looks perfect and no one needs to know!" He bent and kissed her navel.

"I wish I had something to give to you."

"You already have," Albert replied, kissing her tenderly. This time it was not a kiss of passion but one of immense love and tenderness.

Drawing apart was agony for the two young lovers, and when Albert swung her into his arms and spun around with her held firmly against him, Sita clung shamelessly to him, burying her face in his neck.

As her ankle bracelet slid up her shapely calf her spirits soared for a second. "Put me down," she begged, for Albert was making her dizzy.

"How I wish I could take you with me," Albert sighed as he sank with her to the ground.

"I want you to have this." Sita gracefully removed the bracelet from her ankle. Gently taking hold of his hand, she slipped the bracelet over it, and placed a tiny kiss on the inside of his wrist. "There! You cannot ever forget me now!" She attempted a small laugh.

Then, much against her will, she burst into tears, and before Albert could hold her once more in his arms, she fled from him.

Albert watched sadly as she ran from him, and all the time his fingers played with the bracelet around his wrist.

Sita was not able to return to the Big House after what she and Albert had shared. Usually fit, healthy and vibrant, that night she became terribly ill. She developed a high fever, and kept drifting in and out of consciousness, talking incoherently of her one love, which only caused more worry and confusion for Chumpa. Sita refused the soups her mother so lovingly prepared for her, and her anguished cries filled the tiny cottage.

Chumpa, racked with worry, explained the strange illness to Elizabeth Campbell.

"Please make sure that she returns to work only when she is well and strong again," Elizabeth told Chumpa. "And if there is anything I can do to help, don't hesitate to come to me." Chumpa was touched by her kindness.

However, the Sirdar to whom Chumpa reported was not pleased that Chumpa had to keep checking on her sick daughter and was not able to complete the hours required of her. He informed her that her wages would be withheld.

Chumpa grew desperate, as she needed the money for her special home remedies for Sita; she informed Elizabeth Campbell of the situation, and to her relief the matter was resolved without much delay. Chumpa received her wages, together with Sita's, directly from Elizabeth. Chumpa wondered again if they received better treatment because the mistress of the estate had a soft spot for her daughter.

After two weeks of constant caring and worrying and praying, Sita's fever slowly left her and her strength returned, and Chumpa breathed easier. However, Sita looked thin and drawn: she had lost weight, and the sparkle in her eyes was gone, leaving her with a sad, haunted look. Chumpa had realized, through Sita's ramblings, that her once lovely daughter was in love, and that something terrible had happened. She had also discovered the necklace around Sita's slim waist as she bathed her with cool water to help bring down her fever. Chumpa made no mention of this to Sita, although it brought a terrible ache to her heart. Instead, she watched Sita closely, wondering just what type of man could put her daughter through so much anguish. Chumpa found herself actually afraid of discovering the truth, for only God knew what the outcome would be.

Knowing that she could not hide forever until her lover returned to rescue her, Sita returned to work when she felt a little stronger. Elizabeth Campbell met her in the breakfast room as she was setting the breakfast table on her first day back.

"Sita, my dear girl!" she exclaimed, taking in Sita's pale face and the dark circles under her eyes. "You look so thin. Are you sure you are well enough to return to work?"

Sita nodded, and gave her a tentative smile. "Thank you Madam. I am feeling much better."

"That is good news. The children have missed you and so have I," Elizabeth admitted. "More so now that my dear brother has left for England."

Sita's heart began to pound and she nibbled on her lower lip nervously, wondering exactly what Elizabeth was leading up to.

"My father is extremely ill and I pray that he recovers," Mrs Campbell went on.

Why is she confiding in me? wondered Sita, deciding that maybe she just wanted someone to talk to – someone who had been ill and would understand.

"I am sorry to hear of your father's illness," Sita sympathised.

"Thank you, Sita," Elizabeth replied appreciatively. "Now tell me, dear girl, have you made up your mind about the marriage offer?"

Sita went a shade paler and her mouth suddenly felt very dry. The question was so unexpected. "How did you know?" she whispered, wondering just what Albert had said to his sister before he left.

"Please don't be upset," Elizabeth hastened to add. "Your mother is extremely worried about you, and she spoke of her concerns to me. She hoped I would be able to persuade you to accept the Harilakens' offer," she ended gently.

Sita closed her eyes and almost sank to her knees in relief before saying weakly, but firmly, "She really should not have bothered you. I have already given her my answer."

Elizabeth Campbell looked as though she wanted to say something, and then changed her mind. "The children have really missed you, Sita. Why don't you go in and say hello to them and bring them down to breakfast?" she suggested, looking very thoughtful.

Sita did not wait for any further prompting.

Sita's melancholy did not lift. When she began to feel nauseous at odd times, she thought it was just the after-effects of her illness, and she was so caught up in her memories of Albert that she did not realise that she had missed her period. And then Chumpa found her one morning, bent over, retching into a bucket.

"Sita, what is the matter with you?" Chumpa asked, as she took in Sita's pale face and sunken eyes. The girl straightened up and wiped her mouth with the back of her hand.

Seeing the miserable look in Sita's eyes, Chumpa knew, as only a mother could, what was wrong. After all, she had looked and felt just as sick on eight occasions, which had all resulted in her having babies. One of whom was standing in front of her now, looking so young and devastated it made Chumpa's heart break. Yet at the same time it filled her with a deep sense of betrayal and rage, and she too felt sick to the stomach.

Chumpa's eyes narrowed. "Sita, have you been with a man?" she demanded coldly. Although she knew the answer, she still hoped that Sita would prove her wrong.

When Sita did not answer, Chumpa grabbed hold of her and shook her. "Answer me, damn you, I have to know!" Chumpa gave her another hard shake, and Sita's head rolled back and forth weakly.

A pathetic "Yes" escaped through Sita's stiff lips. She did not see Chumpa raise her hand, but felt the impact of the slaps which sent her reeling. Vaguely, Sita heard her mother's angry sobs above her own.

"Do you realise that you are pregnant?" Chumpa pulled her daughter up by her long plait and Sita, who was still too weak to protest, wobbled to her feet. "I cannot believe that you, of all my children, could do something so dishonourable," she cried. "Your father is going to kill you, and the man who did this to you!"

Chumpa sobbed as tears of fury rolled down her cheeks. "Who is he?" she demanded.

"I can't tell you," Sita sobbed, suddenly feeling very young and naïve, and too petrified to think of the consequences.

"Why? Does he not want to marry you?"

"Ma, please don't tell Taj," Sita begged, her eyes welling with fresh tears.

All Chumpa's anger dissolved at the sight of the despair and pain on Sita's face. "Just tell me who is responsible," she pleaded, as she wrapped her arms around her child. Mother and daughter clung to each other as they wept.

"What on earth is going on here?" Sewcharran's booming voice tore them apart. He planted himself between them and placed his hands on his hips, looking first at Chumpa and then at Sita. Sita stared at her mother with beseeching eyes.

Chumpa picked up the edge of her cotton sari to dab her eyes. "You see us in tears because Sita has just agreed to marry Hemith Harilaken." Chumpa forced a smile.

Sita thought she was going to vomit once more. "Ma . . .!" she cried desperately, but Chumpa continued to speak as though she had not been interrupted.

"She will be leaving us shortly," she added as she wiped her eyes again.

"Well, you silly womenfolk," Sewcharran's laughter rang out above their heads. "It is nothing to cry about! I always knew she would come around." He patted Sita on the back, and she pulled away from him as though he had slapped her. Grinning, Sewcharran left the house.

Sita glared at her mother. Only minutes ago they had shed tears together, and now her mother was taking advantage of her condition to manipulate her!

"I don't want to hear anything negative about this marriage, Sita," Chumpa warned with a sharpness in her voice that Sita had never heard before. "You have brought immense shame to me and if you don't do as I say, you will bring disgrace to this family and that is something your father will not take lightly. It is obvious that the man who landed you in this situation does not want to marry you."

Sita closed her eyes against her mother's demanding voice. All she longed for was Albert, for Albert's arms to be around her, to comfort and to love her and to reassure her that everything was going to work out perfectly for them. But how on earth was she to contact him? Soon she would be showing . . .

Her mother was questioning her about the last time she had bled. It felt like such a long time, but in actual fact, Albert had left just over a month ago. That meant that she was into her first month of pregnancy – and already she was feeling the symptoms.

"Just one month, Majee," she whispered.

"Good," Chumpa replied curtly, and Sita wondered just what was so good about her present situation.

"Tomorrow your father will inform the Harilakens of your acceptance, and then on Sunday I will invite them over for lunch and we can finalise everything. Fortunately for you, I did not tell them that you were in no hurry to get married. We will give permission for Hemith to court you, and one evening when he comes by, you will take him for a stroll – some night soon, when the moon is bright and the stars are twinkling."

"But, Ma . . ." Sita's protest was cut short.

"Don't interrupt me," warned Chumpa. "This is for your own good. When you are alone with him I want you to make sure he makes you pregnant."

"But . . . if I already am . . ." stammered Sita in bewilderment.

"He does not know that," Chumpa replied coldly. "He is going to be the father of this child. Is that clear?"

Sita was simply too stunned to speak. Where on earth had her mother come up with such a plan? Her simple, sweet, unassuming mother! Who would have guessed that beneath her warm loving smile lay a brain so sharp and shrewd it made Sewcharran's meanness seem like a mere pebble in front of a mountain?

"Now," Chumpa frowned, deep in thought, "the only problem is, how do we break the news to your father?"

"Papa is improving!" exclaimed Elizabeth to her husband, reading the telegram. "Oh, Graham, I am so glad. He has given us a few scares in the past, but this time I really thought we were going to lose him."

Sita's heart sang when she overheard this. But then she heard Graham ask, "Will Albert be returning shortly?"

"I am so sorry, darling," Elizabeth's voice took on a consoling note. "I know how helpful he was to you, but Papa needs him there as well. He says that everything at the mill is in a mess."

"Well," sighed Graham, "then it seems that we will not see your brother for another year or two."

This news hit Sita so hard she almost reeled, and she had to sink her teeth into her bottom lip to stifle her cry as she sped into the scullery. She felt faint and nauseous, and knew that it had nothing to do with morning sickness. After a few deep gulps of air she felt sanity return; and then anger.

How dare Albert do this to her? What about his promise? How could she face the prospect of having his baby when she had absolutely no idea when or if he would ever return? Hot tears fell down her pale cheeks, but she quickly wiped them away. This was no time for tears, she decided. She would give vent to her pain later, when she had come up with an answer to the problem. Now she had to think, and think very quickly.

Indeed, Sita decided after a few minutes, she would have to marry. There was no way in hell she would allow her precious baby to be labelled a bastard and a half-caste.

Drawing another deep breath, Sita straightened her shoulders, splashed cold water on her face, and pushed the ache in her heart away. Yes, she decided determinedly, she would accept her mother's plan. Sita tried to recall what Hemith Harilaken looked like. All she remembered was that he was a slender, fair-skinned young man of about twenty-one. Being fair-skinned was the deciding factor for Sita: when Albert's child was born there would be no dispute, for she could say that the baby took after both its light-skinned parents.

But first she had to seduce the poor and unsuspecting Hemith.

CHAPTER FIVE

As arranged, Mr and Mrs Harilaken, with all their seven children and their grandchildren, came over to see the girl who had accepted the marriage offer. The Suklals had been over to their home with the good news, and Hemith was thrilled that finally he was going to marry the girl of his dreams. Sita had made him wait a long time for an answer, but it was worth it, and he was going to make sure he did not lose her.

"Welcome to our home," Chumpa smiled at her daughter's future in-laws. Chumpa had really scrimped and saved to make this evening a success, and she was going to ensure that her plans for Sita went smoothly. Soon Chumpa had everyone seated on grass mats.

Chumpa was pleased to see that once Sita had made up her mind to marry Hemith, she had blossomed once more, although the haunting sadness had not left her lovely eyes.

Chumpa had prepared traditional vegetarian dishes of beans, herbs and lentils with flat round roti, made from mielie-meal rations which Chumpa had saved. When Sita shyly offered them seconds, they were only too pleased to accept.

Chumpa was immensely proud of Sita that evening: she carried herself with grace and dignity, wholly befitting a future daughter-in-law.

"Well," began Mr Harilaken, wiping his mouth in satisfaction, "that was a truly delicious meal. Thank you." He smiled kindly at Sita, who hastily lowered her eyes lest he should see the guilt in them.

If only he knew what had prompted this celebration, he would not look at her so kindly, Sita thought as she cleared away the dishes. She could not bring herself to even meet Hemith's eyes, although she was more aware than ever that his gaze followed her every movement. Thankfully, the house was full of people to provide distraction.

She listened half-heartedly as her and Hemith's parents formalised the proposal. When she did finally meet Hemith's eyes, which twinkled with happiness, she felt a complete fraud.

Sita began to have doubts as to whether she would be able to carry out Chumpa's plan. Firstly, she had to summon up the courage – so far, she and Hemith had barely said a word to each other. Besides, he seemed so nice; it was terribly unfair to take advantage of him, she thought ruefully. But, she reminded herself, for the sake of her unborn child, it was important for her to accept Hemith as a husband in every sense of the word.

She was relieved and thankful when the evening came to an end and the Harilakens took their leave.

"You must come by tomorrow evening," Gopi invited Hemith, casually slinging an arm around his future brother-in law.

"Would that be all right?" Hemith looked at Chumpa and Sewcharran with hope in his black eyes.

Chumpa hesitated for just a fraction of a second, casting a quick look at Sita, who kept her eyes downcast, before giving him their approval.

"But you must not stay too late," Chumpa added, not wanting to appear too eager.

When the Harilakens left, Gopi came to Sita and gave her a warm hug. "So my baby sister is finally going to join the rest of the womenfolk and raise a family of her own!" he teased. When Sita stiffened in his arms, he drew away to look into her eyes. Sita's face was filled with sadness. "Hey, what's the matter? You should be all smiles today."

Gopi tipped her chin with a roughened hand, and Sita wanted to lose herself in his arms and weep to her heart's content, and then tell him the whole truth.

"I am all right, Bhai." She gave a weak attempt at a smile. "I am just tired," she added truthfully.

"Don't worry," Gopi smiled at her reassuringly, answering her innermost fears. "Hemith is a fine person. He will take good care of you. Besides, I have seen the way he looks at you. Is that not so, Majee?" he turned to Chumpa for confirmation.

Chumpa smiled her agreement, and Sewcharran nodded with a smug look in his big, round eyes.

The following evening saw Hemith at the Suklals', and Gopi immediately made him feel welcome.

Chumpa, for her part, made sure that Sita looked her best by choosing a buttercup-yellow blouse and a long skirt to show off Sita's still slender figure and small waist. The necklace Albert had given her was still around her waist. Chumpa gave her a questioning look.

"I found it in the field one afternoon and decided to clean it up. It looks so pretty I decided I would keep it," Sita told her.

The look Chumpa gave her spoke volumes; Sita knew that her mother did not believe a word of her story.

"See that you keep it out of sight. I don't want any problems," warned Chumpa.

Pregnancy had lent Sita a special glow, and much to Chumpa's delight she had recovered fully from her illness and was almost back to her old, charming self. However, there were fleeting moments when Chumpa saw the anguish in her daughter's eyes. In those moments Chumpa asked God to forgive her for tying her free-spirited daughter into a marriage of convenience – while also entrapping a sweet young man in a marriage bed that carried a dreadful secret.

That evening Geeta and Anoop also visited. Geeta was in her final month of pregnancy, and the early glow had long since disappeared. Now she was overweight. From the onset of her pregnancy Geeta had developed a gluttonous appetite, wanting everything she saw or smelt, and making the people around her miserable by complaining of every ache and pain. Even Anoop was at her beck and call, and was totally exhausted by her fifth month of pregnancy. Now he simply turned a deaf ear to her complaints, and only gave in to her demands when he felt like it.

"I wish I could stay here with you, Majee," Geeta grumbled as she stuffed a sweetmeat into her mouth. "I feel so tired now, and look," She lifted her sari to show off her fat and swollen ankles. "If I am not careful this baby is going to be born in the field one of these days," Geeta sighed.

"It would not be the first baby to be born in the cane," Chumpa said. "I have helped deliver babies in the field – and their mothers are back at work in a day."

"Why did you make having a baby sound so easy, Ma!" Geeta complained as she shifted her bulky frame into a more comfortable position.

"Hush, Beti," Chumpa patted Geeta's hand. She could not help spoiling Geeta shamelessly. "You have a few weeks to go. Your tummy needs to drop and then it will be all over," she said, eyes on Geeta's protruding belly.

Geeta's small, puffy eyes moved over Sita with envy. "You are so slim and pretty. Please Sita," she implored, "don't even think of having a baby. You will ruin your figure." Geeta popped another sweetmeat into her mouth.

"*Those* are what will ruin your figure," Sita pointed out. It was no wonder that Geeta looked so huge, thought Sita. She was always eating, while Sita herself could not even look at food these days. "Actually Geeta, I think I will start a family immediately." Sita reached out and ran a gentle hand over Geeta's large belly and was thrilled when she felt the baby respond. "Then our children will grow up together, and play together," she said sweetly, as Geeta pulled a funny face which made her chin wobble.

"Don't have such high hopes. Remember how we used to fight over every little thing?" Geeta looked at her sister shrewdly. "And remember how you always hated the idea of marriage?"

Sita knew her sister only too well. Geeta was aching with curiosity as to why she had suddenly agreed to marry Hemith; but Sita was not going to satisfy her. Instead she replied, "I could not help but admire how happy you are, so I decided that marriage can't be so bad after all. Just look at Anoop. He looks so content," she declared brightly.

"He behaves as if he is the one carrying this baby," Geeta snapped, as Anoop's laughter filled the room, sharing a joke with her two brothers and Hemith. Geeta was frustrated. She had planned her marriage so carefully, but somehow things were not going according to her wishes. Instead, she found herself with no say in family matters, and living under the eye of her mother-in-law, whom she was beginning to detest. But after the baby was born, she would show them a thing or two! Meanwhile, Geeta was proving just how shrewd and smart she was. She hid her annoyance well, and made Anoop feel as though he truly were the master in their marriage.

"Come, Geeta. It is time we left," Anoop said, approaching. Immediately, Geeta's expression changed, and she smiled coyly at the man she had just berated.

"Yes, you are right." She gave him her hand, and he helped lift her from the floor where she had been seated. "Sita needs to spend time with her young man, and we have been selfish."

Geeta kissed her family goodbye before leading the way out, with Anoop carrying her small parcel of leftover sweetmeats.

All through the evening, Sita had been very aware of the looks Hemith threw her every now and again. Although Hemith had joined the men in her family, it was very apparent that he wanted to spend time with her, and she felt as though the air were charged with untold expectation. Sita bit her lip nervously. Soon she would have to put her mother's plans into action, before it was too late.

"Tonight is the perfect night," Chumpa whispered to Sita with a warning look in her tired eyes. Sita returned her look helplessly, trying to delay what must occur.

Her brothers were getting on very well with Hemith. However, Sewcharran held himself a bit aloof, adopting the stern persona that was typical of traditional Indian fathers-in-law.

"Is it true that Veerasamy was beaten up again?" Sita and Chumpa heard Gopi ask.

"Yes," Hemith acknowledged. "The Sirdar flogged him in front of his wife and children and the other people from his barracks."

"But why?"

"Apparently," continued Hemith, "Veerasamy came down with diarrhoea after drinking the water from the drums. He could not work."

"Is this Ganga's Veerasamy you are talking about?" Chumpa asked, wringing her hands in concern.

"Yes, he is the one. The sirdar wanted to make an example of him."

"My heart goes out to him," Chumpa's voice cracked with emotion. "To think that we all came here with such high hopes, and now all we hear is that this person or that person was flogged for not being at work on time, or losing a sheep, or something or the other. When will it end?" She wiped her eyes with the edge of her sari.

"At least we are not so badly off here on the Campbell Estate," Gopi put in. "Master Campbell is a fair and good man. We are fortunate."

"Fortunate! Oh . . . oh my boy, you must be joking!" Sewcharran's mocking laughter was like a slap across young Gopi's face. "We are nothing more than slaves here!" Sewcharran's voice lost its mockery as bitterness set in. "We do what the black man will not do."

"The last time I saw Veerasamy he showed me his back. He has been flogged before as well," Hemith informed them. "His back is badly scarred."

"Hare Bhagavan!" Chumpa's eyes widened in horror. She had never heard Ganga or Veerasamy complain before, although she had noticed a look of unhappiness and desperation in their eyes. Gone was the eagerness she had so admired in the young couple. Now she understood.

"Someone should try to . . . do something!" Sita contributed, conscious that she had led a very sheltered life.

"Now listen here, my girl," Sewcharran's voice rang loudly. "There is nothing we can do. We have to shut our mouths and work ourselves to the bone for a few measly shillings."

Bharath had seen and heard a lot for his young age, as his task was to look after the cattle that were kept on the estate and collect their dung for use in the fields. He was terrified that should any of his cattle get lost or stolen he would be held responsible. "We can draw up a letter . . . and send it to the magistrate," he suggested.

"I can help by writing down all the grievances," Sita offered.

"That is the most absurd suggestion I have ever heard of," snorted Sewcharran, and all eyes turned to him.

"Why?" demanded Bharath, with the innocence of youth.

"Because, thick-head," Sewcharran poked Bharath's head emphatically, "we work in the white men's fields and mills and we make them rich. The magistrate is a white man," his voice dripped with bitterness, "and we have sold ourselves to these people for five years. That is why we cannot do a thing."

"Well, at least we are almost reaching the end of our indentured period," Sita put in, hoping to lighten the atmosphere. "Soon we will be receiving our discharge certificates, and then the future is ours to plan."

"Future – what future?" Sewcharran asked. "We thought we had a future when we left India, but so far all we see is disappointment."

"This is all too much for one evening," sighed Chumpa. "Sita," she forced a smile, "why don't you sit with Hemith and get to know each other better? We have had enough serious talk for now." Chumpa lifted her brows knowingly at Sita.

Taking advantage of the opportunity, Hemith looked at Sita. "Let us take in some fresh air." He rose to his feet. "It is a bit too hot in here."

Hesitantly, Sita followed him outside. Her stomach was in knots; she was not sure how to begin. What if Hemith did not co-operate?

"Let us walk for a while," Hemith suggested after a few minutes of awkward silence, taking her by the hand.

Sita was too nervous to speak, so Hemith told her about himself and his family, and how thrilled they were that he was going to marry her. Somehow, Sita found herself walking amongst the rows of sugar cane.

"Wait, don't go any further," warned Sita, putting a restraining hand on Hemith's arm.

"Are you afraid of the dark?" Hemith asked, his voice tinged with amusement.

"No – snakes. You never know what may slither out from the cane," she shivered, suddenly feeling her skin crawl at the thought of a reptile slithering over her body. Sita looked at him from beneath her long lashes, hoping he would not think she was being a silly female.

"Snakes are harmless creatures really," Hemith informed her casually, as he gently steered her towards a soft patch of grass that seemed secluded, yet safe. "If you stay out of their way they don't bother you."

"How do you know that?" Sita asked somewhat doubtful.

"From observing them." He replied as he pulled her down beside him. "At the mill I have seen many."

"I see," murmured Sita, suddenly lost for conversation and unsure of what would follow.

"You have such beautiful hair," Hemith complimented her softly as he placed his arm around her shoulder. As she turned towards him to protest, she felt his lips meet hers. Slowly he pulled her to him, and although she wanted to stop him, she realised that would not be wise. However, she pulled back instinctively, feeling suddenly very shy.

"No . . ." she whispered, lifting her hands to push him away.

"Shush . . . don't talk." Hemith's voice shook, and Sita realised that he was just as nervous. "I have wanted to hold you in my arms for so long. Please don't deny me that."

Sita shut her eyes and clamped her lips tight when she felt his mouth on hers. Slowly, he ran his tongue over her lips. Much to Sita's surprise she did not feel any revulsion; nor did she feel an immense sense of pleasure, but she discovered that it was not an unpleasant kiss. Slowly she allowed her lips to part, letting him wedge his tongue into her mouth. Gently, without wanting to make it obvious, she lowered her back to the ground, and Hemith moved with her until they lay comfortably. A whimper of protest escaped from her as she felt Hemith move his hands over her tender breasts, and she thought she was going to bring up again.

Sita felt Hemith move his hands down her hips and move her skirt aside, and as his cool fingers touched her warm thighs a shiver ran through her. She felt Hemith tense, and forced herself to relax and move her body closer to his. This slight movement was all the encouragement Hemith needed. His fingers fumbled for her undergarments as his kisses grew more passionate. It amazed Sita how quickly he became aroused.

She felt his body tremble, and her womanly instincts told Sita that if they kissed much longer Hemith would want more. With her eyes closed, she felt Hemith slowly slide her undergarments down her slender thighs. He seemed to know what he was doing, and Sita wondered where he had got his experience. He pulled his pants down his hips and then lay on top of her again. Gently, he nudged his thigh between hers and Sita felt his hardness against her belly. Hemith took her lips in a gentle kiss and slid a hand between her thighs to allow him to enter her.

Sita was highly nervous and far from ready for him. She was dry and tight and it hurt when he pushed himself into her.

She winced and found herself stiffening against him, and then she heard Hemith say gently, "It will be all right. It won't hurt much longer," as he moved inside her.

Each time he thrust into her, Sita wanted to cry out, for the pain in her heart was unbearable. She squeezed her eyes shut, wanting to shut out Hemith's glazed look, and the tears she fought back rolled down her face. And then she felt Hemith shudder before falling on top of her, breathless.

He had taken only a few minutes, and yet it had felt like an eternity. She felt him slide out of her, leaving behind a stickiness on her thighs. Hemith rolled off her and pulled up his pants before turning to look at Sita.

"I am so sorry," he whispered, reaching out to gently wipe away her tears; Sita steeled herself not to flinch at his touch. "I did not mean to hurt you," he continued when she refused to lift her eyes to his. Very slowly he straightened her skirt and pulled her up into a sitting position. He took her hand in his as he knelt beside her. "I did not mean to hurt you," he repeated with a tender smile, and Sita wondered just who had seduced whom.

"I have heard that the first . . . time always . . . hurts." Sita gulped as she swallowed a lump in her throat. Then she looked at him with wide, terrified eyes. "Why did you do it? We have just met," she accused. Did he have to move so fast? Now he would think she was cheap and easy, when really she was dying inside.

"Because," Hemith took her in his arms and looked deeply into her eyes, "I wanted to make you mine the day I first saw you. Now I know that you really are mine."

"Now you . . . will not marry me!" She cried out, suddenly horrified.

"Don't say that," Hemith whispered as he pulled her against his chest. "What type of person do you take me for?" he asked as he gently ran a hand through her hair.

Suddenly the strain took its toll, and Sita wept for her unborn baby, for Albert who had betrayed her, and herself for breaking her promise to him. She wept for what she had done and how she had taken advantage of this young man's love for her. Sita wept tears of shame, sorrow and guilt as she clung to Hemith for strength, and found his arms strangely comforting and safe.

"What . . . if I have a baby?" Sita hiccuped as Hemith drew her away from him and wiped her tears away with his bare hands.

"Then, Sita," he answered with great maturity and conviction in his voice, "we will marry immediately. I know what I have done and take full responsibility. Whatever happens from now on, we will weather it together as a couple. I really do love you."

It was his words that warmed the chill in her heart, and she thanked God for sending Hemith to her. He would be her guardian angel. She felt secure in the safety of his arms and, most important of all, her baby would have a name and a loving father.

Hand in hand, Sita and Hemith made their way back to the cottage.

Chumpa was looking out for them. She tried to read the expression on her daughter's face, but Sita could not bring herself to look at her mother. Chumpa ran her experienced eye over Sita's slightly dishevelled, grass-stained clothes, and a small smile of satisfaction crossed her face.

Everything was going to turn out all right, after all!

CHAPTER SIX

A week later, a frantic Anoop arrived at the cottage. It was almost midnight and his urgent banging on the door woke the Suklal household. Anoop rushed in as soon as Gopi opened the door for him.

"Geeta is in labour and she needs you," he cried out, tense as any would-be father could be.

"Hare Bhagavan!" Chumpa exclaimed. "The baby is early! I hope this is not going to be difficult," she worried as she hurried about the cottage, gathering whatever she needed into her little basket. "Come, we must hurry." She rushed ahead of Anoop and was on the cart before he could help her.

"Wish Geeta good luck from me," Sita called out, as she and Gopi watched the cart disappear into the night.

Chumpa found Geeta's in-laws awake and almost hysterical. It seemed that Geeta was in a lot of pain and was being terribly difficult. She did not want anyone with her except her mother, explained her mother-in-law.

"I am so grateful you have arrived." She gave a sigh of relief.

"Where is my daughter?" Chumpa asked, and a horrifying scream of pain answered her question.

Chumpa, clutching her little basket, hurried into the tiny bedroom to find her daughter writhing in pain on the makeshift bed on the floor. Perspiration streaked Geeta's body and her sari clung to her, emphasising her heavy pregnancy.

"I am here now," soothed Chumpa as she wiped Geeta's face and neck with the soft clean cloth she had brought with her.

"Ma, please make the pain go away," she cried, clutching Chumpa's hand tightly.

"Don't panic, Beti." Chumpa picked up Geeta's damp sari and peered between her legs. At least she had had the good sense to remove her underclothes. Chumpa then helped Geeta out of her constricting blouse and sari. "There, you are much more comfortable now." Chumpa offered a smile of encouragement. "Come," she heaved Geeta to her feet. "You have to walk. The exercise will do you good," she advised, leading Geeta around the tiny room.

"How is she doing?" Geeta's mother-in-law inquired as she popped her head through the door.

"Geeta is doing just fine. She is young and strong. Please start a fire and set water to boil. We need lots of hot water," she instructed calmly.

"Are you sure all is well?" Anoop's mother persisted, taking in Geeta's heaving and very swollen body before casting a worried look at Chumpa.

"I am sure," confirmed Chumpa with a tinge of annoyance in her voice. "The baby's early arrival is not a sign of disaster."

"All right. But I can't promise to spare too much water. You know how scarce water is."

"Look," Chumpa, strove for patience. "I do understand, but we will need to clean both mother and baby properly. So please make sure you have enough hot water available when I need it. I have to sterilise the scissors and it is best to keep everything clean. We certainly don't want any infections," she warned, with a tilt of her brow. This was her first grandchild and she was going to ensure its safe arrival.

The hours dragged by, and Geeta was showing signs of exhaustion; but Chumpa knew each minute that passed meant the time grew nearer for her first grandchild to enter this world

"We are almost there now." Chumpa peered between Geeta's legs and saw the baby's head appear. "Time for one big push," she encouraged, and Geeta drew in a deep breath. With eyes bulging with pain and effort, she helped push her baby into the arms of her grandmother.

The Suklals arrived as soon as word reached them, to find the newest member of their family fast asleep, sucking a tiny, perfect thumb, quite unaware of the excitement her arrival had caused.

"She is so beautiful," Sita beamed at her sister when they were finally left alone. "You must be so proud of her."

"It was a lot of hard work," Geeta complained.

"At least you had Majee with you," Sita pacified, "and the next time maybe it will be better."

"Don't even mention a next time," snapped Geeta.

"Why?" The sudden anger in Geeta's voice surprised Sita. "How can you say that when you have such a perfect little girl?"

"Sita, you don't understand," Geeta whispered heatedly. "It is simply an awful experience. I sincerely hope you don't have to go through this."

Suddenly Sita wished Geeta would stop. She was scaring her.

"Look, you are tired and you don't mean what you are saying. Why don't I leave you to rest?" She kissed her sister on her forehead and looked tenderly at her niece before she left the room.

"I am so proud of my girl," grinned Sewcharran drunkenly as he swayed towards Anoop's father, who was distributing drinks freely in celebration of their grandchild's arrival.

Sita wondered just how proud he was going to be when he heard that she, too, would be presenting him with a grandchild before the year was out.

"We have to inform Hemith soon that he is going to be a father," Chumpa reminded Sita as the Suklals walked home, excitement still coursing through their veins.

"I am so scared, Ma," Sita finally admitted. "What if this does not work out?"

"Don't worry, Beti. Leave everything to me." She placed an arm around Sita's shoulders and pulled her closer. "You won't have cause to regret this marriage. Hemith is a good boy and he will make a wonderful father for your baby." Chumpa spoke softly and lovingly to her daughter, hoping to put aside her fears.

When Hemith visited, Sita was relieved to learn how taken he was with Anoop and Geeta's little girl. He very shyly mentioned to Sita that he would love for them to have a baby as well. Sita knew very well what he was hinting at; but to Sita, the damage was already done, so she saw no reason to seduce Hemith again. He would just have to wait until after they were married.

Sita still experienced the odd bout of morning sickness, and one day

Sewcharran caught her in the throes of bringing up the mielie-meal porridge which Chumpa had made for their breakfast.

"What is the matter with that girl?" he asked, taking in Sita's pale face.

"She is . . . with child," murmured Chumpa, taking the opportunity to break the news.

"What?" Sewcharran hissed, his eyes narrowing as Chumpa's words sank in.

Chumpa nodded in affirmation.

"*Nooooo*!" he roared, eyes flashing with anger. "How could you let this happen?" he snarled at Chumpa before turning to Sita. Grabbing her by her long plait, he swung her around.

Sita, weak from the retching and utterly terrified of her father, hung onto him, while turning pleading eyes to Chumpa. As Sewcharran raised his hand Chumpa leapt forward, grabbed hold of his cane knife and held it menacingly in front of him

"You just lay one finger on her, Sewcharran Suklal," she warned in a soft and dangerous voice, "I will not be responsible for my actions." Chumpa reached out and pulled Sita away from him. "You should be ashamed of yourself."

Sewcharran's eyes bulged and his nostrils flared. "What the hell do you mean, woman?" He stepped towards them.

"Stay where you are," Chumpa instructed, holding up the knife, ready to use it if provoked. "You are to blame for this. You insisted that Sita marry Hemith, and then you made us miserable until this poor girl gave in to your demands."

"Ma . . ." Sita was terrified. She had never seen her mother so infuriated before, and the rage seemed genuine.

"Be quiet," hissed Chumpa, before turning her attention back to Sewcharran. "Now that Hemith has put her in a family way you want to strike her. Just what kind of a father are you?"

Sewcharran glared at Sita before he spat in disgust. "She is no daughter of mine. She was trouble from the day she was born."

"How dare you say that?" Chumpa almost screamed at him. Frustration and despair built up in her; she dared not give in though, for her daughter's sake.

Sewcharran turned to Sita and sneered, "You always act so high and mighty around us." His arm snaked out and he dragged Sita from behind Chumpa and snarled into her tearstained face, "I just hope for your sake that boy does not deny this baby."

"You better make sure he does not," retaliated Chumpa sharply. "After all, you are the one who pushed for her to marry, so you have to make sure he *does* marry her."

"Hold your tongue, woman. You have said enough." Sewcharran threw Sita away from him and she landed at her mother's feet, in a small, crumpled heap. "I'll speak to the Harilakens. And you," he shot his daughter a hard look, "stop that snivelling right away."

It was much easier than either Chumpa or Sita had anticipated. Hemith's parents rushed over to discuss how best they could handle the situation, and it was agreed that a small wedding – as soon as possible – would be most appropriate. Sita felt terribly guilty and sorry for Hemith. His parents had certainly given him a piece of their mind for taking advantage of her. He took everything they had to say in his stride, and denied nothing.

After the initial shock and humiliation had died down, Sita's pregnancy was easily accepted by all.

"After all," Hemith's father told Sewcharran, "a baby can only bring joy."

Sita decided to inform Elizabeth Campbell that she was getting married.

"Why so soon?" Elizabeth asked, concerned at the quick turn of events.

"I . . ." Sita bit her lip nervously, and when Elizabeth lifted an inquiring eyebrow as she sipped daintily from her teacup, Sita stammered, "I am . . . with child . . . and have to marry to avoid a . . ." she searched for the right word.

"Scandal," Elizabeth supplied.

Sita nodded, blushing. "I would like to continue working here, if that is acceptable."

"Thank you for your loyalty, Sita," Elizabeth smiled kindly, "and don't worry, I will not turn you out. Besides, you are wonderful with the children. Remind me to give you some of their baby clothes. I am sure they will come in very handy."

"Thank you." Sita's heart contracted with pain. Fate was so cruel, and yet so kind – here was Elizabeth Campbell, who had taken the news in her stride, offering to help her. Were she to discover that the baby growing inside Sita belonged to her brother, how would she react? pondered Sita, as she went about her daily chores.

On the morning of her wedding, Sita was extremely nervous. It amazed her how soon everything had been arranged. It was less than a month since her father had discovered that she was pregnant, and now she was getting ready to leave her home and move in with Hemith and his family.

Geeta arrived with her baby, and everyone doted on the little one. Asha was growing into a plump baby who suckled hungrily, much to the delight of her elders.

"She needs her mother's milk to grow into a fine woman," Geeta's mother-in-law was heard saying each time Geeta took her baby to her breast.

In spite of all the excitement around her, Sita's heart was heavy with sorrow. Albert Sheldon occupied her innermost thoughts, and she still wore the love token he had given her around her waist, fully aware that soon she would have to remove it – for Albert's baby was growing bigger inside her every day. Should Hemith ask about the chain, she was prepared to tell him that she had found it on the grounds of the estate and decided to keep it.

Geeta and Chumpa helped Sita dress for her wedding. Geeta piled Sita's long, black hair into a high knot before helping her drape her sari over her head. Sita, adorned in a simple red sari with white roses that Chumpa had lovingly embroidered, looked beautiful, terrified and very fragile.

"Now remember, little sister," Geeta began, as though speaking from years of experience. "Your husband comes first and foremost in your marriage, and you must always respect what he says."

Geeta's little piece of advice suddenly lightened the intensity of the wedding, and Sita found herself relaxing. "Even if I disagree?" she asked, eyes suddenly sparkling with amusement. "You are a fine one to talk!"

"Don't get smart with me," Geeta said with a straight face before joining her sister in a mischievous grin. "Let me give you a big tip. Even if you disagree with him, no man likes to be told that to his face. You are a woman and women have their ways."

"Really?"

"Just flash him a seductive smile and flutter those long lashes, very subtly give him your suggestion, and then leave it all up to him to decide what is right and what is wrong and who was right in the first place!"

"Is that what you do?" Sita's eyebrows lifted disbelievingly. "Well, I don't think it will work with Hemith. He is a very straightforward and down-to-earth person, and we can have a difference of opinion without any major problems."

"Lucky you. Hope he keeps that attitude once you become his wife."

Sita ignored the anxious tightening in her stomach. "Are you having problems with Anoop?" she asked, intuitively.

"Don't be absurd!" Geeta gave a short laugh.

"Geeta, if you ever need to talk, I will always be here. You know that." Sita put her arms around Geeta.

"Thanks. Suddenly I feel like the younger sister. Where has all that maturity come from?" Geeta smiled, brushing aside a tear. "Anyway, this is your wedding, and here we are having a strange heart-to-heart. This is supposed to be your happiest day, so let us not discuss me any longer!"

The two sisters looked at each other, exchanged tremulous smiles and another hug.

"You know, little sister," Geeta studied her sister at arms length, "Hemith is a very lucky man. You make a beautiful bride and I am sure that you are going to be a wonderful wife and mother. Majee will be very proud of you."

Sita's heart warmed at the genuine praise from Geeta. It was rare to hear sincerity and affection in her voice these days.

Tears shimmered like dew drops in Sita's eyes as Hemith placed the red dot on her forehead, and then completed the rituals which made them husband and wife in the eyes of God. Everyone watched with delight as the couple stood beneath the altar of banana trees and exchanged their vows and garlands before the symbolic fire, under the guidance of their pundit, who worked in the cane fields.

Gopi was somewhat distracted. He had caught the eye of a dark, pretty girl, who was sitting watching the ceremony with a dreamy look on her face. She had quickly looked away; but then, when he stole a look in her direction a few minutes later, he caught her gazing at him again. This time he gave her a small smile of encouragement, and she had blushed delightfully. He was fascinated; after the wedding, he made sure she had had enough to eat, and found little excuses to talk with her. He knew he had lost his heart.

At the wedding party, a sudden hush fell on the crowd as all eyes turned to see the arrival of an unusual guest. Sita was pleasantly surprised to see that Elizabeth Campbell had come to offer them her congratulations. She had certainly not expected Madam Elizabeth to respond to her invitation.

For her part, Elizabeth Campbell, who had never attended an Indian ceremony before, felt herself drawn to Sita's wedding. Perhaps it was because Sita, with her great capacity for love and warmth, had come to her as a young girl and Elizabeth had watched her blossom into a lovely young woman.

Much later that evening, at the end of a letter to Albert, Elizabeth added that she had attended the wedding of her maid, Sita. She wrote that Sita, with her grace and beauty, epitomised the Indian bride, and that she and her new husband made a lovely couple.

After Sita had settled in with her new family, Chumpa, for the first time in many weeks, breathed a sigh of great relief. The small yet gracious wedding so hastily planned for her daughter had gone off without a hitch. Although it had cost them their meagre savings, watching Sita accept her new role made it all worthwhile.

Sita resumed her duties at the Big House, and fell into the routine of visiting her parents every fortnight. Hemith was proving to be a wonderful husband. He was kind and patient, and when they made love he was so gentle, he brought tears to her eyes.

His caring and loving nature filled Sita with remorse, and she knew that the tears she shed were tears of guilt. She tried desperately to make amends by making every effort to be a good wife and daughter-in-law. She was determined to make the best of her life with Hemith and, so far, it seemed to be working. Love and happiness seemed to come naturally to Hemith. Sita found that she had to work extra hard within herself so that her husband would not sense her betrayal and guilt, while she drew strength from his love.

Sita made sure that she did not give her in-laws or anyone else cause for gossip. Fortunately, she did not show her pregnancy too early. Every morning she prayed to the Sun God for forgiveness and guidance and for a healthy baby.

On one of her visits to her mother, Sita found her mother looking tired and depressed.

"Ma, is there something worrying you?" Sita asked as Chumpa pushed an invisible strand of her still-black hair from her face. She looked at Sita with tiredness in her eyes.

"Why, do I look like I am worried?" she returned, tucking the ends of her frayed cotton sari into her waist.

"Yes, Majee," Sita replied candidly.

"Are you truly happy, Beti?"

"Ma," exclaimed Sita. "You know the answer to that, and I am extremely grateful to you. Now don't change the topic. Something is distressing you. Please talk to me about it," she appealed.

"It is nothing," insisted Chumpa, furiously kneading dough for the roti she was preparing for their supper.

"Ma, stop this. I am your daughter and I want to know what is bothering you. Please don't turn away from me. Maybe I can help?" she cajoled.

"You cannot help," Chumpa stated. Then, as if ashamed, she whispered, "It is Gopi," and promptly burst into tears. "I honestly don't know what has got into him." Chumpa wiped her eyes with the ends of her sari. "You know how shy your brother is . . . but lately he has changed so much."

Silently Sita watched her mother as she continued. "Well, Beti . . . I think he is carrying on . . . with that . . ." she broke into fresh sobs, terribly upset.

"Ma . . . calm down. If you carry on like this you are going to collapse," Sita warned, putting a comforting arm around her mother's shaking frame.

After a few minutes Chumpa gained some of her composure. "I . . ." Chumpa inhaled deeply, "I think your brother is in love." Once more she burst into tears.

Sita stared at her mother for a couple of seconds before starting to laugh.

"What are you laughing for? This is not a funny situation."

"I cannot believe it," Sita clamped her hand over her mouth to stifle the laughter which threatened to bubble over as Chumpa glared at her.

"Sorry Ma," she apologised. "It is just that I find it hard to believe that my shy, sweet brother has finally found himself a girlfriend."

"Well, he has. I can still see how his face lit up when he spoke to that girl at your wedding."

"You mean Rani!" Sita's eyes opened wide with amusement. "Yes, I was watching him that day. They could not stop looking at each other. Ma, you should be happy for him."

"She is not what I want for my son," Chumpa's voice dripped with disapproval. "She is so dark . . ."

"That is a horrible thing to say! Just listen to yourself." Sita grabbed her mother's arms. "You are just jealous. Jealous that there is another woman in your son's life!"

"What?" spluttered Chumpa. "How dare you? I knew I should not have confided in you."

"Ma . . . be realistic . . ."

"This is real!" shouted Chumpa. "Your brother is so taken in with this girl he even comes home late."

"Ma," exclaimed Sita. "Gopi Bhai is a grown man. He can do as he pleases! I just think that you are feeling neglected right now and becoming upset for nothing." Sita spoke softly and firmly to her mother: "Listen to me. I know Rani. She is a sweet and simple girl. She is someone who would suit our Gopi well."

"But . . ."

"I know," interrupted Sita calmly, "you always wanted a fair, pretty girl for your son, but look around you. How many fair, pretty girls are there? If Rani makes Gopi happy, then good for him. I don't see what is wrong with that."

"You cannot see what is wrong!" shrieked Chumpa, suddenly losing control. "I'll tell you what is wrong! Firstly your father will never accept that girl . . . nice as you say she is . . . and I, well . . . I just don't like the idea at all. She is not the girl for him," she ended helplessly.

"Majee," Sita continued poignantly, "we do not choose the people we fall in love with. It is something we cannot control."

"I assume you are talking from personal experience," Chumpa retorted.

Colouring slightly, Sita refused to allow Chumpa to upset her. "Did Gopi Bhai mention marriage to you?"

"Just drop the topic," Chumpa sighed. "I have a terrible headache from all this talk." She placed a hand over her forehead.

67

"Ma, what is it that is really bothering you about this girl?" Sita asked in a voice which was soft and comforting. Her mother did look rather strained, but it was better to get everything out in the open before she left.

"Why are you so persistent?" Chumpa asked, wearily, turning away from Sita.

"I only want to help."

Sudden silence filled the tiny kitchen, and it seemed like an eternity before her mother turned to face her. There were tears running down Chumpa's face and Sita saw that there was no longer any anger in her.

"She is not a Hindi girl."

The words were so softly spoken, Sita had to lean towards her mother to catch them. It sent a chill down Sita's spine. What would happen if her family discovered that her own heart belonged to someone from another race group, and that her baby was only half-Indian?

"Oh, Ma." Sita looked at her tenderly. "It is really such a silly reason. After all you have Tamil-speaking friends. Besides, look how you love the Pillais, and they are dark-skinned Tamils," she pointed out.

"I know, but this time it is different. I do not feel comfortable about having a Tamil daughter-in-law."

"It is not what you want, Ma, but what Gopi wants. If Gopi wants to marry Rani, all this ranting and raving is not going to stop him. It will only serve to drive him further away from us," she explained with a calmness she no longer felt. "You know how restless he has been feeling lately – and we will be receiving our discharge certificates soon."

"So?" Chumpa demanded, pinning Sita with a searching look. "What are you trying to say?"

"I know Gopi Bhai wants to . . . leave the estate and move to the . . . city," she murmured, avoiding looking at her mother.

Chumpa's anguished cry pierced through Sita's heart, and she wished she could take back her words.

CHAPTER SEVEN

"Mathaji, this little paper means we are free, free at last!" Gopi waved his discharge certificate in the air like a banner of freedom.

"Stop it," Chumpa scolded, eyes twinkling with delight as her son scooped her in his arms and whirled her around their tiny kitchen.

"Now we can make a life of our own," he grinned.

Chumpa heard the determination and excitement in his voice. How she loved this handsome son of hers! Her face clouded for just a second – what did he see in Rani? – before she forced herself to discard any harmful thoughts in that direction. Chumpa had decided that she loved her son too much to stand in the way of his happiness. Sharing her thoughts and fears with Sita had certainly helped.

Taking in her son's tall, lean frame, his mass of black curls and his infectious smile, she could understand Rani's love for her son. Who could not love him? Gopi was so excited Chumpa wondered if his cheeks were hurting from all the grinning he was doing.

"Don't get your hopes too high, boy." Sewcharran's cold voice fell on them like a shower of icy water. Both mother and son turned to look at him in surprise. "I have decided that we will either return to India or renew our contract."

Chumpa watched in despair the change of expression on her son's face: sheer elation changed to utter defiance and anger.

"Now wait a minute," Gopi stormed, pulling himself upright. "How dare you decide for us? I am sick and tired of this life and I want a change. I am not going back to India, nor do I want to carry on working here! If you want to, you can, but don't you dare assume that I will renew my contract," he warned through clenched teeth.

"You will do as I say," Sewcharran's eyes bulged in anger as he pulled Gopi roughly towards him.

"I've had it with your bullying!" Gopi spat, matching his father in anger. "When you wanted to leave India, that's what we did. We were children then and did as you demanded. Now I am an adult, with choices and opportunities. You, too, finally have the chance to do something meaningful with your life. Take it," he advised unflinchingly.

"Shut up, boy!" bellowed Sewcharran, but Gopi was past caring.

"You have always moaned and groaned about slaving in the fields." Gopi shoved hard at his father. "Why you want to remain here is beyond me. Unless you are a coward and afraid to go out on your own."

Sewcharran roared as he lunged towards Gopi.

"Watch out!" cried Chumpa in a hoarse voice, but Gopi was expecting his father's retaliation: he neatly stepped aside, then grabbed Sewcharran by the arm and twisted it behind his back.

"Don't you dare raise your hand to me again," he warned softly. "I am no longer a puny little boy you can trample on, and I warn you, if you lay another finger on any one of us, I will hit back." His eyes glinted as he shoved his father aside in disgust.

Gopi stalked out of the cottage, clutching his discharge certificate in his hand. It was his passport to freedom and a new life. His heart felt as though it would burst with pain and joy, for he knew that life would never be the same again, for any of them.

"How are we going to survive?" Rani asked, her black eyes filled with apprehension. "All you know is how to work in the cane fields."

"Don't tell me that. I have my certificate here and so have you," Gopi told her. Rani took a step back as he went on: "It is time to move on and make a new life."

Seeing the concern and fear in her eyes, he took a deep breath to calm himself, and drew her gently into his arms. "We don't have to live here anymore. A lot of our people hate it here, but they are too tired to venture out on their own. But Rani," Gopi held her closely, "we are young and we can make a difference."

Rani felt so fragile in his arms; all Gopi wanted was to take her away from the harsh conditions under which they worked, and protect and love her. "Come with me to the city," he coaxed.

"Gopi . . . you know I cannot," Rani protested, freeing herself from his hold.

"What do you have here?" he demanded. "Absolutely nothing." She bowed her head in silence, knowing that he was right. "I love you and want to spend the rest of my life caring for you," he said, cupping her face, savouring the feel of his roughened hand against her smooth cheeks, "but not here. Not in this miserable place." He gazed into her warm black eyes. He looked past her dark skin: all he saw was the woman he loved.

Rani toiled hard in the fields from dawn to dusk, and her once olive skin was now darkened. One had to look at her closely to appreciate the pretty features she possessed. At nineteen her grandparents had given up hope of her ever receiving a suitable marriage offer – her dark complexion had seen to that. But she was a hardworking girl who never complained, and her pleasant, shy disposition endeared her to her friends. Rani's tiny frame belied her stamina and inner strength.

Rani had been in love with Gopi for a long time; and at Sita's wedding he had discovered that he loved her too. He could still recall the exact moment their eyes had met, and he'd felt a wonderful warm glow inside him. For the life of him he could not remember what she had been wearing that day; what blazed in his mind was the expression in her ebony eyes. It conveyed all the love she felt for him, and he knew in his heart that no man could be luckier. He was not going to let her slip away from him, ever.

"Follow your heart and come with me," Gopi whispered, delivering a soft kiss onto her forehead.

"We cannot and you know that."

"What?" Gopi grinned at her, trying to make light of a tense situation. "Can't get married or can't leave?"

"Don't tease me, Gopi," Rani scolded. "Besides, was that a marriage proposal I just received?"

Gopi's face lit up and he almost sagged with relief. For a second he had thought Rani was going to totally reject him and his offer. "Yes, it is, and I'm not taking no for an answer," he told her with a serious look in his eyes. "I have everything planned for us. I have a friend I met on the ship coming to Natal," he explained, "and he is now working at one of the big hotels in Durban. He's promised to help me find a job."

"Doing what exactly?" Rani asked with concern.

"I am not too sure at the moment . . . but I know that hotels are employing Indians. Chin, my friend, has all sorts of contacts," he explained enthusiastically.

The Indian labourers who were now free had many different plans for the future. Some, like Gopi, decided to go their own way. Some large and extended families, having saved very hard and pooled their resources, made tentative inquiries about purchasing land to start their own little farms. Then there were those who decided that they had had enough of this land, and used their money to purchase a passage back to India. Finally, the older generation, who were too tired and terrified to make any major changes in their lives, settled for a small increase in wages and succumbed to the call of the sugar-cane fields.

Chumpa had informed Sewcharran that she had no intention of returning to India. This was now her home, and her family were finally putting down roots in South Africa. Sewcharran was forced to make a decision: he could either return without his family, or stay in Natal. Finally he opted to remain in the employ of Graham Campbell. He refused to admit that Gopi was right, but secretly he knew that he simply did not have the nerve to try something different. The move from India had been filled with hope, but now that hope had died: Sewcharran had settled for a life that brought him no satisfaction.

Gopi was of the younger, more adventurous generation, who could not wait to head for the city to seek their fortune. To many, it mattered not whether they worked for themselves or for the white man, as long as they were not treated like animals, living on rations and in fear of the sirdar's whip.

He was impatient to pack his bundle and leave, but sensible enough to realise that securing a job in the city before saying farewell was vital for his future with Rani. It was decided that they would not share their plans with their families until all the details had been finalised. Everyone knew of Gopi's desire to leave; what they did not know was that he had no intention of leaving alone.

Chumpa had a letter waiting for him. Striving to keep the excitement from showing on his face, Gopi read it carefully, very aware of his mother's curious look. Slowly, he folded the letter and placed it in his pocket.

"Well?" Chumpa asked.

Gopi was unsure how to reply. He was excited and yet he did not want to upset his mother. "You remember Chin, Ma?"

Chumpa frowned slightly before she answered. "He was that young man . . . on the ship."

"That's right," Gopi smiled. "He is now working as a waiter, and he says he is doing very well."

"I am glad for him," Chumpa said, "but what does his letter say exactly?"

"Well, he says that the hotels are taking in more Indians, and I have decided to go and see him. Maybe I will be lucky and find a job I like."

"Is that what you really want, my Beta?"

"Yes, Majee," Gopi answered simply.

"How soon do you plan to leave?"

"Tomorrow morning."

Chumpa gave him a small smile of approval, but Gopi did not miss the tears in her eyes. She was trying hard to be brave. "I will pack a change of clothes for you and some food as well."

"Thanks, Ma." Gopi hugged her.

After a restless night filled with nervous excitement, Gopi rose early. Although he put on a calm front, he was filled with trepidation. He was going into the city: a big move for someone who had spent five years as a labourer on a sugar-cane plantation.

Sita and Hemith arrived early; Hemith had insisted that Gopi make use of the family wagon.

"I was hoping that someone would give me a lift," Gopi said, not wanting to be indebted to Hemith. He wanted to do this on his own.

"On a Sunday? You must be crazy!" Hemith reasoned, and Gopi was forced to accept his logic. Really, he had his head in the clouds! Of course the roads would be empty on a Sunday.

Geeta and Anoop arrived an hour before Gopi was ready to leave.

"So, Bhai, leaving us to seek your fortune in the city?" Geeta put in with a touch of sarcasm. She handed a rather plump Asha to Chumpa, who immediately smothered her granddaughter in kisses.

"Well, not exactly, but yes," Gopi replied humbly, "fortune in the sense of fulfilment and happiness. Although," he added, suddenly grinning mischievously, "I certainly wouldn't mind getting rich and prosperous in the attempt!"

"What a dreamer you are! Hoping to get rich by working in some fancy hotel," sneered Sewcharran, and Gopi's smile slipped away as quickly as it had appeared. His father was spoiling for a fight, but Gopi was determined not to give him the satisfaction.

"Listen everyone," Geeta suddenly clapped her hands together, breaking the tension. "Anoop and I have something wonderful to share, and I think it is best we do so before Bhaiya leaves."

"Are you going to have another baby?" Chumpa asked, as all eyes flew to Geeta's still flabby belly.

"No," retorted Geeta, clearly offended. "What do you all take me for? A baby factory or something?"

Nobody dignified her question with an answer. Geeta looked at them with a haughty expression on her face. "This is better, so much better – and in a way you can call it our 'baby'." She threw Anoop a coy look. "We have saved really hard, and have decided to buy a small piece of land and try our hand at farming."

A deafening silence filled the room for a good couple of seconds. Chumpa swallowed hard in surprise and Sewcharran's mouth dropped open. For once he was speechless.

Gopi was the first to recover. "This is wonderful news!" he beamed, and reached over and kissed his sister on both cheeks before reaching out to shake Anoop's hand.

"Congratulations," Sita smiled and she, too, kissed Geeta, before saying with all honesty, "This is indeed a pleasant surprise. We had absolutely no idea that you wanted to go into farming."

"Well, we had to make a decision. Neither of us want to work for somebody else, and I told Anoop that it was time for us to take our chances." Geeta pulled herself upright, and with her huge breasts stuck out, she resembled a proud peahen. "There's this small piece of property that I've had my eye on for quite a while now, and I have negotiated a good price with the owner," she explained.

"Geeta, starting out on your own is a major responsibility. Are you sure that you and Anoop are ready for this?" Chumpa asked, eyes on Anoop. She knew just how forceful her daughter could be, and hated to think that Geeta had railroaded Anoop into a decision that would affect the rest of their lives.

"We are ready," Geeta replied firmly, without a glance at her husband.

"Good luck then, and you have my blessings." Chumpa reached out to hug her daughter.

"We will start on a small scale, and then grow from strength to strength," Geeta enthused. "I want you all to know that Anoop and I are going to make a success of this. I most certainly don't want to be poor for the rest of my life and make my children suffer."

The family listened to Geeta outlining her scheme until it was time for Gopi to leave. He gathered his little bundle and the food Chumpa had packed for him in a small bamboo basket, climbed onto the donkey-wagon and waved farewell to his family.

On his way to the city it dawned on Gopi that the only person who had not wished him well, nor goodbye, was his father. He pushed away the sudden rush of hurt by thinking about Rani and all their plans.

CHAPTER EIGHT

Gopi arrived at Chin's lodgings utterly exhausted. It was almost dark, and he was so hungry he had developed a raging headache. The food Chumpa had so lovingly packed had long ago been eaten, and to make matters worse, he had got lost, even with the directions Chin had given him. Gopi had lost track of time, and could not say how long it had taken him to find the place. He had to ask a little Zulu boy for help, and finally he found himself climbing the shaky stairs at the front of an old house. Impatient to get in and see Chin, Gopi banged hard on the door, until finally a disgruntled Indian lady opened the door slightly.

"What is the matter with you?" she demanded as she peered through the crack.

"I am looking for Chin. He is tall and skinny with a moustache and the last time I saw him he was almost bald," Gopi explained, hoping he was at the right place.

"Well, he is now completely bald," she replied as she opened the door to let him in, then yelled shrilly, "Chin, there is someone here to see you!"

"Do you have to yell," grumbled Chin as he entered the room. Then he spotted Gopi. "Gopi! Gopi Suklal! It is you, isn't it?"

"In the flesh," grinned Gopi, pushing aside his throbbing headache to embrace his friend.

A little snigger drew them apart as quickly as they had hugged. Chin turned to the woman.

"Excuse me, but I would like to be alone with my friend." He cocked an eyebrow to emphasise the point, and the woman threw him a contemptuous look as she exited the room.

"Old hag," Chin grinned. "You haven't changed much," he commented, taking in Gopi's thin, tall frame, his dancing brown eyes and mop of curly black hair.

"Can't say the same for you," Gopi returned. "Where's all your hair gone?" he teased.

"Since I was losing it anyway, I decided to take the plunge and remove what little I had. This is the new me!" Chin pointed to his bald scalp.

"I have to get used to it," Gopi replied, studying his friend with a critical eye. "It does do something for you, though."

"Scares the girls away, you mean," Chin laughed.

"Well . . . it does bring out a certain seriousness . . ." Gopi replied with a straight face, "until you open your mouth."

"Thanks, pal." Chin's laughter filled the room. "Now tell me," Chin continued, showing him up a short flight of stairs. "Is it the prospect of a job that had you racing to the city, or all my talk of the lovely women?"

To Gopi, Chin's room appeared large and spacious. There was a single bed in the centre of the floor. Against one wall stood a rather old cupboard, and in one corner were a small table and a high-backed chair.

"You can share my humble abode while we find you a job. I know it's not much, but it's home to me," Chin announced, placing an arm around Gopi's shoulders.

"Are you comfortable?" Chin inquired after he had fed Gopi and they were settled in for the night. Gopi's headache had disappeared, now that his stomach was full and he had a bed to sleep in.

"Mmmm . . ." came his drowsy reply. Chin's lumpy bed felt perfect to Gopi. He had never slept on one before: at home they did not possess beds. His sisters were fortunate though. They now had a bed each, for marriage had brought certain privileges. His tired body welcomed Chin's generosity, and he fell into a deep and trouble-free sleep.

"Good morning!" a cheery voice greeted him, and Gopi groaned as he pulled the thin blanket over his head. He heard the curtain being drawn and for a couple of minutes lay absolutely still. "Up you get," the voice commanded as the blanket was pulled off him. The warm, bright sunshine swept into the room, making Gopi squint. "Time to get ready. We have a mission to accomplish," Chin reminded him.

"Mission?"

"Yes, sleepyhead. We can't have you looking the way you do when you go out begging for employment." Chin had brought in a large, steaming jug of hot water, which he put on the table next to a basin.

"What's wrong with the way I look?" Gopi grumbled, taking in his appearance in the cracked mirror on the wall.

"You'll see when I've finished with you!"

Gopi moved to the window and stretched, taking in a deep breath. "Not the same as country air," he commented, examining the view below. "This place seems awfully busy."

"This is nothing," Chin remarked. "Wait until you get near the beachfront."

"Do you think I've got a hope? I mean, what do I know about working in the city?" Gopi asked nervously, hearing Rani's voice in his head. Suddenly the city did not look all that appealing.

"You'll learn. After all, you left your home in India and ventured out here. Think of this as starting afresh," he advised. "And by the time I'm finished with you, you'll be looking so presentable no one will turn you away. Now wash your face. On second thoughts," he looked Gopi up and down, "you might as well have a body wash too."

"Why? Do I smell funny?" Gopi asked indignantly.

"No, but you'll feel better," Chin replied kindly. "I'll be back in a few minutes," he said, closing the door behind him.

Gopi walked over to the table where Chin had placed the hot water, a wash-cloth and a bar of soap. He removed a small piece of charcoal from his bundle and gave his teeth a thorough scrubbing before rinsing his mouth and face. Then he stripped off and washed himself. Looking at his clothes on the bed, Gopi frowned. His mother had packed his best pants and shirt, but suddenly his clothes looked really drab. He could not help but wonder if he stood a chance against the smart city people.

"I'll have to just give it my best shot," he told his reflection in the mirror as he slipped into his shirt.

The door opened and Chin entered carrying a neat brown suit.

"I hope you don't mind, but I took the liberty of sneaking a look at your clothes last night and . . . what you have on . . ." he shrugged his shoulders. Then he noticed Gopi's look. "I'm sorry. I only want to help."

"It's all right," Gopi smiled, weakly. "I suppose you do know what's best." Suddenly, he felt like a poor relative.

"Here, try these on." Chin handed over the dark brown suit and matching shirt. "The pants may be a little short . . . and the coat sleeves. You're taller than I am."

"I can't use these," Gopi protested, looking at the suit. "I'll wear what I have and if – if I'm not suitable, then too bad!"

"Don't be a fool," reprimanded Chin. "Be sensible for once and wear them. You have to look neat and presentable for people at the hotels to even want to interview you. I'm only lending them to you, so don't feel like a charity case."

"And if I am hired – then what do I wear?" Gopi stammered, throwing his arms in the air in frustration. "I can't keep borrowing your clothes, can I?"

Suddenly, as though Gopi had delivered a joke, Chin burst out laughing, and his anger at Gopi's stubborn pride disappeared.

"Now what did I say that was so funny?" Gopi demanded, annoyed with his friend.

"Oh, Gopi. You can be so sweetly naive at times." Chin gave him a playful punch on the arm. "Once you get the job you will be given a uniform to wear to work, like me. So you have absolutely nothing to worry about."

"I . . . see," was all Gopi could muster, not wanting to make an idiot of himself again. "If that is the case, then I will wear these smart clothes. And thank you, Chin."

"Oh no, not so fast, friend." Chin held onto the suit, ignoring Gopi's outstretched hand. "First we have to get rid of that morning shadow and trim your hair. Now sit!" he ordered, as he plonked a rather startled Gopi into the chair.

"What are you up to?" Gopi eyed Chin warily as he brought out a thin and rather dangerous-looking blade.

"Sit back, relax, and enjoy!"

Job hunting was gruelling work. Gopi found himself looked at and spoken to strangely: some people thought he could not understand English, and spoke very slowly. Others tried sign language, while a good few ignored him totally. From moments of utter frustration to moments of hope, Gopi managed to see each day through, and somehow Chin always made him see the humour in his situation. It was just over a week before he landed himself a job as a barman.

"Not bad," commented Chin. "I know people who are still looking for work. You're very lucky indeed. When I was first job hunting," he continued, "I virtually walked the whole of Durban before I found something."

Gopi felt as though he were walking on air. "I was really terrified in there," he told his friend. "The manager looked me up and down and then he said, 'At least you look clean and presentable.' Can you believe it? I have you to thank for that, Chin."

"And then?" Chin prompted eagerly.

"He asked if I had ever worked before, and I told him about the plantation."

"You had no problem with your English, then?"

"No – thanks to my sister, Sita," Gopi replied proudly. "She works at the Big House on the estate and speaks English well. She taught us."

"Really!" Chin's eyes widened in surprise. Most Indians coming to the city spoke only a little English, and with difficulty.

"Yes, and it certainly paid off today. The manager only gave me the job because of my English. It means I can take orders at the bar. Now all I have to do is to learn the names of the drinks!" Gopi's voice rose with excitement. "He even gave me a uniform! Oh, you were right, Chin. I can't wait to let my family and Rani know!"

"Hey, now wait a minute." Chin brought his hand up to stop Gopi's words. "Who's Rani? Have you been hiding something from me?"

Gopi hesitated for a second, and then proceeded to tell Chin about the love of his life.

"Oh, man. You're really asking for trouble. Why don't you stay here and work for a while before rushing into something?"

"What do you mean?" demanded Gopi. "I love her. I don't need time to make up my mind. Now, if you are really my friend, you'll help me find a place for us to live."

"All right," sighed Chin. "It's your life after all, and if she makes you happy then good for you. I'll see what I can do."

"I can't believe it. You actually have a job in the city!" Chumpa exclaimed, and then promptly burst into tears. "Now you will definitely leave us," she sobbed, and Gopi felt the first pangs of guilt.

"Please don't cry, Majee. It's not like I won't be visiting," he consoled his mother, wrapping his arms around her.

"That'll be the day. When you leave here you leave for good, is that understood?" Sewcharran's eyes flashed venom. "I don't want to see your face here again. You are no son of mine – deserting your family!"

"Sewcharran," shrieked Chumpa. "How can you be so mean?"

Dumbstruck, Gopi stared at his father. He'd always known that Sewcharran detested the close relationship he had with his mother, but hadn't expected such animosity. But he should have known better: his father, whether drunk or sober, always tried his hardest to belittle him.

"You want to leave? Then leave now. Go on, get out!" Sewcharran pulled Chumpa away from her son and pushed Gopi out of the cottage, throwing his bundle of clothes after him.

Sewcharran's ranting brought a crowd of curious onlookers. Hurt and humiliated, Gopi retrieved his bundle. It broke his heart to walk away from the place he had once called home, particularly when he heard his mother's anguished sobs. To twist the knife his father had plunged into his heart, he had to leave without bidding his sisters and brother farewell. Slowly, with shoulders bent like those of an old man, he made his way through the crowd.

Realising that they weren't going to be entertained, the crowd slowly dispersed. Only Rani was left. She ran to Gopi, who lifted a sad face to her.

"I am so sorry, Gopi," she whispered softly. "What are you going to do now?"

"I'm leaving as planned!" he answered, shifting his bundle from one shoulder to the other. "I'm not going to stay here another minute and listen to him. Are you ready?"

Rani bit her trembling bottom lip. Leaving with him would cause an immense amount of hurt and embarrassment to her grandparents – but she loved Gopi too much to see him walk away without her. He had made her come alive, and now life without him would be impossible.

"Where must I meet you?" she asked before she could change her mind, and her heart leapt when she saw his smile. "I need to say goodbye to my grandparents and get their blessings."

"You know where the road divides in two at the end of the estate?" he asked. "I'll be waiting for you, sweetheart." He gently touched her cheek before turning and walking away.

But Rani's grandparents did not give her their blessings. Instead, she received their bitterness and anger: they refused to accept that their sweet, gentle granddaughter wanted to run off to live with that Suklal boy in the city.

"He is trouble, that one!" declared the old lady.

"You are so wrong," Rani sobbed. "Gopi is a good, kind person who has promised to take care of me. We love each other!"

"You are going to end up just like your mother," the old lady warned. "Loving that man didn't help her!"

"But Aiya..."

"Go to bed, child," she interrupted. "No more talk about leaving with that boy. This is where you belong. With us."

Rani knew it was useless to explain that her love for Gopi was real, as real as her parents' love had been. Her grandparents would never allow her to leave.

"I am sorry, Aiya. I don't know what possessed me," Rani murmured. She bent and kissed the old lady's wrinkled cheeks, closing her eyes to savour the moment, before turning to her grandfather.

"Very sensible, my child. Now we will not mention his name again," he said as he kissed Rani.

Rani's heart ached, for although she dearly loved these two old people who had given her the best years of their lives, she knew she could not live with them any longer. Her heart belonged to Gopi, and follow it she must. But she hated the deceit this involved; and she knew her grandparents would never forgive her for deserting them in their old age. Once she left, she would not be able to return. She and Gopi would both be exiled from their families.

That night in bed, Rani curled into a ball and sobbed until she felt as though her heart no longer belonged to her. We love each other and that is what really matters, she told herself.

Rani waited until she heard the even breathing of her grandparents, then stealthily crept from her bed. Earlier, she had chosen some clothes and bundled them up to take with her. Her fingers quickly searched through the bundle until they felt the soft velvet pouch in which she kept her only piece of jewellery. Relieved, she kept her hand around it, afraid that if she let go it would disappear.

The extremely valuable gold necklace, set with precious stones, had been a gift to her mother from the man she had loved and lost; the man who had fathered her lovechild. The beautiful necklace had never been worn. Before Rani's mother died, she had given it to Rani; three days later she was discovered hanging from a tree with a sari twisted around her neck. It was said that she could not live without her rich lover, who had been found dead one morning. His wife was suspected of his murder, but no evidence was ever found.

Rumours were rife in the little village after the suicide, and so Rani's grandparents decided to leave the bad memories behind and start again in a new land – to give Rani a chance in life. Now, she was going to take that chance with Gopi.

Rani could never bring herself to wear her mother's gift of love. She believed that the necklace was cursed: it was so beautiful, but it had never brought her mother any happiness. Quickly she withdrew her hand from the bundle of clothes.

She looked over at her sleeping grandparents; she longed to place a kiss on their brows before she left, but knew that her gesture of love would wake them. And so with a heavy heart she crept out of the door, turning back quickly for one last look at them as her tears fell. One day, perhaps, they would forgive her.

Gopi paced the dirt road until he was sure he was wearing away the soil. The sun had long since sunk in the west and the summer moon glowed brightly in the night sky, accompanied by twinkling stars.

"Please, dear God," he prayed. "Don't make her change her mind." It was late and Rani should have shown up ages ago; he was worried, and yet he could not leave. He would wait the whole night if he had to. He had enough time, he decided.

Then he heard her light footsteps and ran to meet her.

"Oh, thank God you are all right! I thought that you had changed your mind, or that something dreadful had happened!" Then he noticed her red, swollen eyes and the tears on her cheeks. "Rani, what is the matter?" His arms went around her as she sobbed out her story.

"It's all right. Everything will work out," Gopi whispered, close to tears himself, for he felt the same ache in his own heart. "We don't need anyone's blessing. We have each other," he added bravely. "I promise you, with all my heart," he took her hand in his and placed it over his heart, "that I will take good care of you and give you no cause to regret your decision."

A small hopeful smile broke over Rani's sad face. Suddenly their future did not seem all that bleak. She was Gopi's, and together they were strong.

Gopi refused to even consider how his family would react when they learnt of the elopement. They were sure to disown him. After they were married and had found a place to live, he decided, he would write to Bharath to ask after his mother. He hoped that she would understand and forgive him for causing her so much pain and embarrassment, but if she could not accept Rani as his wife, then he would have no regrets whatsoever about leaving his home and family.

"Come." And with Rani's small hand trustingly placed in Gopi's, together they began their long walk into a future neither of them could predict.

CHAPTER NINE

Chumpa awoke the next morning to a blaze of gossip. Everyone seemed to know that Rani had eloped with her son sometime during the night. She had hoped that, working in the city, Gopi would forget about Rani; but no, he had to take her with him! The knowledge filled her with shame and anger and a deep sense of betrayal. She had never expected this!

Finally, when there were no tears more to shed, dry, racking sobs were all she could muster by way of grief. Chumpa wanted to be left alone to lick her wounds: even her daughters, who had come round on hearing of this startling turn of events, were sensible enough not to intrude.

Only when Sewcharran gloated about how he had thrown Gopi out of the house, and sniggered that he was a "good-for-nothing majee's boy", did Chumpa finally come to her senses. The quiet fire that simmered inside her erupted like a volcano in defence of her child, and everyone around her felt the heat.

"Don't you *ever* tell me that I cannot mention my son's name again!" she snarled at Sewcharran. "He is my firstborn," she declared in all her fiery glory, thumbing her heaving breasts to emphasise her words, "I was the one who felt his first kick, and it was I who struggled to give birth to him. Not *you*. You were too busy getting drunk!"

"Shut up!" Sewcharran roared as he stepped towards Chumpa, ready to strike. But seeing him approach, she bent down to pick up a piece of wood from the fire; just as he was about to deliver his blow she hit him in the face with the burning end. Sewcharran howled in pain, bringing his hands up to his scorched face.

"Majee, what have you done!" Sita cried.

"I can't see," Sewcharran groaned, moving blindly towards Chumpa.

"Taj!" Geeta ran to his side. "Let me have a look at your face."

"Leave me alone!" he bellowed. It was a few minutes before he calmed down sufficiently to allow Geeta to examine his face.

"Anoop," Geeta said, taking in the amount of damage done. "Go and get Sumi. She will know what to do." She turned accusingly to her mother. "How could you do such a thing?"

"Ask your father why!" Chumpa retaliated, shaking with anger and shock.

"What do you expect me to do?" yelled Sewcharran, despite his pain. "Pat him on the back, after the disgrace he's brought to this family by running off with that . . . *girl*?" he spluttered as he paced the small cottage, glaring at Chumpa with one eye.

"Taj is right, Ma," Geeta added coldly, and all eyes flew in her direction. "She is nothing but a manipulator and Gopi Bhai fell like a fool right into her clutches." She looked at everyone before going on, "Rani used him as her ticket out of this place."

"Geeta!" Sita broke in, horrified at her sister's attitude. "How dare you say that? Rani would never use Gopi. They are in love!"

"Well, Miss High and Mighty," Geeta retorted, "how are you going to face your in-laws after the disgrace your brother has brought this family?" Her voice shook with emotion. "I promise I will not rest until I get Bhaiya back, and make him admit what a fatal mistake he has made." Then she turned to her father: "And then, Taj, you can hold your head up again with pride."

"How wrong you both are!" Sita shot out angrily. "I cannot believe we are of the same flesh and blood."

Anoop arrived with Sumi, who rushed over to check on Sewcharran, while the two sisters glared at each other.

"What is going on here?" Anoop asked, taking in his wife's red face and her uneven breathing.

"You stay out of this," she snapped at him. "This concerns my family. Not yours."

"Geeta!" Chumpa, who had been crying softly while gathering her strength, turned around, appalled at her eldest daughter, and struck her across the face.

Geeta gasped in surprise.

"I did not raise you to speak to your husband in such a manner," Chumpa reminded her sternly – and was amazed when a slow, arrogant smile broke across Geeta's face.

"Well. Majee, you can say what you like, but after seeing what you did tonight to Taj, I think you should heed your own words."

"Geeta," Anoop grabbed hold of her fat arms tightly. "Apologise to your mother this instant!" he demanded, his features contorted with anger.

"Whatever for?" Geeta retorted, and then turned to her mother, smiling ever so sweetly, as though all were forgiven. "Majee, I promise that I will get Gopi Bhai away from that girl."

"You will do no such thing!" Chumpa cried, infuriated. "I know my son. If he has chosen Rani then he must have his reasons, and I will respect and accept his decision. If he ever visits with his wife, I for one will make them welcome!"

"Ma, I am so proud of you." Sita, eyes misty, hugged her mother.

"How can I remain bitter and unforgiving when your father and sister are so hard on our Gopi?" Chumpa asked, as she too wiped her eyes. "Besides, I cannot hate any of my children. You are the fruits of my womb. You are the children of Chumpa," she emphasised, "and no matter what any of you do, I will always love you."

"Well," interrupted Sumi, "I have looked at Sewcharran's eye." She glanced at Chumpa worriedly. "Only time will tell, but . . . he must see the doctor. It doesn't look good."

Rani could not believe that four hard months had passed since Gopi had brought her to the city. When they first arrived, Chin had taken them to the small temple of Hindu worship. There, they were married by the local pundit, who then gave Rani and Gopi his blessings, and the blessing from the Gods above. Thanks to Chin, they had found a room to rent in one of the barracks used by Indians. They purchased second-hand furniture, and Rani went out of her way to make the room as warm and comfortable as she could. This was their first home as husband and wife, and she was proud of it. Gopi's job as a barman brought home a small income, but it was the tips which helped put food on their table. Rani, too, contributed: she took on jobs washing people's clothes, and collected a few regular clients. Although she missed her grandparents, being with Gopi eased the pain, and she was happy.

Gopi never mentioned his family, but Rani knew how much he missed them. As the months went by, the strain of the separation became evident, and Rani tried her utmost to make it up to him. However, one evening Gopi came home much later then usual, and Rani, who had stayed awake waiting for him, caught the heavy smell of whisky on his breath as he got into bed.

"Gopi, you have been drinking!"

He turned to her and gave her a lazy look, and then grinned that crazy grin of his, which always sent her heart racing. "Do I look drunk, my queen?" he teased.

"Yes, and you smell awful, too!" She wrinkled her nose in disgust, which made him burst out laughing.

He laughed so hard tears rolled down his cheeks; and then suddenly they became serious tears. Rani put her arms around him.

"Gopi, what is wrong?"

"I just miss my family. I never knew it would be this hard."

Rani knew only too well what he meant, and she held him close as he let go of his grief. Raksha Bandan had come and gone, and she knew it broke Gopi's heart not to have his sisters tie the sacred silken thread, the rakhi, around his wrist, reaffirming their love for him and his promise to always protect them.

"I am so sorry," he said, pulling himself upright. "I have been very selfish. You, too, have left your family behind, and here I am, snivelling like an idiot."

"You are only human, Gopi." Rani ran a gentle hand through his curls. "This was bound to happen. But you simply cannot drown your feelings in alcohol."

"You are too good to me," Gopi whispered as he gathered her in his arms, drawing from her courage and strength. "I really do love you."

"I know that, and I also know how much you love your family. I think it is time to write to them and let them know how we are," she added encouragingly. "And I should write to my grandparents, too."

Gopi's eyes shone with renewed hope as he brought his lips down to meet hers. That night they made slow and tender love and fell asleep in each other's arms.

The following evening Rani was pleased to see that Gopi came home immediately after his shift, and that he had not been drinking. Together they sat down to write to their families.

"Majee, Majee!" cried an excited Bharath.

Chumpa stood up and wrung the excess water from the sari she was washing.

"Look what has arrived!" He waved a letter under her nose.

"From Gopi?" she asked, terrified he would say no.

"Yes!" Bharath shouted the magic word, and ripped open the envelope.

Chumpa almost snatched the letter from his hand. "Well?" she demanded. "Is he all right?"

"He is, Ma." Bharath replied. "And he says that he misses us and wishes us well, and that he and Rani were married in a temple and are very happy together."

"Is that all?" Chumpa was hungry for more news. "What is that other piece of paper?"

"Gopi Bhai has given us his address so we can write to him, and Rani has sent a letter for her grandparents."

Rani's grandparents had never forgiven the Suklals for what had happened, and no amount of explaining from Chumpa or Sita could dampen their animosity.

"Beta, I don't want you to show this letter to your father," Chumpa instructed, as she wiped her eyes.

"He's half blind anyway, so I'm sure he won't even notice this," he replied, waving the letter in the air.

"Bharath!" admonished Chumpa, feeling a stab of guilt. Sewcharran could no longer see out of one eye – the eye that she had struck in anger.

"Sorry," Bharath apologised quickly. "What about Geeta?"

"I don't think it would be wise to tell her. Not yet anyway," Chumpa advised. Geeta's mission to separate Rani and Gopi had left Chumpa with a hollow, apprehensive feeling in her stomach. "Sita will be happy, though."

The following day saw Bharath heading for the Big House.

"Are you all right?" he asked Sita with brotherly concern, noticing the slightly swollen ankles revealed by her sari, which rode high over her protruding stomach.

"I am just swelling, as you can see," she grinned as she wiped the breakfast dishes. "How are Taj and Majee?"

"Taj, I am not sure about. But Majee is very excited," he replied, grinning mischievously. He popped a piece of leftover toast into his mouth, keeping an eye on the door lest someone catch him with his mouth full. "Look what we got!" He waved the letter in front of Sita.

"A letter!" Sita reached out and snatched it from his hands. She read it twice to make sure she did not miss anything. "Oh, Bharath," she sighed, as tears shimmered in her eyes. "I am truly pleased for them."

"I'll mention it in my letter," Bharath teased, as he swallowed his tea and held out his cup for a second round.

"No, you won't!" Sita gave him a playful smack on the head. "I will write to him myself, and I will send him that rakhi I have been saving for him. Now wipe your mouth. You have crumbs all over you," she chided as she wrapped a piece of chocolate cake and some leftover pancakes for him. "Here, take these home and don't eat them all by yourself. Share some with Majee and Taj."

"Thanks, Sita." Bharath gave her his quirky, lopsided grin before taking the parcel and racing off. He dared not be late, for he might just receive a taste of the sirdar's whip.

Sita watched her baby brother run off. It was not often she saw him so excited, these days: since Gopi left, Bharath had not been the same. The bubbly boy had turned into a serious young man; but today, she had caught a glimpse of the boy again.

There had been other changes at home. Her father, always so forceful and fierce, had become subdued since losing sight in one eye. The spark seemed to have slowly died in him, while Chumpa had grown more confident and forthright.

Suddenly the baby kicked, and Sita ran her hand lovingly over the swell of her tummy. The days were drawing closer to her baby's arrival, but she would continue to work at the Big House for as long as possible.

She still walked to work every day, telling a concerned Hemith that the exercise did her good, and that Elizabeth made sure she rested during the day.

Sita found that living with her in-laws was a pleasant experience. They spoiled her endlessly, fussing over her health and making sure she ate well; but she was careful not to take advantage of their good nature. Sometimes their kindness made her burden of guilt heavier.

Sita learnt from conversations between Elizabeth and her husband that Albert Sheldon was making good progress at the cotton mills, and that his life was filled with new responsibilities. It would be some time before he could even consider visiting. Sita breathed a sigh of relief, for although her heart ached for Albert, she knew that marrying Hemith had been the right thing to do. What she and Albert had shared was a once-in-a-lifetime love affair, which she would always carry in her heart. But they had found and lost each other under strange circumstances, and she realized now that their love had never really stood a chance.

She thanked God for her mother's common sense, for Hemith was everything she could ever hope for in a husband. He was kind and caring, and so delightfully impatient for the birth of "their" baby, as she had come to think of the child she carried. Her son – no little girl could kick so vigorously, she thought – would be the most loved baby around, and his birth was the most anxiously awaited event of the year.

She had already decided that when the child was born, she would say that he had come early. Since Geeta's daughter had been born a bit premature, there should be no cause for speculation. Early births, she could explain, ran in her family.

It happened when she least expected it. Sita was serving lunch to Elizabeth, Richard, Charlotte and their governess when she felt a warm sensation running down the inside of her thighs, and she looked down to see a puddle of water.

"Oh, my!" she cried out, panic-stricken. "What have I done?"

"What has happened?" Elizabeth Campbell saw Sita's terrified expression, and then followed Sita's gaze to the floor. "It's natural, Sita," she said softly and firmly. "You are going to have your baby." Then she turned to her daughter. "Sweetheart, please ask Sumi to come here immediately, and then I want you and your brother to take your plates and go outside," she instructed calmly.

Suddenly Sita felt very alone, and it terrified her. When she saw Sumi she burst into tears of relief.

"Hush now, child," remonstrated Sumi. "This is no time for tears. You have a job to do, and that is to make sure your baby arrives safely."

"I want to go home." Sita cried. She could not deliver her baby here – it was not proper!

"Sita, you are not going anywhere. Is that clear?" Elizabeth's voice left no room for argument. "Your waters have broken and you could deliver at any time." Then Elizabeth turned to Sumi: "Send Indar to fetch her mother."

Sita clutched her tummy as she felt a contraction come on. She was suddenly frightened that her son would not be perfect, and that he would suffer for her sins. When Chumpa arrived an hour later she found Sita pacing the kitchen floor, refusing to lie down as Elizabeth Campbell had instructed.

"Majee, I really want to go home," Sita cried.

"Beti, take it easy." Chumpa wiped Sita's forehead with a damp cloth. "The baby seems to want to make an early arrival," she stated, mostly for Sumi's benefit, "so it is wise not to move you."

"Is she comfortable?" Elizabeth asked Chumpa after Sita was installed in the spare bedroom.

"Yes, thank you," replied Chumpa. "You are most kind."

When the time neared for the actual birth, Sita insisted that Sumi leave the room. She wanted only her mother to be with her.

"Please go," begged Chumpa to the reluctant Sumi. "We really cannot have her upset. I will call you if there are any complications." Sumi, looking none too happy, left the room.

Sita's muffled cries filled the room, but she handled the pains bravely, and Chumpa could not help but admire her younger daughter. She was enduring this labour in such a dignified manner, with a minimum of fuss, biting down hard on a piece of wood to prevent herself screaming.

"Not much longer," Chumpa patted Sita's hand after taking a quick look between her daughter's legs.

"Ma . . . I feel as though I want to push . . . *hard*. The pain . . ." Sita flung her head back in agony as she clutched Chumpa's hand.

"Go, ahead, sweetheart. Push if you want to. You baby is eager to come into this world."

With her mother's encouragement, Sita inhaled deeply and gave a final heave, and Albert's son slipped from the safety of his mother's womb into the world. The baby gave a lusty yell and Chumpa, smiling, placed him in Sita's arms without cutting the umbilical cord. The bond between mother and child was forged.

"Majee, he looks perfect," cried Sita in delight as she ran her hand over his slippery body. Instantly the baby stopped yelling and stared at his mother. And he is such a lovely colour, she thought as she gently wiped his tiny arms. "You are just my perfect little boy." Sita closed her eyes to say a silent prayer. Her son did not take after Albert, nor, from what she could see from his tiny perfect features, did he look like her: it was a combination of both their features that made him unique. This child was going to be his own special person.

"Sita," Chumpa whispered, cutting the cord to separate mother and child. "Who is your baby's father?"

Sita's head shot up instantly as she stared at her mother. It seemed like hours before she found her voice. "Please don't ask me that, Majee. You know that I cannot give you an answer," she whispered, her eyes on Albert's son. "I have married Hemith as you planned, and he is the father of my baby."

Gopi swung Rani around in his arms. "I am an uncle again and look, my Sita has not forgotten her older brother!" he laughed, filling their room with laughter and happiness. The letter announcing the birth of Sita's son, Mukesh, had arrived, together with a rakhi from Sita. "We will send something lovely for the baby. You can pick it, and I will choose a sari for Sita. Oh, Rani, let's celebrate with Chin." He put her down but did not let her leave the circle of his arms.

Rani shook her head. "I think it is best that you two go and celebrate."

"Why? Is something wrong?"

Rani's heart filled with pain. She could not bear to tell him how she really felt. "I'll just be in the way," she smiled tremulously as she propelled him towards the door. "Go and enjoy yourself, and when you return I will have supper prepared," she promised, as she handed him his old black coat.

"Sure you will be all right?" Gopi hesitated at the door.

"Positive," she returned, lowering her eyes so that he would not read the pain in them. Closing the door behind him, she caught his happy whistle and felt a stab of pain go through her.

Making no effort to wipe away the tears that fell, Rani fell to the floor, clutching the letter. She finally gave way to the pain buried deep inside her, which had deepened as the months had passed. How she ached to give Gopi a child of his own! There was a void in their lives, about which neither could bring themselves to speak. Rani had hoped that a baby, *their* baby, would fill that gap. Instead, as each month went by she felt a greater sense of loss. She knew Gopi's yearning for a child was as deep as her own, yet he managed to remain patient, loving and uncritical of her inability to conceive.

"Dear God," she sobbed passionately, "what is wrong with me? Am I so different from other women?" The tears ran down her cheeks and throat, but she was past caring. "Am I being punished for running away with Gopi?" Maybe she was suffering because of the hurt she had caused her grandparents. These questions nagged her endlessly. "Too many tears have fallen, dear God!" she cried. "Now, I ask for your forgiveness, and beg to be blessed with a baby."

It seemed like hours before Rani finally rose from the floor. She looked at herself in the old, tarnished mirror, and almost did not recognise herself. Her eyelids were swollen shut from crying, and she felt drained and exhausted. She forced herself to splash cold water on her face, hoping to relieve some of the puffiness. She then ran a comb through her long, thick, curly hair, and re-draped her cheap cotton sari.

Almost in a trance, Rani began to prepare supper. She placed a cupful of mielie rice over a small open fire. Then she cut up some vegetables she'd received from old Widow Roberts, her favourite client, as part payment for her weekly washing services.

While she waited for the supper to cook, she began to idly cut up an old newspaper, without much thought for the end result. When she opened the newspaper she found that she had transformed it into a pretty tablecloth, which she used to cover the old table Gopi had found and brought home. These simple actions calmed her.

She had almost thrown the drab old table out, but with Chin's assistance, Gopi had made it fairly presentable, through patience and many hours of stripping and polishing to bring back some of the shine to the wood. With a week's hard-earned tips, Gopi had purchased four old chairs, and although they did not match, they served their purpose.

Rani was so engrossed with setting the table that she did not hear Gopi come in, and jumped, startled, when he shut the door.

"Something smells good." Gopi sniffed the air.

Rani smiled nervously. Would he be able to tell that she had been sobbing her heart out? "Wait and see," she said, putting out the fire and placing two enamel plates on the table. "How is Chin?" she added, avoiding Gopi's eye.

"He's fine." Gopi removed his coat and pulled out a chair. Then he looked at Rani. "Is something the matter?"

"I am fine," she replied, a tad too quickly, as she turned her back to him. She heard Gopi push his chair back and heard his soft footsteps approach. Still she found that she could not look at him. She felt his hands on her shoulders, and he turned her around to face him.

"Look at me," he instructed, and when she did not, Gopi placed his hand under her chin and tilted her head back, forcing her to meet his eyes. "You have been crying," he stated.

"No," she lied, quickly turning her head away.

"Don't give me that," Gopi said softly as he ran his fingertips gently over her swollen eyelids. "I know my Rani very well."

"It's nothing," Rani insisted, trying to twist out of Gopi's hold, but he held her firmly, pulling her into the warmth and comfort of his arms. His actions brought a fresh flood of pain through her, and again she started to weep.

"Please talk to me, Rani," he pleaded, wanting to understand the sadness that surrounded her.

"I am so . . . sorry," she gulped. "Just that, after I read the letter from Sita, and saw how happy you were . . . I felt awful. I cannot . . . seem to be able . . . to give you a baby."

"Hey," Gopi tried to laugh. "Is that what's bothering you?" He bent and very slowly wiped her tears away, before placing a soft kiss on her forehead. "I would love to make a baby with you, but you don't have to cry about it. I am sure that we'll have a baby soon."

"How can you be so sure?" Rani whispered as she slipped her arms around his waist.

"Because two people who love each other as we do," he grinned mischievously, "are bound to produce a baby as proof of our love." He gathered her in his arms and carried her over to their bed. "Let's start practising right away," he whispered into her ear. "Trying to make a baby can be such fun."

Much, much later they realised they had skipped supper.

Six months passed, and still there was no sign of a child. Rani sought solace in her work and tried hard not to focus on her heartache. One morning, she awoke with a slight cramp, which she ignored, and went to work. It was while washing the clothes of Widow Roberts that the cramps in her belly worsened, and she doubled over in pain, crying out loudly.

The old lady, who had been basking in the warm morning sunshine, hurried over to her. "Are you ill, child?" she inquired, taking in Rani's heavy breathing and the thin film of perspiration which broke over her forehead as the pain intensified.

"I don't know . . . what is wrong," she gasped, clutching her belly.

"Come, lean on me," Widow Roberts offered – and then she noticed the blood. "Oh, dear." She turned wide, startled eyes to Rani, and then back to the blood which was seeping through Rani's thin cotton sari.

"What's happening to me?" Rani cried out in distress.

"You must lie down," the old lady said as she helped Rani into her bedroom and placed a pillow under her head. "I'll be back shortly."

The pain seemed to take over Rani's body. She wanted to scream. Instead, she bit hard on her bottom lip, drawing blood. She had to fight to keep the blackness from swallowing her. Somewhere, far away, she heard a stranger's caring voice talking to her. She felt hands running over her stomach, and her blood-soaked clothes being gently removed. Her body was drenched in perspiration and the blood kept flowing from her; and she knew that she was losing something more than blood. Eventually she gave in to the pain and the darkness that surrounded her.

When Rani opened her eyes, she blinked in confusion. What was Gopi doing here?

"Something terrible has happened, hasn't it?" she whispered.

For a few seconds, he stared at her with a terrified look on his face. And then he came over and placed his arms around her.

"Thank God, you are all right." He held her tightly, refusing to let her out of his arms.

"Gopi, please tell me."

"How are you feeling?" The stranger's caring voice took over, and Rani's gaze flew to meet the man who spoke. She looked into a pair of compassionate blue eyes set in the most kind and wrinkled face she had ever seen.

"My dear, you have just been through a terrible ordeal and you must rest." The old doctor took her hand in his. "I'm sorry," he continued in a soft voice. "Unfortunately, you were not able to carry your baby to term."

His simple words struck Rani dumb.

The doctor then looked at Gopi. "Your wife is very weak and frail at the moment. She will need lots of rest, and lots of love and care, before you try again," he warned as he gave them both a small, hopeful smile; but Rani just stared blankly past him as she held on to her husband.

Only later, at home, when she heard Gopi's muffled sobs, did the reality of the situation hit her. Then they clung to each other and grieved together for the baby they had so desperately longed for, and so quickly lost.

The loss of their unborn baby affected their lives far more than either one expected. Gopi began to stay away from home, terrified that wanting to hold Rani in his arms and make love to her would only cause her more hurt – for she still looked so frail, and he kept hearing the doctor's warning.

For a long while Rani did not care that Gopi stayed out late; she was too wrapped up in her own grief. There were days when she did not bother to get out of bed at all. Now Gopi often came home with liquor on his breath. They did not quarrel, but a host of unspoken words lay between them.

There was also no talk of another baby. As the months went by, Rani's strength returned, and the longing for a baby had never left her; but when she turned to her husband for love and comfort, he would either pretend not to be awake, or moodily reply that he was too tired. They would end up falling asleep with their backs to each other.

Gopi worked longer hours, and his tips increased, so he insisted that Rani stay at home and not work until she had fully recovered. This meant that Rani had time on her hands to brood, and brood she did. Alone, she would remove her necklace from its little velvet pouch and gaze at it for hours. She had never before been tempted to pawn this beautiful gold chain, with its shimmering set of stones: topaz, ruby, emerald and diamond. Rani would watch as the light caught the stones, adding life to the necklace, and wonder whether she should sell it. Maybe then they could get out of this dreary little room which only brought her misery. And yet, something always held her back. Maybe someday it would come in useful, she decided as she locked away the necklace,.

In the meantime, she decided that she had had enough of the way this marriage of hers was going. Gopi was drifting away from her, and it was time that she fought for what they once had.

Chumpa received a letter from Gopi informing her of the loss of their baby. His letter was short and poignant, and Chumpa's heart ached for them.

"Is life always going to be so cruel to my Beta?" she cried, as she showed Geeta and Sita the letter.

"Probably all her fault," Geeta remarked, through narrowed eyes.

"How can you say such an awful thing?" Sita gave her sister a startled look.

"Well, whose fault can it be? I mean, there are no problems on our side. After all," she pointed out, "you have a handsome son and I have a beautiful daughter, and another one on the way." Geeta moved her hand over her round tummy. "She must be barren."

"Don't be silly." Sita was annoyed. "How can she be barren when she did conceive?"

"Sometimes a woman loses a baby and goes on to have others," Chumpa told her daughters sharply as she placed a pot of tea on the table. "Help yourself," she added, leaving the room without a backward glance.

Geeta sniffed in defiance of her mother's snub, and Sita shot her a look of utter disgust.

Sometimes, sighed Chumpa as she stormed out of the cottage, Geeta acted as though she knew it all. Now that the small farm was proving profitable, Geeta had adopted an air of superiority which was beginning to annoy her humble family. In her simple yet firm way, Chumpa tried to cut her daughter down to size whenever she felt that Geeta was overreaching herself.

Sita, on the other hand, had blossomed into motherhood, and Chumpa could not help but feel proud that her little rebel had settled into marriage without losing her independence. If only her Gopi could find the same contentment!

In the year that followed, Geeta gave birth to a set of twins and named them Ramu and Krishna, and when Mukesh was three years old, Sita had a baby boy whom they called Sunil. Much to his father's delight, Sunil was a miniature of Hemith. Mukesh, it was said, had taken after his lovely mother, and Sita always gave a wistful smile in response.

Sita continued to work at the Big House, and Mukesh and Sunil were taken care of by Hemith's mother during the day. Elizabeth Campbell was very generous, giving Sita her son's old clothing for Mukesh and the new baby – which certainly made them stand out among the other children on the estate.

While Geeta and Anoop's farm prospered, Sita began to wonder if her life should also change.

"Why don't we take the plunge and start a small farm as well?" she suggested to Hemith one evening, while breastfeeding Sunil.

"Do you know what a difficult venture you are suggesting?" he asked seriously, pacing their bedroom. "Anoop is always anxious about his cabbages and herbs, and how much damage he has suffered through the summer storms. He is worried that they have taken on more than they can handle."

"I did not realise that the situation was so bad," Sita murmured as she tucked her breast into her blouse and placed Sunil over her shoulder to burp him. "Every time I see Geeta, she and the children are always dressed so smartly, and from what she tells Majee, they seem to be making progress..."

"Your sister is a bully," Hemith stated. "She does not give that husband of hers a chance. Poor man, the farm is not easy for him to manage on his own."

"How can you say that!" Sita defended her sister. "My sister is an excellent businesswoman, and the brains behind their success. She puts many a man to shame!"

"She is a shrewd –"

"Hemith, not another word about my sister, please. I was talking about us," she reminded him in her quiet and firm manner. She looked at him shrewdly: Hemith had been preoccupied recently. There was something he wasn't telling her. "What is really the problem?"

"Sita," he sat next to her and took her hand in his. "I understand how you feel – I also want to be independent. But we have to be realistic. Hemith hesitated for a few seconds. "Right now we are at a crossroads at the mill. Many of us are fed up with the way we are treated, and because I tend to voice my opinions, I have been approached to start a small group to represent the workers." He turned Sita's palm over and ran his rough fingers across hers, enjoying the softness. "At the moment we are still in the early stages of planning, and there is a lot to do. I have to make sure that the right people are involved. People who are not scared to talk about what is going on." He looked at Sita, determination on his face. "Sita, I feel the need to be there for our people. We cannot stand back and allow this kind of suffering to go on. We have to pave a better life for our children and grandchildren, and their children too."

He spoke with such sincerity and conviction Sita felt a rush of guilt. "Oh, Hemith," she sighed, as she laid her head on his shoulder. "I had no idea that you felt this strongly. I mean," she added hastily as she felt him tense beside her, "I knew that you were unhappy about the conditions at the mill, and that you always wanted to do something positive, but saying and doing are two different things."

"I am aware of that, Sita. And I fully understand the implications. I will not be popular with the plantation owners, but I am prepared for that."

"I am sorry for even suggesting a farm at a time like this. There is too much going on here, and I am glad that you are standing by what you think is right and necessary." She took hold of his hand. "You have my support, Hemith."

Sita set off happily for work the next morning. However, she could not help but notice Elizabeth Campbell's troubled mood: Elizabeth sat in the breakfast room gazing distractedly out of the window, every now and then turning back to her embroidery. Her children were almost teenagers now, and took their lessons with their governess, Mildred: the morning was quiet.

That changed suddenly with the arrival of Master Browne. Sita saw him ride his horse at a furious pace up the drive and halt outside the main door. He was not alone: accompanying him was the short and stocky mill overseer.

The noise startled Elizabeth. "What is going on?" She placed her embroidery down and stood up.

Sumi, inquisitive as ever, rushed to open the door – and stepped hastily back as the mill owner and his overseer walked in, both looking pale and worried. The two men asked to see Elizabeth, and Sumi showed them into the morning room.

Sita looked at Sumi inquiringly, but she could only shrug her plump shoulders in response. Then both women heard Elizabeth's anguished cry, and knew that something terrible had happened. Sita's hand flew to cover her mouth in surprise.

The overseer suddenly opened the door and demanded a bowl of cold water and a towel. A quick glance past him showed Sita that Elizabeth was lying on the couch with her eyes closed.

"Call the governess as well," he instructed, "and hurry." Then he closed the door.

"What is going on in there?" Sumi followed Sita into the kitchen.

"I have no idea," Sita answered. "All I could see was Madam lying on the couch, as white as a ghost. I think she fainted," she added, quickly filling a bowl with water.

Very softly Sita knocked on the door, which was opened by the overseer. He took the towel and bowl from her without so much as a thank-you.

"Excuse me," the governess said behind her, and Sita moved out of the way to allow her to enter the room. Once again, Sita found the door shut in her face.

"I hope that it's nothing serious," remarked Sumi, although she looked fearful. "I know that Master Campbell was going over to the mill to check on how far they had got with crushing his cane. Maybe the governess can tell us what is happening."

However, they were disappointed: the governess soon left the house, with Elizabeth and the two men. Elizabeth Graham looked pale but composed.

What began as a pleasant day for Sita became one of worry and unanswered questions. At home she fed her sons and put Sunil to sleep; Mukesh was far too energetic. As the hours passed Sita became anxious, for Hemith had not returned from the mill and the sun had long since sunk in the summer sky.

From her bedroom window she saw him. He was walking slowly, his head bent, and he looked tense and preoccupied. Sita ran to him.

"Something terrible has happened, hasn't it?" She reached him, breathless and scared. "I was so worried about you. You did not come home, and there seems to be a problem at the Campbell Estate and no one is talking!" she babbled.

"Calm down," Hemith took hold of her shoulders to steady her. "Something did happen, something awful." He took her hand in his. "It is better if I tell you this before we go inside."

Sita's eyes searched his face for answers. She saw how tired he was.

"Your Master Campbell came in for his weekly inspection at the mill. Everything was going well, when suddenly . . ." He shuddered at the memory. "You know how we stack the cane, in high bundles ready to be crushed? It seems that a family of snakes had made a home for themselves in there. Master Campbell wanted to check on his stock, and insisted on moving the bundles himself . . . and before we knew what happened, we had angry, hissing reptiles everywhere!"

"Oh, no . . ." Sita's eyes widened in horror. "Did anyone get hurt?"

"Yes, I'm afraid three people were bitten. And one of them was Master Campbell."

"Will they be all right?" Sita asked, fearing the worst.

"Sita, honestly, I don't know. Master Campbell was in a worse state than the others . . . he is still unconscious. Someone has gone to fetch a doctor."

Sita's lips trembled. "He is such a kind man . . . He cares about his labourers, you know that, Hemith." Sita's voice shook as she put her arms around him. "I simply cannot imagine what Madam must be going through, and those poor children! Do you think he will die? Did Master Browne say anything?"

"We have not been told anything further," Hemith's voice hardened. "You know how it is with these people. They never tell us anything, but expect us to do everything."

Sita remembered the morning's activities at the Big House, and knew her husband was right.

The following morning Sumi filled her in: "Madam did not come home at all last night, and I heard the governess tell the children that Master Campbell was unwell, and that the doctor had issued strict instructions that he was not to be moved." Sumi looked worried. "Sita, I think he is very ill."

The labourers on the Campbell Estate had heard the news by now, and they got together and held a prayer session for their Master, and for the two bitten workers who were also ill, but recovering. The Big House was filled with tension. Two days went by without any news, and then on the third day they heard that Master Campbell had died without regaining consciousness, Elizabeth Campbell by his side. It was indeed a day of bereavement for everyone on the estate.

With a calmness that surprised Sita, Elizabeth Campbell began to make the necessary arrangements for her husband's funeral. Sita and Sumi kept their grief to themselves, for they had to prepare meals, and ensure that Elizabeth's wishes were carried out.

"Maybe she will sell up and return to England. After all, what does a woman know about running a sugar-cane plantation?" was the general speculation. Rumours went around that Master Browne was even thinking of taking over the estate.

"God help us if he does," Sumi voiced everybody's fears. "I simply will not be able to work for that man. He is as different to Master Campbell as night is to day."

Sita knew how right she was. However, she did not want them to lose hope. "Let us wait and see," she advised cautiously, "what Madam plans to do."

CHAPTER TEN

A month after the tragic death of Graham Campbell, Mukesh had an attack of measles. He had never been this sick before, and Sita was extremely worried, although she knew that all children had measles at some time or other. Sita took time off to stay at home and nurse him, with the assistance of her mother-in-law. She carefully followed the old homemade Indian remedies, cooling Mukesh's heated and itchy little body by gently covering it with a mixture of turmeric powder and leaves that

Hemith had brought home from a Syringa tree, which helped prevent Mukesh scratching himself.

Sita spoiled her son during this time. She used the hours to teach him the English and Hindi alphabets, and told him stories she had heard the governess read to Richard and Charlotte when they were much younger. She acted out little scenes for him, and his delighted laughter filled the room. Sita wished she could stay at home all the time and take care of her little boys. There was so much she was missing: their innocent looks, their inquiring minds and numerous questions, and even their sense of humour, which kept her enthralled.

Three weeks later Mukesh recovered fully. By this time he was extremely restless and bored, and wanted to go out and play with his little brother and the other children on the estate. Sita let him have his day of fun, and watched later that evening how her two boys snuggled next to each other, after she had caught them and given them a hot, steamy bath, like two little angels sleeping off their exhaustion.

Two days later, happy that her son was healthy and energetic, she decided to visit Sumi at the Big House and catch up on what had happened during the weeks she had been away. She really did not want to leave her boys. So, as a little treat, she took them with her.

Sita got up early, bathed and washed her hair. It gleamed black and shiny in the sunlight as it dried. She chose for her visit a pretty, hot-pink cotton sari. She loved bright colours and they suited her: the pink brought out her creamy complexion and contrasted with her black hair, which fell down her back, thick, long, and straight. She decided to leave it loose – she put her hair in a bun or a plait when she worked, and today she was definitely not working.

Sita dressed Mukesh in an old sailor suit which had belonged to Richard Campbell, and Sunil matched his brother in an outfit that she had sewn for him.

"You look very pretty Ma, and you smell so nice!" Mukesh beamed.

Sita returned his smile and ruffled his dark brown hair playfully, and his laughter filled her heart. Together, mother and sons set off towards the Big House. Sita carried Sunil on her hip and held onto Mukesh's hand.

"Now, when we see Aunt Sumi I want you both to be good boys. Remember to say 'please' when you want something and 'thank you' when you receive it." Sita instructed in a soft, firm voice. Mukesh nodded his small head and Sita felt a tug at her heart. Sometimes he reminded her of his father, and then she loved her special son all the more. It was not that she loved Sunil any less, but Mukesh was a baby born of true, pure and innocent love, and he held a very special place in her heart.

Sunil, from his hypnotic black eyes to his mischievous little smile, was every bit Hemith's son. He was a strong-minded little boy too: at almost two, he knew what he wanted and always got his way. He did not throw tantrums nor did he sulk, but he was a baby you could not say no to; he made Sita laugh with delight at his funny little expressions.

"Ma, I promise to be good," Mukesh said in English, speaking slowly and clearly. Sita smiled down at him, pleased. Besides the Hindi that they spoke at home, she spoke to her boys in English a lot. Sita was extremely proud of Mukesh: although he was younger than Geeta's daughter, Asha, he spoke with confidence and was always eager to learn.

While Sita was making her way to the Big House, someone else was doing the same. Albert Sheldon was returning. But this time, he was not alone. Sitting beside him in the coach was his wife, Helena; and opposite them were their son Joseph and his nanny.

Albert Sheldon rested his head against the backrest and closed his eyes. The journey from England had been a long and arduous one, and when their ship finally docked in Durban harbour he was relieved to find that a coach had been made available for them.

"How on earth did you put up with this dry, intense heat, Albert?" rasped Helena as she fanned herself. Albert opened his eyes and gave her an amused look. Helena was, as usual, decked out in her English finery, all satin and lace. Suddenly she seemed terribly out of place, waving her jasmine-scented handkerchief in the air. Soon, Albert sighed to himself, Helena would have to accept the fact that South Africa was very, very different from her home.

"Nanny," she called out in her thin, shrill voice, "Wipe Joseph's forehead. The child is simply wilting."

When Helena started in her officious tone, Albert switched off mentally. His mind wandered back to the letter he had received from his sister, and the shock he had felt on learning that Graham Campbell was dead. When he left for England nearly six years ago, he had promised

Graham that he would return to help run the estate. Now he was indeed returning, but under tragic circumstances.

He had not wanted to come back earlier – not since Elizabeth had written, shortly after his return to England, that her little helper Sita had married. This news, delivered so casually, sent his life spiralling in a totally different direction. With his heart broken, he lost control for a while. He forced himself to work like a demon beside his younger brother, Rory, at the mills; when he wasn't working, he was drowning his heartache in liquor.

Sita occupied his thoughts during the day and his dreams at night. When he could bear it no longer he went out, and saw Sita's lovely face in every female he turned to. Albert found himself invited to many parties, and accepted nearly every invitation he received. Young debutantes found him available, very handsome, and utterly charming; yet he carried himself with an air of mystery and aloofness, and this made him unattainable – a challenge.

At every party he attended, he met a lovely, green-eyed blonde who was a few years older than him. Albert, wrapped up in his heartache, did not think it strange that the cool blonde, the daughter of one of his father's business associates, was so often at his side.

The moment Helena FitzGerald saw Albert, she knew that she wanted to marry him. He was young, good-looking and very wealthy: all in all, a wise investment. Her father was on the verge of bankruptcy, and this young man suited her needs perfectly. She wanted to live in style, and she was not going to settle for a middle-aged man who was set in his ways. It mattered not that Albert seemed to be nursing a broken heart: this made it all the easier.

Albert had no idea what was in store for him. When she befriended him, he thought it was out of the goodness of her heart. For Helena, the seduction had just begun. She made sure that she knew which parties he was invited to, and got herself invited as well. She watched the eager young ladies and lonely widows surround him, and when he looked desperately in need of escape, she would suddenly appear at his side and whisk him away.

Albert was thankful for her help, and, often under the influence of liquor, would flirt with her charmingly and harmlessly, seeing her as his safety net – until it was too late to escape from her clutches.

Desperate to get Sita out of his mind and heart, he decided to attend one of his aunt's famous dinner parties. True to her reputation, Maureen Sheldon's guests were elegantly dressed and as snobbish as they come. Albert found himself seated next to Helena, and for this he was grateful. Dinner somehow passed without him making a spectacle of himself, despite having one drink too many.

Desperate to escape this stifling company, Albert found his way to the study, a long way away from the dining hall. He lay on the couch with his eyes closed as images of Sita's laughing face danced in front of him – and when he felt soft lips on his, he responded with ardour to the woman in his arms.

Later, Albert could barely recall the events of that night, but it changed the course of his life. On awakening, he discovered a fan with Helena's name on it, the only sign that she had been there with him – that, and the lingering scent of jasmine, which only made him feel nauseous.

Now, whenever Helena was around him she would blush, stammer and send him coy, secretive looks. He did not understand what this was all about, until one day her father stormed into the office at the mill, caught him by the collar and punched his face. Taken totally by surprise, he fell back, and only the wall behind him prevented him from hitting the floor.

"What the hell . . .!" he looked at the older man in confusion as he nursed his jaw, and then at his father, who had followed him in with a stupid grin on his face.

"Does it hurt, son?" his father asked, with a glint in his eye. "Good. I would have reacted in a similar manner had some young man taken advantage of my little girl."

"*What?*" Albert cried, but his father raised a hand to stop him from saying anything more.

"Look, son. I am not pleased that this has happened. Everyone was talking about the attention you were showing Helena, but . . . I did expect you to be discreet."

"Father, I don't know what you're talking about!" Albert's eyes were dark, and he placed his hands on his hips aggressively. His jaw hurt like hell, and he couldn't understand why his father looked so pleased. Helena's father looked like he'd love to land another punch.

"Son, now don't go and deny that the baby is yours. I'll not take that," John Sheldon warned.

"Baby . . .?" Albert's eyes narrowed as the truth finally dawned. "Are you saying that Helena is *pregnant*? But . . ." Albert stammered, " I have not . . ."

"Don't you dare call my daughter a liar!" Helena's father stepped forward threateningly.

"Henry, now don't get upset." Albert's father took hold of Henry FitzGerald's arm and led him to a chair. "Sit down and relax. I'll sort this out."

Albert ran a hand frantically through his hair. He could not remember sleeping with Helena . . . except . . . then it came back to him: the night at Aunt Maureen's, the liquor he consumed . . . soft lips on his, and the smell of jasmine which had made him feel sick. "Oh, dear God," he moaned, feeling as sick as he had that morning.

"Son," John Sheldon spoke sternly, and Albert warily looked at his father. "I have already given my word to Henry, and we Sheldons keep our word." His voice hardened when he saw the stubborn look on Albert's face: "You have to do the right thing."

Albert decided it was time for him to seek out Helena, and so, nursing a sore jaw, he knocked on the door of the FitzGerald's Tudor-style country hideout some distance from London.

"I am glad that you have come," Mrs FitzGerald greeted Albert stiffly as she let him in. "My daughter is most distressed at the moment and I trust that your presence here will soothe her," she added primly, but Albert heard the warning in her voice.

Albert followed the plain Mrs FitzGerald up the stairs to Helena's bedroom. He could not help but notice that mother and daughter were very different: Mrs FitzGerald was a short, plump woman with small brown eyes and mousy brown hair with streaks of grey in it, which she wore in a tight little bun. It seemed strange that a woman whose husband was so wealthy would dress so simply, while their green-eyed daughter always looked like a princess.

When Mrs FitzGerald opened the bedroom door, Albert had to squint to see Helena: the room was bathed in darkness. Heavy drapes covered the windows, as though to hide her from the rest of the world. Helena was in bed, nervously twisting the sheets.

"Hello, Helena," he said, and then gulped in surprise when she began to cry. It was the most unnerving sound he had ever heard.

"Hush now, Helena. This is no time for tears. Albert is here to talk to you." Mrs FitzGerald's voice was as cold as the look she gave him. She closed the door behind her, and he shivered as though he had been hit by an icy wind from the north.

"I am so sorry," Albert crossed the room and sat at the edge of the bed. He took her hand in his, hoping she would stop that horrible sound. "Please stop crying," he almost snapped, and then felt guilty. "Crying is not going to help either one of us," he added in a soft but very firm tone.

"I . . . don't know what is going . . . to happen to me," she sniffed, screwing up her eyes.

"What do you mean?"

"My father . . . almost killed me," she hiccuped as she peered into his face. "Did . . . he do this . . . to you?" She reached out to touch his face, and Albert drew back from her touch. He did not respond to her question.

"Are you," Albert cleared his throat. "Are you sure about the baby? I mean . . . that it's mine . . ."

Helena's eyes widened and she gasped. "How dare you question my honour, Albert Sheldon?" She almost swooned in disbelief. "There has never been another man!"

"I am so sorry," he mumbled. Albert was starting to feel extremely guilty. " I just cannot remember everything . . ."

"You don't want to marry me!" Helena shrieked. "You don't love me and this baby we created!"

When Albert did not respond she began to sob. This time she sounded quite hysterical, gasping for breath and making the most dreadful noise. Her face started to go blue, and Albert was sure she was going to suffocate. Albert's face whitened and his heart raced.

"What have you done to her, you fiend?" cried Mrs FitzGerald as she stormed into the room. "Helena . . . baby," she soothed as she drew her hysterical daughter into her arms and threw Albert a look that was close to murder. "Well?" she demanded angrily. "Will you make an honest woman of my daughter?"

Albert sighed, feeling the dream of Sita slipping away.
"Yes," he said sadly. "Of course, I will marry her."

Now, watching his wife next to him in the coach, Albert marvelled at his naiveté. He could not believe what a fool he had been. Both mother and daughter had played their parts brilliantly. Helena was the perfect wife in the beginning; then, very slowly, her true personality emerged, and it became apparent to Albert why she had married him.

Helena had conveniently miscarried two weeks prior to their wedding, and only informed him after their honeymoon. He began to suspect that she had never been pregnant at all. When he confronted her, she wept at his insensitivity; and when he declared that he was going to have the marriage annulled she straightened up, and with a smug look declared that it was too late – for there was indeed a baby on the way, conceived during their honeymoon.

And so Joseph Sheldon was born.

Helena's father declared himself insolvent after the wedding, and Helena did not waste any time in approaching her father-in-law for assistance – assistance given under duress, for he was told that he would not have the privilege of seeing his grandchild unless he helped the FitzGeralds

Helena proved to be a lavish spender. She enjoyed the wealth and prestige of being married to a Sheldon, but she was cold towards Albert. After the child's birth, she declared that they would sleep in separate bedrooms, now that she had done her duty and produced a son.

"How much further, Albert?" Helena whined as she dabbed her jasmine-scented handkerchief to her slim white throat.

"About another forty-five minutes," he replied noncommittally as he gazed out at the passing scenery.

"Can't that coolie make this coach go any faster?" she complained, and then in the same breath snapped, "Joseph, sit down," as she pulled her son away from the window of the coach.

"Let him look out, Madam. He will learn by observing and it will do him good," advised Nanny Goodson as her grey eyes scanned the countryside, taking in the lush, rolling green hills filled with cane, the cloudless blue sky and wonderful sunshine.

When Albert told Nanny Goodson he was leaving for South Africa and offered her the job of travelling companion to Helena and nanny to Joseph, who at four was more than a handful, she had accepted without hesitation; she was eager for adventure.

"I still cannot believe that I let you persuade me to accompany you to this God-forsaken wilderness, Albert," rasped Helena as she dabbed a thin film of perspiration from her upper lip. "It is indeed very selfish of you to drag me and our son along," she added bitterly.

"Helena," Albert said with exasperation, "we settled this in England. I have never kept it a secret that I hoped to return to South Africa, so please be reasonable."

They had indeed discussed this move, and after much resistance, and realising that she would be left behind without much financial freedom, Helena had relented. However, she had never stopped whining, and Albert was at the end of his tether.

"Look!" Joseph pointed a plump, pink finger in the direction they were heading.

Albert smiled: they were approaching the estate. It seemed as though nothing had changed. Acres and acres of green stretched on all sides of the house, and in the distance he could see the labourers, some with their traditional turbans and others with caps on their heads to protect them from the Natal sun. It was as though he had never left.

"What are they doing?" Nanny Goodson inquired as this rather unfamiliar sight greeted her.

"The men are harvesting the cane while the women are stacking it into bundles," he explained, "so that they can deliver it to the mill where it will be crushed."

The Indian coachman brought the coach to a halt outside the Campbell home, and Albert opened the door, shuddering in the suddenly intense heat. It was almost seven years since Albert had left for England, and since he had last seen his sister.

"Helena," he turned to his wife with a warning look, "I don't want any catty remarks from you. Please remember that this is my sister's home."

Helena's reply was a mere toss of her blonde head as she stepped from the coach. "Nanny, keep Joseph away from that coolie," she said sharply, as though Albert had not spoken at all.

"Helena!" Albert's voice was cold and stern.

"Oh, Albert, you are just too serious," she laughed mockingly as she slipped her arm through his. "Come, I want to meet the great Elizabeth Campbell."

The front door opened and Sumi stood looking at him in disbelief.

"Hello, Sumi," Albert smiled as she stepped back to let him in, "You are looking very well. Getting nice and plump in your old age," he teased. "Now where is my sister?"

"Master Albert," Sumi recovered quickly, casting a curious glance at the trio who followed. "This is a surprise! Madam will be so pleased to see you. Come, she is in the morning room, as usual."

Albert was shocked to see the changes in Elizabeth. She looked older and there were fine lines around her eyes, and she was thinner, much thinner than he remembered. When she saw Albert tears gathered in her sad eyes.

"Albert, oh Albert," she sobbed as he drew her into his arms. "I am so glad to finally see you!" Albert held her until she calmed down. A discreet little cough drew them apart, although Albert did not let go of Elizabeth.

At Helena's raised eyebrows, Albert made the introductions.

"I am very pleased to meet you, Helena," Elizabeth smiled and turned to Albert. "She is very lovely."

Albert gave a small, cynical smile as he noted the pleased expression on his wife's face.

"And this little man is my son," Albert returned, as Elizabeth scooped Joseph into her arms.

"It has been so long, Albert. I cannot believe you have a child." She looked across at Helena. "He looks very much like you."

"Yes, he does take after my side of the family. Doesn't he, darling?" Helena smiled ever so sweetly at Albert as she seated herself.

Elizabeth showed Albert to a chair and seated herself opposite him. "So much has happened. But first, tell me about Father."

And Albert told her about their father and the improvement in his health. He described how well their cotton mills were doing, and how Rory was now a capable young man who was more than able to run the business on his own.

"I am so sorry to be here under these circumstances." Albert's eyes were soft and compassionate, for he read the pain in his sister's eyes. "But now that I am here, you must let me help you."

"Thank you." Elizabeth smiled sadly as she turned to Helena, who had been observing brother and sister quietly. "And thank you, too, for coming."

Sumi served them iced tea, dainty cucumber sandwiches and tiny cupcakes, and when Helena did not hide her surprise at being served in such style, Elizabeth smiled. "I try to maintain standards as much as I can. We have a little garden that produces wonderful vegetables, and Sumi makes the most divine cakes," Elizabeth explained as she handed her nephew a cupcake.

"I suppose it is difficult, though," Helena replied, and when Elizabeth raised an inquiring eyebrow, she added, "Living here in the wilderness with these strange people must certainly be unnerving."

Here we go again, sighed Albert, getting up and walking towards the huge windows which overlooked the back garden.

The sight that met his eyes caused him to catch his breath.

"Is something the matter, Albert?" Helena cast a curious glance in his direction.

Swinging around, Albert found that his heart was racing, and his mouth suddenly felt very dry. "No," he replied softly, before turning back to give the view ahead of him his fullest attention.

Sitting on the lawn, playing with two little Indian boys and Richard Campbell, was Sita. Her face was raised as though worshipping the sun, and he could see her beautiful almond eyes sparkling with laughter as the little boys ran around her, chased by Richard.

She had grown even more beautiful, Albert marvelled. Her body had filled out and become more curvaceous. He remembered her in the long skirts and blouses she had worn as a girl; the sari, although it covered her fully, revealed more of her shape. Her breasts were high and firm, emphasising her small waist and shapely hips. Albert longed to reach out to touch the silky black mane which flowed down her back, just to make sure that she was real and not a trick of the mind.

The love he still felt for her engulfed him. Was she happy? he wondered, and the ache in him to know overtook all the good sense he possessed. When he felt a gentle tug on his left leg he was glad: his son had just given him the perfect opportunity.

"Come on, son. It's time for you to meet your cousin," he said, taking Joseph's small hand in his. Together they walked out of the morning room into the afternoon sunshine, towards the stunning young woman who still held his heart captive.

CHAPTER ELEVEN

Sita almost swooned at the sight of Albert. She had never expected to see him in the flesh again, and now here he was, approaching her with a deeply intense look on his face. Instinctively, she drew Mukesh closer, while Sunil hid in the folds of her sari.

Richard Campbell, after a few baffled minutes, recognised the visitor and ran to meet his uncle halfway. They hugged long and hard before the boy withdrew, turning towards the plump little blond child who hung onto Albert's leg. Sita felt a slow, dangerous heat rise in her as she met Albert's gaze. He turned and spoke a few words to Richard, and Richard led him towards Sita.

"Sita, look who has finally arrived from England. This is my Uncle Albert and my cousin Joseph," he grinned, clearly delighted. "I was a small boy when he left, but I remember him," he declared proudly.

Sita gave Richard a nervous smile as she slowly rose to her feet. When she lifted her head, her honey-brown eyes, frightened but defiant, met his unreadable gaze. Sita almost gasped aloud when Albert delivered a slow, lazy smile, and she shivered in the sunshine.

"And who are these little boys?" Albert inquired.

"They are Sita's sons, Uncle Albert."

Albert's eyes widened ever so slightly, and he bent and held out a hand to Mukesh. Sita's breath caught in her throat.

"Hello, young man. What is your name?"

"Mukesh," piped the little voice confidently, and Sita held her breath. The similarities between them were obvious to her, and she was terrified he would discover the truth. She was not prepared for that confrontation, and knew she never would be.

"Well, Mukesh," Albert smiled, clearly charmed, "this is my son Joseph." He propelled the smaller child towards the boys.

"This is my brother," Mukesh returned proudly, as he pointed to Sunil, who was peeping at them from behind Sita with round curious eyes.

The two little boys assessed each other, hesitating, and then Sunil stepped away from Sita. With Richard's encouragement, Joseph also shyly stepped closer.

"You have a pair of handsome little boys," observed Albert as the children chased each other on the lawn, their innocent laughter filling the air.

Sita fought hard not to meet his eyes or comment, afraid of what she might reveal. Instead, she kept her gaze focused on the children.

The three smaller boys were chasing Richard when Joseph stumbled. Mukesh reached out, but could not steady the smaller boy; both fell to the ground.

Sita rushed forward, all her protective instincts to the fore, and picked up both Mukesh and Joseph. Joseph, who was a little winded, began to howl. She very gently held him in her arms and wiped his tears away with the edge of her sari, as she would have done for her own sons.

Albert was watching her tender ministrations when a shrill, cold voice halted Sita's actions.

"Get him away from her!"

As Sita swung around with Joseph in her arms, her eyes fell on a slim blonde woman, who seemed to be flying, not running, towards her. Before she could move, the child was snatched from her arms.

"Don't you ever touch my son again!" the woman instructed coldly, and Sita took a step back. The blatant hostility in the woman's green eyes was almost frightening. "And," the lady continued in the same tone, "keep those rascals away from him as well!"

She spat out the words as though Sita's sons were lepers. Sita pulled her little boys towards her, shocked – she had never felt more humiliated in her whole life. The children watched with wide-eyed innocence, not understanding.

"Helena, stop this talk immediately!" Albert's voice was tinged with ice and his eyes burned with fury, and he clenched and unclenched his fist to keep himself in check. His anger was terribly controlled in contrast to the woman's outburst.

It dawned on Sita that the woman she was looking at was Albert's wife. Her eyes were flashing green, her lips were drawn into a thin line, and her pale skin had taken on an ugly red hue at Albert's rebuke. Despite her cool blonde looks and striking features, she seemed a cold and heartless woman whose beauty was superficial. This person could make life on the estate unbearable for everyone, Sita concluded. She watched in amazement as the woman gathered her green silk gown with one hand, barely allowing her ankles to show, and holding her son's hand with the other, swept past Sita as though she were non-existent.

Albert turned to Sita: "I apologise for her behaviour." When Sita did not respond he continued through clenched teeth, "I will make sure that such a display never happens again."

Sita read the anger in his eyes before he turned on his heel, his broad and muscled body taut with emotion.

Albert was furious, almost to the point of violence, a feeling he did not entertain very often. Helena's behaviour, acting as though Sita and her sons were untouchables, was deplorable. She had to learn that the people on the estate were good, decent and most of all human, and that they were to be treated with respect.

Storming into the morning room, he discovered Helena sipping tea with Elizabeth as though nothing had occurred. But when she lifted her cold green eyes to Albert, they revealed that she was expecting him. Joseph was nowhere to be seen.

"Please excuse us," he said to his sister, holding Helena's gaze unflinchingly. Elizabeth did not protest. When he heard the door close softly behind her, he yanked his wife from her seat, not caring that she dropped her teacup in surprise.

"Albert," Helena met his eyes coolly. "I was just protecting our son from those . . ." She shrugged her shoulders, as though any further explanation was below her dignity.

Albert felt something wild unleash itself inside him, and for the first time in his life he struck a woman.

"Why . . . you *bastard*! How *dare* you!" she hissed at him, holding her cheek, which was turning a horrible shade of red from the slap.

"And I am not going to apologise either." His voice shook with fury as he clenched his fist and took a step towards her. Helena was forced to step back, and slid into her seat. It was time, he decided, she learnt that this was no place for her snobbery. "You have to drop that 'Lady of the Manor' act, Helena." Albert bent over her as he placed his hands on either armrest, keeping her imprisoned in her seat. "This is Elizabeth's home, and she respects every single person she employs, whether they are African or Indian."

"You sicken me, Albert," she hissed as her eyes flashed venom at him. "First you drag me all the way here, away from my friends and family, and now you act as though this is your home and the people here your family. Damn you, Albert," she swore. "You are English born and bred, and don't you dare forget it!"

"Be quiet," Albert ordered firmly, as he held her chin, making it difficult for her to move. "Another word from you and I will not be responsible for my actions. We will be meeting all sorts of people, and I want you to start treating every one as a human being and not an animal. And," his eyes narrowed warningly, "I don't want any more acidic remarks dropping from that tongue of yours." He jerked her to him, and his fingers bit into her soft upper arms. She stared at him defiantly. "Just remember, if it were not for them, *you* would be doing all the menial tasks you take for granted." Suddenly disgusted with her, he flung her from him, as though she were the untouchable one.

Undeterred, Helena cried out vehemently, "I don't want that woman or her offspring near my son!"

"That is impossible," Albert returned, striving for calmness. Anything to do with Sita could turn explosive, and he was not quite ready for that. "That woman is called Sita and she works for Elizabeth. She has done so for years. You have to accept that. And Helena," he continued firmly, "I want my son – yes, my son," he lifted a hand to stop her from interrupting him, "to grow up into a caring, gentle and unselfish individual who can feel compassion for others – unlike his mother!"

"Why . . . you . . .!" Helena gasped at his insult and reached out to slap him; but Albert was faster, and caught her hand in mid-swing, stopping her with a chilling look.

"Just be careful, very careful from now on. I will be watching you," he warned before turning away. He heard her cry of indignation as he slammed the door behind him.

Albert was exhausted, both mentally and physically. Just one day on the estate, he thought, and so much had occurred. Seeing Sita again had thrown him off-balance. He did not want to think about her. He needed to focus on his sister, he decided.

He found Elizabeth in the study, seated in what used to be Graham's chair.

"Why are you sitting here in darkness?" he asked, moving to open the heavy drapes.

"No . . . don't," whispered Elizabeth, and Albert noticed the shimmer of tears on her cheeks.

"Elizabeth," he drew his sister into his arms, "no more tears. I am here now."

"I am not crying for myself, Albert." Elizabeth managed a weak smile as she brushed away her tears. "I could not help but notice the ill feeling between you and Helena, and I am sorry to be the one to cause it."

"Nonsense!" Albert protested. "She knew what coming here entailed."

"She looks very lovely, but Albert, she also looks fragile. Do you think she will cope?"

Elizabeth's concern was so amusing, Albert found the tension drain from him.

"Don't ever let Helena's fragile appearance deceive you!" he laughed as he hugged Elizabeth to him. "Helena is a tough lady beneath that cool exterior," he warned. "She can manipulate people and circumstances for her own gain. Don't worry about her – or me."

"I'll try," she promised. "But Albert, she did frighten me this afternoon."

"How?" he asked, although he knew exactly what Elizabeth meant.

"Her reaction to Sita and her children, and her attitude towards Sumi when she served us tea," she told him honestly. "I don't mean to sound critical, but it was just too . . . obvious."

"I know," he admitted, not in the least bit embarrassed to be discussing his wife's attitude with his sister. "I have spoken to her already, and I don't think you need to be concerned about her behaviour in the future."

"I sincerely hope not," Elizabeth looked at him directly. "Both Sumi and Sita are very loyal, and the children adore Sita. I really don't want any problems, Albert. My estate has been running smoothly. I have kept up the reputation that Graham built, and I have a reasonably co-operative and content lot of people working for me. I don't need trouble of any kind," she reiterated.

"I'll make sure that nothing changes for the worse here," he promised, taking her hand in his. "You have my word."

"Good," Elizabeth gave a smile of relief, "because I have a few pressing matters which I need to discuss. If you feel up to it?"

"What better time than the present?"

Elizabeth pulled out several thick black leather-bound ledgers and placed them on the desk. "I have an offer to make to you, and I want you please to give it careful thought." She moved to sit next to him on the couch. "I know that Graham left the management of the estate in your capable hands, Albert, and I realise what an immense undertaking it is for you. Uprooting your family and bringing them to a totally new world is quite a sacrifice. Richard is a little too young to take over as you are doing, and who knows, he may even want to settle in England one day. I believe that it is only fair that you own half the estate."

"Elizabeth, no . . ." he protested. "This place belongs to you, Richard and Charlotte –"

Elizabeth placed a finger over his lips to stop the flow of words. "Albert, my dear," she looked at him trustingly, "knowing that you own part of the estate will allow me to relax. I might even go over to England to visit Father, once this is all settled, and stay for a couple of months."

"I think you are being too hasty."

"I am being selfish, Albert," she admitted. "If you go through the accounts you will find that I have not been running at a profit. You will manage the estate so much better – and we will both benefit. I trust your judgement, and will leave all decisions about the estate to you."

Albert had never expected such an offer. He rose to his feet, fully aware that Elizabeth was watching him anxiously.

What have I to lose? he asked himself as he paced the study. "I want to have a look at the books, carefully, Elizabeth," he said, " before I make a decision."

"Of course. Everything is up to date." She too rose to her feet, and paused at the door. "I have thought about this long and hard, Albert. Please consider it," she begged, before closing the door behind her.

Albert poured himself some whisky from the crystal decanter and settled down to look through the ledgers. Two hours of study, and a ride though the estate, brought him to his decision

Supper was served promptly at seven that evening. Sumi had prepared a variety of fresh vegetables from their garden and a leg of lamb, cooked to perfection, served with baked potatoes and gravy. For dessert, she had made a delicious chocolate cake.

"You remembered that I love chocolate cake, Sumi!" Albert's eyes twinkled as he helped himself to a second piece.

Supper, with the help of Elizabeth's gentle and easy manner, turned out to be a little less strained than he had expected. Helena chose to ignore him and he made no effort to speak to her. At this stage, he thought, the less said the better.

As coffee was being served, he turned to Elizabeth. "Would you like to join me for coffee in the study?" he invited, ignoring the sudden look of curiosity his wife shot at him. Then he turned to Nanny Goodson. "Why don't you put Joseph to bed? He must be tired. I will be around shortly to tuck him in." Albert reached over and dropped a kiss on top of his son's blond head on his way out of the dining room.

"Well?" Elizabeth's eyebrows rose inquiringly, the moment they were alone.

"What I have to say must remain very confidential," Albert began, as he took a sip of his coffee.

"I solemnly promise," Elizabeth's eyes twinkled with laughter as she held a hand over her heart.

"I am very serious, Elizabeth." Albert sat opposite her and took her hand in his. "We are brother and sister, and I am most touched by your faith and trust in me."

"But?" the laughter died in Elizabeth's eyes as she searched his face.

"But," he replied, "I want this offer to remain between you, me and the lawyer who will draw up our agreement."

"You mean you accept!"

"Yes, dear sister; but I don't want Father or Helena, especially not Helena, to know."

"Why . . . ? I would have thought she'd be happy." Elizabeth's eyes clouded with doubt, and Albert hesitated for a moment, wondering if he should confide in her.

"If we inform Helena that I am your partner, she will want to take over the entire household and I cannot allow that to happen. If Father knows, Helena's parents are bound to get wind of it, and tell her."

"But . . ." Elizabeth's protests were cut short by Albert.

"No arguments, Elizabeth. I know what I am talking about. This is your home, and Helena can be very domineering and selfish. I would hate this whole agreement to turn ugly. My wife needs to step down from that pedestal of hers; only when she does, will I inform her."

"I see."

"Can I have your word that this stays strictly between us? To everyone else, I am here as your manager."

"Oh, Albert!" Elizabeth reached out and hugged him. "I am so relieved that you have accepted my offer, and yes, you have my word," she promised.

"I heard that Madam Campbell's brother arrived from England," Hemith remarked casually, as Sita was serving supper for the family.

Flushing, she turned away, filling the enamel bowl with more curry. "Yes."

"And Taj," Mukesh tugged at his father's sleeve, "there is a lady and a boy with yellow hair!"

Sita cringed inwardly, hoping that Mukesh would not tell all that had transpired earlier that day. "Be a good boy and eat up," she coaxed, giving her son a smile that would have warmed the coldest of hearts.

Later that night, Hemith brought up the subject of the Sheldons once more. "How does it feel to have so many new people around?" he asked, this time concerned. "You have not said much about them."

"I don't know much about them," Sita said shortly. "I only return to work on Monday."

"You don't seem very happy though," Hemith observed, as he tenderly brushed the hair away from her forehead.

"No, I'm not," she sighed. "I don't think life at the Big House will ever be the same."

CHAPTER TWELVE

Sita woke very early on the morning of her first day of work following Mukesh's bout of measles. She donned a simple, sky-blue sari and plaited her long black hair. The face that stared back at her from the small wall-mirror looked tired and pale. She saw apprehension in her eyes, the faint dark rings under them adding to her look of fragility. I have to get going, she thought, jerking herself upright, or I will be late.

The walk to the house seemed endless. Sita was so deep in thought that by the time she reached the kitchen she had chewed her bottom lip almost raw.

"Good, you are in time!" Sumi was hurrying about the kitchen. "You might as well set the breakfast table," she instructed in the same breath. It was obvious she was rather harassed.

"Good morning, Sumi," greeted Sita, as she tied an apron over her sari. "How many for breakfast?"

"Let me see," Sumi hesitated with a look of concentration on her face, then started counting them off on her fingers: "There is Madam Elizabeth, Miss Charlotte, Master Richard and Governess Mildred..." She paused.

"I know that." Sita got out the cutlery, hoping the visitors had decided to return to England. "What about the others?"

"I'm getting to them. Master Albert..." Sumi smiled. "He has grown into a handsome young man! Not so skinny any more, either," she commented, eyes alight with admiration for her new Master.

"Sumi!" Sita cried out in exasperation. "Hurry up."

"Oh, patience, child," Sumi scolded. "Then there is his snotty wife and their son," she concluded, holding up seven fingers.

"Seven. Are you sure we haven't left anyone out?" This was Sita's first day back and she really did not want it to be disastrous.

"Oh, and the nanny. I almost forgot about the little boy's nanny."

The breakfast room was deserted when Sita arrived, so it did not take her long to set the table. The rolls were freshly baked and, together with the steaming coffee, filled the room with a delicious aroma; it reminded Sita that she, too, had not had any breakfast.

Sita removed her apron in the kitchen, and carried in the eggs and bacon on a tray, which she placed in the centre of the table. She was stepping back to admire her work when she felt herself come up against a hard male form. Stiffening, she pulled away, knowing without looking who he was. Moving away, Sita forced herself to remember that she was here to serve breakfast. "Coffee?" she asked, without turning around.

"Yes, please, and I'll have some of those delicious-looking rolls with some bacon and eggs," Albert requested as he seated himself at one end of the table.

Sita placed the food on a warm plate and poured his coffee, careful not to spill. She was fully aware that her hands trembled. When she cast Albert a look from beneath her lashes, she realised that he was watching her closely, and could see her nervousness.

"The others will be here any minute now."

Sita wished that he would not speak to her. His smooth voice sent a delicious warmth through her body.

"Good morning, Albert! I see you are ready for the day," Elizabeth greeted him, before turning to Sita as she seated herself at the head of the table. "How is your son, Sita?" she inquired.

Sita gave her a warm smile. "He has fully recovered, and is up to his little pranks again."

"I am glad," Elizabeth returned.

"I want Joseph to sit next to me," Richard interrupted. He pulled out a chair for the little boy as Albert's wife made her entrance into the breakfast room.

Helena glided into the room, trailing a faint smell of jasmine. She wore a white silk gown which flowed around her slender form as she moved. Her blonde hair, stunning green eyes and red lips highlighted her pale skin. As she slid into her seat and helped herself to some coffee, Sita watched, mesmerised by her beauty – and actually jumped, startled, when Helena requested toast with a little butter.

The talk at the breakfast table centred on lessons for the children, and it gave Sita a chance to observe the newcomers. The nanny, a short, plump, motherly figure, looked like a kind and gentle person, thought Sita. She was older than Chumpa, and her once-brown hair, wound into a tight bun, was streaked with grey. Her soft grey eyes had a faded look; Sita sensed sadness in them, but marvelled at how they sparkled whenever Albert spoke to her. When her double chin wobbled with laughter, Sita decided that she liked this simple, plain-looking woman.

"Excuse me."

Sita felt the chill in the voice that was directed at her, and blinking, found herself looking into Helena's cold green eyes.

"The coffee-pot needs to be refilled," Helena ordered, as though she were the head of the house.

Sita removed the coffee-pot and turned to make her way to the kitchen. She heard Helena say, "Really, Elizabeth, I think you must get someone efficient. That girl was daydreaming."

Sita felt a shiver of doom run through her, and the fine hair on the backs of her hands stood up. Already, she was experiencing animosity from Albert's wife. She returned as quickly as she could and placed a cup of steaming coffee in front of Helena, hoping she would scald her tongue.

The morning sunlight caught the diamond ring on Helena's finger, sending off a shimmer of beautiful colours, and reminding Sita who this woman really was: Albert's wife. She is as hard and beautiful as her diamonds, Sita thought. Her beautiful gown did nothing to soften her, and Sita wondered what had made Albert marry such a cold woman.

"Sita, you may clear the table," Elizabeth's soft voice broke her stream of thought and she coloured guiltily. She shook her head quickly to clear her mind.

"Well, how did it go?" Sumi inquired, taking in Sita's harried look as she brought in the dirty dishes.

"I don't think she likes me at all," commented Sita, her thoughts still on Helena Sheldon.

"I hope you mean Master Albert's wife?"

"Who else?" Sita almost snapped, and then tried to pull herself together. Unkind and very unladylike thoughts about Helena were entering her head.

"Well, I'm not going to let her upset me," Sumi said vehemently. "She must just get used to living here! Besides, she is not the lady of the house. Madam Elizabeth is."

"Do you mean they'll be living here indefinitely?" Sita's heart sunk as her worst fears were confirmed. "I had hoped they were just visiting."

"Oh, no," Sumi lowered her voice into a conspiratorial whisper. "I overheard Master Albert tell her off the first day they arrived. She has to learn to adjust because nobody is going to change to suit her," she ended smugly.

"I see," Sita murmured, chewing on her still-sore lip, wondering how on earth she was going to contend with the situation. This woman might just turn her into a little she-devil!

Chumpa turned forty-five that September, and her family gathered around her to celebrate. She still looked young and lovely for her age, and it was hard to believe that she had five grandchildren.

"Nani, we brought you a present!" Asha, Geeta's plump daughter, excitedly pulled out a lovely shawl from Geeta's bamboo basket.

Chumpa's eyes lit up with pleasure. "This is very pretty!" she exclaimed.

"It is for you. For your birthday." Asha jumped about excitedly before rushing into Chumpa's arms to give her a big hug.

"Thank you, sweetheart." Chumpa kissed her round cheeks.

More hugs and kisses followed, and then Geeta turned to Sita.

"And what have you brought for Majee?" Geeta's voice held a hint of challenge, which her sister did not miss.

Sita handed over a small jewellery box, covered with a beautiful array of seashells. Chumpa gave a small gasp of pleasure as she opened the box and found that it was lined with red satin.

"This is simply exquisite!" Chumpa marvelled at the handicraft.

"Hemith made the box and the boys picked up the shells from the beach, for decoration," Sita explained. "I put it together with the final touch of red satin."

"Thank you," Chumpa hugged her excited grandsons. "I will treasure these gifts forever."

"I hear you have a beautiful new Mistress," Geeta remarked casually after supper. The two sisters were cleaning up the kitchen for their mother, who was surrounded by her grandchildren. "What is she really like, though?" Geeta's eyes were lit with curiosity.

"I really don't know," Sita replied, preferring not to gossip. Geeta was known never to keep a secret – Sita often found herself hearing things she had told her sister, repeated with colourful exaggerations. "We don't speak to each other. I go there to work, not socialise." The topic of Albert's wife always made her irritable and snappish.

"I'm just curious, Sita. There is no need for you to get so cross," Geeta admonished. "By the way, how is the new Master? I heard that he is even better-looking now." Geeta did not hide her smirk.

"Geeta!" exclaimed Chumpa, who had come into the kitchen unexpectedly.

"Oh, Majee. I was only joking," Geeta giggled mischievously.

"You are a married woman, Geeta. You must behave respectably," Chumpa reprimanded. Sita's cheeks stung: she felt the heat of her mother's words.

"Oh, Majee, you have been on edge lately," Geeta sulked.

"Have I? I didn't realise it." Chumpa sighed. "I think it is on occasions like this that I really miss Gopi."

Suddenly the atmosphere in the room changed. The three women looked at each other sombrely.

"Majee, how can you mention him after the disgrace he has brought to this family?" Geeta was the first to break the silence. "This family was the centre of gossip and the laughing stock of the community for months – until we heard that Nanda's wife was sleeping with the white overseer for extra rations. Did I not thank her for getting the people's attention away from our family?" Geeta's mouth twisted into an ugly line.

Sita stared at her sister, appalled at what she was hearing. "I cannot believe that you still harbour such bitterness. Why can't you let go of the past? It is water under the bridge now. Gopi is, and always will be our brother. What has happened to you, Geeta? You frighten me when you get like this!"

Sita's eyes reflected all that she felt at that moment towards her sister. Geeta was only in her mid-twenties, but she had let herself go. She was now overweight and expecting her fourth child. As the years passed, pride had entered her life. Sita felt sadness in her heart for those years of sisterly talks, which were now a thing of the past. Now, all Geeta seemed intent on talking about were her children, the success of her farm and how important it was to maintain the perfect social image.

Work for Sita fell into a routine, and she did her best to avoid Albert and his wife. Fortunately, she almost never saw Albert. He had adapted to the work pattern set by Graham Campbell, either leaving very early in the morning or returning late in the evening. Helena, it seemed, was on a mission to make Elizabeth's staff miserable, and was often rude and abrupt to them when Elizabeth was not present. Sita did her best to avoid a scene.

The fact that the Sheldons did not share a bedroom was no great secret in the Campbell household, and Sita wondered what kind of a marriage they had. Albert occupied the spare bedroom next to the study, and she suspected that he often worked late through the night.

On the rare occasion when Sita served him a meal, she would notice a strange look in his eyes: his gaze would darken, and his expression become unreadable. Watching her closely, he played with the bracelet he still wore on his wrist. Words were seldom spoken between them, yet whenever their eyes met, something fleetingly passed between them. Then their masks fell back in place. He made Sita terribly uncomfortable.

It was now almost a year since the Sheldons had arrived on the Campbell Estate, and it was thriving under Albert's management. He made sure his workers were treated with respect and kindness, and met with the sirdars and foremen regularly. Albert was extremely proud of how cooperative the labourers were, and how well the estate was running.

At least, he sighed, this was one area of his life where everything was going smoothly. Albert looked at the letter in his hand. Helena's father had written to say that his wife was extremely ill, and requested that Helena be sent home with Joseph.

"I insist on going, Albert." Helena had been firm and determined. "How can I not? This is a family emergency."

"I am aware of that," Albert placated, "but you have to understand that I cannot just leave."

"I am not asking you to accompany me," Helena hit back, her green eyes flashing in defiance.

"Helena, you know that it is not safe for you to travel alone. Besides, you hate travelling, if I remember correctly," Albert reminded her.

"How can you be so cruel and so selfish!" Helena turned on him angrily. "My mother may be dying, and you don't want me to go to her. All you can think about is this damn plantation!" she shrieked.

Albert ran his hand through his hair as he tried to shut out Helena's hysteria. It wouldn't surprise him to discover that the mother was faking her illness so that her daughter could return to England. Lord only knows, he thought, what lies Helena had been feeding her parents about this country.

Elizabeth entered the study and took in the unpleasant scene. "What on earth is going on here?"

"My mother is terribly ill and Albert is being difficult. He does not want me to go home," Helena accused, crying hysterically.

Albert did not bother to defend himself. Instead, he handed the letter over to Elizabeth, who read through it quickly.

"I will accompany her to England," Elizabeth said unexpectedly. "It has been years since I saw Father and the rest of the family, and I think it is time the children got to know their kin. What do you think?" she smiled as Helena's sobs slowly died down.

"That would be wonderful," Albert replied, suddenly deeply grateful for his sister's interruption. "But I am going to be very lonely in this big house," he teased, relieved to have the problem solved.

"No, you won't," Helena said tartly. "You'll be too busy running the estate, as usual."

Albert organised their travel arrangements as promptly as he could, and Elizabeth took charge of all other matters. It was decided that Nanny Goodsen and Mildred, the governess, would accompany the children on the journey. Sumi, too, would go along to help the ladies.

It took two full weeks to get everything organised for the big trip, a frantic time for the servants. There was excitement in the air as the Indian seamstress on the estate made new gowns for the ladies; even the boys had suits made for them.

Soon it was time for them to leave. After helping pack all the family's trunks and making sure that nothing was left behind, Sita was almost ready to drop from exhaustion. The house was in a state of total chaos. Elizabeth, caught up in the excitement of packing, told her not to worry:

"You can clean up once we are out of your way, Sita."

The family made quite a troop, in their fine, elegant clothes, waving to Albert on the dock as their ship set sail for England. Helena, looking cool and elegant as always in a cream silk gown, had actually kissed him on the cheek before leaving. She had become warmer towards him once the travel arrangements were finalised: astonishingly, the night before they departed, she had come to his room and hinted coyly that she was available to perform her wifely duty. Albert had almost laughed aloud. He could not remember when last she had been so generous.

"It is a little too late to play the dutiful wife, Helena," he had replied in a mocking voice.

Elizabeth, for the first time in months, looked relaxed and happy, and filled with enthusiasm for the trip. Albert had promised to keep her well informed about estate matters during her absence.

Joseph looked very dapper in his new suit. It was a replica of the one worn by Richard, who was growing quite tall and handsome, and, Albert thought, very responsible as well. He had promised his uncle that he would take care of the ladies.

"Especially Charlotte," he had teased, and received a poke from his sister.

Charlotte had grown into a lovely, intelligent young woman, and Albert was sure that her father would have been very proud of both his children.

Albert felt a great sense of relief as he waved goodbye.

Hemith was pleased when the party finally set sail for England. "I can get my wife back," he teased as he put his arms around her that night.

Over the last fortnight, Sita had come home every night too exhausted to give her family and her husband the attention they deserved. She was even too tired to make love.

"At this rate, we're never going to add the daughter we want to our family," he had grumbled.

Sita sighed, deeply troubled. Since Albert's arrival she had not been quite herself. She was aware of the growing distance between Hemith and herself, and now this unexpected turn of events was placing immense strain on her. She had omitted to tell Hemith that now she would be alone in the Big House with just Albert to take care of: she had to face the months ahead with the man who still possessed her heart.

That night, Sita turned to Hemith for comfort. She curled up against him and put her arms around him. He always made her feel safe and secure, and she longed for those feelings once more. Thinking that she finally wanted to make love, Hemith eagerly pushed up her clothes and entered her. Sita lay beneath him as he moved over her. She waited for his moan of satisfaction, which did not take long to come; then he placed a gentle kiss on her forehead, and turned away to fall asleep. She lay beside him, listening to his gentle snore as the tears ran down her cheeks. Does it always have to be this way? she wondered. Hemith, although very gentle in his lovemaking, seemed to always take so much from her. She knew he loved her, for he showed it in so many ways, yet their coming together always left her feeling dissatisfied.

Sita simply accepted this routine lovemaking as a punishment for the immense pleasure and love she had shared with Albert, and for bearing his son. However, she could not deny that her body craved a satisfaction of its own, and her heart ached with the knowledge that the love she felt for Albert had never died.

Thoughts of Albert entered her mind and she felt terribly guilty. This is no time for that, she admonished her inner self, as she tried to shut out images of the intense look in his brown eyes.

After a restless night, Sita rose before the sun cast its first golden hue over the horizon. She completed her morning chores, had the fire blazing and was dressed before she shook Hemith awake. He had to be at the mill before the horn was blown, and there was always trouble for a latecomer. She prided herself on making sure that he was always on time for work, and thus would never feel the sting of the sirdar's whip or bear the brunt of his foul language. Sita knew how affected Hemith was by the treatment they received.

As Sita let herself into the kitchen of the Big House with the key Elizabeth had given her, she recalled Elizabeth's words: "No use expecting Master Albert to open the door for you, Sita. He will be out in the fields by the time you arrive. You know the routine?" Sita had smiled in response. "Indar will continue to maintain the gardens as usual and will go into town for your shopping." Elizabeth had given Sita a couple more instructions, and informed her that Albert would pay her wages.

Sita took into the empty kitchen, and found herself missing Sumi's warm presence. It was now her task to care for the house and its master. Sighing, she set about lighting the fire.

Some time later, Indar came in. "Good morning," he greeted her as he took the steaming cup of coffee Sita held out to him. "Thanks," he took a sip. "Where's the Master this morning?"

"I haven't seen him. Madam Elizabeth said that he would be in the fields."

Indar grinned at her.

"What?" she looked at him in confusion. "Did I just say something funny?"

"Well, I know for sure that he is not in the fields. In fact I think he spent the night in Durban, enjoying his freedom, no doubt."

"Indar!"

"Well, who can blame the poor man?" Indar said sympathetically. "Anyway, he should be back for lunch. Anything you need, you let me know," he offered, handing back the empty mug.

Three hours later, Sita looked around her. She had worked tirelessly through the morning, and was finally satisfied that the house was restored to its former neatness.

Walking down the hall, she noticed that the study door was slightly ajar. Strange – she was sure that she had shut it earlier on her way to the bathroom, where she had splashed cool water on her face and hands to refresh herself. She went towards the door. Suddenly it was pulled open, and Sita jumped back in surprise.

Albert's brown eyes burned into Sita, and she felt her cheeks sting under his hot gaze.

"I am . . . sorry. I did not know you were . . . back," she stammered, and then deliberately added, "Sir."

Neither moved from the doorway. Albert stared at her as though mesmerised by her flushed cheeks and shining eyes. A thin film of perspiration broke out on her forehead, and when she bit her bottom lip nervously, he almost groaned aloud with desire for her.

Dear God, he prayed. It was such a long time since he had held this woman in his arms. This was the woman who had deprived him of countless hours of sleep. The woman who had betrayed him and married someone else, when she had promised to wait for him. "I apologise for taking you by surprise, Sita," his voice came out dry and hoarse. "Come in." He moved into the study, forcing her to follow.

"Do . . ." Sita's voice trembled slightly. "Do you want me to get you anything?" When he turned and raised an eyebrow, she hastily added, "Lunch, Sir?"

"Nothing for the moment." He stepped closer to her and she took a step back. "And Sita, don't call me 'Sir' ever again," he warned softly. He watched closely for a change in her expression, or for a little message in her beautiful eyes. Albert stood directly in front of her, inhaling her scent. He reached out and ran one long tanned finger along her satin-smooth cheek. "You have not changed at all, Sita."

Sita pulled away from him sharply. His touch left her cheek burning.

"I apologise for that." However, he did not look in the least bit sorry. "I should not have done that. You are a happily married woman now. Am

I right?" His eyes glinted mockingly at her. "Do you love your husband?" he asked, moving to lean casually against the edge of the desk as he folded his arms across his broad chest.

Sita could not believe his audacity. "Do you love your wife?" she retaliated, suddenly angry. They had barely held a conversation all year, and now he was prying into her personal life! His sudden burst of laughter only increased her annoyance.

"You are still the same, smart Sita," he laughed, noting her outraged expression. At least she was not intimidated by him. It was not yet midday, and he felt light-hearted, reckless, and quite intoxicated by the sight and scent of this woman. He wanted to gather her in his arms and make passionate love to her; he wanted her to feel all that passion she had hidden away, and make her regret breaking her promise to him!

But she remained silent and composed. It unnerved him.

"Um," he cleared his throat and pulled himself upright. "I won't have any lunch and I will be at the Browne's mill for the afternoon. You can leave something simple in the oven for my supper," his voice came out strong and firm, and the teasing note was no longer there.

Sita did not wait for him to tell her to leave. She slipped out of the study as quickly as she could.

It had taken every ounce of strength she possessed to remain calm and unaffected by Albert Sheldon. For a few minutes he had seemed like the young man she had fallen in love with, and her heart had raced crazily. His eyes had softened and shone with mischief – but he had so skilfully evaded her question about his wife. Just as she had avoided talking about her marriage. So, Sita thought, two can play at the same game. This time, she decided, she would be mature and sensible; she would not let her heart rule her head.

True to his word, Albert left the house shortly afterwards. Sita was glad for Indar's presence. He kept her sane with his silly jokes while she baked a steak pie for Albert's supper and left it in the oven.

For the next month Sita and Albert did not speak to each other unless it was necessary, and only during meal times. Albert avoided Sita's eyes as often as he could, but she caught him looking at her a few times and deliberately ignored him.

An ache began to grow in Sita, which she could not explain, even to herself. Hemith noticed her sadness, but he put it down to the fact that she had not conceived the daughter they longed for, and did not pressure her in any way.

"Try not to worry so much, Sita. We will have our daughter. I promise," he said, and kissed her gently. Then he swung Sunil up into the air, and the child's laughter brought a smile to Sita's lips.

CHAPTER THIRTEEN

Sita closed the cupboards and handed Indar a list of the items she required.

"Don't forget to tell the shopkeeper to tick off the items on the list," she instructed as she watched him climb onto the horse-drawn wagon. "And don't be too long!" She knew that these shopping expeditions gave Indar an opportunity to enjoy a bit of socialising.

"The Master said that I could take the whole day off," Indar informed her with a smug smile. "I think I'll visit a few friends in town. I'll try to be back before dark. Oh," he turned to her one last time, "before I forget, don't bother with lunch for the Master. He won't be back for the rest of the day either."

"Strange," murmured Sita. "He didn't mention anything to me." But then, reflected Sita, we are not exactly on speaking terms.

"He said something about spending time at the Browne Mill until evening," Indar supplied as he cracked the whip. The horses moved steadily away.

By the time Sita had spring-cleaned the kitchen, cleaned the carpets and washed the windows she was exhausted, hot and very sticky. Stripping off her damp clothes quickly, she soaped herself and rinsed the dust and perspiration from her body in the bathroom allocated to the servants. Her people, as she fondly referred to the Indians on the estate, either stood or sat on their haunches while they soaped and scrubbed and then poured water over themselves. They did not believe that it was hygienic to lie in a bath filled with water before the dirt was washed from their bodies, and thought that the white people had a strange way of bathing.

Once she was clean, though, the idea of a long soak was very appealing. Sita had always fantasized about luxuriating in the huge tub in the

Campbell's main bathroom. And now, for the first time, she was entirely alone in the house . . .

On impulse, Sita decided she would finally give in to the urge. Wrapping herself in a gown given to her by Elizabeth Campbell, she made her way to the main section of the house, first stopping in the kitchen to make herself a drink.

In the main bathroom, she filled the tub with warm water and threw in her favourite rose-petals. After making sure one last time that she was alone, she stepped into the bath, lay back and closed her eyes as she felt her muscles relax. Her body seemed weightless.

For how long she had dozed she had no idea, but the water, grown cool, woke her. Lazily, Sita reached out and took a sip of the iced tea she had carried in with her. She closed her eyes and lay back as she placed the glass back on the chair next to the bathtub. Because she was not looking, she misplaced the glass and it came crashing down on the tiled floor. The tranquillity that she was so enjoying was shattered, and Sita's eyes flew open. Seeing the mess on the floor, she slowly rose from the tub. She was cautiously putting her foot down, avoiding the shattered pieces, when the door flew open and Albert rushed in.

Shock registered on both their faces. Sita's cheeks burned with embarrassment, and she quickly reached for her gown and clutched it to her body.

Albert was taken aback at the sleek, naked, glorious sight of her. Slowly he moved towards her, his eyes never leaving her face, and scooped her into his arms, ignoring the crunch of glass beneath his boots. She was dripping, but Albert did not care. Finally, she was in his arms, and that was all that mattered.

He held her so closely, Sita could feel the wild thud of his heart and the warmth of his breath on her cheek as he carried her into his bedroom and gently laid her on his bed. The fire in his brown eyes terrified her, and yet she was spellbound.

"You are so incredibly beautiful," he whispered as he ran his eyes down the slim length of her body. His heart felt as though it would burst in his chest, as it filled with a mixture of love and a wild desire to possess her again and again. He wanted her so desperately he thought he would die if she turned away from him. With hands that trembled, he cupped her face, fingers travelling tenderly over flushed cheeks; when at last they touched her full lips, a tiny moan escaped from her. The air between them sizzled.

Albert felt his self-control, which he had fought so hard to maintain all this time, slip away as he took her soft lips in a kiss of sheer hunger. Sita responded with a passion that matched his, and all the years apart simply fell away. The pain, the heartache and the loneliness they had survived diminished, as sensations only they could create, rose between them.

"Sita," Albert moaned, as his lips slid to the curve of her neck. "You have been driving me absolutely crazy." As Sita's lips parted, he captured them once more, and her hands moved over the small of his back to draw him closer.

Breathless, Albert was the first to break their hot and hungry kiss.

"Do you know how many sleepless nights I have had?" his voice was hoarse with desire as he looked deeply into her eyes. He did not want to let her go, lest she disappear from his arms. "Dreaming of you, wanting to hold you, day after day, night after night. This past year has been hell. I longed to tell you . . . but it was impossible. You have been so cold and aloof and proud, and I have been torn up inside from wanting you so much!"

Sita's eyes filled with tears, which threatened to spill over as she closed her eyes and turned her head away. Such magical words! He was voicing what she had felt all along, but had never ever admitted to herself. Sita ached to reach out and touch him, and yet she knew it would be wrong, so very wrong.

"This is not right," she whispered, struggling to her feet, trying desperately to focus her mind not on the flames of passion she felt within, but on the sacred fire before which she had taken her wedding vows. She picked up her gown from where it had fallen to the floor and slipped into it quickly.

"Sita, I love you!" Albert's brown eyes were dark with passion.

"And I have always loved you," she admitted, "but Albert, we are different people now, with different lives and responsibilities. We cannot go back. It is too late."

"It is never too late to love."

"It is for me. I have taken vows and I cannot and will not break them. I will not betray my husband. He does not deserve that. If you truly love me then you will respect my wishes." Sita's voice trembled as she brushed back her tears.

"Sita, you are killing me slowly," he moaned, running his hand over his face in frustration. "I have dreamt of making you mine for so long." His voice cracked with emotion as he pulled her back into his arms.

"I am not yours, Albert. Not anymore. I stopped dreaming a long time ago." Sita's voice was soft with love and regret as she gently pushed him away. "I never thought our paths would cross again."

"But you still wear my gift." His eyes, soft with love for her, fell to her slim waist, where the necklace lay under her gown.

"Yes," Sita smiled tremulously, pulling the gown closer to her, "and you still wear this." She picked up his wrist, where the bracelet shone. Her eyes were full of pain. "You were my first love. You stole my heart and never bothered to return it to me. Why did you do that, Albert?"

"I never expected to fall in love with a lovely Indian girl, Sita. And when I asked you to wait for me, I sincerely meant it. But you did not wait." There was no accusation in his voice, only pain. "You got married. When I heard what a beautiful bride you made I thought I would die. Why did you not wait, Sita, as I asked you to?"

"You will never know the kind of pressure I was under." Sita's voice trembled as the memories flooded back. "I waited and I prayed for you to come back and rescue me. Albert, I felt so betrayed and angry when I heard that you were staying in England. Then I had no choice. I had to marry." For Mukesh's sake, she decided to hold on to the secret of his birth.

Sita felt him flinch at her words. "Besides," she reminded him as she wiped her tears away, "you also married."

Albert's colour heightened at her words. "Helena entrapped me, and since I could not have you as my wife, Sita, I allowed myself to become a father. My son is the only thing that brings me joy and happiness in this farce of a marriage."

The sadness and honesty in his voice touched Sita deeply. She longed to wrap her arms around him and to comfort him. Instead, she cupped his cheek tenderly for just a second before turning away.

Sleep evaded Albert once more. Sita's scent clung to him, and tortured with desire, he almost screamed in frustration. Albert buried his face in his pillow and moaned her name over and over again, but the ache in him only intensified. He could imagine her now as she lay next to her husband, and he burnt with jealousy, and began to detest a man he did not know. He knew that she would not be unfaithful to her husband: her marriage and her family meant everything to her. He was too late.

"Damn, you, Sita Suklal, damn you!"

That same night, with tears rolling down her cheeks, Sita removed the necklace from around her waist, and knew with certainty that she would never wear it again.

"I am so proud," beamed an excited Anoop. "Our own stall, finally! We can now sell our own produce fresh from the farm, without a middleman cutting our profits to the bone."

"Well done!" Hemith shook Anoop's hand and Sita gave Geeta a warm hug.

"And what are your plans now?" Chumpa inquired, sensing that there was more to this venture.

"Majee, we are going to build ourselves a house on the farm. It is a strain travelling to and fro from Anoop's parents at the moment," Geeta explained, overflowing with confident expectation.

"And if we are living on the farm we can make sure that no one steals the vegetables," Anoop added practically.

"It sounds perfect. I'm sure you will reap the rewards of your hard work," Sita said encouragingly.

"Nani, I am hungry!" Mukesh interrupted the adults by tugging at his grandmother's sari.

"I think all this talk is too much for the little ones," Geeta grinned. "Time to fill those little bellies."

"Come," Chumpa called out to her grandchildren. "Nani has made some sweetmeats for her little angels."

The children followed their grandmother excitedly into the tiny kitchen as though she were the pied piper.

"Just look at them," sighed Geeta in contentment. "Can you believe how they have grown, Sita? Your two boys and my three. I simply cannot believe that I am the mother of that adorable little girl and those two imps."

"And another on the way," Sita reminded Geeta, keeping an eye on

Mukesh. Every day that passed she could not help but notice how very similar Mukesh was to Albert Sheldon.

"Remember when you refused to marry Hemith!" Geeta's teasing voice broke Sita's train of thought. Geeta ignored Sita's alarmed look, and continued, "Now you look so happy – so all that fussing was definitely a waste of time."

Sita attempted a weak smile. "How we all have changed over the years," she remarked lightly.

Geeta ignored her sister's comment with finesse. "Marriage to Hemith must be great," she persisted. "You are positively glowing. Are you sure you are not in the family way, too?"

"No." Sita's face flamed with colour as she discreetly crossed her fingers under the pleats of her sari. She had not told Hemith yet that she was late. He was hoping their third baby would be a girl.

"I think you are," Geeta continued, "and it is time anyway. You don't have to blush, you are a married woman, you know." Geeta playfully tapped her sister's arm. "When is your Mistress coming home?"

Sita cleared her throat in surprise. Trust Geeta to jump from one topic to another without blinking an eye! "I'm not sure."

"So . . . it's just you and . . ." Geeta's eyes opened wide with innocence. "What is his name?" Not waiting for Sita to answer, she clicked her fingers: "Ah, yes, now I remember, Albert. Albert Sheldon. I believe it's just the two of you in the Big House."

Oh, dear, thought Sita. Here she goes again. "Well, not really," she smiled, adopting a casual air, while her heartbeat picked up. "There is Indar."

True, Indar's presence was a good buffer – but he was not always available. Sita was very aware of Albert's heartwrenching glances and his soft butterfly touches. She knew he would willingly drop his promise not to touch and hold her close to him again, given the slightest encouragement.

Sita fought hard to avoid leading him on, for both their sakes; but Albert could not be oblivious to the passion in her eyes at times. When temptation threatened to overwhelm her, Sita forced herself to focus on her loving family: she knew that if she gave in, she would lose both them and her dignity. There was no going back.

Thankfully, the ruckus from the kitchen interrupted any further discussion.

"I think Majee needs rescuing." Sita laughed, secretly blessing Geeta's sons for starting a fight.

"Those rascals!" Geeta was on her feet too.

"Sit," ordered Sita, as she gently pushed Geeta back into her seat. "I will check on them. They don't need their mother yelling at them as well."

"Thanks," Geeta replied, as she watched Sita's graceful exit. There was something different about her sister, Geeta reflected, her eyes narrowing shrewdly, but she just couldn't put her finger on it. "She's concealing something," Geeta muttered under her breath, "but I will find out what it is, in due course."

"The boys are friends again," Sita smiled on her return. "They can be quite a handful."

"So you really don't know when they are coming home?" Geeta rubbed a plump hand over a swollen belly as the baby kicked her.

"Who are you talking about?"

"Your Mistress, silly, and her troop!"

Sita shrugged her shoulders in a show of indifference.

"I mean, what are they waiting for?"

Sita wanted to give her sister ten out of ten for persistence. "Really, Geeta. It is none of my business. I just work there." Sita strove for calmness, although she was highly irritated by Geeta's questions. "I can see Majee has been filling you in on what's been happening on the estate."

"You know Majee," Geeta complained bitterly. "She never tells me much, either. I have to pry the information out of her. You are both so much alike."

"And you are so much like Taj," retorted Sita.

"Come on, now," Geeta placated, reading the sudden anger in Sita's eyes. "I'm not asking you to gossip; I'm just curious." She took hold of Sita's hand. "You tell Majee everything that happens at the Big House. Why don't you share it with me? Everything I hear is second-hand. I am your sister, after all."

"All right," Sita gave in. "What is it you want to know? But remember," she warned, "I cannot promise to know everything. After all, I do not sit chatting at the table with the Master, like friends."

"I wonder what Albert Sheldon gets up to now that his wife is away?" Geeta's eyes lit with mischief.

"What do you mean?" Sita already regretted her weakness for giving in to Geeta's demands. She should have known better!

"Well, you know . . ." Geeta lifted her eyebrows expressively and laughed at Sita's blank look. "My dear sister, for a mother of two sons, your naiveté astounds me. You know how grumpy men can become when their urges are not fulfilled."

"Geeta!"

"Oh, don't be such a prude," Geeta cackled.

"I think it is time you gave up on your obsession with the Big House, Geeta. There is more to life than the goings-on on the Campbell Estate." Sita delivered a disarming smile together with her words of advice. "Now, what size house are you and Anoop planning on building? After all, the family is expanding."

Gopi folded the letter and placed it carefully in the inside pocket of his well-worn coat. Bharath had written to him of Geeta and Anoop's success. Apparently, each week they brought their produce into Durban, to their stall at the Indian Market in Pine Street. He had had no idea they were so close. Gopi ached for a glimpse of his sister.

Too many years had passed, and he and Rani had resigned themselves to living in exile from their families. They were very isolated: even Chin had left for the Transvaal, hoping to try his luck on the diamond mines. It was a sad day for them when they had said their goodbyes.

Bharath's letter was like a light at the end of the tunnel. The sudden burst of excitement lent him courage, and the following Saturday morning he decided to seek out his sister and her husband.

"We are going to the Indian Market, Rani. Why don't you wear your prettiest sari?" he suggested, trying to keep the thrill out of his voice. Gopi hoped Rani did not notice his nervousness, which was becoming more apparent by the minute. But of course she did notice: she felt his every nuance of emotion.

"What's the special occasion?" she asked, for it was a long time since she had seen him this light-hearted. His eyes sparkled with excitement, reminding Rani of the young man she had fallen in love with.

"I have a surprise for you, so no questions." He kissed her on her full lips. "It will spoil it if you know too much." He swung her around until she giggled with happiness.

"Let me help you," she offered, as he struggled with his necktie. "There. You look very handsome," she complimented, standing back to admire him. She still could not believe, after all these years, that he still belonged to her.

"And you look very pretty, too." Gopi returned the compliment as he hugged his wife, and then looked at his pocket watch. "It's time we left."

"That thing loses time, Gopi. How on earth you can go by it, is truly a wonder," she teased.

"Don't forget your basket for the vegetables."

"You mean we dressed like this for the vegetables?" she giggled as she slipped an arm through his.

As usual, they turned a few heads at the marketplace. She knew they made a startling pair, for often people turned around to stare at them: he was so tall and slim, while she was petite and ladylike; he was fair-skinned and very handsome, while she was darker.

The market hummed with activity: people crowded the street and the noise was deafening. Everyone was rushing around, too busy to bother about the next person. The place was extremely colourful. Ladies, young and old, were dressed in brightly-coloured saris; some were even brave enough to wear their gold jewellery to come out shopping. The stalls were overflowing with fresh produce, from fruit and vegetables to fresh fish and poultry, and somewhere amidst the great din of the marketplace someone was playing the sitar.

Rani had to cling to Gopi as he wove his way through the crowd.

"Where are we going?" she shouted as the crowd jostled them.

"It's not too far now," he shouted back. "Just don't let go of my hand!"

Usually, Rani preferred to do her shopping at the local shop, not far from where they lived. She hated the hustle and bustle of the marketplace with its smell of fish; and the sight of people earning a living cleaning trotters and sheep's heads to sell tore at her heart-strings. They all worked so hard in order to survive – and survive they did.

Suddenly Gopi came to a halt, and Rani almost banged into him.

"Why are we stopping here?" When Gopi did not reply, she followed his gaze – and went pale beneath her dark skin. Geeta and her husband were standing at a stall.

Recovering, Rani wanted to laugh hysterically. The last time she had seen them was at Sita's wedding, and both Geeta and her husband had really changed. Geeta's double chin wobbled visibly as she spoke and laughed with her customers. She was wearing a green cotton sari, which was draped over her head. She was either very overweight, or pregnant again, Rani decided, because her sari rode high over her stomach, to reveal fat, swollen ankles and feet squashed into flat sandals.

Anoop, whom Rani barely knew, matched his wife in size. One would have thought that with all the hard work involved in maintaining a farm and stall, they would be lean and muscular individuals; instead they looked soft and prosperous, as if life had been kind to them. From Bharath's letters she knew they had three children; Rani wondered what *they* looked like.

Gopi appeared dumbstruck.

"Gopi . . . is that . . . who I think it is?" stammered Rani, bringing him back to reality.

He finally nodded. "Yes. Come – let's say hello."

He tugged at her hand when she hung back, eyes wide with apprehension. Rani had always been wary of Geeta; it was Sita she knew and liked. But Gopi seemed so nervous and hopeful, Rani could not deny him his wish.

Geeta was bending down to pick up a bunch of fresh herbs when Gopi reached her side. He bent down to pick it up for her. Their fingers touched, and Gopi found himself looking into a pair of eyes very similar to his own – and yet so different. Geeta's jaw dropped and she gulped for air, wide-eyed.

"Bhaiya . . . it's *you*!" she cried out, reaching with her fat hands to touch his face, making sure he was real. "Anoop! Look who's here, after all these years!"

Astonished, Anoop engulfed Gopi in a bear hug, and then Geeta was crying in her brother's arms, ignoring the curious glances from customers and passers-by.

Rani stood by, her heart aching, as she watched this reunion – for she, too, wished that she could be reunited with her family. Would her own kin be so pleased to see her?

Wiping away their happy tears, Gopi and Geeta drew apart. Gopi, his heart singing, held out his hand to Rani and brought her forward.

"Geeta," he said, "this is my wife, Rani."

The sudden change on his sister's face froze his proud smile. Geeta cast Rani a look of pure hatred before turning to Gopi.

"Is this the reason you broke Majee's heart?" she demanded, pointing to Rani. "You almost killed our mother with your selfish actions, discarding the family who love you. The shame we felt when we learnt that you had run off with this . . . this *tramp* . . .!" she spluttered, her eyes blazing with fury. Geeta threw Rani a look of utter contempt. "She is not welcome at home, Bhaiya." Then her voice dropped coaxingly, and if one had not been there to see it, one would never have believed that she could change so swiftly: "But you . . . *you* can come home anytime."

The elation Gopi had felt at their reunion was swept aside by disgust and rage: who gave Geeta the right to dictate to him?

"How dare you! You are worse than our father!" Gopi retaliated, his voice trembling with fury as he held onto Rani, who appeared too stunned by Geeta's venom to move an inch. He pushed Geeta's hand away as she reached out to touch him. "Don't you ever touch me again," he hissed.

Rani did not realise that she had tears streaming down her cheeks until her vision became blurred, and she had to wipe her eyes to see the hazy figures in front of her. She could not deal with Geeta's anger and hatred any longer. Wrenching her hand from Gopi's strong grip, she fled from them. She ran through the crowd, not even stopping when she heard Gopi cry out her name: she dared not show him her tears and her hurt. The tears she shed were for her husband; the ache in her heart was for herself.

She ran all the way home and slammed the door behind her. The sobs she finally gave vent to, sounded like the cries of a wounded animal.

Gopi pushed open the door. "Rani," he panted, "why did you run away like that?" Perspiration dripped from his face as he tried to get his breath back.

"Why?" choked Rani. "You have the nerve to ask me why, after that little performance from your sister!" she screamed at him. "Just how do you think I felt, standing there watching you two, and then hearing her speak about me as though I were lower than the dirt beneath her feet?" Brushing away the angry tears with the backs of her hands, she searched Gopi's face for an answer.

Gopi reached out to hold her, but his gesture only infuriated her further. "Get away from me!" she yelled. "Go, go to your precious family and leave me alone. You have been yearning for them from the first day we came here."

"Rani, stop this now!" Gopi took hold of her slender shoulders and shook her. "You are letting Geeta and her vindictiveness get to you, and come between us. How do you think I felt, listening to her condemn you?" He pulled her into his arms and held her close to his heart as she wept. "Yes," he said, "There are times I miss my family and wish I could be there with them, but if it means losing you, then I can do without them. I would never give you up. Never!" he promised, stroking her hair with infinite gentleness until she calmed down.

He knew he would never forgive Geeta for hurting the one person who meant everything to him.

"I cannot accept that Gopi Bhai could turn his back on our family for a girl like *that*." Geeta's voice dripped with anger and bitterness as she remembered their meeting.

"Geeta, why can't you just drop it?" Anoop was clearly annoyed. "Your brother looked perfectly content to me. You had to go and spoil it by calling his wife names."

"Oh, is that what you think?" demanded Geeta. "If they are so happy, why has she not given him a child?"

"Geeta!"

"Well, I'm right. They have been married for years now. What kind of a life do you think he leads? He looks so thin and under-nourished. I wonder if she can even cook."

"They both looked perfectly fine to me. What does it matter that she is Tamil?"

Clearly, Anoop did not share her feelings. An idea was forming in Geeta's mind, but she would need his co-operation.

That evening she put the children to bed early, and carried a tray of their favourite Indian delights – syrupy, orange-coloured jaleibs, pink-and-white coconut fudges and gulab jamoons – to bed with her. Knowing how much Anoop favoured his sweets, Geeta made sure she had enough on the tray before settling into bed with her husband. First, she chuckled to herself, she needed to put plan one into action before plan number two could be launched.

Popping a sweet gulab jamoon into his mouth, her free hand roamed tantalisingly over his hairy chest. Slowly, watching the change in his eyes, she continued the exploration over his protruding belly and down his fleshy thighs, smiling at his arousal.

"I still satisfy you after all these years, don't I?" she purred as she licked at his earlobes. Anoop gave her a lazy smile. "Come on, admit it," she coaxed, running her hands over him. She may be overweight and pregnant, but she knew what excited her husband.

"You are my wife," he replied. "If you cannot satisfy me then who can?" he teased, eyes twinkling with mischief as he placed his hand between her warm thighs.

Geeta smiled at him seductively as she spread her legs apart; and Anoop, who could never resist his wife's bedroom allure, succumbed with a groan.

As he positioned himself and moved into her, Geeta made all the obligatory sounds to excite him, moving her ample hips to encourage his thrusts. When he climaxed, she moaned in feigned ecstasy, while her mind busied itself with how to introduce plan number two.

"Now, that was something," he panted.

Geeta could not wait for him to slip out of her. She needed to work on him quickly, for he was at his weakest while still in a state of euphoria.

"Anoop, my dearest heart," she whispered into his ear. "Don't fall asleep on me just yet."

"Uh," he grunted as he cushioned his head against her billowy breasts.

"Do you think you can obtain some information about my brother and that woman for me?" she asked, running her fingers through his hair.

"Why?" Anoop mumbled, almost asleep.

"Well . . ." she drawled, "who knows? Maybe she is just using him – and if we can obtain some evidence, show him just how manipulative she really is, then – "

"Are you insane!" Anoop's eyes flew to her face and he sat up abruptly, fully awake. "I cannot believe that you would stoop to such a level, Geeta."

"Anoop," Geeta's voiced dropped an octave as she reached out to stroke his chest. "You know how happy Majee will be when we get Gopi back for her." She leaned over to drop feather-light kisses on his neck and shoulders. "Just listen to me, please. I'm sure that we can pay for some information before . . ."

"*What*? Now you are definitely insane, to think that I will use my hard-earned money to dig up dirt on your brother and his wife. Just leave them alone!"

"Shush, keep your voice down. You will wake the children," she scolded, before noticing the angry glint in Anoop's eyes. "All right," she conceded. "I'm sorry for suggesting something so despicable." She leaned over and kissed him full on the lips. "But I know a few people who owe us a favour." She snuggled into Anoop's arms.

"So?" Anoop looked at her in exasperation, trying hard to ignore her attempts to seduce him.

"So, don't you think it's time they did something for us?" She slid her arms around him. Anoop found himself closing his eyes and falling under her seductive spell once more.

"Just say 'yes, I promise to help' . . ." Geeta whispered, as she bent her head to kiss Anoop – but stopped inches away from his lips. "Say yes and I will be yours," she teased, slipping a caressing hand down his body, yet not quite touching him.

"Fine," Anoop groaned, "I'll see what I can do."

He saw his wife's smile of triumph as she straddled him at last. Too late he realised what he had committed himself to.

Anoop groaned aloud, and it had nothing to do with the ecstasy she had made him feel. Men, he thought with disgust, were such weak creatures – and women were master manipulators!

CHAPTER FOURTEEN

"It's time to leave, Gopi," instructed Raymond, observing the dwindling pile of notes at Gopi's side.

"Just a little longer." Gopi's words were slurred as he waited for the next hand to be dealt.

"Is he in or not?" a harsh voice demanded.

"Out," Raymond declared with finality as he pulled Gopi from his seat and ushered him into his coat.

"Why did you have to do that?" demanded Gopi, glaring at his friend. "I would have won my money back."

"Not at the rate you were losing," Raymond retorted, as he propelled

Gopi out of the door. "Count your blessings you didn't blow all your money."

Six months ago, Raymond Lazarus had strolled into the bar where Gopi was working the late shift. It had been a lazy mid-week evening and the atmosphere in the bar was relaxed, with Boxer, an elderly black man, playing the piano. Gopi watched as the smartly dressed Indian gentleman moved with long easy strides towards the bar and seated himself at the counter. His air of confidence caught Gopi's attention instantly.

"I'll have a whisky – neat," the man said, looked around the bar with a bored expression.

"New in town?" Gopi placed the tumbler in front of the stranger, and watched him gulp down his drink in one swallow and order another.

"You could say that," he drawled, before delivering a magnetic smile.

He was a handsome man and he knew it, Gopi saw. When he smiled, he revealed small white teeth and his cheeks dimpled. His hair was black, wavy and carefully styled. His sooty black eyes were fringed with long lashes, and his whole demeanour spelt "moneyed gentleman".

"Are you here on business?" Gopi was suddenly very curious.

"Sort of," the gentleman replied somewhat mysteriously as he sipped his drink.

Gopi felt himself drawn to this arrogant stranger. He put his hand out.

"My name is Gopi Suklal."

Something flickered in the man's eyes, and he hesitated for a second before reaching out to shake Gopi's hand.

"Raymond Lazarus." He delivered another of his smiles. "Nice meeting you."

And so a friendship was born with a handshake. Raymond began to frequent the bar late at night, just before closing time.

"For a night-cap and the fantastic company," he would say as he shuffled a pack of playing cards.

Although curious, Gopi never questioned his new friend about his daytime business. He sensed that Raymond was a very private person.

"The less you know about me the better," Raymond had remarked in passing one evening.

But Gopi observed how well he dressed and that he always had cash on him – a lot of cash. Raymond never seemed to be short of female company either: women loved him. Gopi envied his good looks, his confidence, his charisma, and his ability to make money; and when he saw Raymond flash a few crisp notes one evening, his curiosity got the better of him.

"Why do I always see you at night and never during the day?" Gopi ventured as Raymond shuffled his cards.

Raymond looked up from what he was doing and gave Gopi a long hard stare. Gopi held his gaze just as steadily.

"Can you keep a secret?"

"What do you think?"

There was a couple of minutes' silence before Raymond grinned. "All right, I trust you. Don't ask me why, I just do. You see these cards?" He held them up for Gopi's inspection.

Gopi nodded, wondering what this was leading to.

"I am what you call a professional gambler," he supplied smoothly, watching Gopi.

"You're joking," laughed Gopi, thoroughly amused. Then he saw Raymond's serious expression. "You're not really serious, are you?"

"Laugh all you like, my friend," Raymond's voice was deadly soft and brought Gopi's laughter to a dead stop. "Where do you think I get the money from, to dress well and look successful and wealthy?" He stood up and turned around for Gopi's benefit.

"Well, you certainly have excellent taste," commented Gopi.

"Which does not come cheaply. And let me tell you something else – women are just as expensive," he added with a glint in his eye and a lift of an eyebrow.

"Teach me."

"What?"

"Teach me how to make money," Gopi's eyes shone with enthusiasm. "Not for women, Raymond," he explained urgently. "I'm sick and tired of this dead-end job and I'm always working so damn hard to make ends meet. I could do with a bit of extra money."

"What I do is illegal. I cannot encourage you to do it. It could get you into serious trouble, and –"

"Doesn't get *you* into trouble," Gopi retaliated smartly. Adrenaline was pumping through him. "Just think what I could do with the extra money. Rani will never have to work, and we can move out of that dump we live in." His eyes danced with possibilities.

And so, after much debate, Gopi got his wish and the lessons began. They shared many an evening laughing together, while Raymond taught Gopi a few tricks and all the different card games. Gopi latched on to everything Raymond showed him with a hunger that left a worried look on Raymond's face.

When Raymond was confident that Gopi was ready, he took him along for his first evening with the gents.

Gopi was very surprised to discover that a leading Indian businessman was playing host to the gamblers. He entered the house of the Sen brothers with Raymond leading the way – an entry that would haunt him in years to come.

The room was dark and smoky, making faces hard to see. Apparently there were many prominent men from all sectors of the community there.

"You don't need to make friends with these people, Gopi. You are here to win and that's all," cautioned Raymond. "And remember – as soon as it looks like your luck is running out, it's time to quit. Don't ever make the mistake of thinking that it'll get better. It never does. Understand?"

"No problem," Gopi grinned, as he rubbed his hands together in anticipation.

Now, half a year later, Gopi was hooked on gambling, and Raymond had to keep his eye on him. Together, they made a formidable pair, although Gopi was still a little in awe of his friend.

They made their way home together in the silence of the night. Eventually Gopi turned to his friend. "Thanks, pal. I suppose you were right to haul me out of that game," he admitted.

"I'm always right," said Raymond.

"See you tomorrow night?" Gopi asked, giving Raymond an anxious look.

"I'm sorry, I should have told you earlier – I have to go out of town tomorrow. I'll be back in a week's time. And I don't want you going near the Sen brothers while I'm away – they'll eat you alive," he warned.

Gopi missed Raymond. He also missed the gambling rush, and when he heard nothing from Raymond for a week, he decided he was big enough to enter the Sen brothers' den alone. Besides, he was a bit upset that Raymond hadn't contacted him.

"Ah, look who's come," the eldest of the six brothers remarked sarcastically as Gopi sauntered in. Although nervous, he adopted the confident attitude that he admired in Raymond.

Sam Sen did not gamble. He was a lean, tightly muscled man in his forties who looked taller than he actually was. Wealth lent him style and he dressed immaculately. He was also known to be quite ruthless, and the men who frequented his place feared him. The Sens' gambling den was at the back of the large house in which all six brothers lived with their wives and their children. It was a perfect set-up: no one suspected that the wealthy Sen brothers had any business other than their thriving import and export concern. To the wealthy they sold beautiful oriental carpets, exotic brassware and other interesting items from the east. They were well-dressed, well-known, and gave to charity freely.

On entering the den, one's first impression was that it was a huge warehouse. However, behind the beautiful Persian carpet which covered a whole wall, lay a secret door. This protected gentlemen with a penchant for gambling from the outside world. There they could eat, drink and spend their money until sunrise.

"Sit down." Sam pulled out a well-padded high-back chair for Gopi. "Men," he declared with a grin, revealing stained yellow teeth, "here is your sixth player." And he bowed slightly, as though he had just done them a great service.

When Raymond arrived at the hotel and headed for the bar, he discovered that Gopi was not working the late shift. He was immediately sure that he would find him at the Sens'.

Now, unseen by Gopi, Raymond paced the gambling den with a look of grave concern on his handsome face. Gopi was heading for trouble in a big way. Raymond had learnt through the grapevine that his friend already owed the house almost one hundred pounds – for Gopi, an enormous sum of money. He would never be able to repay it, unless his luck changed fast.

"Damn," Gopi swore as he threw down his deck of cards. Standing up, he reached for his coat. "Excuse me gentlemen, I have to call it a night," he declared, maintaining his nonchalant air. Although he was wound up as tight as a spring, he could not let these people know.

"Not so fast, hot shot." Sam put out a long arm to prevent Gopi from moving. He shoved a piece of paper under Gopi's nose.

"What is this?"

"How much you owe us, with interest." Sam's eyes narrowed shrewdly. The pressure on Gopi's arm increased very slowly, until he was sure the blood circulation was cut off.

"Just keep your filthy hands off me," Gopi retorted with just the right amount of arrogance in his voice, pulling his arm away. "You don't scare me."

"You better watch out, boy," Sam whispered menacingly, and clicked his fingers.

Immediately, Shan, the second youngest of the six brothers, appeared. Gopi threw him a look of sheer dislike. Shan was known at the club as the muscleman, and dangerous. He was in his early thirties, but looked much older. His beard gave him a piratical look, and he was born cross-eyed, so one was never sure exactly whom he was looking at or what to expect from him.

"Show the boy out, Shan." Sam commanded, and Shan moved to Gopi's side, grabbed hold of his arm in another tight grip and propelled him towards the door.

"Don't touch me," snapped Gopi, jerking his arm away fiercely and glaring at Shan. He was not going to give the Sen brothers the satisfaction of intimidating him. Besides, he could handle himself: Raymond had taught him how to box, and he had been in a fair number of training fights.

"Just do as the big guy says and there'll be no trouble," Shan warned, smiling at him nastily. And with that, he caught Gopi by the collar and hauled him out into the cold night.

Pulling himself upright, Gopi heard Shan's taunting voice: "Payment is due a week from today – or else!"

Gopi viciously kicked at a stone. He was furious with himself. He should have heeded Raymond's words; but no, he'd known better. He heard footsteps hurrying behind him and felt a hand on his shoulder. Instinctively, Gopi swung around with clenched fists, ready to deliver his first blow. Raymond caught his hand.

"Hey, take it easy. It's only me."

"Come to laugh in my face and say 'I told you so?'" Gopi gave a short, bitter laugh. "What a fool I was not to listen to you!"

"Gopi, this is serious business. Those guys are very dangerous," cautioned Raymond. How he wished he had not been the person responsible for introducing Gopi to the Sen brothers. The worst part was that he had turned Gopi, a decent, loving man, into a totally different person where gambling was concerned. "What are you going to do?"

"I don't know. I honestly don't know," Gopi repeated, totally dejected. "I just have to come up with the money." Gopi looked at Raymond. "This is my problem. If you are too scared to be seen with me, then go. I'll survive without you – and don't give me that guilty look, Raymond," he said curtly. "I landed myself in this mess. I understand if you choose to disassociate yourself from me."

Raymond's mouth dropped open in surprise as Gopi swung on his heel and left him standing there, alone and speechless and feeling horribly guilty.

Gopi wiped the counter for the umpteenth time and each time he wiped it, he gave a silent prayer for some kind of assistance. "I am a fool of all fools," he swore under his breath. "The only person who knows about this is Raymond, and I have rejected him."

Raymond had stayed away from Gopi since Shan Sen had thrown him out. Every day that passed Gopi received a little note from Sam Sen reminding him that his deadline was drawing closer. He had just two hours to go before the deadline and he had only fifteen pounds. It was all of his and Rani's little nest egg, and it hurt like crazy to use it. He was tempted to pawn Rani's only piece of jewellery to pay his debt, but he could not bring himself to stoop to such a level. He dared not tell Rani about the Sen brothers, and spent many sleepless nights, keeping his nightmare to himself.

"Oh, God," he moaned as he buried his face in his hands. "How on earth did I let myself get into this mess?" A tiny voice inside his head nagged: *Raymond, Raymond, Raymond.* "No . . . no . . ." Gopi shook his head to clear away that voice. "It is all my fault for being so weak, gullible and greedy in the first place."

How could he blame his friend when, right from the beginning, Raymond had warned him about gambling, and particularly borrowing money to gamble? *If you run out of cash, leave the game. Never borrow from the Sen brothers, no matter how tempting the offer . . .* Yet he had ignored those words of wisdom, and now he felt as though he were drowning, drowning very, very slowly.

Hot tears of frustration blurred his vision, and he hastily wiped them away. It was only then that he noticed the solitary figure sitting on the other side of the room, watching him closely.

"What are you doing here?" Gopi hoped that he had not seen his tears.

Slowly, Raymond unwound his tall frame and walked over to the bar, his gaze never leaving Gopi's face.

"Have you managed to come up with some cash?" he asked. Gopi did not reply. "That's bad," Raymond said in a grave voice. "You have an hour to go before they send Shan over."

"I know," Gopi acknowledged, "and I suppose I have to face up to whatever they dish out. Thank you for the boxing lessons, by the way." He gave Raymond a grin.

Raymond looked at his friend seriously. Gopi had so many good, admirable qualities: there was no indication, for example, that his friend was afraid of bodily harm from the Sen brothers.

"All right, Gopi," he sighed. "I'll help you, and I don't want that stupid pride of yours to stand in your way. Now, how much do you owe them?" Raymond seated himself at the counter. "I won't move until you tell me."

Gopi hesitated, taking in the stubborn look on Raymond's face. "Okay," he said grudgingly. "One hundred and fifty pounds, including interest."

Raymond let out a whistle, which did not make Gopi feel any better. "Well, my dear friend. This isn't much but it's all I could rake up under the circumstances." Raymond reached into his pocket and pulled out a wad of notes, which he placed on the counter right in front of Gopi.

"Where did you get this from?" Gopi asked, not touching the money.

"Don't ask questions," Raymond's voice was gruff and he avoided Gopi's eyes. "Put on your coat and let's get out of here before the muscleman arrives." He tried to sound light-hearted but failed miserably.

In his relief, Gopi wanted to laugh and cry at the same time; but then, much to his surprise, he found himself pushing the money away. "I'm sorry, Raymond, but I can't accept this."

"Are you insane?" Raymond shouted. "I know it's only eighty pounds, but damn it, Gopi, at least it will keep those money-hungry mongrels off your back!"

Gopi pushed the notes even further away, unperturbed by Raymond's outburst. "It belongs to you and I cannot take it."

"What is the matter with you?" Raymond yanked Gopi by his collar. "Now listen my friend. I have worked damn hard to come up with this money, and now you tell me you don't want it. You can pay me back – all of it, with interest, if it makes you feel better!" Then he released his hold, and his tone softened: "Please. Take the money."

Gopi looked at Raymond, touched to the core. "You are truly a good friend, and I will never forget this," he said. "I am sorry for the way I've treated you."

Gopi walked around the counter and they hugged, but not before he saw the sudden flicker of pain and guilt in Raymond's eyes.

"Hey, come on," Raymond's voice was thick with emotion, "Lets get going."

"Well, well, well. Look who's here," drawled Sam Sen as Gopi and Raymond entered the den. "I was about to send Shan out for some fresh air and exercise."

"What's stopping him?" Gopi asked calmly, holding Sam's stare.

Sam let out a guffaw before replying. "You, tough boy!" When Gopi showed no emotion, he added, "Follow me." He led the way to his office behind the gambling room.

It was the first time that Gopi had been inside Sam's "special den", as he liked to call it. "This is where I conduct all my legal business. For you, my friend," he gave Gopi a wolfish smile, "the very best seat in the house."

"I prefer to stand, thank you."

"Well, then," Sam rubbed his palms together, "let's get down to business."

"Firstly," Gopi began, keeping his voice steady and confident. "I would appreciate a little understanding . . ."

"You don't have it, do you?" Sam interrupted, his voice like thunder and his black eyes hard as marbles.

"Actually, I do," Gopi informed him smoothly. "Just not all of it."

"How much do you have?"

Gopi told him without blinking an eyelid.

"You could not come up with the balance?"

"If I could, do you think I would be standing here?" Gopi replied, sounding very young and arrogant.

"Don't smart-talk me, boy." Sam growled, pulling Gopi closer to him. "Now hand it over."

"Let go first," Gopi shoved him away and took a step back. He ran a hand through his hair and straightened his coat. His heart was racing madly and he most definitely did not like the murderous glint in Sam's eyes, but he held the older man's gaze unflinchingly. He took the thick envelope out of his coat pocket and tossed it on the desk.

Sam reached out and counted the crisp notes. Gopi watched in fascination as he removed the oil painting of the Taj Mahal to reveal a wall safe, opened the door with a tiny key, and placed Gopi's payment inside. Gopi's eyes caught sight of the bundles of notes stashed away in the safe, and he swallowed hard. He had never seen so much money in all his life.

"Look all you like," sniggered Sam as he caught Gopi's eye in the mirror inside the safe. "Just keep your mouth shut and nothing will happen to you." He replaced the painting. "Now, about the balance. You have ten days," Sam warned. "That is all. Now leave the way you came in." He dismissed Gopi with a nod, and then sat down, taking out a small black book from a drawer and making an entry in it.

Gopi met Raymond at the back door and gave him an appreciative hug. "You're a friend in a million."

But when Raymond heard about the ten days, he did not look happy. "That is how they fill their coffers," he explained. "They give extensions, but they keep adding interest."

Nonetheless, Gopi felt temporary relief. Tomorrow he would think of a way to come up with the balance. He was never going to gamble again, he decided; he wasn't cut out for it. And he was most definitely not going to confess to Rani about this dark period in his life. He could not have her tainted as well.

CHAPTER FIFTEEN

There were just three days left before the new deadline. Gopi had received a note stating that all outstanding monies, with interest, were to be paid in full; there would be no second chance. Gopi spent sleepless nights wondering how he was going to come up with the cash: his tips barely covered the Sen brothers' interest.

On the way home from an early shift, he met Rani returning from her weekly shopping. She was carrying a basket full of fresh vegetables, and looked happy and relaxed – as though she didn't have a single care in the world.

"Hi there, my beauty," Gopi greeted her. It pleased him to see that she still delivered that wonderful coy smile whenever he complimented her. He took the basket from her, and they walked on hand in hand.

"You seem rather pensive," she observed after a few minutes of silence.

"It's nothing," he replied shortly.

"Are you sure?"

"Rani, I'm fine." Gopi tried to keep the impatience out of his voice.

Looking up, he wished suddenly that they had taken another route home: approaching them was Shan Sen, with a henchman on either side of him. "Damn," he swore under his breath, and was aware of the startled look Rani threw him. Then they were face to face with Shan.

"Is this the little lady you've been hiding away?" Shan's eyes moved over Rani.

Gopi was tempted to remove that lecherous sneer by punching him in the face.

"Excuse us," Gopi hissed; but the three men blocked their way.

"Who are these . . . these people?" Rani's voice trembled.

"Don't worry." Gopi drew Rani closer to him, and tried to step around Shan and his men.

"What's the matter?" demanded Shan, again blocking their path, and bringing Gopi and Rani to a halt.

"Keep away from us," warned Gopi through tightly clenched teeth, eyes flashing with anger.

Shan placed his face close to Gopi's. "If you cannot come up with the payment in cash," he whispered intensely as his eyes swept over Rani again, "she will be more than adequate."

"You . . . *bastard*!" Gopi felt something wild unleash itself in him.

Before he could stop himself, he punched Shan in his stomach with all the force of his white-hot fury. Not expecting the blow, Shan staggered under its force. The men on either side of him grabbed hold of Gopi before he could land another punch.

"Want us to finish him off?" the short, overweight man on the right asked, as Shan made a swift recovery.

Shan glared at Gopi and then, with a sadistic twist of his lips, moved his eyes once again to Rani, who was too terrified to scream. A tiny whimper escaped her.

"No," Shan answered, and suddenly grinned maliciously. His eyes lingered on Rani, and the message in them was clear. Then he turned abruptly and walked away, followed by his men.

"Gopi!" Rani cried, horrified. "Who on earth is that creature?"

Gopi was still shaking with fury. When she got no response, Rani grabbed hold of his arm. "What is going on?" she demanded.

"Don't worry about him." Gopi tried to give her a casual look, but failed. They were near their home and he did not want to make a scene in public – one was more than enough.

"Don't tell me that," Rani's voice shook. "You saw the way he looked at me!"

Gopi felt as though someone had taken a knife and was twisting it into his heart. He pulled her closer, hoping to take away the fear in her eyes. "He's not going to hurt you," he placated her. "Come, let's get home."

They walked home in silence, Gopi with a deep feeling of foreboding gnawing inside him.

Once inside the house, Rani could restrain herself no more. "What was he saying about payment?" she persisted as Gopi closed the door behind them.

"I told you not to worry about it."

"Gopi, this concerns me as well!" Rani cried out, almost hysterical. "Maybe I can help . . . I love you and I don't want anything to happen to you. Talk to me, please!"

Gopi looked at his wife silently, not knowing what to do. He hated himself for what he had just put her through, but it was too late to turn back the clock. He pulled out a chair, drew Rani onto his lap and held her closely, soothing her until he felt her calm down.

When Rani could bear the silence no longer she lifted her face to his. "Are you in some kind of financial trouble?" she asked gently, holding his face between her palms.

He looked at her intently for a moment. "Yes, I am."

"With those people," she prompted, and when he nodded her eyes revealed her confusion. "Why?"

"Because your husband is a fool. That is why," his voice cracked.

And then, with her gentle coaxing, he told Rani every little detail, including his friendship with Raymond. "I am so ashamed, Rani. You will never know how much."

Rani stood up and looked at Gopi. She was horrified by what she had just heard. "I cannot believe that you would keep such a thing from me," she declared. Many emotions ran through her: anger, betrayal, fear. But in the end, her loyalty and love for Gopi won through, and she cried in his arms.

"We certainly have a problem," she said, wiping away her tears and returning to her sensible self.

"Not you, Rani. *I* have a problem," he corrected.

Rani shook her head. "We are in this together. I should have realised that there was a problem a long time ago – there were lots of signs. You were working late too many nights . . . and then you started buying me pretty saris and shoes and even some nice clothes for yourself. And your erratic moods . . . I was too afraid to ask, but I should have," she ended, seeing the pained look in Gopi's eyes.

"What a fool I've been. I have two very dear people in my life, you and Raymond, and with your help I could have avoided this mess."

"How much do you need?" Rani asked. When Gopi told her, her eyes widened in disbelief. "How on earth are we to come up with that kind of money?" she gasped.

"I really don't know," he sighed, and when he saw her look of despair, he tried to give her a brave smile. "But don't concern yourself, Rani. I'll think of something."

Suddenly Rani's eyes brightened – but she knew in her heart that if she shared her idea with Gopi, his stubborn pride would surely reject it.

"Gopi – can I meet Raymond?" she asked softly, her mind already formulating a plan.

The following evening Rani waited for Gopi and Raymond. She had decided that they would have supper first, and when she was satisfied that she could trust Raymond she would let him in on her plan. When she heard the door handle turn she began to feel terribly nervous. She was very afraid of the consequences if her idea did not work.

Rani took in Raymond's immaculate, stylish attire as he followed Gopi into their modest home. This was the man who had tempted her straight, decent husband with his fancy lifestyle. When he smiled at Rani during the introductions, she saw something in his eyes which troubled her, but she could not quite put her finger on it . . . But he carried himself well, she thought; and she immediately picked up the rapport between the two friends.

As the evening progressed she felt herself drawn to Raymond, much against her will. He was charming and gentle and he had a great sense of humour. But she could not fathom why that nagging feeling did not leave her.

I have to think of Gopi, she scolded herself, and this is the only person who can help me to help him.

Rani waited until Gopi had to visit the outside lavatory before she addressed Raymond with a beguiling smile: "I am so glad Gopi has a friend like you to turn to."

"Thank you for the compliment," Raymond returned, "but right now I feel extremely helpless." He wished he had never befriended Gopi. He had never planned on actually liking the man, and to make matters worse, he found he also liked this lovely dark-skinned woman, who had the kindest eyes he had ever seen. She looked at him so trustingly that guilt twisted his guts and he felt sick. Those dark, trusting eyes would haunt him for the rest of his life.

The honesty in Raymond's voice touched Rani, and she knew that she could rely on him. "I have a plan . . ." she began.

Rani paced the small room impatiently. It was almost ten o' clock, and it seemed as though Gopi and Raymond were taking forever. Please have the money, she prayed, knowing that although Gopi put on a brave front for her benefit, he was slowly killing himself with worry. "Hurry, please hurry home," she whispered fervently.

A tap on the door brought her pacing to a halt. "Thank God," she cried out, relief flowing through her as she rushed to the door and pulled it open.

The expectant smile froze on her face. Her heart contracted with fear, and she moved instinctively to shove the door in the face of the man standing on her doorstep. But it was too late. The man, using his superior strength, easily pushed his way inside.

"Get out of here," Rani's heart pounded, so loud she was sure he could hear it.

"I've come to collect," the man drawled as he slammed the door shut and moved towards her.

Rani backed away from him. His cross-eyed stare was so obviously lecherous that it made her skin crawl. But she dared not show him her fear and disgust.

"Get out of here – or I'll scream," she warned.

"Scream all you want," he answered mockingly. "My men outside will stop anyone from entering. Anyway, everyone will think you're screaming because of the pleasure I'm giving you." He grinned sadistically as he advanced slowly towards her.

"You touch me and I'll kill you," spat Rani as she grabbed an iron poker, the nearest thing on hand.

He merely laughed, and reached for Rani. She screamed.

"Shut up," he hissed, clamping a huge sweaty hand over her mouth. "Your man failed and I have come to collect." He licked his lips hungrily as his hand tightened over her mouth. "No more yelling," he instructed. "I'm going to let you go slowly, and if you know what's good for you, you'll do as I say. Got it?"

Rani, who was struggling to breathe, nodded, and to her relief he let her go.

She took in great gulps of air. "What kind of people are you to go back on your word?" she whispered.

When he just laughed again, something snapped inside Rani. Reasoning with this monster was impossible, she realised. He was insane.

"You crazy man!" she screamed.

In desperation Rani swung the poker and struck him on the side of his head; but this did not deter him. Instead it unleashed his anger, and he slammed her against the wall.

"You bitch," he snarled as he slapped her hard across the face a couple of times.

For the first time in her life Rani tasted blood, and her head began to swim as she felt his large, fleshy hands all over her. Her puny efforts to fight him off merely added to his fury. From a distance she heard, and felt, him rip her clothes. She hit out blindly, and more violent blows were delivered. A fist landed in the middle of her stomach, and she doubled over in pain.

He yanked her up by the hair and forced her to look at him. A whimper of pain escaped through her swollen and bruised lips: she felt as though she were being slowly stretched to reach his height. Then, to her disgust, he ground his fleshy lips into hers. She almost choked. She tasted her own blood and tears and felt his tongue invading her and without thinking of the consequences she bit him, hard.

The man pulled back in pain and shoved her away from him, but not before he delivered another blow, which sent Rani reeling.

"That's the limit, you bitch," he snarled as he tore again at her clothes. Her sari ripped in several places as she desperately tried to hang on to it to cover herself. Her blouse was torn right down the front and her worn underclothes did not stand a chance under his vicious assault. Rani shut her eyes tightly, wanting to erase the sight of his evil face, and a scream rose deep inside her. As she opened her mouth, he clamped his big hand over her swollen lips; with the other, he held her small hands over her head.

Terror gave way to strength and Rani fought against him; but the more she fought, the harder he laughed. Rani drew in a deep breath and spat. A mixture of blood and saliva flew at his face. This enraged him further, and he kicked her as though she were a dog. Her scream became a whimper of pain as she felt him land a kick to her stomach.

"You bastard . . ." Rani's voice was a mere whisper. Her head rolled back and forth and a terrible pain attacked her lower body where he had kicked her.

Just as a tidal wave of darkness swept over her, she heard a bang on the door and someone calling out, "Hurry Shan, someone's coming!"

When Gopi saw the door left ajar he instantly sensed that something dreadful had occurred.

"Something's wrong," he cried, breaking into a run.

Lying on the floor, barely breathing, was a crumpled, bloodied figure. Gopi's heart began to thud wildly, and he let out an anguished scream.

"Rani, oh my God!" He scooped up her beaten and near-naked body and rocked her in his arms.

Raymond gasped as he entered the room, and Gopi lifted his tearstained face to his friend: "Just look what those bastards have done to her!"

Raymond was beyond words; he numbly covered Rani with a blanket. He had never seen anything like it in his life: Rani's face was horribly bruised, her eyes swollen to twice their normal size; and her body – that was something else. He shuddered. What kind of a monster would do this to a woman?

"Try and get a grip on yourself, Gopi," he muttered. He wanted to sound firm and strong, but the horror of what had transpired left him weak and torn inside.

"This is all my fault . . ." Gopi sobbed as his tears fell on Rani's battered face. Raymond left the two of them together, and returned with a bowl of water and a towel.

"Hold her gently, Gopi," he instructed. "I'll clean her face."

Gopi gently pushed the hair away from Rani's face as Raymond wiped it. "I'll kill him, honest I will," he swore as he carried Rani's still form to their bed. "Why is she not moving?" he cried, turning to Raymond, almost hysterical.

There was blood seeping between Rani's legs. Raymond did not know what to do. "I think it's best if I get a doctor."

Outside the house, Raymond let go of his feelings. He bent over and brought up his dinner. Dear God, he prayed. Please forgive me.

While Raymond was gone, Gopi touched Rani's face tenderly, all the time talking to her, telling her how much he loved her and how sorry he was. "Who did this to you, Rani?" he wept, although he knew the answer in his heart.

As his tears fell on her face, her eyelids fluttered weakly. Rani looked at her husband through swollen lids and whispered, "Shan . . . that man . . ."

Gopi held tightly onto her hand as her voice faded and her eyelids dropped again.

The doctor was the same one who had seen to Rani when she had her miscarriage.

"Thank you," Raymond said as he led the doctor to Gopi's door. "You are very kind to come out to help an Indian, this late."

"It is my job to serve humanity," the doctor replied with a kind smile.

When he saw Rani's condition the doctor caught his breath. "Move out of the way," he instructed, pulling out a stethoscope which he placed very gently on Rani's chest. He noted her shallow breathing, and turned to Gopi and Raymond. "Please wait outside while I attend to her," he ordered.

"No," Gopi refused.

"Come on, Gopi." Raymond directed him to the door, and Gopi had no choice but to follow him outside.

"I never meant this to happen, Raymond." Gopi's whole frame shook with anger. He had already cried tears of pain. "I love her so much, and for the Sens to do this to her . . ." his eyes were hard and filled with hatred.

"We don't know if it was them for sure." Raymond hated himself for trying to cast doubts on what was obvious.

"Oh, it's them all right." Gopi stormed. "None other than Shan Sen himself." His voice was aching. "God, Raymond. How could I let this happen to her? I am to blame for everything. I was weak and arrogant and my wife has paid for my actions!"

Raymond was at a loss for words, and silently thanked the doctor for interrupting them just then by opening the door. He nodded towards the doctor, and Gopi straightened up immediately.

"How is she, Doctor? Is she going to be all right?" Gopi reached out to this man who had been so kind and compassionate the last time he tended to Rani.

"I have to be frank . . ." The doctor cleared his throat. "And you have to be very strong for the sake of your wife. What she has been through is traumatic, and there is internal bleeding. She is also losing a lot of blood from the blows she received to her stomach. I am afraid . . . she has lost the baby."

"Baby . . ." Gopi's eyes widened with shock. "What are you saying?"

"Your wife was about eight weeks pregnant."

"Oh no . . . *no!*" Gopi's cry of anguish was heart-wrenching. He sank to the ground, burying his face in his hands as he wept. He wept out of anger and pain, and most of all out of guilt. He wept for the loss of their unborn child, and he wept for the terrible ordeal he had put his wife through.

They let him sob for a while, and then the doctor pulled him to his feet.

"You both must think I am a weakling." Gopi brushed back his tears, ashamed.

"It is human nature," the doctor smiled sadly. "I have seen a lot of grown men cry in my time."

"Is Rani going to die?" Gopi asked, desperation in his voice.

"If the bleeding stops, then she will recover, although she will never be able to have another baby. Her other internal injuries will take time to heal."

"Doctor, what do you mean *if* the bleeding stops?" Raymond, who had been listening quietly, asked. His voice was tense and anxious.

The old doctor could only shake his head.

"If anything happens to my Rani," Gopi's voice broke the silence, cold and ruthless, "God be my witness, I will get that bastard!"

CHAPTER SIXTEEN

Hemith had wrapped his arms around Sita's growing waistline, and quite unexpectedly felt a kick – their baby, responding to his touch. He smiled in delight, and a warm glow of happiness spread through Sita.

"I hope it is a little girl," he whispered "Two sons and, I hope, a daughter. What more could a man ask for?" He grinned at her: "I was beginning to get worried there for a while. At the rate we were going, I didn't think we would make another baby."

Sita's heart contracted. "What do you mean?"

"There was a time when we barely made love," he reminded her. " I know I have not been the most attentive husband recently. Work has also taken up a lot of my time and energy and I have been neglecting my wife."

Life on the estate was currently very unsettling for Sita. Almost into her ninth month of pregnancy, she continued to work, for her family needed her income – the mill workers were striking, and they were not being paid. Hemith had organised the strike.

"No work, no pay. Those are Browne's rules," he told her.

It was a week since the workers had downed their tools. From their point of view, the timing was perfect: it was the busiest time of the year at the mill. But for Sita the timing was terrible.

"Did you have to organise this now? The baby is due shortly, and what happens if I deliver early?" she asked, worried.

"Please try to understand, Sita." Hemith paced their small bedroom. "We have suffered and some of our people have died because of our working conditions, and for far too long our grievances have been ignored." He took hold of Sita's hand. "I have always said that one day, I would do something constructive to help our people. Now is the time. I know how difficult this is for you, but please, I need your help."

He looked at her with weary eyes, and Sita's heart went out to him. He was exhausted, and yet still radiated that inner strength that she had come to admire and rely on so much.

"What can I do?" she asked, puzzled. Hemith was very careful not to involve her in the problems at the mill. He often said that strikes were a man's business.

"We need you to write down our grievances. If we present something to Browne and the other estate owners who use the mill, it has to be done properly, so that they know we are serious. You are the only person I know whose English is good enough.

Although Sita understood everything her husband was saying, she felt torn in two. This strike was affecting the Campbell Estate, for their cane was crushed at the Browne Mills. By assisting her husband and her people, she was turning against her employer –and the man who possessed her heart.

However, her people were oppressed, and she felt their agony and heartache more than ever; she also knew what her assistance would mean to her husband. In the end, her loyalty to them was stronger.

"All right. I'll do it," she decided, and Hemith gave her a quick hug. "You will have to tell me exactly what you want written down. All I know is that the wages paid are not enough to live on."

"That is just one of our grievances," Hemith filled in, as he handed her paper and pen. "We want better working conditions. The mills are overcrowded and infested with rats, and it is very unhealthy."

A shiver ran through Sita as she settled down to begin the list. Finally, she was making a valuable contribution to society!

"We need another section built to store the crushed cane, and we definitely need shorter hours," Hemith continued. "I suggest that the men work shifts, instead of having too many exhausted men trying to work at the same time, causing accidents."

Sita paused in her writing, her eyes shining with unshed tears. "I don't think I have ever told you this before, but I am proud of your courage and strength," she smiled.

Hemith returned her compliment with a kiss on the top of her head. "Now, about an increase in wages."

He gave an amount which Sita felt was not unreasonable, given that for the past three years they had received no increases whatsoever. More grievances followed, and Sita made sure that she wrote down everything.

"I had no idea that the situation was so bad," she sighed, as she put down her pen and handed the list to Hemith.

He read through what she had written. "I like this one here that you added," he smiled.

"Well, I thought I'd sneak that in. After all, it's time we had a small school for the children," she replied with an impish grin.

"I think we need to make a few copies of this. Can you manage?"

Sita was on tenterhooks the next day. Hemith, with four other representatives from the mill, had gone up to Browne's office with the list she had compiled. She would have to wait until evening to hear the outcome.

While Sita was serving lunch to the family at the Big House, Albert rushed in. His face was flushed beneath his tan and he looked hot and bothered.

"Albert, what is the matter?" Elizabeth asked, and Sita's eyes flew to his face.

"It's this damn strike! We are into the second week already, and now the men have come up with a list a mile long!"

"Typical," Helena remarked.

Sita ran her tongue over her suddenly dry lips.

"Does it affect our production?" Elizabeth placed her fork down.

"Yes, it does!" he stormed, clenching his fist. "I'd like to get my hands on the person who helped draw up that list."

Sita's head shot up, and when she spoke her voice was clear and firm: "I did."

"*What?*" both Elizabeth and Helena gasped, and Albert's mouth dropped open.

"I mean," she stumbled over her words, and then pulled herself upright when she caught the hostile look in Helena's eyes. "I wrote down the grievances, but it was my husband who dictated them to me."

Albert stared at Sita in utter disbelief. "You mean to tell me that . . . that the instigator of this strike is your *husband*?"

"Yes," she replied, "but he is not an instigator. He is a leader." A touch of pride entered her voice.

"I want to see you in my study, now!" Albert thundered as he stormed ahead of Sita, totally ignoring Elizabeth's protest.

"Just what the hell is going on, Sita?" he demanded, as she closed the door behind her.

"What do you mean?" She gave him a wide-eyed stare.

"Don't you dare play stupid with me. I know you too well." He towered over her, his eyes blazing with fury. "You know what this strike is costing us – and then you do this, behind my back!"

"Now wait a minute, before you start throwing accusations at me!" Sita's eyes matched his in fury. "I am sorry if you are suffering the consequences of our actions, but my people have suffered for too long. At least now you might be willing to do something constructive." Her voice filled hopefully, for beneath that anger lay fairness and justice.

"What are you talking about?"

"You may not own the mill but you give Browne a fair amount of business, so why don't you acknowledge some of the grievances?" Sita saw his look of astonishment, but refused to slow down. "You and Elizabeth have always been fair and just with your labourers. Everyone talks of how well you treat them, and that you have upheld Master Campbell's standards. If you speak to Browne you may just get through to him," she implored.

"Sita, I cannot tell him how to run his mill, for God's sake!" Albert ran his fingers through his hair in frustration as he turned away from her.

"I am not asking you to do that, Albert. Just point out what you think is wrong and offer suggestions." Gently, she turned him to face her. She noted the softening in his eyes, and knew in her heart that he would do anything she asked. "Please." She placed her hands over her protruding belly, and her eyes begged for his understanding. "Those grievances are not unrealistic, Albert. My people are not animals. We have feelings and needs. We are hardworking and loyal, and right now we need all the assistance we can get. *Your* assistance," she whispered, and her voice held an aching note which she was quite unaware of. "I have never asked you for anything. Now all I ask is for your help to right the wrongs that have been done."

Albert felt torn. Sita was right. She had never asked him for a single thing. He knew how Browne treated his workers, but had never felt that it was his place to intervene. He stared at her for a minute before turning away and walking to the window.

He was silent for so long that Sita thought he had forgotten about her. Suddenly he turned, and Sita's breath caught in her throat. His eyes burned with intensity, but when he spoke his voice was cold and hard:

"Why should I do this, Sita?"

Sita felt faint with helplessness, but she refused to surrender.

"You are under no obligation to help," she replied, her voice barely a whisper, "but if you cannot help now, what kind of a life do you think this baby, and others, are going to lead?"

His face was an iron mask; Sita held his gaze.

"All right," he sighed at last. "I'll see what can be done." Then his mask dropped. "So I have finally met your husband, Sita. He seems to be a decent and caring man."

Sita's eyes misted. "He is," she affirmed. "Sometimes, when I look at him, I feel so lucky. I do not deserve to have him."

"Don't!" Albert's voice shook with emotion. "He is the lucky one, to have someone like you in his life."

There was an abrupt knock before the door was flung open and Helena strode in, followed by a rather apprehensive Elizabeth.

Albert did not move away from Sita. Instead he calmly handed her his handkerchief.

"What is going on here?" Helena demanded, appraising the scene.

"Come in," Albert invited sarcastically, ignoring Helena's suspicious eyes as she looked from Sita to him. "Don't go yet, Sita," he said, holding her back as she turned to leave. "I want to get my sister's opinion on this situation. Sit down." He showed her to the nearest chair and moved to sit behind his desk. "Why don't you ladies sit down as well?" he continued, looking at his wife and sister.

"This is not a tea party, Albert," sneered Helena, throwing Sita a cold glance.

"No, it's not," he agreed, "and no one is insisting you stay. In fact, I would prefer it if you left," he issued coolly, and took pleasure in watching her face turn an ugly red.

"Albert!" she almost gasped with embarrassment, for he had humiliated her in front of a servant – a servant she found herself hating at that moment. "We will discuss this later," she returned coldly, then stormed out of his study and slammed the door behind her.

"That was quite unnecessary, Albert," Elizabeth reprimanded as she sat opposite him.

"Was it?" he returned with a lift of his brow. "I believe we have more important things to discuss, Elizabeth." He then explained everything to her, including Sita's role. "So what do you think?" he asked, sitting back in his chair and putting his booted feet up on the desk, ankles crossed. He watched his sister carefully, through narrowed eyes.

Slowly Elizabeth turned to Sita. "I must say that your involvement does not surprise me at all. I have always known that one day you would be of assistance to your people."

"It is to my husband, Madam, not I, that credit should be given," Sita said.

"It is time Mr Browne became aware of the situation, Albert." Elizabeth's eyes suddenly twinkled. All apprehension vanished as she was filled with enthusiasm. "Graham always maintained that in order to get the best from our workers we had to treat them like people, for that is what they are. And," she turned to Sita with a brilliant smile, "I am proud of you, and in a way proud of myself too. Proud for taking you in hand and giving you some form of education. Maybe we can do something after all!"

"You mean you are not angry with me?" Relief flooded through Sita. It was a long time since Elizabeth had seemed so motivated.

"Not at all," Elizabeth smiled. "I want to help. Albert, we must set up a meeting with Mr Browne and his labourers."

The following day Albert called Elizabeth and Sita into the study. "I have seen Mr Browne and he has set up a meeting," he informed them. "Today at three o'clock."

"Is that not short notice?" Sita asked, hoping that Hemith would be ready.

"Not to the strikers. Browne's overseer has notified the leader of the strike."

Sita could not help but notice that Albert did not acknowledge that he knew it was her husband, nor call him by name.

"Does Mr Browne know that you are sympathetic to our grievances?" she asked.

"Not yet. All I said was that if something was not done soon, our production and profits would take an even deeper nose-dive, and the best thing we could do would be to listen to what the workers have to say."

"Did he accept that? You know how ruthless and underhand he can be at times," warned Elizabeth.

"Well, my dear. So can I," Albert grinned.

"I suggest we take Sita along," Elizabeth's eyes were alive with challenge. "She can act as interpreter."

"My husband is there and he speaks good English," Sita put in hastily. What would Hemith say if she arrived with them?

"All the more reason to come along. Give him moral support as well. After all, Sita," Elizabeth went on determinedly, "you helped him and should be there. We must remember that we are dealing with a very shrewd businessman here . . . sometimes a woman in a delicate condition can be very persuasive."

Sita's worried look caught Albert's attention. "Will you be all right, Sita? We would hate to throw you into the lion's den," he teased, making light of the situation.

I have to be strong, she told herself. Here are two people who are going out of their way to support us, and the other estate owners may well spurn them for their efforts. How can I not contribute to this fight as well?

Squaring her shoulders, Sita picked up her head proudly. "I will be fine. Just fine."

Sita arrived at the Browne Estate with Albert and Elizabeth. Her quick gaze took in the tired faces of the strikers. Some were standing in groups while others sat on the ground, talking quietly amongst themselves. Sita's eyes scanned the crowd for Hemith.

A hush fell over the workers at the sight of the newcomers. Hemith's eyes widened in surprise: Sita was being assisted from the carriage by Albert Sheldon, who was handling her as though she were the most delicate thing in the world. He watched as the man's eyes tenderly passed over Sita's body and her protruding belly. Behind them, Hemith recognised Elizabeth Campbell.

Although the Campbells crushed their cane at the mill, Hemith had never spoken to Albert Sheldon. He could not understand this strange feeling which was coming over him – he wanted to rush over and pull Sita away from him. She was already walking towards the entrance of the building, with her employers on either side of her.

"What is your wife doing here?" Harry, one of the crushers asked, as his gaze followed Hemith's.

"That's what I'm going to find out," Hemith snapped as he headed towards the building.

"Where do you think you're going?" O'Grady, Browne's overseer demanded

"Inside, for the meeting." Hemith glared at the red-haired giant. At that moment he was too infuriated to be intimidated by this man. "You have a problem with that?" His eyes followed Sita.

"The meeting is to begin at three sharp, coolie. What's the matter with you? Can't wait to get your hands on that . . ." he moved his large, beefy hands in the air, visibly drawing Sita's figure and sticking his belly out to emphasise her pregnancy. "Pity she's so huge," he sniggered.

Hemith's temper rose. Calm down, he warned himself. To retaliate now would be detrimental to our goals. He knew that the overseer was baiting him, and he was not going to give him the satisfaction of losing his temper.

"She is my wife," he announced, and almost grinned when he saw the stunned expression on the man's face. Hemith took advantage of the moment to call out, "Sita!"

The overseer blinked, and just as Hemith was about to call her name again he was grabbed by the neck.

"Shut up, you bloody coolie," O'Grady snarled. He threw Hemith to the ground and kicked him viciously in the ribs; as Hemith tried to get up, he was kicked down again. The crowd gathered round, and began shouting for the overseer to stop. He held Hemith down with a booted foot and stood over him with his arms crossed over his chest.

"What the hell is going on?" Albert pushed through the crowd, followed by Sita and Elizabeth.

"Oh my God, it's Hemith!" Sita cried as she ran forward. Hemith was struggling to get up.

Albert took in the arrogant stance of the overseer. "O'Grady, I want to see you inside. Now," he ordered, his voice tight with fury.

The very sight of Sita stooping over her husband had brought a burning desire to hit out, and in the office Albert gave vent to his anger and jealousy.

"Just what the hell were you up to?" he shoved the man against the wall.

"Take your bloody hands off me," O'Grady shoved back at Albert, who retaliated by smashing his fist into the man's smug face.

"You are nothing but a fool," Albert ground out as O'Grady slid to the floor.

"Albert!" Elizabeth rushed in, together with Henry Browne, a thin, long-faced man with cold grey eyes.

"Looks like you knocked him out," Browne observed as he bent over his overseer. "I hope you are satisfied."

"Satisfied!" cried Albert. "This has probably ruined our chances of getting those people back to work."

"Just remember that this man works for me and follows my instructions."

Albert's eyes narrowed. It was clear that this meeting was not going to be easy.

"Well, learn to control him," he retorted crisply, as O'Grady opened his eyes and groggily sat up.

"What are you doing here?" Hemith demanded, ignoring Sita's attempts to help him to his feet. Anger emanated from him.

Sita's eyes filled with hurt and she felt the prick of tears. "I am here to act as interpreter and to give you moral support," she whispered.

"This is no place for a woman, especially one in your condition," he pointed out sharply, holding his side, in pain.

Sita was all too aware of the curious stares they were receiving, but she refused to give in. "Madam Elizabeth suggested I come along and act as interpreter. After all, I did help write down the grievances."

But the fire in Hemith's eyes burned through Sita and her heart pounded. She had never seen her husband so enraged.

"Are you telling me that we, the workers, would not understand what we are discussing? Don't insult my intelligence, Sita. I may not have had the education you had, but I certainly can hold my own against those people. Now I want you to leave." His voice was firm and final.

"How can you be so horrid?" she whispered desperately. "I have as much right to be here as you do. There are women who work on the estates too, and when you asked for my assistance you made me aware, more than ever, of our situation."

"The other wives are just as aware, but you don't see them here, do you?"

"I think it is time you realised that I am not like most wives, Hemith. I want to do something meaningful with my life too. You should feel proud of me."

Hemith drew in a deep breath just as the bell rang, loud and clear. Someone shouted that the meeting was ready to commence. Sita turned away from Hemith.

"Stop!" Hemith turned her around, and took her hand in his. "If you insist on going in, then we go in together, as a team."

CHAPTER SEVENTEEN

Almost four hours later, when the meeting drew to a conclusion, Sita was dropping with exhaustion.

"I want it noted that I am not satisfied with the results of this meeting at all. However, since we have arrived at some sort of middle ground, I want the mills operative immediately," Browne concluded, his discontent clearly evident.

Albert, acting as Chairman, ended the meeting as they all rose to their feet.

Hemith turned to Sita, his expression unreadable. "I'll see you home, but first I have to speak to our people." She nodded in response, but he was already walking away from her.

Outside the building, as they waited for Indar to bring the carriage round, Sita took Elizabeth's hand in hers. "Thank you so much," she smiled tiredly at Elizabeth before turning to Albert. "Both of you. It means a lot that we had your support, and I am very appreciative of your help."

"And we are very proud of the way you handled some of the difficult areas," returned Elizabeth, her eyes soft with pride. "You made Mr Browne understand your set of grievances without losing your temper when he became difficult. I believe he knew he was cornered."

Admiration shone in Albert's eyes: what had impressed him the most had been Sita's ability to remain calm and logical in her negotiations.

"You and your husband make an excellent team, Sita," Elizabeth continued. "Both of you came across with such honesty and conviction."

"Moreover, I don't think that the men would have been able to accomplish much if you hadn't been there today," Albert added, hoping that the touch of jealousy he was feeling was not evident in his voice.

Indeed, Sita and her husband had an excellent rapport, he noted irritably. During the meeting they had communicated with each other in Hindi, before turning to address the others in English. Although Hemith's English was not as fluent as his wife's, he was easier to understand than the other Indians on the estate.

"Thank you." Sita smiled graciously as her eyes scanned the crowd for her husband; their eyes met and locked across the distance which separated them. Sita turned once more to Elizabeth and Albert: "What I said in there came straight from my heart."

Her simple words tore at Albert's heart, and he ached to enfold her in his arms and take her away from what he knew was a very harsh and difficult life. And yet he knew it was impossible. She did not belong to him. She had never really belonged to him, and even now that acknowledgement made him want to scream.

Today had been a revelation to him. Once and for all, he had discovered where Sita's loyalties lay. She had proved to be strong and courageous, and it was obvious she loved her people; that made him love her even more.

"Come, we must leave as well," Elizabeth interrupted his thoughts, and he gave her a small, tight smile which did not reach his eyes.

"You are right, " he murmured, giving Sita a melancholy look. "There is nothing more we can do."

Sita's ambivalent feelings gnawed away at her: she felt elated and depressed at the same time. Elizabeth and Albert had seemed so proud of her and what she had helped to accomplish for her people, and she felt as though she had finally achieved something worthwhile. Yet Hemith's attitude was causing her such pain – pain she never thought he could evoke.

It was very late, almost one-thirty in the morning, and she had not seen Hemith since he brought her back from the mill. Their journey home had been made in silence. Hemith had made sure that she was safe, and then left again to meet with the strikers. She had fought to stay awake and wait up for him, but her eyes had grown droopy and she had succumbed to the exhaustion and strain of the day. During the night she turned in her sleep and felt the chill of an empty space beside her. Slowly she opened her eyes and reached over for her husband, only to confirm her fear: Hemith's side of the bed was smooth, cold and empty. She had never felt more lonely in her whole life.

Restless, Sita got out of bed and made her way to the kitchen, where she found her husband, asleep at the kitchen table. She could not see his face. Her heart contracted at the sight of him – he had looked so exhausted earlier on. Gently, so as not to startle him, she tapped him on his shoulder.

"Hemith," Sita called out softly. "Wake up."

He groaned in his sleep and she gave him another gentle nudge. Wearily he opened his eyes. "What do you want?" he grumbled.

"Come to bed. You must be exhausted."

"Leave me alone." He drew away from her, as though her touch pained him.

"Hemith, please. You cannot sleep at the table. You are exhausted and need your rest. Besides, what will your parents say when they wake up and find you here?" she tried to reason with him. For all the years of their marriage they had never slept apart, no matter how much they argued.

"I really don't care. Besides, you should be more worried about what they'll think when they hear about *you*." He was now fully awake, and just as hostile as he had been earlier.

"They already know and they support me," she replied with quiet dignity.

"Well, good for you. I, however, feel like a bloody incompetent fool. You, my dear wife, did not have to be there at the negotiations." Anger threaded his voice as he got up and moved away from her. He was now fully awake.

"At least Browne listened to me when you were too hot-headed in there."

"Do you blame me?" he cried, anger turned his eyes soot black. "You were the last person I expected to see arrive with . . . Albert Sheldon!"

Sita flinched at his words. Hemith was jealous! Had he seen more than he was supposed to? "I came at Elizabeth Campbell's invitation," she reminded him. "All I wanted to do was help and . . . and you are very ungrateful!" Tears of hurt filled her eyes. "I refuse to let you put me down."

"What?" Hemith gasped. "You put *me* down!"

"No," Sita shook her head. "I did not, and I am sorry that you are ashamed of me. However, I am not sorry that I was there with you and was able to help. You should at least be thankful that Browne gave in."

"Oh, I am," he returned coldly, "but I still maintain that it was not your place to be there."

"Hemith . . ." Too late, Sita realised that she had hurt his masculine pride. "It is over now. As a team we have achieved what seemed like an impossible dream." She gave him a tearful smile as she held out her hand to him. "Let us not spoil it by fighting."

Hemith stared at his wife long and hard. He heard the appeal in her voice and knew that she was right. "I felt as though I was the joke of the community, having my wife fight our battle," he finally admitted as he took her hand in his and drew her into his arms. "I had no idea that she was such a cool and confident negotiator, who could wrap men around her little finger with just one look." A reluctant twinkle appeared in his eye. "You are truly amazing, Sita. You even got them to open a school for our children!"

Sita's heart soared with relief and her face lit up with a dazzling smile. "I did, didn't I? But, Hemith, I bet that most of the men are thinking you are a very lucky man indeed, with me for a wife." Her eyes sparkled with laughter.

Hemith's face reddened, and he had the grace to look embarrassed. "Well, they did tell me that, but I was so angry I thought they were mocking me," he admitted as he hugged her to him and looked into her radiant face. "But Mrs Harilaken, I think you are the lucky one, working for the Campbells. At least they have compassion for our people."

Together they went to bed, and when Hemith wrapped his arms around her, he placed a gentle kiss on her forehead and whispered: "I am proud of you. Very proud to have you as my wife, Sita." She knew that everything would be just fine.

She was Hemith's wife and the mother of his children, and for the first time it felt completely right. That night she came to a painful yet final conclusion – a conclusion her heart had not wanted to accept for a long time. The love she and Albert shared would always be precious to her, and she would carry it in her heart to her death. But she had another life now; and as long as she kept that chapter of her past closed, no one need to know or be hurt.

She felt as though a great weight had lifted from her, as she slid closer to her husband and felt his arms tighten around her swollen belly. She fell asleep as the tears rolled down her cheeks for an impossible love – a love which had held no real future. Her future was with the man who held her so lovingly in his arms.

Sita decided that once her baby was born she would resign from the Big House. This decision hurt, for she loved working for the Campbells. They were like another family to her, and she knew that saying goodbye would break more than one heart. Sita could not bring herself to say anything to Elizabeth Campbell at this point, and so she went about her daily chores as best as she could.

Sita had served breakfast and was clearing the table when Albert handed the newspaper he was reading to Elizabeth.

"Such a pity we always receive the news two weeks late," commented Helena. "In England we never have this problem."

"This is not England," Albert reminded her calmly, as he drank the last bit of his coffee.

"I never said it was, my dear." Helena returned with an icy smile.

As Sita reached over to remove Elizabeth's plate she heard a gasp. Elizabeth's face was pale, and her hands trembled as she dropped the newspaper.

"Madam." Sita looked at her with concern. "Are you all right?"

Helena was already picking up the newspaper, peering at the article that had caused Elizabeth's dismay. Sita leaned over to read it too.

"Don't show it to her!" Elizabeth cried out.

But it was too late. Sita had caught the headline: *Indian Gambler accused of murder.*

"Oh, my God," whispered Sita, stunned, as she scanned the contents of the article. Suddenly her knees buckled, and with Elizabeth's help she sank into the nearest chair. "It cannot be true," she moaned, shaking her head in disbelief.

"Sita?" Albert asked, concerned.

"Why is she reacting like this? Does she know this murderer?" Helena demanded, and Sita lifted her tear-filled eyes to Elizabeth.

"Yes," Elizabeth answered honestly, as she quickly drew in deep gulps of air to keep calm.

"How?" Helena's voice was sharp and cold, and she directed the question to Elizabeth, as though Sita did not exist.

"He is my brother."

A silence fell over them and no one moved. Sita watched Helena's eyes widen and her mouth fall open.

"Why, Elizabeth!" she gasped. "Do you think we are safe?"

"What are you talking about?" Albert asked.

"I mean," Helena's hands moved dramatically to her throat, "he will want to return and perhaps hide here amongst his family. Who knows what he is capable of? Our children will no longer be safe with a killer on the run!"

After the shock of reading the article, this was too much for Sita to bear. "Stop it!" she cried out, tears streaming down her cheeks. "My brother is not a murderer! You have no right to say such awful things."

"Hush, now," Elizabeth instructed firmly. "This is no time for hysterics, from either of you." She looked at both of them sternly, before directing her next words to Helena: "Sita has just received some shocking news, in the most unpleasant manner. It would be appreciated if you could refrain from making derogatory statements."

Helena sniffed haughtily, "Albert, we simply cannot be charged with harbouring a convict."

"Now wait a minute," said Albert with rising anger, putting his hand up to stop her continuing. "What makes you think he will be heading for the estate? According to this article, he is being held in prison, and the case is to be heard in the Pietermaritzburg Supreme Court."

"He has to be innocent," declared Sita passionately. "He is the kindest, most gentle person in my family. There must be some mistake!"

Albert wanted to take her in his arms and kiss away the pain from her eyes. Instead, he said, "Elizabeth, ask Sumi to bring her some strong coffee. She needs it."

Helena grabbed hold of Albert and pulled him towards the window as Sita wiped away her tears with a trembling hand.

"Albert, I don't think it is wise that she stays on," she whispered, soft enough for it to appear as though she were having a confidential talk with her husband, but not so softly that her words did not go unheard by Sita. "I mean," she explained as Albert tilted a brow questioningly at her, "with a criminal brother . . . imagine having her here, taking care of the children." She shivered visibly. "It simply terrifies me to think of Joseph being exposed to the likes of her."

"Helena!" Albert, astounded by the shallowness of his wife's thinking, jerked her to him. "What the hell is the matter with you? Does she look like a criminal to you?" he demanded, eyes flashing with anger, as his fingers bit into her arms.

Helena refused to look at Sita, which only infuriated and disgusted Albert even more.

"Sita has been with this family for nearly ten years. I don't want to hear this kind of talk ever again. Do you understand me?"

"She is right," a quiet voice interrupted, and Albert swung around to see Sita standing a little away from them. "I have decided to leave here, permanently."

"No, Sita!" The cry left Albert's lips before he could stop himself. He refused to hear the finality in her voice. "You don't know what you're saying. You are just overwrought."

"I have made up my mind and it is best for all." Her soft and gentle voice hit him in the centre of his heart, while the message in her eyes was clear: there was no second chance for them, ever. This was goodbye in every sense.

Albert knew that he would never love another woman.

"We have to go and see him before they take him away." Chumpa wiped away her tears with the end of her old cotton sari.

"No," Sewcharran almost growled. "That boy has brought us nothing but disgrace, and I will not have you mention his name to me." His hand moved over his partly closed eyelid. It angered him to know that he carried the scars of Chumpa's defence of their eldest son.

"How can you be so unfeeling, Taj?" Sita's eyes begged for forgiveness. "He needs us. According to this article, he is to be sentenced next week.

We are his family and we should be there – to support him, and to give him a chance to explain to us what went wrong."

"Hasn't that article given you all the details?" Geeta's voice matched her father's. "Taj is right. Why should we add to the pain he has caused us?"

"Look," Hemith decided that he had heard enough. "I have a solution. Bharath and I will go to Gopi and find out what can be done to assist him. We will leave tomorrow. Since Geeta feels so strongly about the whole situation, I doubt that Anoop will want to accompany us."

"You are damn right. I wouldn't . . ."

Geeta's sentence was interrupted as Chumpa struck her oldest daughter across the face. Sita gasped.

"Watch your tongue," Chumpa warned, her eyes bright and furious.

"Ma, this is no time to lose your temper." Sita stepped between them as Geeta's face reddened and she began to fume. "Go on," Sita prompted Hemith.

"Didn't you hear me, boy!" charged Sewcharran and everyone looked at him, astonished. Over the past few years his temper had simmered down, and they had grown to believe that the grandchildren had brought about a drastic change in him.

Hemith met Sewcharran's glare with one of his own. "You can dictate to your wife and children, but please don't try it on me. Gopi has been a friend to me, and the least I can do is be there for him."

"And if I was not going to have this baby, I would accompany you." Sita took hold of Hemith's hand and placed it over her stomach. "But you will have Bharath with you," she smiled, trying to look brave and encouraging.

"Bharath, are you out of your mind?" Geeta turned her anger on her youngest brother.

"No, Geeta. I have never felt better – and please don't think that you can come in here and tell me what to do." Bharath turned to his father: "And Taj, you cannot stop me either. I am no longer a little boy. You drove Gopi away, and for all I know you may be part of the reason this has happened to him."

His words brought a silence upon them, which hung thick and heavy until Chumpa could bear it no longer.

"Go, my Beta," Chumpa put her arms around Bharath. "And tell your Bhaiya that our prayers are with him, and that we love him."

Sita stayed with Chumpa during this trying period in their lives. Chumpa began to look older than her years: her hair, the pride of her youth, turned white overnight, and the smiling lines on her face deepened with worry. She would rush anxiously to the door whenever she heard a wagon approaching. "Please, Hare Bhagavan," she prayed fervently, "don't let them send my Gopi to prison."

Finally, when she thought she would die from not knowing what was happening, she heard the sound of a wagon in the still of the night. Grabbing hold of a clay lamp, she raced barefoot to the kitchen door, flinging it open before Bharath reached it.

"Beta," she grabbed hold of him. "Did you see your Bhai? How is he?" The words tumbled from her wildly.

"Majee, let's go inside." Bharath put his arms around her shoulders and guided her back into their cottage. He was shocked at the change in her appearance, and prayed silently that what he had to tell her would not throw her totally off balance. Hemith followed behind.

Sita, awakened by the disturbance of their arrival, waddled into the kitchen. "What happened?" she asked as she went to Hemith, who gave her a hug and held her tightly in his arms.

"How is my Gopi?" Chumpa was impatient for information, any information.

"Majee, please sit down." Bharath pulled out a chair for her, and when she was seated, he knelt beside her and took her roughened, hard-working hands in his. "Majee, we don't have good news."

The look in his eyes made Chumpa pull her hands away from his and place them over her mouth to stifle her scream of pain. All that escaped was an anguished moan.

"Did he actually kill that man?" Sewcharran asked, and all eyes turned to him, waiting for an explosion. But Sewcharran's voice was no longer loud and booming. "Well, Beta, did he?" he aked his youngest son, wanting him to deny it.

When Bharath did not respond, Chumpa let out another terrified wail and collapsed in a faint. Hemith hurried to fetch a cup of water, which he sprinkled over Chumpa's pale face. It took her a few minutes to recover.

"Ma, are you okay?" Sita wiped her mother's face with the end of her sari. Chumpa just stared at her in a daze.

"Ma," Bharath shook her by the shoulder. "Listen to me. He is going to be all right." He hoped Chumpa could hear him – she had an almost insane look in her eyes. "He sends his love, and he has one very specific request." He turned his attention to Sita. "If you have a little girl he would like you to call her Rani." Tears shimmered in Bharath's eyes. "He loved her with all his heart."

"Oh, God." Sita cried and buried her hands in her face. His request tore at her heart. Hemith, who was just as moved, drew his wife into his arms.

"I want to know exactly what happened!" Chumpa's voice, hoarse with emotion, startled them, and all four swung around in her direction. "Bharath, I want to know all the details."

"Majee, I don't know where to begin," Bharath tried, tears streaming down his face.

Chumpa took his face in her hands and gently wiped away his tears.

"Gopi blames himself for everything," Hemith began, for he could see that Bharath was too distressed to explain anything. "He got involved with some gamblers."

"Gamblers!" Sita turned her bewildered eyes to Hemith.

"No . . . no . . ." Chumpa shook her head in disbelief. "Not my Gopi. He would never do that."

"I am sorry Majee, but it is the truth." Hemith found it difficult to continue, but knew it was best to get it over with. And so he related the whole sad story of Gopi and the Sen brothers, and the attack on Rani. "Rani . . ." Hemith felt the tears at the back of his eyes, and for an instant he saw Gopi's pathetic face as he told them the truth. "Rani was badly beaten."

"No . . ." moaned Chumpa, and Bharath placed his arms around her as she began to rock to and fro.

Bharath, afraid that his mother was losing control, looked at Hemith worriedly. "I don't think we should continue."

"We have to know everything." Sewcharran's voice cracked with emotion. It seemed that he did have feelings for his eldest son, after all.

Hemith cleared his throat. When he spoke, his voice was thick with unshed tears. "Rani . . . lost their baby and . . ." he drew in a deep breath, "she never recovered. Rani bled to death."

"I don't want to hear the rest," Chumpa wailed, pulling at her hair in agony and grief.

Sobbing quietly, Sita fell to her knees in front of her mother and tried to still Chumpa's frantic movements. "Majee, Taj is right. We have to know what happened," she cried, as she caught hold of Chumpa's hands.

"My sympathies lie with Gopi. I would have reacted similarly," Hemith said, trying his best to ease their pain. "He knew the name of her attacker . . ." his voice shook with emotion and he found that he could not continue.

Chumpa turned questioning eyes to Bharath, who buried his tear-stained face in the folds of her sari. "How did he kill him?" she whispered hoarsely.

"He strangled him, Majee." Bharath wept. "That animal deserved to die."

Together, the family shed tears for Gopi, and the heartache he and his wife had suffered. Vengeance bore tragedy in more ways than one.

"My poor Beta," said Chumpa at last. "Now, please tell me – what happened in court?" The question came out in a calm whisper, for she had stopped her rocking. But her eyes betrayed the emotions raging inside her.

"Majee, you would have been so proud of Gopi." Bharath held her hand. "He stood up in court, tall and strong, and spoke so clearly and honestly. He was not afraid to tell the truth."

"And what is going to happen to my Beta?"

"Because he assisted in exposing the Sen brothers, he has not been sentenced to death. Instead he is to get life imprisonment, with hard labour," Hemith choked out.

"Life!" Chumpa screamed, suddenly coming alive. "It is as though he is dead. What kind of a life is he going to lead? You tell me!" she wailed.

"Majee," Bharath tried to quieten her down, but Chumpa was hysterical. "Sita," Bharath appealed to his sister, who was sobbing in Hemith's arms. "If Majee does not stop she is going to get very ill."

Chumpa's hysterical wailing drew much attention, and soon her little cottage was filled with people. They came out of curiosity, but many left with sympathy in their hearts – for life had most certainly served the Suklals a cruel blow. Even Sewcharran was at a loss for words, and when the men shook his hand in sympathy Sita saw the pain and guilt in her father's eyes. He no longer looked enraged and bitter whenever Gopi's name was mentioned. Instead, he seemed utterly devastated at what might have been the result of his own harsh words and arrogant actions. Something died in Sewcharran Suklal the night he learnt that his eldest son was imprisoned for life; it was a burden he would carry to his grave.

Everyone was behaving as though her brother were dead, and Sita could bear it no longer. He was alive, no matter what. She brushed back her tears and pushed aside the women who surrounded her mother. She grabbed hold of Chumpa by her shoulders and forced her to look at her. "Majee, you have to stop this right now. Gopi is alive, and for that we have to be thankful." But Chumpa seemed past the stage of hearing – and Sita found herself reaching out and slapping her mother across the face. People gasped; and then there was silence as the older folk looked at Sita and shook their heads in bewilderment: no child was brought up to hit a parent.

A sudden burst of pain struck Sita which such intensity, she almost doubled over. Her baby was ready to make its appearance.

"Majee, I need you." Sita clutched her swollen belly as she sobbed, terrified. "I am going to have this baby soon!"

The sheer intensity of desperation in her voice finally got through to her mother. After what seemed like an eternity, Chumpa looked up at her daughter and whispered in a dry, hoarse voice: "A new life."

Sita's daughter, Rani, came into the world with a loud, energetic cry; and while Chumpa was cutting the umbilical cord to release her granddaughter into the world, a warden was locking iron chains onto her son's ankles and wrists.

PART TWO

1908

CHAPTER EIGHTEEN

Stepping from the train at the Durban railway station, Gopi took in the changes. Everything looked very different after fifteen years. Time had not stood still while he was in prison, and life, both the good and the bad, had gone on.

The initial anticipation Gopi had experienced when he first heard that he would be pardoned was now replaced by fear. Fear of finally being free, long after he had given up all hope of seeing beyond the prison walls. He had not informed any member of his family of his release, and had decided to stay out of their lives. He had never responded to letters from them, nor to the numerous letters sent over the years by Raymond. Expecting to die in prison, he saw no reason to keep old ties.

And now too many years had gone by.

Slowly he made his way to the station exit. He was drained by exhaustion and hunger, and he had no place to rest his head for the night. Prison and hard labour had taken its toll. A glimpse of himself in a windowpane showed a man older than his forty-five years: he was emaciated, and his once black hair was sprinkled with grey. The bad lighting in his cell had caused his eyesight to deteriorate. Gopi now looked and felt like an elderly man.

Seeing all the happy couples in the station filled him with overwhelming sadness. The years had not healed his wounds, and although he had served time in prison, the guilt and heartache he felt at the loss of his wife had never left him. Now he was free, free to go his own way and build a life for himself. But he had nowhere to go, and no one to live for.

Gopi's despondency did not go unnoticed. His observer was leaning nonchalantly against a shiny black Daimler, dressed in an expensive grey suit, white silk shirt, red necktie and a charcoal-grey hat which matched his shiny shoes. Oozing wealth and confidence, he drew looks of admiration and envy from those who passed him. He drew casually on his cigar and watched Gopi through the smoke.

He was not too surprised at the changes in Gopi. The wardens with whom he had communicated over the years had informed him of Gopi's condition, and of his eventual release. Now he was on a mission. Finally, he had been given the opportunity to put an end to the guilt and grief he carried inside.

Gopi passed the man without so much as a glance. He might as well leave Durban, he decided. There was no future here. He heard the tapping of a cane behind him, and when he glanced back he saw a man hurrying along, slowed down by a limp.

"Damn," swore Gopi in English as he reached the ticket box. It was closed.

"This is pathetic," added the man with a limp.

There was something vaguely familiar about the voice behind him. "It is," returned Gopi. "I have to wait until morning to buy a ticket." Gopi turned to face the stranger, and found he was looking into old, familiar eyes.

"Raymond! Is it really you – after all these years . . .?" There was hesitation in Gopi's voice, and yet he knew in his heart that he would recognise Raymond anywhere, no matter what. The years had seen changes in him as well, but he was still the same confident, well-groomed gent who had befriended Gopi years ago. He emanated style from his well-cut hair and neatly trimmed moustache down to his shiny grey shoes, and beside him, Gopi felt old, dowdy and very tired.

"It's me." Raymond hugged Gopi to him. "And you have no idea how wonderful it is to have my old friend back again. It is time for you to come home."

"Home?" Gopi's face clouded with sadness. He had no home. At this moment in his life all he wanted was to purchase a ticket, and see what the next stop brought him.

"Yes, I'm taking you home." There was finality in Raymond's voice as he took hold of Gopi's arm, and before Gopi could argue any further, led him away from the ticket box. Together, they walked outside onto the street.

"What a beautiful car. Does it belong to you?" Gopi asked.

"Yes," Raymond grinned excitedly, like a little boy showing off his favourite toy. "Second-hand – I bought it from an old white couple." He opened the car door for Gopi.

"It certainly looks expensive. I have never been in one before," admitted Gopi, feeling a thrill go through him as Raymond started the engine.

As they drove, he looked around him in awe. In fifteen years there had been much change: new buildings were everywhere, and people were driving fine-looking cars. The horse-drawn carriages people travelled in were also very fine. Everything looked modern, and he felt quite out of his league.

"I have a home on the Bluff, also bought from the people who sold me this car," Raymond was saying. "I actually live further down south, but I often come to Durban on business. I was spending too much money on hotel bills, so I found it was cheaper to buy a house."

Gopi nodded, but his eyes were on Raymond's hands as he changed gears and manoeuvred the big car with ease. Everything he did seemed so poised and elegant.

"We're home," announced Raymond as he turned into a driveway.

Quickly Gopi followed him into the house. After spending years sleeping in a cold, stinking cell, Gopi's eyes widened in amazement: it was as though he had walked into a hotel. The house was warm and welcoming and very tastefully furnished, and he caught the smell of food cooking. Raymond removed his hat and coat and placed it in a tiny closet while Gopi waited uncertainly in the hallway.

"Come, take a seat. What would you like to drink?" Raymond offered graciously.

"Anything," Gopi replied. He was very tired, and fought to stifle a yawn. As Raymond left the room, he sank into the maroon, velvet-covered couch, and thought about his unlucky life. If only he could turn back the clock. He would have loved for Rani to have lived in a home like this, he thought as his eyelids drooped. He lay back on the couch, using his small bag as a pillow.

By the time Raymond limped back into the room, carrying a tray filled with hot spicy buns and two cups of steaming coffee, Gopi was sound asleep on the couch, totally drained and exhausted. A small, tender smile broke over Raymond's face as he took in Gopi's sleeping form. Carefully he placed the tray on the table, and then fetched a blanket with which he covered his friend.

As he straightened up a gasp escaped from him. It was that dreaded pain again: for the past two years he had suffered from it, and he did not know how much longer he would be able to cope. His doctor had been honest with him, and warned him that if he didn't cut down his drinking, he would not have long to live.

He could not follow his doctor's orders: the drink helped bury the guilt that had eaten away at him, year after year. He could only fall asleep when his brain was numb with alcohol.

Raymond dragged himself across the carpeted room to his cabinet, wrenched open the door and pulled out a file. He limped back to his favourite chair and reached for his medication, which lay on the small round table beside his chair. He swallowed the pills his doctor had given him, washing them down with some brandy, and lay back, eyes closed, waiting for the drugs to work.

"Please, dear God," he prayed, "don't let me die until I have righted my wrongs. I owe Gopi that much." It did not take long for him to feel some relief from the pain. The spasm left him drained and exhausted, but he still concentrated on the file in his lap. It was marked PRIVATE AND CONFIDENTIAL. Quickly he scanned the contents; satisfied that everything was just as he wanted it, he placed the envelope in the draw for safe-keeping and slipped the key into his pocket. How weak and vulnerable he had been all those years ago! How he wished he had been strong – strong enough to fight and reveal the truth and not to worry about the consequences. How he wished he could change the past.

A moan shattered the silence in the room, and his eyes flew to the figure on the couch, which had started to thrash and writhe.

The old dream was back to haunt the sleeping Gopi. The woman in his dreams was clearly exhilarated, and then her expression changed to anger and bitterness at the sight of another woman who entered the room. Gopi strained to see who had evoked such animosity in her. Then a man laughed, and the woman lost her angry expression and joined his mocking laughter. As they turned to Gopi, their amusement increased until they had tears streaming down their faces. Gopi tried to move towards them, but he found that he was bound to a chair, and Rani, his dear Rani was locked in a cage like an animal and he could not reach her, no matter how hard he tried.

"Let her go . . . let her go!" he cried, but the couple ignored him. The more frantic his cries became, the harder they laughed, and Rani seemed to move further and further away from him.

"Gopi, wake up. It is only a nightmare."

Startled, Gopi's eyes flew open and he looked into Raymond's concerned face. Perspiration ran down his face and his clothes felt damp. Slowly he sat up, his eyes, filled with confusion, never leaving Raymond's.

"What is it? Are you all right?"

"I . . . I sometimes have this dream and it leaves me in a cold sweat. But don't worry. I'm okay." Gopi tried to smile as he got up and straightened his clothes. "I'm sorry to have given you a scare."

"I can't imagine what you've been through; but Gopi, remember I am here for you, no matter what." Raymond took hold of his friend's hand. "It is rather late and you look exhausted. Why don't you have something to eat, and we can talk tomorrow?"

"I can't believe this." Gopi sipped his coffee as he looked across the table. He was finally able to have a decent breakfast, and it gave him immense pleasure to be sharing it with Raymond. "After all these years, you never did forget about me!"

"How could I? Especially after the mess I landed you in. I wrote to you, but you never replied . . . and so I bribed the wardens instead. You'd be amazed what a little bit of cash can do. I know everything about you!"

"You look well – and you haven't lost your style," Gopi added with admiration. "But I see you have acquired a limp . . . what happened?" he asked, concerned.

"Accident. A while back."

"Are you married?" Gopi looked around the room, filled with brilliant sunshine which streamed through the big bay windows. There were fresh flowers everywhere and it all looked perfect, as though a homecoming had been planned. The room definitely had a woman's touch.

"No," Raymond answered, and when he saw the look of disbelief on Gopi's face, he burst out laughing. "Sorry to disappoint you, Gopi, but I never did meet the right girl. But I am married to my business. I own a banana plantation further down the coast."

Gopi's eyes widened. "I would never have thought of you as a farmer – you, the ardent gambler . . . never!" Laughter bubbled up deep inside him; it was the first time in many years that Gopi had laughed with such glee.

"What's so hilarious about being a farmer?" growled Raymond as he bit into his toast. But his eyes were twinkling as much as Gopi's.

"Well . . ." Gopi tried to smother his laughter and failed. Raymond lifted an eyebrow. "You hardly look like a farmer . . . and you certainly don't have farming in your blood." He waved his hands at Raymond's attire. "Your clothes are far too elegant!"

"I don't mean to burst your bubble, but I have owned this plantation for the last thirteen years," Raymond stated. "I have built it up from virtually nothing, and today I have a thriving business. I basically supply the whole country with bananas," he added proudly. "But you are right. Farming is not in my blood."

Raymond knew that he had been driven by something far stronger: guilt.

"I knew it," Gopi grinned. "So where is your plantation?"

"Just before you get to Port Shepstone."

"Have you got someone running it while you're in Durban?"

The question was a godsend to Raymond: he had been wondering how to approach Gopi with his proposition. "At the moment I have someone managing it. But he will be leaving shortly, for a tobacco plantation in Zululand. I am looking for someone to take over. Actually, I think I've found him. I haven't asked him yet, but I am hoping he will accept."

"I'm sure he will."

"I would like you to take up the position, Gopi."

There was silence in the room as Gopi slowly put down his coffee mug and looked at the man sitting across the table from him.

"Me. You want *me* to run your plantation. An ex-convict." Gopi slid his chair back.

"Yes, I do . . . where do you think you're going?" Raymond pushed Gopi back in his chair. "I need someone I can trust."

Gopi's voice dripped with annoyance. "Don't give me that line. I don't need your charity!"

Raymond sat back in his chair and crossed one leg over the other as he watched his friend's reaction. "You, my friend, have not changed at all."

Gopi glared at Raymond. "What do you want from me?"

Raymond gave Gopi a calm smile. Gopi may look war-beaten and weary, but there was a fire that lurked in his depths; if carefully stoked, he would still develop to his fullest potential. All was not lost!

"I want you to come and work with me." He did not say "for", because he did not want to offend his friend. "I need your help, Gopi."

"How can I help you? I don't know a thing about running a plantation. Have you forgotten that I have spent the last fifteen years in prison?"

Raymond ignored Gopi's sarcasm. "We go back a long time, Gopi . . . and right now I think we need each other. Besides, you don't have anywhere else to go." His lips twisted into a knowing smile. "I know that for a fact."

Gopi's brows lifted: Raymond certainly knew how to score points, and he didn't mince his words. As Raymond calmly finished the remainder of his coffee, Gopi tapped the tabletop with one long finger, in deep contemplation.

He had made no specific plans, and he certainly did not want to be reunited with his family. He could not bear to put them through the shame and embarrassment of having the family convict return. They had their own lives to lead; and now he had a new beginning.

He had made his decision.

CHAPTER NINETEEN

"Happy sixteenth birthday, sweetheart!" Sita woke her daughter up with a kiss, and watched with pride and joy as Rani unwound her tall, lithe frame and rose from her bed, wrapping her skinny arms around her mother in a sleepy hug.

"Thanks, Ma," she responded, her voice drowsy.

Rani had a head of curly dark-brown hair which she controlled with coconut oil and wore in two long plaits, and was tall and slender for her age. Whereas Sita had been well formed at sixteen, Rani was still boyishly built, and this made her shy around the opposite sex. Perhaps, Sita reflected, she inherited her slenderness from her father.

"Come, young lady," Sita pinched her cheek affectionately. "Your bath is ready, and once you give thanks to God for keeping you well and healthy for the past sixteen years, your father and brothers want to congratulate you."

Hemith was seated at the kitchen table with their two sons. There had been no more children after the birth of Rani, and although her family was quite small by the standards of the community, Sita would have it no other way.

They now lived in a simple but spacious cottage on the Campbell Estate. After the strike and the negotiations, Hemith had been promoted at the mill and his salary increased. They moved into a house of their own, and Sita had stayed at home to bring up their children.

The years had been good to Hemith, and the muscle he had put on through physical work gave him a lean, masculine look.

Sunil, their second-born, was identical to his father, and reminded Sita of the days when Hemith had courted her. He was slightly above average height, with almost black hair, and he had his father's soft velvet eyes. He had also inherited his father's inner strength, which Sita had come to love and admire. Sunil was the calm, gentle son who was often the peacemaker in the family.

Mukesh was totally different. At almost twenty-two, he showed no signs of wanting to settle down and have a family of his own. In fact, Mukesh was the estate Romeo, breaking the young girls' hearts. A hard worker and well liked on the estate, he was forever talking about his political hero, Gandhi. His favourite pastime, besides teasing the girls, was making Sita laugh with his delightful sense of humour. Sita loved the way his tall, strapping frame would shake with laughter, and the sparkle of mischief that lit his brown eyes. Yet she knew beneath his jovial exterior lay a determined, razor-sharp mind, and she prayed he would not get into trouble: he was not afraid to speak his mind about the oppression of the burgeoning Indian community.

"Here comes the birthday girl!" Mukesh sprang to his feet and hugged his sister close to him, and they all chorused, "Happy Birthday, Rani!"

Lots of love, hugs and kisses flowed in Sita's home, and this filled her heart with happiness.

"Thanks," Rani grinned at her family.

"Very soon we are going to have the boys banging on our door," Sunil teased as he tweaked her cheek playfully.

"Don't you dare say such things." Rani looked embarrassed. "I am hardly pretty."

"Now don't be modest," Hemith chided gently as he took his daughter's face between his hands. "You are a lovely young girl who is blossoming into womanhood, and if I were young and single I would be the first to line up at your door."

Rani's brown eyes shone. "You only say that to make me feel better, but thanks, Taj. You are always first in line where my heart is concerned." She placed a loving kiss on his cheek, ignoring the teasing moans from her brothers.

Smiling, Sita turned away from the warm, loving picture father and daughter created as Hemith hugged Rani to him once again. Quickly she handed out her family's lunchboxes. "Don't forget to be back early," she reminded her sons as she ushered them out of the house. "We can't be late at your aunt's place this evening. You too, Rani."

Today was Rani's first day as a teacher at the school, and she could barely stand still with all the excitement and nervousness building up inside her.

"Wish me luck!" she called as she left the house, waving at her parents.

"I can't see why we couldn't have the party here," remarked Hemith, taking his lunchbox from her hand.

"You know why," Sita nudged him knowingly, her soft brown eyes twinkling with secrecy.

"Still, I don't like feeling obligated to Geeta and Anoop."

"Now you are being silly," she scolded. "I bought everything we need. The only reason we're having it there is that we don't want Rani to suspect anything."

"I just hope she doesn't wear one of those silly outfits Elizabeth Campbell gives her."

"I'll make sure she doesn't," Sita reassured him, knowing how much he resented seeing Rani wearing handouts from Elizabeth and Charlotte. Although the clothes were out of fashion, they were neat and presentable and made her stand out from the other Indian girls. The long, cool cotton gowns, buttoned high at the neck with long sleeves, looked very prim and proper, and they fitted Rani after her mother had done a few alterations.

Tonight, however, Rani would be traditionally dressed. Sita had chosen for her daughter a simple rose-pink silk sari, knowing that it would compliment her daughter's colouring perfectly, and had sewn a blouse to match. She had saved hard for this purchase, but it was worth it: Rani would look beautiful.

Her little girl was growing up fast. She was growing into a kind, loving and gentle person, who carried herself with dignity and respect. Sita knew that her daughter could never hurt anyone and prayed that she would not be hurt in turn. Her brothers were terribly protective, and it made Sita feel better to know that Rani would always have someone to look after her; but still she worried. Although Rani was a bright, articulate girl who excelled in the classroom, she was still innocent when it came to the opposite sex.

Because Rani had done so well at school, the teacher hired by Albert Sheldon, Miss West, had informed Hemith and Sita that she would like Rani to stay on at the school and help with teaching, starting with the smaller children. She could also continue her own education and become a qualified teacher. Rani jumped at the opportunity, and her parents encouraged her.

Most young girls were forced to leave school as soon as they turned thirteen or fourteen. Many were already engaged and getting ready for marriage, while others had to find work to help their parents before marrying. Poverty was rife in the Indian community, and many parents looked forward to the time when their children would be old enough to work and contribute financially towards the upkeep of the family.

Education was something the Indians strived for, and Sita and Hemith realised that if they allowed their daughter to teach, it would open the door for other young girls and encourage them to continue with their education.

By evening, Sita's tasks for the day were completed. Her baskets were full of delicious treats, and she covered them carefully. She had bathed and dressed, ready for her family to return from their day at work.

Sita was still slim and curvy and carried herself gracefully. Gone was the rebellious teenager; instead, here stood a woman who was happy and content as wife and mother. She had settled into marriage and her love for Hemith was steady and strong and gentle – and very real, for it had grown out of respect, admiration and tenderness. The deep, passionate, impossible love she had shared with Albert was buried deep within her, although Mukesh was a constant reminder of it.

Albert had found there were ways in which he could demonstrate his love for Sita without their relationship becoming physical. He had gone all out to establish a school, and recruited qualified teachers to help educate the children on his and the surrounding estates. It was a gesture that filled him with pride and hope for the future, but one which was frowned upon by the more conservative estate owners, who felt that they would lose their labourers.

Sarah, Albert and Helena's second child, had attended the same school, much to the annoyance of Helena. Finally, however, Helena insisted that her daughter complete her education in England, as Joseph had done. Sarah's enthusiasm and Helena's constant nagging eventually wore Albert down, and he gave his consent.

Sita never returned to work at the Big House. She rarely visited her old friends there, but when she did, it amazed her how fast Richard and Charlotte Campbell had grown. They were adults now, and often spent holidays in England.

Rumour had it that Joseph, who had spent most of his teenage life in England, was returning to spend some time with his family, while Richard took a break and visited his English relatives.

Sita shook her head to clear her thoughts. Why was she thinking of Albert and his family at a time like this? It was her daughter's sixteenth birthday!

As always on family occasions, she tried hard not to think of her two dear brothers: Bharath, who had died so tragically after catching tuberculosis, helping the injured soldiers during the Anglo-Boer War. Like so many young Indian men he had served under the simple yet forthright politician, Gandhi, as a stretcher-bearer. Within a year he had been snatched from his family.

And of course Gopi. She had kept her promise and named her newborn daughter after his wife, and she knew that Rani would have made her uncle very proud.

"Ma, I'm home." Rani's happy greeting broke her reverie. "Oh, Ma, I had a wonderful day. I love teaching!"

"I'm so glad," Sita smiled, taking in her daughter's shining eyes. "Now come, it is time for you to get dressed. We are going to visit your Nani and Nana."

Sita helped her daughter dress and stood back to admire her. Rani's long, dark brown hair fell to her waist in soft waves, while the beauty and innocence of her large brown eyes were enhanced by their long, curly lashes. Her lips were full and rosy, as though she had rubbed them hard to get some colour into them.

"Oh, sweetheart, you look absolutely beautiful." Sita brushed back her tears of pride. "I know it is bad for a mother to say such things, but I cannot help myself, Beti."

Rani blushed prettily as they hugged. Three wolf whistles drew them apart. "My heroes are back," Rani giggled at her brothers' admiring looks.

"Stop it, you two," scolded Sita as her sons got hold of Rani and tickled her playfully, mussing her hair. "If we don't leave soon we are going to be late. And Rani, you need to brush your hair." She shot a warning look at her boys.

They just laughed and tousled their sister's hair again. "Oh, Ma. Rani loves it!" Sunil grinned, tweaking Rani's cheek playfully.

"No. I don't." She stuck her tongue out at him and scooted from the kitchen before he could add anything else.

"Hurry up," Sita called out to her family. "I don't want to keep your grandmother waiting. You know how she gets at this time of the year."

Chumpa missed her sons, but as each year passed, she found increasing joy in Rani, who filled the void. And so, a tradition had been created: on her birthday Rani spent time with her grandmother. Today was really not very different, except that they were all going to her Aunt Geeta's home; and her mother seemed to have prepared very well for the evening.

As Hemith brought their wagon to a halt outside Geeta's palatial home, Sita reminded herself that she and Hemith had different values from her sister and brother-in-law. While she and Hemith had fought for their people's rights, Geeta and Anoop had been too busy providing for their family's material needs. Today they were filled with pride, for they were among the few well-to-do families in the community: they owned their own property, prospered at farming and were respected for their wealth.

Sita did not feel any jealousy. Although she loved her sister, she did not like the Geeta the years of material wealth and success had created. She had become hard and domineering, often trying to bully the Harilakens as well. However, Hemith had made it clear where he stood: no one was going to interfere with his family – and Sita could still remember the day he had told Geeta so.

Rani's cry of delighted surprise as she entered her aunt's home made

Sita smile: they had planned a surprise dinner party for her, and the dining room was beautifully laid out.

"Happy Birthday!" cried the family in unison.

"This is so unexpected!" Rani hugged her cousins. "I don't know what to say."

Around her were all her family – people she loved and respected. Smiling, she went to Chumpa, who enfolded her in a warm embrace. Of all her family, Rani admired her grandmother the most. White-haired, strong and very wise, she had remained a pillar of strength to her family.

Chumpa wiped the tears from her eyes. As much as she loved her granddaughter, her heart still ached with emptiness for her sons.

Sewcharran was now an old man. He wore a black patch over his right eye, but none of the grandchildren knew the secret of how he had lost half his sight. It was a forbidden topic. His soft spot was his love for his grandchildren: it seemed that he lavished on them all the affection and love he could never display towards his own children. Chumpa always remarked that the grandchildren had mellowed him, and Geeta agreed.

Geeta had become a very motherly figure in her middle age. Her round, earthy physique belied her razor-sharp brain and business acumen. Rani remembered fondly all the times Geeta had hugged her or carried her. She loved the feel and comfort of her aunt's soft, fat arms and bosom, and with her childlike innocence, she did not see the shrewdness that lay behind her aunt's high-toned laughter and narrowed eyes.

Anoop, her devoted husband, also carried too much weight. Once their farm was established and making a profit, Anoop did not do too much physical work, and that was when the fat had crept on. After his heart attack, his doctor had warned him to slow down and take things easy. The children were grown up now, and he found that leaving the daily running of the farm to them was a relief.

Asha, Rani's eldest cousin, was a replica of her mother. Now that she was expecting her second baby she was gaining a lot of weight; to pacify herself she kept saying that her body was merely retaining water.

Rani's favourite cousins were the twins, Ramu and Krishna, who resembled their father except that they had inherited their mother's small eyes. They were huge, strapping young men, and when they joined forces with Mukesh and Sunil, they were very popular amongst the fairer sex – even though they already had wives chosen for them by their mother.

Smita, older than Rani by two years, had her father's facial features, but her mannerisms and the way she held her curvy form reminded everyone of Sita at that age. Smita was engaged to a young man, and could not wait to start a family of her own.

Ajith was the unplanned and most welcome child in the family, after his mother had thrown tantrums about being too old to mother a newborn baby. He was fourteen years old and enjoyed being the baby in the family. His family spoilt him, and he was growing up to be as demanding and arrogant as his grandfather had been.

Although her aunt and her family oozed wealth and prosperity, Rani knew that she was indeed blessed to be born of parents as wonderful as her own, and thanked God for the family he had given her. They might not be wealthy materially, but they were rich in the love and happiness they brought to each other.

Looking at her parents, Rani's heart was filled with love and joy. Her mother looked young and lovely, and looked perfect next to her handsome father. She smiled at her father, who lifted an eyebrow at her. Then she realised that everyone was seated and waiting for her to join them.

"Sorry, everyone." She cleared her throat and grinned at them happily. "I was just counting my blessings and marvelling at my wonderful family here. I love you all!"

"Yeah, yeah, yeah, we know," teased Ramu as he got up, scooped her into his arms and carried her to the chair beside his, as Rani's tinkling laughter filled the dining room.

Chumpa watched, misty-eyed. "This is such a joyous occasion." She turned to Sita. "How I wish my boys were here to complete our family."

For a fleeting second Sita's eyes filled with pain, which she successfully hid. "Majee, don't dwell on the past. Think of the future and what it has to offer this new generation."

"Let Bharath rest in peace, Ma," Geeta patted her hand. "He has done us proud by being so brave and strong."

"I know, Beti," Chumpa wiped a tear with the back of her hand, "but I cannot forget my sons – and today is the day Gopi was sent to prison, sixteen years ago." Her voice cracked with pain: "God knows whether he is alive or dead!"

Geeta's small eyes hardened instantly. "Majee, this is Rani's birthday party and don't spoil it by talking about . . . *him*," she hissed under her breath. Chumpa's face crumpled.

At the sight of her mother's shattered expression Sita turned to her sister, infuriated. "What is the matter with you, Geeta? How can you say such mean things to Majee? You never give her a chance to say what she feels about Gopi. He is part of our blood. Don't forget that."

Geeta's lips thinned and she gave Sita a cold, hard stare. "Do you want the children to know about him?" she returned in a heated whisper. "I certainly don't, and while you are in my home, I expect you to respect my wishes."

"Geeta!" Chumpa, shocked at her daughter's words, turned to her in astonishment.

"It's okay, Ma," Sita pinned Geeta with a look of fury. "She has made her wishes more than clear. I don't think she is right, but I won't walk out – much as I want to – and upset her plans for the day."

"Supper is ready." Asha announced, unknowingly breaking the tension between mother and daughters, and Sita heaved a sigh of relief.

Geeta mystified her. Outwardly, her sister's life was a great success: her children were adults, except for Ajith, and as a family they worked together to maintain their prosperity. They owned acres of fertile land and lived in a beautiful house, filled with beautiful furniture, with more than enough room for all of them. The Balraj children worked hard on the farm under their mother's iron leadership, tolerating her constant reminders that she had come from a poor background and had striven hard to achieve what they had. And Geeta made it very clear that her reputation was to remain untarnished, no matter what.

But now, watching Geeta in her home, Sita felt that there must be something wrong: why was Geeta so terrifyingly bitter and aggressive? Suddenly it seemed to her that Geeta and Anoop were harbouring some secret – a secret that held their life together, and one which Geeta was determined would remain hidden from the rest of the family.

CHAPTER TWENTY

"I am very sorry, Mr Suklal." The doctor's tone was grave.

"I . . . don't understand." Anguish filled Gopi's eyes. "I know that he's not been himself lately, but he was well last week . . . I cannot believe what's happening."

"Raymond should have taken my advice a long time ago." Dr Welles sighed deeply as he took a seat opposite Gopi. "His liver is badly damaged. Whatever treatment I give him is not going to help at this stage."

"Is it the drinking which has caused this illness?" asked Gopi as he watched Dr Welles through horn-rimmed spectacles.

Gopi had lived with Raymond on the plantation for over a year, ever since meeting him at the station. During this time Raymond had hid his illness well, until three months ago when he had suddenly collapsed.

"I am afraid so," the doctor replied honestly.

Gopi closed his eyes. The last time he found Raymond drunk he had given him a lecture on his alcohol consumption, and Raymond had just laughed: "The damage has already been done, my friend."

Gopi's heart ached. "Is there anything I can do for him?"

"You can help by making sure he's comfortable – please don't deny him anything, Mr Suklal." Dr Welles opened his black bag and handed Gopi a small box. "In here is a drug to ease the pain. I will be in every morning to check how he is doing and to give him the morphine. However, if I am not around, you will have to do it. I have written down the instructions so it shouldn't be a problem. Give him small doses – but if the pain worsens, increase the dosage. I will also arrange for a nurse to be with him daily, to see that he eats and that his basic needs are taken care of."

Gopi's hand trembled as he took the box from Dr Welles. "I would prefer to take care of his needs myself. There is no need for a stranger to be around him at this time. He needs his family, and at the moment, I am the only family he has . . . and Dr Welles, please call me Gopi."

After the doctor had left, Gopi went into Raymond's room. Leila, the pint-sized housekeeper, had drawn the bedroom curtains and the afternoon sunshine streamed in. Gopi felt something touch his soul: there was an air of deep serenity in the room.

"Come and sit with me," Raymond invited weakly.

Gopi's heart contracted painfully. He could not believe that his friend's health had deteriorated to such an extent: he was now so frail that Gopi had no problem carrying him. He was merely skin and bone, too weak to even leave the room.

"Don't look so sad, my friend," Raymond patted the bed beside him.

"It is all right. I have to finish something before I can go with the angels." His voice was faint as it floated across to Gopi.

"Hush . . . don't talk. You have to save your strength." Gopi took his place beside Raymond and wiped away the perspiration that had gathered on his friend's forehead.

"I have to tell . . . you something. It is very important." Raymond's words were interrupted by a spate of coughing which racked his already worn and weary body.

"You don't have to tell me now. We have plenty of time . . ." Gopi began. He was silenced as Raymond grabbed his hand in a suddenly strong grip. Gopi was surprised at how cold Raymond's hand felt.

"I have to. I will . . . never be able to go with the angels . . . otherwise. I have to let go of this burden . . . I have carried around for so long." Another short spell of coughing interrupted him. "I . . . know," he croaked, smiling. "Too many expensive cigars."

Gopi returned his smile, although he was filled with immense sadness. How brave is the spirit, he thought.

"I am so glad . . . you are with me," Raymond whispered, struggling to breathe. "Now . . . I have to tell you everything. Allow a dying man his wish. Gopi, I have to confess . . ."

"Raymond . . ."

"No! No more interruptions, please."

After a pause, Gopi gave his consent with a small nod.

Raymond's voice trembled as he began. "Remember the first time we met, Gopi?" His eyes shone with remembrance. "How young and naive you were. How I wish those days were back! But now, I have to beg for your forgiveness." He struggled to pull himself upright, declining Gopi's help with a small, sad smile. "If it were not for me, Rani would still be alive today and you would have a family of your own," he whispered, clutching Gopi's hand desperately when he saw the confused look on his face.

"What? . . . I don't understand." Gopi's voice trembled with emotion as the muscles in his stomach knotted painfully.

"Oh, Gopi . . . you will when . . . I have finished." Raymond was forced to stop as his body shook with intense pain. Fighting for breath, he waited before taking a sip of water from the glass Gopi held out to him. "I was . . . blackmailed into befriending you, Gopi," he began again when he felt a little stronger. "My task was to introduce you to the evil world of gambling. You see, my friend . . . my father . . . my father was a gambler and he taught me to play cards." Raymond swallowed hard, as though his confession were far more painful than the physical pain he was experiencing. "I was not a gambler . . . when I met you, for I had vowed never to end up like my . . . father. When he died he left behind a huge debt, and the burden fell on me to settle it." His voice was filled with sadness as the memories rushed back. "My father had borrowed money from your brother-in-law, Anoop, with interest, to settle part of his debt. My family did not know of this until Anoop arrived very suddenly with your sister, demanding that we settle the debt immediately. Oh, Gopi. How my mother cried!" Raymond closed his eyes as though to shut out the image of his mother's heartbreak, which he had always carried in his heart.

"We were not rich and we did not have the money to repay the debt. My mother wanted to pawn her jewellery but I could not take that away from her. You must understand this, Gopi. I never meant to hurt you . . . honestly I did not."

Not a muscle in Gopi's whole body moved.

"Your sister then came up with a plan. She would cancel my debt, if . . . if I introduced you to the Sen brothers, and . . . Gopi, I had no choice. You must believe me!" he cried, holding unto Gopi's arm.

Silence, deep and hurting, filled the room.

"I begged her to change her mind, but she was so adamant, so filled with hatred . . . and she terrified my mother." Raymond sighed. "When I met you it became even harder . . . I liked you – and then I began to hate myself. You see . . . it was too late. You had already fallen into the web she had so skilfully weaved."

"But why? Why would she want to do something so hateful?" Gopi felt as though his head might explode – and yet he had to know everything. "Did she hate me so much?"

"No, she did not hate you. I think she loved you too much, and wanted you back in the family. The only person she hated was Rani."

"I don't believe this," Gopi shook his head, wanting to scream at Raymond, tell him to stop lying. And then the image of Geeta and her hostility towards Rani at the market came rushing back to him; and in that instant he knew that Raymond was telling the truth. Gopi searched deep inside himself for the right words. Words that would somehow make it easier for both of them. "You were a victim of her manipulations, Raymond." His words were simple and truthful, but his eyes reflected how astounded he was by what was unfolding, after all these years.

"She felt that if you landed yourself in trouble you would turn to her for assistance."

"I did . . ." Gopi whispered, as memories flooded him, "but I did not accept her terms. She demanded that I give up Rani."

"I know," Raymond acknowledged quietly, but Gopi was past hearing him.

Gopi was unaware that tears were rolling down his cheeks until he felt the saltiness on his lips. "She helped kill my wife and unborn child." This finality tore at him, and the walls he had built around his heart came crashing down.

In his weakened state, Raymond gathered a sobbing Gopi in his arms, and both friends cried. Gopi clung to his friend. They had both lost so much through one woman's conniving: he, the one woman he loved, and Raymond, his self-respect. Gopi felt a growing hatred fill that emptiness which he had carried within himself for too many years. After what seemed like an eternity he drew away from Raymond.

"That is not all," Raymond whispered. He was emotionally and physically exhausted, and yet he knew that he had a mission to accomplish. There would be no more half-truths. "When Rani learnt of the trouble you were in, she gave me her necklace to pawn." He heard Gopi's gasp. "I was not to tell you a thing: she could not hurt your manly pride. She made me swear that it would be our secret." Raymond's weak attempt at a smile of remembrance failed.

"She did that for me?" Gopi's eyes welled with tears, as his heart swelled with love that had never died.

"She loved you, and would have followed you to the ends of the earth if you had asked her," Raymond stated simply. "I had the cash from the necklace in my pocket that evening, and it was more than sufficient to get you out of trouble. But it was too late. When I saw what those animals had done to her . . . I could not hand over the money. They did not deserve it." He choked back his sobs as Gopi handed him some water to drink. "No chance of some brandy, my friend?" he managed to tease, before drinking thirstily.

"No chance," Gopi's smile wobbled as he took the glass from him. He gently massaged Raymond's back to ease the sudden bout of coughing which racked his frail frame.

"I could not give them the money, Gopi, and after you were sent to prison I used it, and some of my savings, to purchase this farm. You see, I knew that you would be free one day. I spoke to the prison authorities and made sure that you were all right. Even when you did not respond to my letters, I kept in touch with the prison wardens."

"I cannot believe this."

"I know how this must sound to you, Gopi . . . but I swear on my deathbed that it is the truth. I even know about the time you were terribly ill and they thought you were dying. I prayed for God to spare you. I needed you to live so that I could tell you everything. It is only right that you should know. I am just so sorry that it hurts so much."

"Don't be, Raymond. I am so grateful to you for having the courage to tell me everything." Gopi tenderly wiped the perspiration from Raymond's forehead. Every word Raymond uttered was such an effort.

"I am not finished." Raymond's voice was barely a whisper, and Gopi found himself leaning forward to capture his words. "In the second drawer of my cupboard you will find a black velvet box. Please bring it to me."

Wondering how many more unpleasant surprises there were in store for him, Gopi found the box without much difficulty and handed it to Raymond.

"Open it, please."

Gopi obliged, and an agonised moan escaped from him when he saw the contents of the box. Inside, nestled against the black velvet, lay Rani's necklace.

"It is beautiful, isn't it?"

"Yes, it is . . ." Gopi's sorrow filled the room. He closed his eyes as the image of Rani, beaten and left for dead, filled his mind. "I don't understand . . . You told me you pawned it."

"Yes, and I did. But I managed to buy it back from the pawnbroker that same year. It was hard, but I just could not let it go. And now it belongs to you. She wanted you to have it, Gopi."

Overwhelmed, Gopi started sobbing again as he clutched the box to him. "I don't have a single thing of hers."

The two friends clung to each other as the necklace sparkled in all its glory between them.

"She was someone special," Raymond whispered. There was a sense of peace within him: he had finally put her soul to rest.

"I really miss her, Raymond. You will never know how much." Gopi caressed the necklace tenderly, as though he were touching Rani. "She was everything to me."

"As you were to her, Gopi. In the short space of time I knew her, I saw what you meant to her. You were fortunate to be loved by someone like that." He smiled sadly at Gopi.

"I loved her but could not take care of her, Raymond. She died because of me." His voice ached with grief and guilt.

"There is no need to punish yourself. You brought her killer to justice. It was the bravest thing you could ever do." Raymond closed his eyes as the pain engulfed him once more. "Oh God, it . . . hurts like hell."

Gopi could not bear to see Raymond in such agony. He took hold of Raymond's arm and gently cleaned it with the small bottle of alcohol Dr Welles had given him. He then drew the liquid from the tiny bottle into a syringe and tapped Raymond's forearm steadily until a vein stood up. He quickly inserted the needle under Raymond's skin and emptied the contents of the syringe. He was suddenly grateful for the years he spent in prison, where he often helped out in the small clinic for the prisoners, after he had recovered from the pneumonia that almost killed him.

"Is this for the pain?" Raymond's voice was barely a whisper as he watched Gopi's actions.

Gopi nodded.

"Why don't you just put me out of my misery? No one will ever know, Gopi," Raymond pleaded, clutching at Gopi's arm in desperation.

"Don't ask that of me, Raymond. I cannot survive with another death on my conscience. Come . . . this will help you to rest for a few hours."

"You must rest as well," Raymond murmured, his eyelids growing heavy as his hold on Gopi's arms relaxed.

Gopi tucked the blankets around him, before carrying the jewellery box into the study. He closed the door and poured himself a whisky. It was the first time since his release from prison that he felt the need to drink something stronger than tea to calm his nerves. Gulping down the drink, he gagged as the spirit's sting hit him hard. He refilled his glass and carried it and the decanter of whisky back to the desk. Leaning back in the chair, he opened the box on the table. His fingers ran over the necklace caressingly as memories of Rani flitted through his mind, and his heart ached with remembrance.

After all these years, he finally understood the dream which haunted him so often. The woman laughing mockingly at him could be none other than Geeta.

"How could she be so cruel, Rani? Why did she have to part us?" He clutched the necklace to him. "I will make her pay for this," he vowed, "for depriving us of a life together. She destroyed you and our baby while her family grew and prospered . . . I promise you, Rani, I will make her regret the day she was ever born." He clenched the whisky glass so hard that the glass shattered and the pieces cut into his hand. He watched as his blood mingled with the whisky. The only pain he felt was the intense grief he carried in his heart.

Gopi sat alone in the study as darkness fell, completely immersed in his grief and anger. When Leila walked into the study to check on him, she found him staring into space with pieces of glass scattered around him. Then she noticed his hand. "Gopi, what happened?" She moved towards him with surprising speed, and, when he did not respond, picked up his hand.

Startled, Gopi pulled away. Blinking hard, he looked down at the blood, which had dried on his hand. "It's okay," he said, and slowly unwound his tall frame from the chair. "I need to check on Raymond."

Leila watched him leave the study. He moved, she thought, like a cat: softly and stealthily; and then he would surprise her by his capacity to increase his speed, to pounce when the time was right.

Gopi had grown so much stronger over the past year. His thin frame had slowly filled out, and now there were muscles where previously there had been just skin and bone. It was difficult to believe that he had spent years in prison. He loved the sunshine, the outdoors, fresh air and manual labour, and he no longer walked like an old, beaten man. Although there was fire in his eyes, sadness lingered there as well. The spectacles he wore hid his pain and gave him an air of authority.

Under Raymond's tuition, he had learnt all about running the farm; and when Raymond had looked at their year-end financial report he had declared, with pride in his voice, that their profit margin was higher than ever.

"You were a terrible gambler, but you have proved to be an excellent businessman," Raymond had complimented him. "You certainly have grown this past year, in more ways than one."

Looking at his sleeping friend, in the throes of death, Gopi could not believe that this skeleton of a man had once been so vibrant, so suave, so charming and alive. He could never hate this man, who had carried such a grievous burden for so long. "You have punished yourself for far too long, Raymond," he murmured. "You are a victim of all this, and have endured too much."

As though sensing his presence, Raymond opened his eyes. "How long have you been here?" he whispered, struggling to breathe.

"Not too long. Can I get you anything?" he offered lamely, taking Raymond's hand in his. It felt cold and clammy, and Gopi's heart clenched fearfully. "I am getting Dr Welles now."

"No . . ." Raymond rasped. "There is no need . . . Please . . . forgive me, Gopi . . . for everything . . ." he stammered, looking at Gopi with desperate eyes. Eyes that were tired of living with a heavy burden.

Tears, which Gopi had been holding in check, streamed down his cheeks as he gathered Raymond in his arms. "You have done nothing wrong. You are more than a friend to me. You are my brother . . . my only family." Gopi felt the sigh of relief and very gently set Raymond against the pillows. "There is nothing to forgive."

"Thank you," Raymond whispered. His eyes sparkled with vitality for a second before the spark died, and Gopi felt the life flow from his closest and dearest friend – the only family he had known this past year. It was as though Raymond had been waiting for him to utter those words before letting go.

Gopi lost all sense of time: he had no idea how long he sat holding onto Raymond's hand. The lamp he had lit burnt out. Eventually, the sun rose on a new day. When Leila came in to draw the curtains, she discovered Gopi sitting beside Raymond, and looked at him questioningly.

"He is gone," Gopi stated simply.

Raymond was buried on the estate, as he had requested. Gopi, grief-stricken, had returned to the study after the funeral and closed the door behind him. Work on the estate had come to a halt. Raymond had left behind a will, but at this stage Gopi was not ready to meet and discuss anything with the attorney handling Raymond's estate. Days slipped by, until now a week had gone past.

As he lifted another glass of whisky to his lips, he heard Leila's hurried footsteps outside the study. He gulped down his drink.

"He's in there. He's hardly come out since we laid our Mr Lazarus to rest," he heard her complain.

"Don't worry. I will speak to him."

It took Gopi a few seconds before his befuddled brain recognised the stern, authoritative voice. It belonged to Anthony Rands, Raymond's attorney.

The door burst open and a tiny white man entered.

"Just what do you think you're up to?" he demanded in a booming voice, belied by his slender build.

Gopi did not flinch at the thunder in this diminutive man's voice. Instead, he stared stormily back at Anthony Rands, taking in his neat attire, from his immaculate blond hair and well-fitting suit down to his shiny black shoes.

"What the hell do you want?" Gopi retaliated, turning his back on Anthony as he took another swig from the glass in his hand.

"This place smells." The little man waved his arms about and wrinkled his nose in disgust.

"Then don't stay. Leave." Gopi whirled around and pointed to the door, anger cutting through the air. "I would like to be left alone."

"Stop it," Anthony ordered. He stood on tiptoe and wrenched away the glass which Gopi had lifted to his lips once again. "Sit down." He pushed Gopi into his chair. "Just look at you. You need a shave and a bath. Raymond must be turning in his grave. You . . ."

"Shut up," Gopi snarled, wanting to smash the little man's face in.

Anthony took hold of Gopi by the shoulder and shook him hard. He saw how Gopi clenched his fists to prevent himself hitting out. "You are grieving, I know, but you are also filled with self-pity. Your friend suffered too much and it is time he lay in peace. You are alive and healthy and have an estate to run. Now, I am giving you until tomorrow to pull yourself together. The will is scheduled to be read on Friday at nine a.m. sharp, and I want you to be sober and well-presented." In the same breath, Anthony pulled open the door – and found a rather guilty-looking Leila eavesdropping. He ignored the reddening of her face and instructed: "Get this place cleaned. When I return on Friday I don't want it smelling like a brewery. Is that clear?"

"Yes sir," Leila whispered, terrified.

Anthony Rands turned to Gopi, giving him a hard, penetrating look, which Gopi started to return – before sighing deeply, and running his fingers through his already tousled hair. The attorney was right. Raymond would be so ashamed of him. "All right," he relented. "I'll be ready and waiting for you.'

"Good," Anthony replied curtly before turning on his heel.

Leila helped Gopi to his feet and into his bedroom. Before leaving the room, she ran his bath and set out fresh clothes for him. Gopi undressed slowly. When he looked in the mirror he was horrified to see how exhausted he looked: his eyes were red and tired and full of pain and anger. He turned away and stepped into the tub. Reaching for the soap, he scrubbed himself so hard he felt as though every nerve in his body were awakening slowly. He closed his eyes, and felt the tension he had carried around for so long slowly leave, until he almost fell asleep in the tub. He dragged himself out and crawled between fresh sheets, naked and wet, and for the first time in weeks managed to fall into a deep sleep.

"Well," Anthony Rands smiled as he shook Gopi's hand. "It is certainly nice to see you more like your old self again."

Gopi shook his hand without returning his smile.

"I see you are growing a beard," the attorney remarked as he moved to his place at the desk and opened the case he carried. "Makes a nice change to your appearance."

"Cut the small talk, Rands." Gopi growled.

Anthony's eyes sparkled with amusement, although his face was set in its normal serious expression. "I need Leila and her husband to sit in on the reading of the will," he stated, suddenly back to the firm, businesslike role that Gopi was familiar with.

Gopi obliged by opening the door and letting the pair in.

Both husband and wife were startled, caught eavesdropping once again. Gopi almost laughed at the guilty expressions on their faces. It was a well-known fact that they were a highly inquisitive pair, but also very loyal and compassionate. Besides, they were excellent in their roles as housekeeper and gardener.

"Let us begin." The attorney opened his file and drew out the necessary documents. "This is the last will and testament of one Raymond Lazarus . . ." he began.

He went through the formal part of reading Raymond's will, and then began on the bequests. Two sets of eyes widened in surprise at his next words:

"To Choonilal and Leila Ramsuth I bequeath one hundred pounds, and ask that they remain in service for as long as they wish, with free board and lodging, and annual increases."

"We will stay," Leila wiped the tears from her eyes. "This is our home. God rest his soul!" She hiccuped.

Anthony Rands nodded approvingly before returning to the document he held in his hand. "To my old and dear friend, Gopi Suklal, I bequeath all my worldly possessions, including my estate, both the houses and their contents, and my car – which I know you are simply dying to drive."

Gopi could not help but smile. Even in death, Raymond's humour lived on.

Anthony continued: "I know, my dear friend, that you will find this unbelievable, but everything belongs to you, as I have explained. I want you to carry on with what I have started, and make Rani and myself proud."

Gopi did not see the startled and curious look he received from Leila and her husband. He swallowed a lump in his throat and fought back the tears which threatened to spill over. Anthony's voice droned on. Raymond had left some money to a few charities, but Gopi was too stunned to take in the details. When Anthony drew the meeting to a close, Gopi stood up automatically.

"Mr Suklal," the attorney held out his hand. "You are a very rich man now, with a lot of responsibilities. According to Raymond's instructions, I am to remain your attorney, so should you require any assistance whatsoever; please don't hesitate to call me."

"Thank you," Gopi gripped Anthony Rands' hand firmly as the facts slowly sank in. "I'll do the best I can. I won't let Raymond down."

CHAPTER TWENTY-ONE

At seventeen, Rani carried herself with confidence. She had begun to fill out: her tiny breasts became fuller and her hips more rounded, and the gowns which had hung on her boyish frame now clung to her soft curves. She was very popular among the children, who adored her smile, her laughter and her funny jokes. Her gentleness made it easy for them to relate to her. Rani's passion for knowledge and teaching made the children want to excel – they loved being taught by her, and were eager to impress their kind, lovely teacher. The parents began to look at the bright young woman with renewed interest, and their admiration grew.

The young ladies on the estate envied Rani. She epitomized the modern Indian woman, and set an example for others to follow. Other young women still toiled in the fields, much to their disadvantage, and many fought with rigid, orthodox parents for some freedom to educate themselves. Some approached Rani to teach them to read and write in English, and she found herself using the school in the evening to educate and empower these women. And so Rani's career was set.

One of the pleasures of teaching, Rani discovered, was taking the children out of the classroom to enjoy fresh air and wonderful sunshine. One beautiful, sunny day, perfect for the outdoors, Rani decided to treat the children during the last hour of the school day. She took them down to the clearing by the river – where, unknown to her, Mukesh had been conceived many years before. The area had since been turned into a beautiful picnic area. The pool was safe for children to play in, and once they had overcome their initial shyness Rani found that this was their favourite pastime.

She settled against the big oak tree, keeping an eye on the children splashing in the cool, clear pool. Their laughter and zest for life filled the air, and Rani could not help but smile. Such simple things could bring such pleasure, she thought.

Watching the carefree scene in front of her, Rani had no idea she was being observed – until she felt the tap of a riding crop on her shoulder. She spun around in surprise, and her brown doe eyes widened as they clashed with hostile green ones. The imposter, intruding on the children's hour of fun, seemed anything but pleased by the sight of them.

"What are they up to?" he demanded, and Rani flinched at the coldness in his voice. It matched the glacial green of his eyes . . . suddenly Rani realized that she was looking into the eyes of Helena Sheldon's son.

Her eyes rose to his challengingly. "What does it look like to you? They're having some fun." She threw him a look of disdain before turning her back to him.

"And who gave you permission?" The green eyes bore into her back relentlessly.

"I teach at the Sheldon School, and one of the perks for the children is that they use the pool. Besides, I cannot see how this is any of your business," she retorted smoothly. She was not going to let this cold stranger intimidate her with his obvious prejudice.

"Is that so?" He cocked an eyebrow arrogantly as he tapped his riding crop impatiently against a black, shiny boot. He scanned the pool again through narrowed eyes, before heaving himself onto his big black stallion. Throwing Rani a last hostile look, he flicked his crop against the flank of his magnificent horse, which responded immediately by setting off at a gallop.

The fine hair on Rani's arms stood up. His icy stare had unnerved her, and she did not like that uncomfortable feeling that had settled in the pit of her stomach. A sixth sense warned her to be careful; she put it down to the glint in his green eyes.

"Madam, are you all right?" a little boy tugged her arm.

Rani looked down at him. "I'm fine," she replied with a shaky smile. "But I think it is time for us to get back to the classroom."

That evening, Rani chewed on her bottom lip as she washed the dinner dishes, wondering if she should tell her mother what had happened. The thought of the sinister Joseph Sheldon made her blood run cold.

"You're awfully quiet this evening, Rani," Sita observed, drying the dishes next to her daughter. Rani had seemed preoccupied the whole evening. "Is something wrong?"

"I hope not." Rani replied, casting her mother a worried look. "I met someone today. Someone you once knew."

"Really! And who is this, who has taken over your thoughts for the evening?"

"Joseph Sheldon."

The plate that Sita was drying almost fell from her hands, and she threw her daughter a startled look.

Rani missed her mother's reaction as she busied herself with the last of the dishes. "He is so unlike his father. So cold and rude and full of himself!" Her voice trembled with anger as she recalled his insolence.

"Beti, did he do anything to upset you?" Sita searched Rani's face for an answer.

"No..." Rani replied hesitantly, turning away from her mother's probing eyes. "Well, yes," she admitted. "I did not like his attitude when he discovered the children playing in the pool. It was as if he personally owned it."

"What did he say?" Sita did not trust Helena's son at all. That sweet young boy she'd met so many years ago seemed no longer to exist.

"He interrogated me and tried to intimidate me as well, but I stood my ground," Rani replied proudly. Then finally she voiced the concern that had been gnawing at her the whole evening: "I just hope he doesn't think he can interfere with the running of the school."

"He must take after this mother," Sita commented, and Rani caught the strangest of expressions on her mother's face.

"Well, I for one don't care who he takes after. I don't like him at all." Rani's firm tone startled Sita. "And I pray that our paths do not cross, for I will not tolerate his arrogance and insolence at all!"

But their paths did cross.

Some days later, Rani was teaching the children their English alphabet when she felt, rather than saw, someone staring at her. The hair at the nape of her neck stood up, and a cold shiver ran through her. Instinctively, she turned her head slightly, and caught Joseph Sheldon's scrutiny. He stood just outside the door of her classroom, positioned in such a way that he was not visible to the children. Their eyes clashed. Defiantly, she moved to the door, and held his cold, hard, mocking look as she shut it in his face.

Gopi slowly sipped his tea as he put down the newspaper. It was futile trying to concentrate on the news. It was almost three months since Raymond's death, and he still missed him. He missed their long chats about the past, and their friendship which had been forged through one woman's vengeance.

Gopi closed his eyes as a vision of Rani filled him, and he knew that it was now time: time for the woman who had destroyed his life to pay. He vowed that Geeta, too, would feel the pain and heartache she had inflicted upon him. And if her family got caught up in it, well, he had decided, that was just too bad. She was going to learn what it felt like to be destroyed – as he had been destroyed, for loving a kind, beautiful woman; one who had made him happy, and who had been about to give him the baby they so desperately wanted.

Gopi swallowed the lump in his throat: this was no time for tears and sentiment. He shook his head to clear away the memories of the past. It was the present that mattered; and he looked forward to the future. He had been through much anguish and turmoil, but he was still a fighter.

Slowly he rose to his feet and walked over to the window. The plantation was doing well under his guidance. It had become his life, and he was reaping the rewards – thanks to Raymond's trust in him. His eyes were drawn to his desk. The man he had hired had finally given him the information he needed. Now all he had to do was dangle a suitable bait, and wait for Geeta to swallow it.

He walked over to his desk and pulled out a red folder from the drawer. He did not have to open it – he knew its contents by heart. While he languished in prison, Geeta's power had grown, and she had become very wealthy over the years. She now owned vast acres of land, and her fresh produce and tea farming made her one of the most respected and wealthy people in the growing Indian community.

Geeta also had quite a family. Gopi knew all about her children, and that she was now also a grandmother. He was not truly interested in them – they seemed just as rich and spoilt as their mother – but he needed to know how many lives he was going to change.

Prior to his death, Raymond had wanted to expand his farming venture. He had purchased some land just outside Geeta's boundary – rich, fertile land, with a stream flowing through it, making it extremely valuable. The land was vacant and ready for farming. Raymond had wanted to start keeping cattle, and had just arranged to purchase his first herd when his health took a turn for the worse.

Now, the land all belonged to Gopi, and it played a vital part in the plans he was laying. Geeta hungered for more land; and the piece which suited her needs perfectly was the land Gopi owned. She had inquired as to the ownership of the land, and made it clear that she wanted to purchase it.

There was only one minor problem: Geeta needed capital. Most of her cash was tied up in assets, and she did not have enough cash to put in an offer. Gopi had discovered this weakness. He smiled a slow, sad smile as he put his final plans together.

"And then, my dear Rani," he whispered, "I will avenge your death."

He pushed the red folder aside and took out a pretty yellow folder with Sita's name on it. His expression softened as he looked at the report. Sita was still married to Hemith and was the mother of three grown children: two sons, and a daughter whom she had named Rani, after his late wife. He had not thought she would; the gesture truly touched him.

Memories of his beautiful, headstrong younger sister filled him with pride. How she had stood her ground and refused to consider marriage – and then, just when he had her figured as a young rebel, how she'd done a complete turnaround and agreed to marry Hemith Harilaken. Not long after that, she had become a mother and settled into marriage. From the report in front of him, it seemed she was still a rebel, but in a much subtler way; and for that he was still very proud of her. Her family radiated a warmth and compassion that stemmed from the love and values she so strongly shared with her husband, and which they had passed on to their children.

Those values were what impressed Gopi the most about the Harilakens. They did not believe in material possessions at all. Instead, it was clear that their concern was for the rights of their fellow man. Gopi wanted more than anything to be reunited with this family, and to get to know his nephews and Rani's namesake.

Both his parents were still alive; they were older, but they still had their health. The only thing that saddened him was that they had recently moved in with Geeta and Anoop. Although Gopi did not care where his father lived, he cared about the effect his plans would have on his mother.

The hand of sadness which gripped his heart quickly erased the happiness he had felt when reading about Sita. Tears rolled down his face as he reread the news of Bharath's demise. His kindness and loving spirit lived on in Gopi's heart.

Now, Gopi sighed deeply, he was left with two sisters. One whom he adored and the other whom he detested. Feeling quite sick at that thought, he slowly returned the folders to the drawer. The investigator he hired had done an excellent job: everything he needed to know was in the files. All he had to do was drop the bait and let Geeta swallow the worm.

After all, he sighed as he ran his hand through his hair and stretched his neck from side to side, she was the biggest fish in this deadly game; a game she had started almost two decades ago.

"Ma, I think you should wait until we have enough cash between us before we purchase that extra piece of land," Ramu offered.

"Beta, we cannot afford to wait. The timing is perfect," Geeta insisted. "If we don't snatch this offer we are going to lose. We have to come up with the cash, one way or the other." She spoke passionately, and her gestures made her determination apparent to her family. "I want only the best," she went on. "That land is very fertile and it has a great source of water." Her eyes narrowed as she pinned the male members of her family with a hard look. "I want it."

Silence fell.

Anoop read the stubbornness in his wife's voice and face. Even after all these years she still had the ability to amaze him. He admitted that she was the strength and brains behind their wealth and status, and he admired and loved her determination, but there were times when he had to bring her back to reality. And this was one of them.

"We simply cannot afford it," he stated, breaking the spell.

Geeta glared at him fiercely. "Don't tell me that," she snapped. "Since when have we let the lack of money stand in our way? I have weighed the options, and by purchasing that valuable piece of land we will become one of the biggest landowners in the area. Besides, that land has water, which we need."

"If we are going to expand we will need more labour and . . ." interjected Krishna.

"We can do it," Geeta insisted excitedly, looking at the serious faces around the dining-room table. She had had not expected this much opposition. Her sons were proving to be excellent farmers and businessmen but they were cautious, just like their father. It was time they took some chances, like she did, she decided.

"Think how much we will make within a year," she coaxed.

"That is, if we can weather the storms we've been having these last few years," Ramu reminded her.

"We were almost ruined," added Krishna.

"But we were not! Since when did I raise my boys to be pessimists?" she demanded.

"Geeta, I think our sons are realists." Anoop looked at her sternly. "They have learnt to take care of what we have acquired over the years, and –"

"And here is an opportunity to expand," Geeta interrupted. "I have almost a quarter of the amount in cash. I just need to come up with a little bit more . . ."

"I feel disaster in my bones," Anoop warned, "but as a matter of interest, just how do you plan to raise the balance?"

"The land is sold privately by an attorney. He's told me that he can arrange credit for me, at a lower interest than the bank charges. It shouldn't be a problem – we have sufficient assets to put up as collateral."

"This sounds too easy. There must be a catch somewhere!" Ramu interjected.

"Ramu," Geeta gave her son a smug smile. "I have done my homework. The owner died a little while ago and his heir has no interest in the land. He wants to sell and I want to buy. It is that simple. If I don't buy then someone else will."

"I still don't like the sound of this, but I think before we make our decision we should meet with the attorney," Anoop suggested.

"I agree," Geeta beamed as she clapped her hands, failing utterly to hide her look of triumph.

"I am so glad you have decided to take up my offer." Anthony Rands shook Geeta's hand before turning to Anoop. "Please take a seat." He waved them towards the chairs and watched as the Balrajs took their places in front of him. He noticed the look of suspicion that passed between the sons.

"Mr Rands, we have a few questions for you before our parents sign any documentation," Ramu began, with a cool smile.

"Mr Balraj, please feel free to ask your questions. Remember that you are under no pressure whatsoever to buy. I already have someone who is very interested in purchasing the land, but I thought I'd give your parents the first option as it is virtually on their boundary."

"Thank you for the consideration, but I would like to know about this loan you have so kindly arranged. Is it from your own funds?"

Anthony gave them each a small smile and leaned back in his Queen Anne chair as he clasped his hands in front of him. "No," he replied casually. "To be honest, I am not a wealthy man, Mr Balraj, and would not be able to assist your family with a loan. But I do have wealthy clients who trust me to invest their money. These people are very committed to the community, and often we loan out money to families who want to start their own businesses. We charge a low interest rate, and we don't pay attention to race. If a family shows business potential, we invest in them. Everyone wins," he smiled.

"I understand. However, is it not possible for us to pay the seller directly, in instalments, instead of borrowing from your client?" Krishna asked in his quiet, careful manner.

"No, I am sorry. The seller is in urgent need of funds. He wants the full price immediately."

"I see," murmured Krishna, casting an anxious look at his parents.

"Look." Anthony leaned forward and his voice took on a serious business tone. "If you're not comfortable with this arrangement, you need not purchase the land. I will put this offer to the next client on my list, who is very anxious . . ."

"No," interrupted Geeta as she slid warning looks at her family. "We want that property, and we do not have a problem with what you are offering."

"Mr Rands," Ramu cut in, "before we finalize everything I want to go over the contract."

"Son," Geeta turned to him, impatience obvious in her voice. "I have already discussed the finer details with Mr Rands prior to this meeting, and a contract is being drawn up at this moment. I cannot believe that after all my years as a businesswoman, you have the audacity to doubt my instincts and ability!"

Ramu felt his face redden, but he refused to be intimidated by his mother's manner.

"Mrs Balraj," Anthony cut in. "I can see that your family is not happy with this venture. I will explain the contract in layman's terms so that there is no doubt in anyone's mind that everything is legal."

Anoop nodded, and Anthony began explaining the various clauses of the contract. "Should you have a financial problem and cannot pay an instalment, my client will be understanding and merely increase the term of the loan. We would require notification in writing if the payment cannot be met for any reason. I doubt you will have that problem. However, should you miss more than two instalments, then we will have to repossess the land." He smiled at Geeta as though that were surely impossible.

Anoop cast his wife a warning look before turning to Anthony. "Mr Rands, I would like to speak to my wife before we go any further."

"Certainly." Anthony rose and closed the door behind him.

"Are you mad?" Anoop glared at Geeta. "Do you know what that man has just told us?"

"I know exactly what he said. I am not an idiot," she hissed. "Why are you all so pessimistic? I have always made excellent decisions and you have all benefited from them. If this was going to fail, I don't think Mr Rands would risk his client's money and trust by investing in us."

"Something just does not feel right here," Anoop insisted. "Why do we need to put up the house and all our land as collateral?"

"There is no other way," Geeta's patience was running thin by now. "The amount we are borrowing is considerable. Have faith, Anoop. We have taken chances before, and so far we have not failed."

"Well, how did it go?"

"I had a few uneasy moments there, but you were right, Gopi. Your sister wanted that property so desperately she put up her freehold property as collateral. She is a gutsy lady."

A cold, hard look entered Gopi's eyes. "Don't refer to that woman as my sister – and she is not gutsy. Just bloody greedy."

"I'm sorry," Anthony apologized. Gopi had taken him into his confidence, and his heart went out to the man, who he felt had been dealt an unfair blow. Besides, he loved helping the underdog, and he wanted Gopi to win this battle. "But I must warn you, she is tough. She dresses very well too – her clothes and jewellery must cost a small fortune. Geeta Balraj is the very image of success."

"Has she impressed you that much?"

"Please give me some credit," laughed Anthony. "I happen to be a good judge of character, and I know exactly what type of woman we are up against. She is extremely intelligent, manipulative and ambitious. She is also very greedy, and that is her downfall," he summarized. "And, Gopi, your major advantage."

Gopi leaned back in his chair, tapped his gold pen against his chin and gave Anthony a slow, lazy smile. "Don't I know it? All we need to do is give her the cheque and then wait. In the meantime, I want the river that is running through her property to be diverted. Soon she will discover that her stream is a mere trickle . . . and that the best part of the land has not been sold yet."

"You mean we merely whet her appetite."

"Exactly," Gopi grinned, enjoying the chase.

"How long do you expect to wait for results?" Anthony was intrigued. The more he dealt with this case the more interesting it became.

"If I have to wait a year, I will."

"Remind me never to cross swords with you, Gopi. I would far rather be your friend than your enemy."

"A very smart decision," Gopi grinned as he handed Anthony the cheque. Together they lifted their glasses.

"Here's to the downfall of the Balrajs," said Anthony.

"No," corrected Gopi. "Here's to Rani and Raymond. May they rest in peace."

CHAPTER TWENTY-TWO

Rani's heart soared with happiness: finally, Balu Pillai had noticed her. Just thinking about him sent a shiver of delight through her body as she sank down beneath the old oak tree near the pool. Closing her eyes, she saw his face in front of her, and a slow, dreamy smile broke across her face.

When she was a little girl Chumpa had taken her along to visit the Pillais, and Rani knew the story of how her grandmother had delivered Balu on the ship before they reached Natal. Now he was a tall, good-looking and intelligent young man.

She sighed deeply. He was also so mature and serious about life. As a child she had followed him everywhere, until one day he wasn't around any more. She had learnt from her parents that he'd been sent to England by Albert Sheldon to further his studies. Master Sheldon had seen a need for an Indian doctor in the community, and Balu had jumped at the opportunity to go to medical school. Now he had returned to serve his people.

Rani was very impressed with him, and shy whenever they met. She had fallen a little in love with the intense young doctor.

When Rani took one of her pupils who had suddenly become ill to see him, he expressed his delight at seeing her. He told her he was thrilled that she, too, had taken advantage of Mr Sheldon's generosity and educated herself. Balu was also impressed that she played such a vital role in empowering the women in their conservative community.

"Our people need a teacher like you," he said. "You are kind and gentle and you have a way with the children."

Rani's heartbeat was loud in her own ears. Balu was so different from the people she dealt with daily. He was serious about his calling, but he had a wonderful sense of humour once one got to know him.

"What made you want to take care of the sick?" she asked. She wanted to know everything about him.

"I remember a time when my father was beaten very badly, and there was no one to tend to his wounds. I was very little then, but I made a vow that I would not let it happen again."

He replied matter-of-factly, but Rani saw the hurt in his black eyes when he looked at her. No matter how much life had improved through their hard work, the pain of the past could never be erased. That pain moulded the future for generations to come.

Now, weeks after that conversation, something had at last developed between them. It happened when she visited his family with her parents and Chumpa. Diwali – the festival of lights – had come and gone; Chumpa realised she had not seen her old friends for a while, and wanted to share with them a belated parcel of sweets. The reunion was a pleasant and lively affair. After lunch, Rani excused herself, saying she needed to stretch her legs. Balu offered to accompany her. When she looked at her father for his approval he nodded ever so slightly, and she gave Balu a shy smile.

They walked side by side, hands barely touching, and talked about work, their families and everything else except their growing feelings for one another. Not looking down, Rani caught her heel on a loose stone and stumbled. Balu reached out to catch her.

Later, she wondered exactly when it was that he realized she was no longer a girl but a woman – for he suddenly let go of her as though she had burnt him. And then, when she looked at him with confusion in her eyes, he drew her into his arms and kissed her.

Her first kiss was everything she had dreamed it would be. He made it perfect: his lips when they touched hers were soft and so very gentle. As Rani's heart beat furiously, he kissed her tenderly, with just a hint of passion, so as not to frighten her.

But it had ended too soon.

Now, the sound of a galloping horse broke her reverie. Her eyes flew open as Joseph Sheldon brought his horse to a halt in front of her. He looked at her so deeply and intently that it frightened her. Rani stood up: she did not want to be at a disadvantage.

As she got to her feet in one graceful movement, Joseph decided that she had to be his.

"You don't have to leave on my account," he smiled, keeping his voice light and friendly as he dismounted and walked towards her.

"I'm not." Rani lifted her head and looked at him. "It's late and I must be getting back."

"Don't leave," he whispered, putting out a hand to stop her. She stepped away from him to avoid his touch, and he felt a rush of anger at her snub. The girl was acting as though she were too good for him. "What's the matter with you?" he demanded, green eyes growing stormy. "I try to be friendly, but you're all high-and-mighty just because you teach at the school."

"Excuse me, but I am late."

Rani turned to leave, but he stepped in front of her to block her path, swearing angrily beneath his breath. He caught her arms and gently applied pressure as he drew her towards him. He saw the hint of fear lurking in her beautiful eyes, and a surge of power ran through him. He wanted her!

Rani tried to pull away from his grasp. She did not like the glint in his eyes. "Let me go or I'll scream," she threatened.

"And who will hear you?" He threw back his head and laughed as he jerked her closer to him.

"Let go of me!" Rani cried, as fear gave way to fury.

She tried kicking at his booted shin; amused at her feeble attempts, he laughed louder. As she turned to swing away, he let her go, but stuck out his boot to trip her. Before she could get up from the ground he was beside her, and then she felt his weight on top of her.

"Get off me, you animal!" she spat, as she struggled to get out from under him.

Joseph Sheldon chuckled. He had never been denied a single thing in his life, and this beautiful young coolie would not be the exception. Besides, it was time for him to have some fun, and he found Rani extremely intriguing. In England the girls were forever chasing him, which was terribly boring.

Now, Rani was different. She excited him and made him giddy with desire, and she was a challenge. He could feel her soft curves beneath him as she tried to push him off. His breathing deepened and he pulled her closer. Her lips, so perfectly shaped, looked inviting as they parted to let out a gasp – he could not resist. He crushed that soft mouth in a hungry, bruising kiss, running his hands over her body.

When he released her lips, a soft whimper escaped, but she continued to struggle. "Don't fight me or you won't enjoy it," he hissed as he cupped one firm breast.

Pure white fury, mingled with terror, filled Rani as her voice rose in a scream. "*Get off me, you crazy bastard!*"

"Stop fighting," he snarled as he slipped a hand under her dress. Rani reacted by sinking her teeth into his neck.

"Bitch!" Joseph's temper snapped as he felt the bite and rolled away in pain.

Rani took the opportunity to escape.

"So . . ." Gopi sat back on the couch and stretched out his long legs in front of him as he fixed Anthony with an inquiring look. "They have not defaulted on a single payment, and six months have passed."

"Yes. She is smart and driven."

"Too smart and driven for her own good," responded Gopi with a chilling smile. "I know for a fact that she's battling to keep up with the payments and is in need of some capital. It is just a matter of time before she starts to crumble."

"I had no idea . . ."

"Well, my man, now you know," grinned Gopi. "It hasn't rained for months and Geeta, like other farmers in her area, is feeling the drought."

"What about the stream?"

"Drying up slowly. She needs to improve her irrigation system – something she didn't think about very carefully." Gopi's eyes danced. "And now she desperately wants the land I haven't sold her yet. Offer her more money by way of assistance. She won't turn you down," he said with certainty.

A month later, Anthony met Gopi at the Royal Hotel to report back on his meeting with Geeta. "You were right. She is getting desperate: it was either the loan or repossession."

"Excellent," chuckled Gopi. "She's going to sink so deep, there will be no way she can surface."

It wasn't long before Geeta started to regret taking the second loan. The farms were not turning in the profits she had calculated, and the stream on the new property she had been relying on so heavily was also drying up.

"We need to improve our irrigation," she told her family, "or else we are going to be ruined."

"And whose fault is that?" Ramu interjected sarcastically.

"Bring me those contracts you signed with Mr Rands," instructed Anoop. Indeed, this situation was very worrying. Two months had gone by without paying towards the loan, and to add to their problem, Geeta had taken out this additional loan to buy them some time.

After careful scrutiny of the documents, Anoop raised very concerned eyes to his family. "We have a major problem here. If we don't come up with the instalments soon, we are going to lose everything we have worked so damn hard for."

"Rubbish," snapped Geeta as she snatched the papers from Anoop. "We are only two months in arrears! Perhaps we can speak to Mr Rands to get us an extension . . ."

"Ma, sit down." Krishna took the contracts from his mother's hand and looked them over.

Geeta sat back fuming: she hated not being in control of the situation.

When Krishna lifted his eyes to his mother, it was with anger. "Did you even read this added clause in the second contract?" he demanded, as he slid the contract back to her across their huge dining-room table.

"How dare you!" screeched Geeta, looking at her family with wild eyes. "All I did was try and give you children everything you ever wanted, and now you talk to me with no respect. All we need is time and some rain," she added stubbornly.

"Well, why don't you order some?" Ramu put in. "You give orders very well."

"Don't get smart with me, young man," Geeta lashed out. "I have been trying my best here."

"Well, your best is costing us our home and everything we have worked for. Do you understand, Geeta? We will lose everything!" Anoop too was shouting now, out of frustration and fear.

"What is going on here?" Chumpa walked in on the meeting.

"It seems that we are going to lose everything, Nani." Krishna gave his mother a disgusted look as she started wailing uncontrollably.

Chumpa looked at her family in confusion, taking in the angry expressions all round. She had never intervened in any business discussions, but this appeared to be very serious: Geeta was devastated. "What are you talking about?" she asked.

"We are about to be thrown out of our home and off our property, Nani," Ramu replied bitterly, "and it is all because of her." He pointed to his mother.

"Your mother is a smart businesswoman and would never do anything foolish," Chumpa reprimanded.

"Well, I am sorry to disappoint you, but she has," Anoop responded. "Geeta has taken out a second mortgage and did not have the decency to discuss it with her family, and now we are running into arrears with our payments. We will have to go to Mr Rands and explain our situation. In the meantime, we better pray that the heavens open up and it rains. We need water."

"All I wanted was to make a success of our lives!" cried Geeta. "I wanted my children to lead good lives." She looked at her sons for understanding.

"I should have gone ahead with the building of a few catchment dams like I wanted to. But you said that it would cost us labour, and you wanted to buy land we did not need," Ramu reminded his mother accusingly.

"That piece of property was to be our source of water."

"Well, Ma, you should have given your sons more credit. We would have made it work, and it would have cost us nothing but sweat," Krishna added sadly. "We are adults and we have made good business and farming decisions before."

225

"I know that son, I know," wept Geeta, feeling terribly afraid for the first time in her life.

"You want an extension?" Anthony looked at Geeta as if her request were ludicrous.

"Yes, we do," Ramu answered for his mother. "Please liase with your client and let us know as soon as possible. We would certainly appreciate your help."

Anthony was impressed. Ramu and his twin brother were intelligent and well-spoken, and they seemed to know what they wanted. Pity, he sighed, looking at Geeta. They are going to lose everything through your greediness and manipulation. "You do understand the danger you are in? After all, the first loan was not paid back. Your mother then borrowed more, but no payment has been made as yet on that loan – which carries the clause that if you default on even a single payment, you stand to lose everything," he warned cautiously.

"We are fully aware of the problem, but you did mention that your client is very wealthy and he does own a plantation. I am sure that somewhere along the line he has hit a bad patch in his life too. Perhaps if we met him personally, and explained our plight, he would be sympathetic," Krishna requested very politely.

If only you knew of his bad patch, thought Anthony, as he took in their desperate faces. "Is that what you want?" he asked Geeta.

She was hardly dressed as a pauper. She was wearing a beautiful silk sari and her jewellery itself looked as though it would pay a portion of her debt.

"Anything to help us," she answered, grasping at straws.

"So they want to meet me." Gopi sighed. "The timing is not right."

"What do I tell them?"

"Give them ten more days as an extension, and not a day more," Gopi replied. "They are so close to ruin I can almost taste it. I have waited for far too long to make a mistake now."

"What if they come up with some money?"

"They won't." There was confidence in his voice. "I have had their financial situation investigated and they are stone broke. The banks are loathe to loan farmers money at this stage. The ten days I am giving them is to watch them squirm."

"You are bad, Gopi, very bad," Anthony said, with a mischievous grin on his face.

"No, my friend. It is merely time to settle some old scores. It is a pity that there are going to be some innocent casualties in this war," he replied, somewhat sadly.

"Only ten days!" Geeta was aghast. "What can we do in ten days?"

"Perhaps we can sell some of your jewels," Anoop suggested.

"What?"

"You heard me."

"Our family heirlooms? No." Geeta's face was set in her usual stubborn mask. "My jewellery is for the children and you know that."

"Then I give up!" Anoop snapped, totally fed up with her attitude. He was exhausted. He had approached a few of his friends for assistance, but had been turned away very politely. It seemed as though even the gods were turning away from them now. There was just no answer.

Watching them, Chumpa felt helpless, and even Sewcharran was at a loss for words. The Balrajs were the talk of the community. Geeta had always been so proud of their achievement and her status; but now she hid indoors and wanted to die. They were not even in a position to pay their labourers, and even though they sold some of their most beautiful and expensive pieces of furniture, it was not enough to tide them over. Their debt was increasing.

Every effort they made failed. At the end of the tenth day, they were frustrated and terrified. Their carefully built-up life was falling apart before their eyes, and there was nothing they could do to save their farm.

"No news from the Balrajs?" Gopi inquired, as he watched the sun slowly set in the west. The sky was awash with golden hues of pink and blue and the evening air was warm and still.

"They are desperate to meet you," Anthony reported.

"I know that." Gopi spoke calmly, but a deep and dangerous fire ran through him. Memories of Rani, bruised and battered, dying in his arms, filled his mind and heart. "But there is just one person I want to meet, and that is the great Mrs Balraj herself."

CHAPTER TWENTY-THREE

Geeta sat upright and proudly outside Anthony's office, in the chair she normally occupied while waiting to keep her appointments. Her demeanour belied the apprehension she was keeping at bay – and she had good reason to feel apprehensive. She needed her wits about her when she finally met the man who had advanced her all that money.

At the time, the gesture had seemed so generous. Now, the thought of losing everything she possessed terrified and angered Geeta. Discreetly, she wiped her sweaty palms against the beautiful purple silk sari she had chosen to wear, and her breathing deepened. The intricately designed gold choker adorning her neck felt tighter, and tiny beads of perspiration sat on her nose, where her diamond nose-ring sparkled.

Why did he ask to see *her* specifically? Anxiously she glanced at the clock on the wall, and noted that it was still working – although the sound of its ticking was drowned by the rapid thud of her heart. It was now almost ten-thirty, and a full half-hour had passed since her arrival. Slowly she got to her feet and walked over to the window. The cool air from the opened window helped dry the perspiration on her face as she brought her palms together in silent prayer. Down below, she could see her two sons and her husband. They would soon burn a hole in the sidewalk, she thought, as she watched them pace back and forth. How she wished this feeling of impending doom would simply evaporate!

"Good morning, Mrs Balraj," Anthony's cheery voice startled Geeta, and she swung around. "Sorry to have kept you waiting." He smiled charmingly at her – and in that instant Geeta saw past his sweet smile and realized that his charm was deadly as sin.

Still smiling, he led her into his office. "Please take a seat," he offered, and Geeta, sick with worry, sank into the leather chair he pointed to. It was then that she became aware of a third presence in the room. Her mouth felt very dry.

"Have you managed to come up with the outstanding payments, Mrs Balraj?" Anthony inquired politely.

Geeta's voice betrayed her, and the only response she could give was a shake of her head. This failure to speak infuriated her. She had never felt such defeat before, and her fingers itched to slap that polite look off Anthony Rands' white face.

"You are fully aware of the consequences?" Anthony waited for her response.

Geeta cleared her throat, very conscious of the tall, well-built man standing gazing out of the window with his back to her. She knew that he had a perfect view of her family down below. Curiosity got the better of her: "I would like to meet your client," she said.

From the corner of her eye she saw him turn, as though on cue. Geeta watched him with narrowed eyes. Something about his stance was vaguely familiar, and yet she could not quite put her finger on it . . . What surprised her most was that he was an Indian, just like herself. She had assumed the client was white, like Anthony Rands. It was certainly something for a white to be representing an Indian – but then, she thought bitterly, money talks, and it appeared that this man had a lot of the stuff.

He stood tall, strong, and confident. His neatly trimmed beard and horn-rimmed spectacles gave him an air of distinction, and just for a second she envied him and his success, and wondered if he had a family of his own – and if so, did they know how fortunate they were?

The man returned her silent stare. His eyes were expressionless as they raked her from head to toe.

"I want to speak to her alone."

Although he directed his words to Anthony, his gaze never left the woman who remained seated, watching him scornfully. He spoke as though she were insignificant, and Geeta clamped her teeth together in anger. Didn't he know that she was a highly respected businesswoman? How dare he treat her like this! Maybe, she thought, her mind turning windmills, I can coax him into an extension with payment over five years . . . The idea lifted her spirits. After all, he was a man and men normally succumbed to her charms. She gave him a tentative smile.

"What have you come up with, Mrs . . ." He paused, as though he did not recall her name.

"Balraj," Geeta supplied sweetly, although she was seething inside. How dare he not even remember her name! "Mr . . .?" Geeta paused dramatically, but all she received was cold silence. "I cannot pay you all that I owe you right now. Please give me more time." When she still received no response she continued, hoping he would relent. "We have worked extremely hard over the years to acquire what we have, and now . . . this." Her voice grew thick with emotion and she wrung her hands together.

The sound of her gold bangles made her recall Anoop's suggestion that she sell her jewellery. "I'll even leave these with you as a guarantee," she offered, quickly starting to remove her jewellery; but when she saw his look of contempt she shuddered and stopped. Now it was time for pity. "Our property is everything we have. It is my children's future," she implored, and even let a few tears fall. Then in a voice that shook with hate for him, for he was making her grovel, she added shrewdly, "You don't look as though you need the money, or lack for anything."

"Well, you are wrong!" The man startled her by replying in a tone that bordered on violence, and Geeta felt scorched by the blaze in his eyes. "You are damn wrong. You —" he came forward for the first time, and in one swift movement yanked her from her seat. "You don't remember me at all?" And then, as though she were disgusting, he let go of her so abruptly that she stumbled back and grabbed the side of the desk to keep her balance. "Look at me carefully," he instructed, whipping off his spectacles.

In a flash, it was as though the present no longer existed, and the past unfolded before her. Geeta went as white as a sheet. Her breathing quickened and her knees buckled as she held on to the desk. "Gopi Bhai," she whispered, and then, to make sure this was not some nightmare, she reached out a trembling hand to touch him.

"Don't," he warned in a quiet, deadly voice as he stepped away from her. "I am not your brother. You gave up that right the minute you so maliciously engineered my imprisonment."

"No!" cried Geeta, terrified by the look in his eyes.

"You make me sick!" Gopi raged. "Don't bother denying your involvement in any of it. You hated Rani so much you could not see the love we had. *You*," he spat as she recoiled in terror, "you cold-heartedly manipulated an innocent man to play on my weakness, and in doing so you destroyed three lives." He brought his fist down on Anthony's desk. "What the hell were you doing the night my wife was beaten, almost raped and left to die!" he demanded. "Making love to your husband, and increasing your family?"

"Bhaiya . . ." Geeta cried out, wanting to stem the flow of such angry words. It seemed as though her whole world was crumbling, and the past was back to haunt her. She had never dreamed that he would return. She had simply cast him from her mind and heart and moved on with her life – she had to, in order to succeed. But now he held the future of her family in the palm of his hand. "Please," tears rolled down her fat cheeks, "can't you be forgiving?" Even as the words left her mouth, she heard how futile they sounded. "You cannot let your own flesh and blood suffer!" She allowed herself to sob shamelessly, while Gopi stared at her with loathing. "I have regretted everything!" she whispered, wiping her tears away. "I prayed day and night for your safety."

Liar, screamed Gopi silently, as she sank to her knees before him in desperation. He stood rock-still as he watched her clutching his legs and crying for forgiveness. All he could see was the beaten image of his wife. Feeling his stillness, Geeta realized that she was not going to win this way. Slowly she rose to her feet, and when she finally looked up at Gopi, her eyes were hard and bitter and her voice was strong. "All right," she began. "I am truly sorry that you had to end up in prison. But you should have listened to me. You dug your own grave." Her voice grew shrill: "And I'm not sorry about what happened to that Tamil bitch you married. She deserved what she got!"

Gopi almost reached for her. He so desperately wanted to place his hands around her fat neck and squeeze and squeeze until she screamed and begged for mercy, and the life drained from her. But he knew that this was not the way – it would be too easy. Instead, he clenched his fists, fighting for control. This time, he was not going to let her get to him.

Suddenly, from deep down laughter bubbled, until it erupted like a volcano dormant for too long. He laughed so hard that tears flowed down his cheeks.

"You are insane. Do you know that?" whispered Geeta.

She slowly backed away from him.

"No," he replied, sobered, after a few minutes. "I am perfectly sane. I have never been saner in my life than at this precise moment. You," he snarled, swallowing his hysteria as he approached her slowly, "have just dug your own grave, and now I am going to watch how you bury yourself and your family in it. Ironic, isn't it?" He gave a soft and dangerous laugh.

"You think you've won?" Geeta stormed furiously.

"I don't think. I *know*," he replied smoothly, in control of his emotions now. "Tomorrow, I will be looking over my new property with my attorney. Be ready to vacate when I say so." His voice was cool and self-assured.

"How can you be so cruel? You are willing to kick out your own sister!"

"I have one sister only, and it is certainly not you. This is a simple business transaction, Mrs Balraj, which went very wrong for you. So don't call me cruel. And for your own sake, don't refer to me as your brother ever again." He turned away from her as though she were dirt. "Now get out of my sight."

"You planned all this, didn't you? You planned my downfall down to the last detail!"

"No. You did." He spun around to look at her, contempt alive in his whole body. "It was your own selfishness and greed. I merely held out the bait, and you so typically gobbled it without thinking of the consequences. There is no one to blame but yourself."

"Why . . . *you* . . ." Geeta lost control and flew at him, reaching out to scratch his face.

He thrust her easily aside and she fell to the floor. "Next time don't play games you cannot win," he warned, before calmly strolling out of the office without a backward glance.

Geeta stormed out of the building in fury. Even a stranger would have been kinder! How on earth was she going to break this news to her children, and worse, how would Anoop deal with Gopi's sudden and devastating appearance? His heart would not stand the shock – or the truth!

"What happened in there? You were in for such a long time." Anoop took one look at his wife's face and knew they were in trouble. Her eyes were blazing with anger.

"Just take me home," she instructed. "Don't ask any questions yet. All I can say is that it is worse than we thought."

At the house, Geeta's whole family had gathered to hear the outcome of the meeting; they were all anxious about their future. Smita rushed to her mother's side the moment she entered the house.

"Ma . . ." was all she managed to get out before her mother pushed her aside and stormed into the living room. Smita turned to her brother. "What's going on? She's in such a mood!"

"We don't know," Ramu replied, following. "She hasn't said a word to any of us. All we can feel is this immense rage."

Chumpa took one look at her daughter and knew that something terrible had happened. They really were going to lose everything. "Geeta, Beti . . ." she began.

"He's back!" Geeta suddenly screamed with rage as she faced them all. "And he is bent on ruining us!"

Anoop's gasp was clearly audible. His breathing deepened and he broke out in a cold sweat.

Chumpa went as white as a sheet. There was only one person who could evoke such venom in her daughter, and that was Gopi. But that was impossible; her son was in prison. She shook her head in disbelief – and yet her heart soared.

Sewcharran looked at his daughter as though he were seeing her for the first time. "Is Gopi free?" he asked, his voice cracking with emotion.

Geeta's children threw confused looks at each other.

"What on earth are you ranting about?" Krishna demanded, watching his livid mother.

"I never dreamt that he would return and turn against me," she said, her eyes frantically searching Anoop's face, "and we are losing everything because of him."

"No . . ." Anoop groaned, as he felt a sharp pain in his chest. "I warned . . . you," he pointed to Geeta accusingly, "but you refused to listen!" Groaning with pain, he slid to the floor.

"Quick," Krishna was beside his father, "I think it is his heart again. Get Balu."

Even before the words left him, Ramu was out of the house. Smita sank to the floor and cradled her father's head in her lap.

"I knew . . . that someday . . . the truth would surface, and then . . . disaster would strike," Anoop whispered hoarsely. "I warned you not to interfere . . ."

"Shh, Taj." Smita wiped her father's face.

"Ma, what is Taj talking about?" Krishna demanded.

"Nothing!" Geeta mopped her perspiring face as her eyes moved worriedly to Anoop. "Can't you see what is happening to your father?"

"You are to blame . . ." Anoop whispered, before giving in to the pain in his chest.

"Ma, we need some explanation," Krishna muttered, throwing his mother a furious look as he knelt before his father, trying to feel a pulse.

"This is no time for questions," snapped Geeta. "Your father needs to be carried to our bed."

"I don't think we should move him just yet. We should wait for Balu to get here. It will be safer." Krishna turned to look at Chumpa, who was kneeling next to him with tears streaming down her face. "Nani," he took hold of her hand tenderly. "Do you know what this is all about?"

With sadness in her eyes, Chumpa looked at her grandson. "No. I, too, need an explanation." She turned to Geeta for an answer.

"Just don't ask me now," Geeta turned her back on everyone and almost fled from the room, when Ramu and Doctor Pillai's entrance brought her to a halt.

The silence was deafening as Balu checked the semi-conscious Anoop's pulse and heartbeat, noting that his skin felt cold and clammy. "I warned Mr Balraj a couple of weeks ago to take it easy, but I see that he did not take my advice. The best thing for him is to rest in a calm environment."

After he had settled Anoop in his bed, the doctor looked at the family reproachfully. He knew of their dilemma because Anoop had confided in him. "Make sure that absolutely nothing upsets him. I don't think his heart will survive another attack," he warned. "Call me when he wakes."

After Balu left, Geeta just sat there beside Anoop, holding onto his hand and watching him. Oh, what a price to pay, she thought bitterly. Her drastic actions had cost Anoop his health.

Her children wanted an explanation, but they were also worried about their father's condition, and so refrained from questioning her just then. For that she was thankful. As her rage burnt down her maternal instincts took over again: she wanted so much to protect her children from the truth. How could she inform them that the house in which they had grown up – a small house in the beginning, which they had slowly extended as they prospered, until it was one of the best homes in the area – was no longer their home? Now it belonged to Gopi. Everything they owned belonged to him.

"Are you really going to turn them out today?" Anthony asked as Gopi brought the car to a halt outside Geeta and Anoop's palatial home. The home had clearly been built with pride and care. The green lawns were vast, with tall palm trees bordering the path leading to the front door.

Gopi's eyes swept over the property. He felt no regret for what he was about to do. "I will do whatever is necessary to make that woman's life a living hell," he said, meeting Anthony's gaze.

Although Gopi was confident of his plans where Geeta was concerned, he was worried about his mother's reaction. Would she hate him for bringing so much pain and disruption to their well-organized life? And what about the shame she must have suffered when he ran away with Rani, and when he was imprisoned for murder? His heart filled with pain at the thought of his mother's rejection. Or would she understand, and welcome him into her heart and life again?

As he stepped out of the car, the first person Gopi met was his father. The years had not been kind to him, and Gopi was somewhat taken aback. Sewcharran came forward and looked at his son for several minutes, his one eye covered by a black patch that Gopi had never seen before. The eye that was visible spoke volumes, and Gopi felt a tug in his heart for this old man.

"Taj," he greeted, holding himself upright and proud.

"Beta," the old man said. "I am glad you are free," he added before turning away. Gopi was stunned at the change in his father; and in those few moments he knew that he had to let go of the hurt and anger he carried in his heart for Sewcharran.

Krishna came forward to meet Gopi, and Anthony introduced the two relatives. Gopi liked the way his nephew looked at him, unflinchingly. Nodding his head in acknowledgement, Gopi followed his nephew into the house that now belonged to him.

Immediately he sensed that something was wrong. The air was thick with hostility, and something else – something awful that reminded him of the night when Rani lay dying in his arms. Death! A shiver ran down Gopi's spine at the thought.

"Beta, is it really you? He heard an old and achingly familiar voice, and then he found himself in his mother's arms, and Chumpa was weeping with joy. She ran her rough, hard-worn hands over his face and pressed kisses wherever her fingers touched. "Gopi Beta! I have never given up hope. I cannot believe that you are here . . . and you look so handsome!" Overwhelmed with emotion, she stood back to admire him through her tears as she held onto his hands, not wanting to let go of him in case he disappeared again. "You look so healthy and strong too, my son."

"He does, doesn't he, Majee?" Geeta's voice dripped with hatred as she observed this wonderful reunion of mother and son.

Gopi lifted his shining eyes and met Geeta's look challengingly. He was appalled so see how old and haggard she looked – it was obvious that she had not had any sleep. There were dark circles under her eyes, and she looked positively evil as she stared at him. It was as though whatever wickedness she had buried in her was surfacing, and there was no way she could control it.

"Nani," a soft and feminine voice called out hesitatingly, and Gopi saw a pretty, slim young woman. She reminded him of Sita. "Taj is calling for someone called Gopi." As she spoke, she looked at him as though she knew who he was.

"I am here," he replied, "Where is your father?"

"Come with me." She gave him a sad, shy smile as she led the way, ignoring her mother's protests.

Gopi's breath caught in his throat. Just yesterday he had observed Anoop and his sons from the window of Anthony's office. Although Anoop had looked stressed and very anxious then, he had not seemed ill. Gopi was stunned at Anoop's transformation in a matter of hours.

"Taj," Smita called softly as she laid her palms against her father's cheeks.

Gopi found himself swallowing a lump in his throat. That gesture, so simple and pure, was the most loving thing he had seen in a long time.

Anoop opened his eyes slowly, and Gopi realized what an effort it was for him. Anoop was critically ill.

He gave a tired smile. "Smita, Beti. Where is everyone else?"

"Taj. Please take it easy." Smita held his hand as she turned to her uncle and gave him another one of her soft, sad smiles. "He was doing a little better this morning, and then when he heard you arrive . . . he began having pain in his chest again." Her words were delivered without any accusation.

"Please . . . Beti . . . call everyone here." Anoop clutched his chest as another spasm clutched his chest.

Smita ran from the room, and within seconds Anoop's family was around his bed.

Anoop tried to sit up slowly. "Come closer," he invited Gopi, pointing to a spot on the bed beside him.

Gopi sat. Anoop's hand was ice-cold in his, and a sense of dèjá vu came over him. This was just like when Raymond was dying.

"I must beg your forgiveness, Gopi. I never meant to hurt you."

Gopi was stunned. He had wanted revenge so badly, but not in this manner. Raymond too had begged for forgiveness before he died, just as Anoop was doing. Yet, left alone, these two men would not have caused him any pain and heartache. They were merely the useful pawns in Geeta's deadly game. The only person he wanted to see suffer was Geeta. But events, or should he call it fate, had intervened, and now Geeta's family also had to suffer the consequences of her actions.

Geeta had robbed him of a wife and family, and now, ironically, she was losing her husband. Her children were clearly furious and disappointed with her and did not trust her at all. She had just cost them their home and their father.

"I want my children to know that this is not their fault, and that they must not blame you in any way." Anoop, in deep pain, appealed to his children: "This is your mother's eldest brother, Gopi. Your mother and I have caused him immense pain and . . . grief." He looked at Gopi. "I don't blame you for wanting to extract your revenge. Please forgive me . . . and promise me that you will tell my family everything, so that they will understand and accept what has happened."

Tears welled in Gopi's eyes as he embraced his brother-in-law. They could have been good friends had it not been for Geeta. "Everything will be alright," he whispered. "I promise."

"Thank you . . . " a small, relieved smile broke over Anoop's pale face. He clutched Gopi's hand tightly. Then he cast his tired gaze on each member of his family and whispered, "I am so sorry," before he closed his eyes.

Gopi was welcomed into the bosom of Sita's family with immense love. Sita and her family arrived at the Balraj house soon after receiving the news of Anoop's demise, unaware of Gopi's arrival. She rushed up the stairs and was heading for Geeta's bedroom when Chumpa stopped her.

"Sita, Beti, wait. There is someone here you have to see."

"Ma . . ." she protested as her mother led her into the dining-room.

The instant Sita's eyes fell on Gopi, they widened in utter disbelief as her hand flew to her mouth. Gopi would always recall the expression on Sita's face in that moment.

"Gopi Bhai . . .? Oh my God! . . . It *is* you . . . after all these years . . . and you look wonderful!" she cried, as tears of joy fell. She ran into his arms, hugging him to her. "I have dreamed of this for so long!"

The funeral was over and still Geeta and her family remained in the house. Gopi had taken over the management of the farm, but he had not been able to bring himself to turn the Balrajs out of their home.

Chumpa mourned the death of her son-in-law, but found it difficult to restrain her joy and amazement that her son was back in her life. He made her heart sing with happiness and pride, and she was always hugging him to make sure that he was real.

Although pleased that Gopi was free and well, Sewcharran could not talk to his son. It seemed that he was ashamed of what had happened, and did not want to relive the past.

Geeta was filled with bitterness and blamed Gopi for the death of her husband. *Murderer!*, she had screamed at him as her husband's body burned on the funeral pyre. She was dressed in a white sari, free of jewels and the red dot that she had worn with pride. Geeta had cried bitter tears as her bangles were broken. Now she was a widow.

Gopi had not said a word. How many more people would pay for her actions, he wondered solemnly. His outward indifference merely enraged her further, and her family was exposed once again to the ugliness of their mother's vindictive nature.

As the days went by, everyone in the family wondered about the feud between brother and sister. Gopi decided eventually to set the record straight, but first he felt that he owed his mother a private and personal telling. One evening he sat down with her and gave her the details, leaving nothing out.

"Hare, Bhagavan," she cried, "how they all have suffered just because of Geeta! I am so sorry for the pain she has caused you . . . so very sorry."

"Majee, I have to tell the family. They have not asked me any questions, but I know that they are confused and want answers – especially Geeta's children. The truth needs to be told."

"I know, Beta. And I know how painful all this must be. I heard Geeta screaming at you the other night when you were going through her records," sighed Chumpa.

"She accused me of enjoying all this – but I get no enjoyment from it at all, Majee."

My husband and I worked like animals to get where we are and you just stroll in here and claim everything by some dirty trick! Geeta had yelled. *We paid our taxes and it wasn't easy, you bastard!*

"Majee, this Saturday I want to have a small dinner party, and I'd like Sita and her family to come as well. Make sure that everyone's favourite dish is prepared. I want to make my entrance into the family official, and I will disclose everything then. It is time."

"But Beta . . . what about the cost? I know that you have spent a lot of money putting up those dams on the farm . . . and you paid the workers their back pay, as well as giving them an increase . . ."

"Don't worry, Ma." Gopi hugged her. "If you have not realized it by now then something must be wrong. I am a very wealthy man. Your days of scrimping and scratching are long over – so don't spare any expense."

CHAPTER TWENTY-FOUR

Gopi nursed a glass of whisky as he watched his family. They had certainly come up in the world. Gone were the days when they looked like skin-and-bone scarecrows, with their clothes hanging loosely on their bodies; when they sat on grass mats on floors that smelled of cow dung, and ate from banana leaves and tin plates. Today, they all looked so well and healthy. They dressed well, ate off glass plates, and were educated, poised and sophisticated.

The food being laid on the table was fresh and wholesome. Chumpa had caught and cooked chickens from their own back yard, and the vegetables were from their farm. With the help of her granddaughters, Chumpa had prepared quite a feast indeed.

Gopi was very aware of Geeta: she sat as though carved out of stone, with fingers clasped tightly, as though if she moved she would fly straight to him and strangle him with her bare hands.

Hemith and his sons were talking politics and sport with Ramu and Krishna. The young Harilakens were both handsome boys, and yet they looked quite different. Mukesh belonged to the local Indian cricket team, and he loved sport. His popularity on the playing field made him a favourite with the young ladies, and he was not scared to voice his political opinions, either – a trait that ran in the Harilaken family. Gopi had overheard Sita warning her son that his big mouth would land him serious trouble – which made Gopi smile, because she reminded him of Chumpa. Mukesh had just laughed mischievously and said, "We Indians are made of strong stuff. The white and the black man think that because we wear garlands and pray to statues we are weak and ignorant, but Gandhi has shown them differently. We don't need a rifle to fight. We have words and pen and paper."

Sunil was more Hemith's son, particularly in his appearance. He was the more serious of the two brothers, being calm and slow to anger, while Mukesh moved through emotions at a drop of a hat. But although they were so different in looks and temperament, they shared the same blood and the same ideals.

"Dinner is ready," Rani called out as she placed a steaming dish of vegetable curry on the table.

Gopi had instantly taken to Rani, who had been named after his beloved. As she ran to and fro from the kitchen to the dining room, helping set the table, she kept giving him the sweetest smiles. She seemed loving and caring, and indulged by her overprotective brothers. Although they all spoke Hindi at home, her English was flawless. If it weren't for Geeta, Gopi thought, I could have had a daughter just like her.

During dinner, conversation flowed between sports, politics, general gossip and Gopi's recent improvements to the farm. But there was an underlying tension, which Gopi sensed and thrived on. He was charming, gracious and very attentive to his nieces and nephews. He knew that his sudden appearance had piqued their curiosity, and that Geeta's silence at the table added more mystery to his life and the feud between them.

For desert Chumpa had prepared his favourite: sweet rice with raisins and almonds. As Gopi savoured its melting sweetness in his mouth, he wished that time would stand still and capture this moment with his family . . . before he opened the floodgates of deep dark secrets.

Hemith seemed to read his mind. "Gopi," he said, laying down his spoon. His tone made every member in the family stop and look up at Gopi in expectation. "We know that you called this dinner for a reason, and I am sure that everyone here wants to know what it is, although we have politely said nothing. Please don't keep us waiting any longer."

Trust Hemith to be so direct and open. Chumpa reached out to clutch her son's hand, and Gopi responded to her smile of encouragement by giving her hand a gentle squeeze. He settled back in his chair and looked at every member of his family, his gaze lingering on Geeta. Then he began speaking in a voice devoid of all emotion.

He spoke of his love for Rani and the happiness they had shared together. He told of her tragic and untimely death, and how it had changed his life forever. "The years spent in prison were the toughest," he said, looking straight at Geeta. "The cold nights, the hard labour and the terrible food." He was not ashamed of disclosing the facts, and as he spoke he felt the raw bitterness he had carried with him for so long fall away, like layers of an onion; the sting brought pain to his eyes. There were tears in the eyes of his family too as they sat listening to him.

Geeta's gaze never wavered. She looked at him with hard, hateful eyes and did not seem touched by his revelations. Gopi was past caring. He told them of his release, and how Raymond had taken him in; and how he had finally learnt the truth.

Astonished gasps and exclamations erupted, and accusing eyes flew to Geeta.

"Geeta!" Sewcharran turned to his daughter. "What on earth were you thinking of?"

"I was doing what I thought was best," she retorted, determined to have her say. "After all, Taj, you remember how angry you were. You felt that Gopi had disgraced us," she reminded him. "I wanted you to be able to lift your head up and walk with pride."

"What you thought was *best*?" Sita turned to her older sister, eyes filled with horror. "You never did know when to stop, did you?" Her voice dropped to a pitying note. "And now your family must suffer for your sins."

"You don't have to rub it in," sneered Geeta, and Gopi knew it was time to intervene. Given time, Geeta would turn the whole situation around to suit herself, and he would end up the villain in this mess. It was time to go one better.

His voice was soft, yet clear and full of authority: "Now, although I am owner of these farms, I have my own property to run. I will be needing reliable people with experience to assist me. But I want to have their trust and full co-operation."

From the corner of his eye he saw Sewcharran sit up and cast a warning look in Geeta's direction. It was uncanny, Gopi thought: his father finally saw Geeta for what she was.

"I am offering you the chance to repair the damage your mother created," Gopi continued, looking steadily at Ramu and Krishna. "How do you feel about running this farm for me?"

Silence fell. Then Geeta stood up, and with her hands on her ample hips she shrieked, "You thief! How dare you offer my sons what belongs to them!"

"It is no longer your land," Gopi informed her curtly. "This land is mine. It belongs to a Suklal. Now sit down," he ordered, and then dismissed her with an uninterested glance.

"Why . . . you . . ." she spluttered, clenching her fist.

"Ma, that is enough," Ramu interrupted. "You have done nothing but create disaster."

"Don't talk to me like that," Geeta hissed, reaching out to slap him – but Gopi's hand shot out to halt her action.

"Another word from you and I will have you thrown out of this house," he warned, and then turned to the twins with a raised eyebrow. "Well?"

"We would like to discuss this before we give you an answer," Ramu replied cautiously.

"Don't take your time. I need an answer before this evening ends." Gopi knew he was being difficult, but to hell with it. What they were experiencing was not a quarter of the ordeal he'd been through.

Ramu and Krishna left the room, and Sewcharran followed them.

Geeta's angry snarl brought him back to reality. "Are you satisfied?" she demanded, glaring at Gopi and then at her daughters, who had been crying quietly.

Gopi felt sorry for his nieces, but he was not going to show them any sympathy – their mother would just pounce on it. Instead, he turned his back to her and gave his attention to Hemith.

"I would like to keep the second property separate, and I will make it worth your effort if you manage it and oversee this farm as well. Keep an eye on the youngsters," he told him with an easy smile. "In addition to a salary, I will give you forty percent of the farm's profits and the option to buy me out in ten years. I will also donate the funds to build Sita the home she's always dreamed of."

The room fell silent as Hemith and Sita looked at each other in shock, aware that they were the focus of attention.

"Gopi . . . I don't think it would be right," Hemith said. "I mean . . ."

Sita refused to meet Geeta's eye.

"You are feeling awkward because this was Geeta's property," Gopi intervened. "Remember, she never really owned it. I do, and you deserve to be rewarded for always standing by me. Besides, I need someone I can trust."

"Gopi . . . Bhai." Sita's voice thick with emotion. "We don't have to be rewarded. We have always loved you."

"I know. And this is my way of expressing *my* love."

"How dare you?" Geeta suddenly raged, eyes blazing with fury.

"I dare because it all belongs to me," Gopi reminded her yet again.

Ramu and Krishna re-entered the dining room with their grandfather.

"We have reached a decision." Krishna looked at his uncle. "What has happened to you is terrible, and I am sure that no apology from us will remove your hurt and anger; and although we cannot take responsibility for Majee's actions, we must suffer the consequences."

Gopi cocked a brow at them. By now they realized that it was his sign of impatience.

Ramu took over. "What Krishna is saying is that we do not have a choice in the matter, and we accept your very generous offer – but," he added quickly, "there is one condition. You allow my family to live in this house and carry on as normal."

Gopi did not bat an eyelid. "Is that all?" Ramu nodded. "I agree – but I will be taking my mother back with me."

A hushed silence descended. No one dared object, not even Sewcharran. He knew it would be wrong to tear mother and son apart again.

After much heart-searching, the Harilakens accepted Gopi's offer. Gopi kept his promise, and Sita and her family settled into a beautiful new home – the kind of home Sita had never thought would be her own. Often, as she prepared breakfast for her family in her new kitchen, she was reminded of the days when she worked in the Campbell's lovely kitchen and had longed for one of her own.

Both farms were producing good fruit and vegetables and the profits were high. The weather was holding up and the dams that had been built were serving the family's needs perfectly.

Rani still taught at the Sheldon School. Every morning Mukesh used the family's horse-driven cart to take her to the Campbell Estate, and she walked home when he was too busy to fetch her.

In the short time she had known him, Rani had grown to adore her uncle. He was the most dynamic man she had ever met, and she knew that beneath his tough exterior lay a heart of gold. He had proved that by not turning Geeta out of her home. It made her happy to learn that he was so taken with her, and admired her for her achievements.

At eighteen, Rani had received many offers of marriage. Each one she turned down, much to the dismay of her family.

"Rani is so stubborn," Sita, who worried that her lovely daughter would become the estate's spinster teacher, complained to Gopi.

"She takes after her mother," he reminded her. "I remember a time when you did not want to marry Hemith, but when you came finally around there was no holding you back."

"Ma," Rani laughed, thoroughly amused by this revelation. "You never told me that! What other secrets have you been hiding?"

Her mother turned away, but not before Rani saw her flush and lower her eyes. "Don't you change the topic, young lady," she scolded. "Bhai, if you find a nice boy for Rani let us know. It seems that the boys around here are not good enough for our little queen."

"Ma . . ." Rani's protest died on her lips as a blush stole across her cheeks. Her heart belonged to Balu. He wanted to ask her parents for her hand in marriage, but Rani had talked him into waiting – she wanted to enjoy their secret romance for a while longer, without the added pressure of finalizing a wedding date. But she knew that it was almost time to let her parents know.

Joseph Sheldon had not forgotten Rani. He watched and waited for her.

It was Friday and Rani was looking forward to the weekend. Her uncle and grandmother were extending their visit, and Rani wanted to spend time with them. Mukesh did not arrive to fetch her after school, and she decided to take the coastal route home and enjoy the scenery.

Lost in her own perfect little world, Rani had no idea she was being followed. Not long after she started walking, Joseph Sheldon appeared suddenly before her on his horse, and Rani screamed with fright as in one swift action he grabbed her and pulled her up onto his saddle.

He rode with her along the beach until they were out of sight of the road.

"Let me go," Rani screamed as she squirmed in front of him. "What kind of man are you? Will you get some kind of satisfaction from raping me?"

He threw back his head and roared with laughter. "This, my dear, is not rape. You want me as well. Besides," he grabbed her chin and forced her to look at him through her hysterical tears, "no one would believe a coolie."

Joseph brought his horse to a stop, threw her roughly onto the sand and jumped down beside her. She scrambled to her feet.

"Don't you dare touch me."

He gave her a cold smile as he reached out for her. "You like it," he sneered as his hand snaked around her waist. "Now don't get coy with me."

Rani, filled with disgust, lifted her hand and struck Joseph across the face. Taken by surprise, his hold on her slackened. Rani turned to run, but she was not fast enough; he caught her, and together they came tumbling down. Rani felt herself pinned to the ground. She pushed away from him with all her strength, but he was strong and determined.

She felt his cold, hard hand against her thighs as he ripped at her underclothes. She kicked and clawed and fought like a wildcat – and the more she fought, the more aroused he became. He ground his lips into hers until she tasted blood. His hungry hands tore her blouse and bruised her breasts, and he showed no mercy as he drove himself into her.

Rani cried tears of anger and bitterness as she lost her innocence in such a vile way. She had wanted this to be special; she had wanted Balu to be the person she shared her body with for the first time. Sobbing, she wondered what sin she had committed to suffer at this man's hands.

"I hope you burn in hell, you son of Satan!" Rani cursed, tears coursing down her cheeks as he drew himself up and straightened his clothes.

"Don't you dare talk to me in that superior English tone of yours." Joseph Sheldon's eyes blazed with fire as he held out his hand.

She hit his hand away. "Get away from me, you bastard! I could fall pregnant..."

The blood drained from his face, and his pallor made him look ugly and cruel. Before Rani had time to get to her feet he struck her across the face. "You bitch," he snarled as he yanked her by her hair and shook her until her teeth rattled. "Don't you dare even think that you can lay that problem on me. I'll deny this ever happened, and say that the brat belongs to that coolie doctor you've been carrying on with!"

"No!" screamed Rani, anger giving her strength. "You have raped me and you have spoiled me for the man I love. I was a virgin until you, you . . ." She spat at him.

She felt the back of his hand against her cheeks and saw stars dance before her eyes; and then she felt another blow to her head as darkness took over.

Mukesh and Sunil were on their way back from the market. Both were satisfied with the profits they had made that day.

"Did you see how Muthoo's daughter kept sneaking looks at you when you went to buy curry powder from her father's stall?" Sunil cast a teasing look at his brother.

"What are you talking about? All I saw was the way Deeplal's daughter was eyeing *you*."

"These girls of today," sighed Sunil. "They are not shy at all."

"Our Rani is so different," remarked Mukesh. "She hates it when men look at her."

"She's changed these past few months. So quiet . . . and I've caught her with her head in the clouds a few times. Something's happened to her."

"She must be in love."

"Nani says it's time Rani married and settled down, and Majee said she would have a word with Uncle Gopi. Perhaps he can find her a good husband."

"I thought Dr Pillai was interested in her." Mukesh mused as he flicked his whip against the horses' flanks. "I wonder what happened?"

"I hope there won't be a problem because he is Tamil." Sunil's face clouded. "There have already been too many unnecessary problems in the past."

"Mm, I agree . . ." Mukesh murmured, before bringing the cart to an abrupt halt, almost throwing Sunil out.

"Hey, watch out!"

Mukesh had already clambered out of the cart and was running to the figure lying on the ground. The woman's long, dark brown hair hid her face and her clothes were torn.

"Rani!" Mukesh's cry of shock filled the air as he pulled his unconscious sister into his arms.

"It looks like she crawled from the beach . . . Who could have done this awful thing to her?" Sunil's voice trembled as he tried to straighten his sister's clothes.

"Whoever he is, he is going to pay for it," Mukesh swore as anger coursed through his body. "He will regret the day he was born. I will kill him with my bare hands!"

"Mukesh Bhai, we have to take Rani home and call the doctor."

"What happened?" screamed Sita when she saw her bruised and beaten daughter in her son's arms. "Who did this to my baby? Tell me," she demanded, grabbing hold of Sunil; but he had no answers for her.

Chumpa followed Mukesh into Rani's room. "I'll take care of her. Get the doctor," Chumpa instructed, as she pushed aside the bedspread and Mukesh placed Rani down. "And please get your father here. He is the only person who can keep your mother calm."

"What is going on?" Gopi, hearing Sita's cries, came to investigate. When he caught sight of Rani through the bedroom door, he felt the old rage course through him again; all the anger and grief that he had buried deep down inside him. "Oh, dear God, this is a nightmare." His voice shook with emotion as he embraced a sobbing Sita. "I should never have asked you to name her after my Rani! That name is cursed!" But after a moment he collected himself: "This is no time for hysterics," he said, picking up Sita's chin and looking into her tear-filled eyes. "Rani needs you."

Sita took strength from his words, and drew in a deep breath. "You are right, Bhai," she said, and made her way into Rani's room.

Chumpa was very gently cleaning her granddaughter. Sita silently thanked her mother, for once again her quiet strength and courage were needed.

Slowly, ever so slowly, Rani's eyes flickered open, and when she saw the concern on her family's faces she knew that she had been found and brought home. She felt bruised and very sore and so ashamed she wanted to die.

"Baby, you are safe," Chumpa whispered as she brushed the hair away from Rani's forehead. "Everything is going to be alright."

Rani turned away and shut her eyes.

"Rani." Mukesh, who had not left his sister's side, knelt down beside her and took her small hand in his. "Who did this to you?"

A moan escaped her, and she slid even further under the bedding.

"Please, sweetheart," he coaxed, touching her swollen face with his big, gentle hand. "You must not be afraid to tell me."

Rani looked at her brother, whose eyes were identical to her own. Eyes that gazed into hers deeply and with such determination. Eyes that demanded the truth.

"Joseph Sheldon," she whispered through lips which barely moved. Mukesh gave her hand an encouraging squeeze as he sprang to his feet.

"Mukesh, no . . ." Sita jumped to her feet and ran behind her son as he stormed out of Rani's room. "Wait!"

"What is there to wait for?" Mukesh swung around in anger. "Your daughter has just been beaten and raped by an animal called Joseph Sheldon," he yelled, "and you ask me to wait. No, I will not wait!" He grabbed hold of his sjambok, and without a backward glance unharnessed the horse from the cart and mounted it.

"Do something!" Sita turned to Gopi. "Mukesh has a terrible temper, and where is Sunil?" she demanded, eyes wild with terror as her body trembled uncontrollably.

"He went to get the doctor and to find Hemith."

"Just do something, anything, Bhai," she begged. "I don't want my son killed!"

"If he is going after the man who did this to our daughter, then I won't stop him," interrupted Hemith, who had just come in and seen Rani. "That bastard deserves what's coming to him."

"Violence is not the answer, Hemith," Gopi tried to restore some sanity to this mess. "I know that better than anyone else. Come," he told the distraught parents. "We have to stop Mukesh before he commits murder, no matter how justified it is."

Mukesh had caught up with Joseph and had him tied to the huge oak tree they had played under as children. But that was a lifetime ago, and now he was using his sjambok on young Master Sheldon. There was no one around to stop him – until he heard his mother's scream.

"Oh, God!" Sita cried out when she saw the red stripes on Joseph's pale body, and the blood flowing from his wounds. "You are going to kill him. Hemith!"

"This is no way to fight, son." Hemith ordered sharply. "Untie him."

Mukesh turned around, defiance and hatred written on his face.

"I said untie him, Mukesh. Don't be like them, using a sjambok. Use your fists like I taught you.."

Joseph staggered as he was suddenly released. Mukesh grabbed him by the neck, and before Joseph could stand up he took a blow to his stomach that left him gasping. Then he crumpled to the ground as he felt the impact of Mukesh's knee into his groin.

Hemith stepped forward with clenched fists.

"No, you don't," Gopi held him back. "Let the boy deal with this."

Mukesh pulled the groaning Joseph to his feet. "You bastard, fight like a man!"

Suddenly, a shot rang out, and all eyes swung towards the man who approached with a rifle in his hand.

"Take your hands off my boy!" Albert Sheldon ordered, and Mukesh replied with a further kick to Joseph's groin as he held him up.

Albert stepped forward and wrenched Joseph away from Mukesh's unrelenting hold. "You lay one finger on him and you are dead," Albert warned, pointing the rifle at Mukesh.

"Don't you dare threaten me – after what this animal . . ."

Albert raised his rifle as Mukesh lunged for Joseph, who whimpered like a terrified child behind his father.

"No!" screamed Sita. Suddenly her legs moved, and she flew in front of Mukesh.

"Majee, get out of the way." Mukesh tried to push his mother away, but she stood her ground.

"If you are going to shoot, you might as well shoot me," Sita challenged, meeting Albert's fierce gaze with tears streaming down her cheeks.

"Move away, Sita." Albert's face was set in anger. "Your son had no right to trespass on my land, or to lay a hand on my son."

Mukesh tried pushing her aside, but she clung to him, crying out, "Do you know what your beloved son has done? He has beaten and raped

249

my daughter and you," she shrieked uncontrollably, "you want to shoot one of your sons for the sake of another!"

"Get ou–" Albert's sentenced halted in mid-air as Sita's words fell on him. "What the hell . . .?" He paled beneath his tan as he looked at Sita, and then at Mukesh – and suddenly the truth was staring him in the face. The boy never had looked anything like Sita's husband. There was only one person he really resembled . . .

"Yes," she answered the question in his eyes, the word falling from her lips without her control. Sita had forgotten her audience – until she heard Hemith's voice.

"Sita . . . what you are saying?" Hemith's eyes narrowed in disbelief as he turned towards Albert Sheldon, and then to Mukesh, who was staring at his mother.

"Hemith . . ." Sita held out a trembling hand to her husband.

She almost fainted when she saw the look in his eyes. Hurt, anger and betrayal were emotions she had never thought she would see reflected there. Turning her anguished gaze towards her son, she saw his confusion.

Then the meaning of her words sunk in, and Mukesh covered his ears and screamed: "*Nooo* . . ."

In that one afternoon, more than one life was shattered.

CHAPTER TWENTY-FIVE

Champa paced her granddaughter's room with grave concern.
Balu Pillai had arrived, with his black medical bag and a great sense of urgency. "Where is she, Nani?" he asked, trying to keep the professionalism in his voice while his eyes told a different story. His love for Rani was more apparent than ever.

"Come." Chumpa led the way.

Rani was curled in a fetal position on her bed, facing the wall.

"Rani," Balu's voice was soft and tender, as he touched her gently on the shoulder – afraid that she would recoil from him. "I am so sorry . . ." The love poured from his voice, and Rani heard it through her pain. She turned instantly towards him, seeking the comfort she knew she would find in his arms. He held her, not as a doctor but as a man offering whatever was needed from him.

They did not even notice as Chumpa and Sunil slipped out of the room.

"Let me look at you, Rani," Balu tried to pull away from her gently, but she just sobbed harder and clung tighter.

"No . . . *no*," she sobbed. "I look awful . . . and I am so ashamed."

"Sweetheart," he murmured, smoothing her hair tenderly. "There is nothing to be ashamed about. I am just so sorry I was not there to protect you." Anger coursed through him. "I love you."

"How can you love me? I am now . . . damaged . . ."

"Nonsense, you are perfect, perfect for me." He held her gently and rocked her in his arms as her sobs subsided. "Sweetheart, I need to tend to you. Will you trust me?" He asked as he lifted her chin. Her beautiful face was swollen, and she looked black and blue from her terrible ordeal. She must have fought Joseph Sheldon desperately to come away looking so bad. Time, he hoped, would heal more than her physical wounds.

After what seemed like eternity, she nodded. Balu had to remind himself that he was a doctor, and that he had attended to rape victims in the past as part of his job. Yet taking care of Rani was one of the most difficult things he had ever done. He knew that he had to be strong for her.

"She should sleep for a while, Nani," Balu said on his way out. "She needs her rest."

Finally, Rani fell asleep – unaware of the upheaval in her family that her rape had triggered.

The sound of Gopi's car screeching to a halt had Chumpa running from Rani's room. Instinctively, she sensed disaster, and when Gopi carried Sita into the house she knew that something awful had happened.

"Where are Hemith and Mukesh?" Chumpa looked frantically from Gopi to Sita. "Did something happen to them?" Sita looked as though she had just lost her entire family.

Gopi drew in a deep breath as he cast a worried look at Sita. She was in a state of shock. "No . . . and yes."

"What . . .?" Chumpa looked at him for an answer as he set his sister down.

Sita sat as still as a statue, looking at them and yet not seeing them. It was as if she were in a trance. And then she hugged her stomach, and a soft moan escaped her. "Hemith . . . I want Hemith. I have to tell him the truth," she whispered.

Gopi sat next to her and took her hands in his and gently rubbed them. She was so cold, almost frozen. "He is not here, Sita. I sent Sunil to look for him."

"Majee . . ." Sita turned to her mother, and Chumpa looked at her daughter with eyes that were old and so very tired. Tired of the years of carrying secrets and the heavy burden of guilt. "Hemith knows that our firstborn is not his."

Her eyes flew to Mukesh as he entered the house. There was a look of torture on his face.

"I knew it!" Chumpa spun around as guilt wrapped its hand around her. "I knew that one day disaster would strike," she wailed, clenching her fists and bringing them to her mouth. "Oh, Bhagavan, what have I done?" She reached up and pulled her grandson into her arms.

Mukesh, who had always loved it when his grandmother hugged him, suddenly wept. The feeling of security he had always felt when she held him against her was no longer there, and it terrified and angered him. He did not know who he was and where he belonged. His family no longer seemed whole: Hemith, whom he loved, cherished and hero-worshipped, was not his father. The blood which ran through his veins was not that of a Harilaken. Instead, a man whom he had never really liked, without understanding why not, had given him life – and he had a half-brother whom he hated with a passion.

Chumpa held him and rocked him in her arms until his sobs subsided.

"Mukesh . . ." Sita held out her hand, but he did not return her gesture of comfort. "Beta, there is so much you have to understand," she cried. "Please let me explain . . ."

Mukesh looked at his mother with eyes that were suddenly filled with hatred. And then he turned his back on her and walked away. His rejection was like a knife twisted into her heart, not once, but over and over again.

Chumpa watched as her daughter buried her face in her hands and ran from the room. She too hoped for forgiveness, and prayed to God for courage to explain to Hemith what had happened. Perhaps he would find it in his kind heart to understand, and forgive mother and daughter for deceiving a smiling, fresh-faced young man who had been blinded by love.

Ironic, she thought, how the truth always seemed to cause havoc; and yet one cannot live life to the full carrying the heavy weight of deception. Now she must repair the damage she had helped cause.

Gopi watched his mother carefully. "So," he said, "you knew the truth and kept it hidden. This family is great at keeping secrets." His laugh echoed with remorse.

Chumpa lowered her eyes. "Yes," she admitted, with a deep sigh. "I did know, and for that I am guilty as hell. I should never have forced Sita into marrying Hemith, but she refused to tell me who the father of her child was, and . . . I had to do something. You know what your father was like then." She choked at the awful memories that were coming back. "I still don't know who the father is, Beta. I suppose when the time is right Sita will tell me."

"Oh, Majee," Gopi sighed. He hated to see her cry. She had been strong for everyone for so long. Now in her son's arms she let go of that strength and clung to him, drawing comfort. "Majee, you don't have to explain anything to me. The person you owe an explanation to is Hemith." Gopi brushed the snow-white hair and placed a tender kiss on her forehead.

"I know," she whispered, "and it is going to break his heart."

It was very late when Rani finally awoke. Her throat felt dry and sore. In fact, she hurt all over. Closing her eyes, she tried to push away the haunting images of the afternoon's events. She felt sick and impure. She hated Joseph Sheldon and she hated herself.

Rani desperately wanted something to drink, but there was no one around. Slowly she got to her feet and made her way along the passage to the kitchen, a pain-filled feat. She was almost there when she heard voices coming from the dining room. The anger in her father's voice was like a slap in the face.

"And don't even think you can lie to me this time, Sita. Mukesh is Albert Sheldon's son! I cannot believe you would do this to me."

Rani felt the blood in her veins freeze as she waited for her mother's reply. How could her father say such an awful thing?

"Yes," sobbed Sita, and this unleashed an anger in her father which terrified Rani. Her father had never really lost his temper with her mother: he had always treated her as though she were the most precious thing in his life.

"Damn you!" he shouted. "How could you allow him to touch you?" Hemith's voice shook with emotion. "I love Mukesh with all my heart, and to learn that he is not mine . . . Can you imagine what this is going to do to him, and to this family?"

Rani's mind began to spin as the words unfolded and her world crumbled. She could not bear to hear the betrayal in her father's voice one second longer. Careful not to make a sound, she tiptoed down the passage and crawled back into bed.

So Joseph Sheldon was Mukesh's half-brother. They shared the same blood. The fact almost drove her mad as she retched into the bucket by her bed.

To hear that the man whom Mukesh loved with all his heart was not his father only confused her more . . . but looking back, the pieces of the puzzle fitted. The special treatment she received from Albert Sheldon finally had meaning. The education, the clothes, the kind and gentle smiles just for her – they were because she was Sita's daughter.

Rani's heart ached. Albert Sheldon may be the man whose seed had created Mukesh, but Hemith was the father he knew and loved, and they had all been brought up never to disgrace him. She was determined to get well and never let this rape divide her family, no matter what it took.

In the following days, Rani sensed the enormous tension between her parents. Mukesh watched her with eyes that matched hers in pain. Yet they all behaved like a united family in her presence, pretending everything was perfect.

Although Rani burned to press charges against the man who had stolen her virginity and caused such havoc in her family, she looked at her father, and could not bring herself to be the cause of further humiliation for him. The family could not understand why she refused to go to the police.

The only thing that had not changed was Hemith's affection for his children – all three of them. For that alone Sita loved him more than ever, and she deeply regretted deceiving him. Hemith spent a lot of time with Rani. He told her that he loved her and that she was still his little angel, and that he would never let anyone hurt her again. Hemith and his children grew closer, and Sita felt like an intruder.

One evening, Sita found Mukesh sitting in Rani's room, watching his sister sleep with an unfathomable look in his eyes.

"Beta, what is the matter?" Sita sat facing him and took hold of his hand.

Mukesh stared at her resentfully. It was so much easier to love his father. His mother he could easily hate, now that she had turned his safe little world upside down. He snatched his hand away and walked out of Rani's room, into his own.

Sita followed, and pushed open the door he almost shut in her face.

"Mukesh . . ." she began.

"How could you? Don't you have any morals?"

She did not have to ask what he was referring to. "I was young," she whispered. "So very young and so naïve, and I fell in love." She reached out to touch his cheek. "And Beta," she said softly, looking at him with great tenderness, "you were born out of that love."

"You mean *lust*," he hissed furiously as he pushed her hand aside.

It was then that Sita slapped her grown-up son. The sound was sharp and clear and shocking. She shook her head, breaking the angry silence: "Don't you ever, ever say that! I loved you from the moment you were conceived; you meant the world to me, and for that sake alone, I knew that I could never let you be born a bastard." Her voice trembled. "You have no right to stand here and be judge and jury!"

"Did you ever stop to think how I would feel?" his eyes widened as he pointed to himself. "I am a half-caste!" He had been ignoring her since the secret had been revealed, and now finally he was giving vent to his feelings.

Tears rolled down Sita's face, but she refused to give up. "I did not choose to fall in love with a white man. It just happened. I don't regret giving birth to you, but most of all I don't regret marrying your father . . . yes," she stopped him from disagreeing. "Hemith is your father. He loved you from the day he knew you were going to be born."

"I love him too," Mukesh retaliated, coldly, "but do you?"

Sita returned his challenge unblinkingly. "I love your father. It is a love that grew out of respect and admiration, but Mukesh, I did love Albert Sheldon as a young girl and there is no denying that. I am not saying that what I did was morally right, but it felt right at the time. When one is young, one follows one's heart and that is what I did. I give no apology for that. What I do apologize for is for keeping it a secret from your father." Tears filled her eyes. "Please, Beta, I hope you have it in your heart to forgive me. For the moment, I am going to stay with Gopi Bhai. Nani has agreed to stay here for a while. Rani has Balu, who loves her a lot. Your father needs time alone to think about what is going to happen to us. He knows I love him and that nothing can change what has happened. I want you to think about everything as well. You know that you, Sunil and Rani can always talk to me."

Her words cut through him, and he turned away. He could not bear to look at his mother any longer. He was so confused: one moment he loved her, the next he resented her for being weak and foolish. Most of all, he hated her for confessing the love she had felt for Albert Sheldon.

The only person he could speak freely with was Hemith. They confided in each other about the anger and betrayal they felt, but beneath it all they knew that they still loved Sita.

"It is going to take us a very long time to come to terms with your mother's betrayal. I don't know, son, if I ever can. It hurts to know that I never really knew her – never knew of her hopes and dreams, and her love for another man . . . All I know is that jealousy nagged me whenever I saw her with him. It was something special they shared. Something we never had . . ." The pain still ripped through Hemith like a sword. He had never dreamed that his perfect family was not so perfect after all.

"What are we going to do, Taj?"

"I don't know, son. I honestly don't know."

Under no circumstances was Rani going to allow what was inside her to become a human being. How could she ever explain to a child that it had been conceived out of violence and lust?

Especially now that she knew the truth about Albert Sheldon . . . She was not going to add corruption to another life. She would get rid of it, she decided. Rani could not even bring herself to call it a baby. It was something forced on her, and the very idea of her body protecting and nourishing it filled her with revulsion. The sooner it left her womb the better.

She had arranged to meet with the old sangoma who lived in the hills, through her granddaughter who cleaned the schoolhouse. Rani was certain she would know what to do.

Rani was back at the school now and away from her family's watchful eyes. She was starting to put her life back in order – except for the dreadful nightmares that had started to haunt her once she realised she was pregnant. Hemith would stay with her when she woke screaming, and she would lie in his arms until she felt safe and could fall asleep. She turned to him instead of her mother, who had returned home when she heard from Chumpa that Rani was having trouble sleeping.

That evening, she waited until the house was quiet and still before pulling a shawl around herself and sneaking out of the house, with just a small lamp to guide her to the old lady. The sangoma's granddaughter had told her to go to a place just outside the farm where the river formed a gentle curve, and the weeping willows bowed humbly as they swayed in the stillness of the night. It was the safest place the sangoma knew, and it would give Rani the privacy she needed.

Rani reached the curve and held the lamp high as a signal to the old woman – she hoped she hadn't missed her. A shiver ran through her. The night was filled with all kinds of sounds: every now and again an owl hooted, and nearby she could hear the surf as the waves broke gently on the moon-kissed sands. The night air was hot and still, and Rani felt the gods were holding their breath, waiting to see what was she going to do.

Rani's heart leapt as a hand landed on her shoulder. With a terrified shudder she spun around, almost dropping the lamp, her eyes round with shock. She was greeted by a wide, toothless smile and eyes that glinted in the light. The wrinkled old lady had colourful beads encircling her neck, arms and legs, and was wrapped in an equally bright blanket. Rani struggled to get her rapid breathing under control.

Grinning, the old lady reached out and with surprisingly gentle hands touched Rani's tender breasts and slightly swollen belly. She clicked her tongue in dismay, looked into Rani's terrified eyes and shook her head. She then began to chant a prayer, and from under her blanket drew out an old pouch made of cow-hide. She shook it hard a few times, her eyes never leaving Rani's bewildered face, and threw the bones onto the ground. Her chant ended as she bent to read the signs. A wild shriek sprang from her throat as she ran backwards, startling the birds from their resting-place.

"What is it, mama?" whispered Rani in Zulu, the old sangoma's language.

"Bad, very bad news," the sangoma cried out. "Baby come."

"I know that," Rani explained, striving for patience, "and I don't want it."

"Very dangerous," the sangoma whimpered as she drew away from Rani.

"Please, mama. You have to help me . . ." Rani grabbed hold of her wrists as the sangoma tried to twist away. "Look at me," she appealed, and when the old lady finally did, she continued in a voice that trembled with desperation. "I was beaten and raped and I cannot have this. You must help me, please. I want to marry the man I love and have only his babies. Please mama . . ."

"No . . . no," the old lady shook her head stubbornly. Suddenly, hopelessness filled Rani and her body sagged. She slid to the ground, sobbing. The old lady clucked as she went down on her haunches beside Rani. "Child . . . if I help you . . . you can die."

Hope flared in Rani's eyes. "No, I won't," she whispered, "I am strong and healthy. I promise I won't die."

The old lady shook her head. "The bones say differently, my child, and my heart is very sore."

"Then do something," Rani begged, "because if you don't, then I will die tonight, without your help!"

The old lady shook her head again and retrieved the bones, shook them once more and spilled them in front of her. This time she did not run away. Slowly she turned to Rani. "I'll help you, child, but my heart is not happy." Her voice was filled with sadness, but Rani did not hear it. All she heard was the old lady's agreement.

"Oh, thank you mama," she cried, flinging her arms around the sangoma.

"Now listen carefully, child." She released Rani and bent to search in a bag she had brought with her. She handed a small black bottle to Rani. "This is a potion for you to drink. It is very bitter but it will help you."

"What is it?" Rani took the bottle from her.

"Don't ask so many questions," the old lady responded curtly. "Just make sure that you drink every last bit of it. You will get very bad pains here," she touched Rani's lower stomach, " and then you will be free."

"That's all?" Rani took the potion and looked at the sangoma, relief flowing through her.

"There will be lots of pain and blood and perhaps a fever too," the sangoma warned with a worried look. "You must take care of yourself. The bones don't say that all is well."

And then she slipped away into the darkness as silently as she had appeared.

Rani did not hesitate as she swallowed the mixture; even the bitter taste did not deter her. After drinking every last drop she crawled into bed, praying for her nightmare to end.

The pains began in the early hours of the morning. Eventually, she forced herself to wake up, bathe, dress and join her mother and grandmother in the kitchen for breakfast. Conversation lagged, as each woman was in her own world.

"Anyone for more coffee?" Rani asked, hoping her voice sounded cheerful, as another wave of pain hit.

"Yes, please," Chumpa smiled gently at her.

As Rani rose to refill her grandmother's cup, she was hit by a terribly sharp pain, far worse than anything she had felt before, exactly where the old sangoma had touched her. Her hand trembled so badly she could not hold the coffeepot, and it crashed to the floor. The pain ripped through her, as though someone was physically pulling out the thing that was growing inside her. She bent over as the pain grew, and cried out in relief as she felt the warmth of her blood flowing down her thighs.

"Beti!" Sita's cry of alarm coincided with Rani's cry. "Majee, help!"

Quickly, between the two of them they half-carried Rani back to her room. "I think she is losing the baby," Chumpa said softly, face white with shock. She had suspected that Rani was pregnant. "Look at the flow of blood."

"Baby! What are you talking about?" Sita almost yelled at her mother. As realisation dawned, her almond-shaped eyes widened and a groan of despair escaped her. "It can't be. It just can't be. Oh, my poor baby. What did that bastard do to you!"

"Sita, stop this now. I need your help." Chumpa was shaking like a leaf. Through all her years of delivering babies, she had never been more terrified. There was so much blood everywhere . . . Quickly she grabbed some sheets, which she shoved between Rani's thighs. "We have to stop the flow or else she could die."

"Die?" Sita cast a frantic look at her daughter and then at her mother. "Is my baby going to die?"

"Stop repeating everything I say!" Chumpa almost shouted. Perspiration rolled down Rani's face, and as Chumpa leaned over her to dry her face, she recoiled from the heat emanating from her body. "She is burning up. Get me some cold water and another towel, and hurry."

Sobbing, Sita flew into the kitchen where she sloshed water into a basin and grabbed some towels, not caring that she wet her sari in the process. Chumpa stripped off Rani's clothes and sponged her down. All the while Rani tossed and turned and cried out in pain, as the bleeding continued and her strength slowly ebbed.

And then she felt a great wave of pain, arched her back and let out a horrifying scream as a thick clot of blood spewed from between her bloodstained thighs. Sita turned away, unable to bear the torture her lovely daughter was going through.

Chumpa scooped up the bloody mass in a large sheet. "The worst is over," she sighed, as Rani's cries of pain became tears of relief. She carried the sheet outside and placed it in a bucket, and then, saying a silent prayer of forgiveness, dug a hole under the banana tree and buried the sheet and its contents.

Inside, Sita cleaned Rani and placed fresh towels to absorb the flow of blood. Tenderly, almost reverently, she wiped Rani's face and pulled a clean nightdress over her head. Moaning softly, Rani's eyes fluttered weakly as Sita dropped a kiss on her forehead.

"You are free, my baby. It is all over now." She tried a small smile for her daughter's benefit, but failed. She swept aside wisps of damp hair from Rani's face, and held her in her arms until she fell asleep. The entire ordeal had lasted for almost two hours, and it left the three generations of women utterly drained.

"It is better she lost the baby," Chumpa reasoned. "God works in strange ways."

"This is all my fault," Sita cried, unable to comprehend this latest cruel twist of fate. "My daughter is paying for my sins, and I have to watch her suffer. This is the worst punishment a mother could ever experience. How I wish I could take away what has happened to her!"

"Shush, Beti. The past has a way of coming up, no matter what. We cannot escape from the truth, you know. Look at what happened between Gopi and Geeta."

Rani was not yet out of danger. As predicted by the old sangoma, in the following days she became deathly ill, developing a raging fever. Under Balu's guidance, Chumpa and Sita took turns tending to her, swabbing her down and making sure she took in liquids.

There were times when Rani cried out for her father, and Hemith would hold his daughter in his arms. Often during this time he was forced to meet Sita's pain-filled eyes, begging for understanding and forgiveness. When one evening Sita collapsed under the strain, he carried her to their room. As she lay on the bed looking so pale and drained, Hemith was suddenly terrified that he might lose her; he knew then how deeply he still loved his wife.

Slowly, Rani's fever came down and she began to recover.

It was during this period that they learnt that Joseph Sheldon had returned to England after what had happened, and that no charges had been pressed against Mukesh for taking the sjambok to the Master's son.

CHAPTER TWENTY-SIX

1919

From across the Indian Ocean the evening spring breeze gently blew into the white marquee, splendid with a blaze of coloured candlelight. Hundreds of little lanterns lent the scene a soft, romantic glow. It was Chumpa's seventy-fifth birthday, and Gopi was hosting a grand party in her honour. He had planned it, with Rani's assistance, down to the last detail.

Sweet, soft music floated in through Chumpa's open window. Gopi had hired a four-man band for the evening's entertainment and, as usual, he had shown excellent taste. Smiling, Chumpa looked at her reflection in her bedroom mirror. The years had certainly taken their toll on her once-youthful face, but tonight her eyes sparkled with excitement, giving her a glimpse of the lovely, vibrant young girl she had once been. She was dressed in a sari of red and gold, made of pure silk, and to finish her outfit, Gopi had presented her with a beautiful gold necklace with matching earrings and bangles.

Carefully she studied her face in the mirror. Yes, definitely, the soft glow made her look pretty in her old age: her eyes twinkled, and the soft light hid her wrinkles. Chumpa called them the marks of time. Her hair, the pride of her youth, was now snow-white, and tonight it was styled in an elegant, simple knot at the base of her neck. The make-up her granddaughters had forced her to wear was light and beautifully applied, and it made her feel young and carefree. She looked beautiful and dignified, and she knew that her family would be proud of her.

Satisfied with her appearance, Chumpa strolled to the open window. It was still too early for her to make her appearance; Gopi had said he would escort her downstairs. From her window she could see the cars coming up the winding driveway leading to Gopi's mansion. Yes, she smiled, it *was* a mansion. It would put the Campbell home to shame – the old Big House, which had inspired such awe in them when they arrived all those years ago. Who would have guessed that one day she would live in an even grander home?

Indeed, her son had come a long way from slaving in the sugar-cane fields. Today, she mused with the pride that only a mother can have, he was a highly respected businessman. The fact that he had been imprisoned and spoke openly about those years only gave strength to his character, and his honesty brought trust and admiration.

The only sad thing was that he never remarried, and Chumpa had long since given up hope of him taking another wife. Gopi had declared that his love for Rani had never died: *I owe all this to her, Majee, and it will not be fair to have another woman enjoy what should have been hers.* She remembered how his eyes had misted when he uttered those words. He still kept Rani's necklace in a little glass case in his bedroom, and Chumpa knew that it was the closest he could get to being with his wife.

Gopi was in his mid-fifties and carried himself well, and there were quite a few women out there who would love to have him as a husband; but Chumpa respected his wishes and did not press him further.

Chumpa wiped a stray tear. During her years with her son, she had discovered him all over again. He had grown stronger with experience, but his love for his family had not diminished.

She smiled gently as her thoughts went to Sewcharran, the man she married, and who no longer ruled over her. He had chosen to stay on with Geeta. Sewcharran had had a bitter pill to swallow – to accept living off the charity of his son. A son whom he had once declared dead! It had taken time, but it seemed that Sewcharran had finally let go of the past, and tried to mend his relationship with the only son he had left. Father and son had come to some sort of reconciliation that only they understood. Chumpa let it be. Sometimes when she watched them, she felt as though her heart would burst with joy, for finally their differences had been put aside for the sake of family.

Even Geeta, after what she had put her brother through, was fortunate in the leniency he showed her. But then, Chumpa, sighed, Gopi always had a big heart, and Geeta paid a heavy price. She had lost her husband and her wealth, and today she was totally dependant on her older brother. It was that alone which forced her to maintain an air of politeness towards Gopi. Chumpa knew that Gopi merely tolerated his sister.

Geeta's children had taken after Anoop, and Chumpa was so grateful for that. They had none of their mother's shrewd habits. The boys, as she fondly referred to them, had kept their word, and the farm their mother had brought to ruin was now prospering in their care. All Geeta's children were married, with families of their own. It had taken them a long time to get over the death of their father, and to forgive Geeta for their problems.

Chumpa spotted Rani from her window and waved at her favourite granddaughter. Rani grinned and waved back, before linking her arm through Balu Pillai's. She looked positively radiant, and it was all the doctor's doing. He had never hesitated to shower her with love and patience. Watching the glow of love on Rani's face, Chumpa placed a hand over her heart and said a silent thank you to God, for her granddaughter had recovered completely. She noticed how Rani placed a protective hand over her tummy: she was almost due to deliver their first baby, and Balu had promised that he would be there to see their child enter this world.

Chumpa recalled the day Balu was born. It was almost four decades ago, and yet it seemed like only yesterday that she had held his tiny body in her hands and cleaned him. His birth had been a beacon of hope for the voyagers on that ship, and indeed, he had made them proud. He had grown into a mature young man who worked among his people, taking care of them in sickness and in health.

Ganga and Veerasamy had welcomed Rani into their Tamil family, with absolutely no objection to the fact that Rani was a Hindi girl. Even Geeta,

Chumpa recalled, dared not say a word against this liaison, and both the families had given the young couple their blessings.

Chumpa knew how hard it had been for Mukesh to finally come to terms with his birth. But it was a fact that nothing could ever change, and with Sita's gentle persistence and Hemith's encouragement, he had finally made peace with his mother. Now he was more determined than ever to ensure that there was peace and equality throughout the country. The family was a little terrified of his passion for politics: he had lost that youthful gaiety they all loved so much and had turned into a serious man, who voiced his political views with such candour that it was frightening.

Sunil, who was to be married shortly, reminded Chumpa of the young Hemith who had come courting Sita with such love and honesty in his heart. She knew that she would always carry the burden of guilt in her heart for that: she had manipulated a young man's love, and still found it extremely difficult to look her son-in-law in the eye.

Chumpa's heart clenched with pain, remembering the devastation caused by Rani's rape and the horrible truths it had revealed. It had seemed then that the marriage between Hemith and Sita was over. But eventually the tears dried up and the anger burnt down, and the love was still there – although it took a long, long time for the hurt to heal. Chumpa remembered with a mixture of pain and pleasure the day Hemith finally conceded that Sita had proved her love and respect for him over the years. Her heart had sang with pride and joy for the Harilakens: they fought hard to remain a united and loving family.

Chumpa had felt a great sense of relief when Albert Sheldon, after meeting with Hemith and Sita, agreed that it would be best to leave things be.

"We cannot rectify the past, but we can ensure that the future brings peace and harmony," he had said, and the Harilakens knew that there would be no demands from Albert Sheldon. He had promised that no further harm would come to any of their children, and that Joseph Sheldon had agreed never to return to Natal.

Sighing heavily, Chumpa reflected on how some of her mistakes had changed the course of their lives. She had come to Natal, against her wishes, scared out of her wits; today it was her home and she had raised her children here. They were grandparents now, and she a great-grandmother. She remembered with immense sadness the day she heard her last-born had died. Bharath had died a carefree and spirited young man, and she would always carry that memory of him in her heart.

A sharp tap on her bedroom door reminded her that she had a party to attend.

"Come in."

Gopi pushed open the door and stepped in as Chumpa quickly brushed a hand across her face. Smiling, she turned to her son.

"You look beautiful tonight, Majee." Gopi held her at arm's length and looked at her carefully. "Have you been crying?" he asked, taking in her damp cheeks.

"Not really, Beta. I was just thinking back on the past, and how far we have come."

"We have, haven't we?" Gopi hugged her. "But no more tears. Your reminiscing can be done later, when you have your family around you. Now, I have come to escort the beautiful lady to her party," he teased.

"Fool," Chumpa scolded with a grin. "This is your old mother you are talking to. But thank you," she added graciously as she linked her arm through his. "You don't look too bad yourself." In fact, she thought, he looked very handsome and dashing in his formal clothes.

"Thank you, kind lady," Gopi returned, lighthearted and jovial. "Now we have guests to meet."

Chumpa's heart was beating so fast it reminded her of the first time she set foot on Natal soil, and was about to meet Master Campbell. Then she had been poverty-stricken and dressed in a threadbare sari, keeping her children around her like a mother hen. Now she was beautifully dressed and living in luxury – and yet she still felt like a nervous schoolgirl.

Chumpa paused at the entrance of the marquee for a few seconds, drinking in the scene. A huge banner wished her "Happy Birthday", and the main table was arranged with brass vases filled with a multitude of brightly coloured flowers. She was pleased to see her brass lamp standing to one side, carefully decorated and ready for her to light; and next to it milk and fruit, the simple offerings to God. Her guests – family, friends and business acquaintances – were dressed in simple yet elegant splendour. The ladies, adorned in rich silk saris, many with intricately designed gold jewellery, and their spouses in formal suits, some still wearing turbans but minus the dhotis, were seated at long tables covered with red tablecloths. What surprised and charmed her the most was that the snacks on the table were placed on different-sized banana leaves. Her guests had been given smaller leaves to eat off – the way they had done when they first arrived!

She gave a small smile of satisfaction when she noticed how close together Sita and Hemith were sitting, and that their fingers were entwined. It was the most intimate gesture she had ever seen between them in public, and she knew that finally she had no more reason to worry.

It was time for her to make her entry. Her guests stood up as she stepped forward, and loud applause broke out.

"Oh, Beta, everything looks wonderful!" Her eyes fell on the huge cake. "Are there really seventy-five candles here?" she whispered nervously as he led her to the main table. Smiling, Gopi nodded. "How on earth am I going to blow them all out?"

"Majee, you have come such a long way, I don't think seventy-five small candles are going to be much of a problem," replied Gopi confidently.

Indeed, she had come a long way. She had travelled from another country, across the sea; she had lived on rations and worked on a sugar-cane estate for five shillings a month. She had learnt to fight, and had won battles with her husband. She had helped bring a number of babies into the world and had raised her own family, and had paid the taxes the government demanded. She had made some major mistakes; but in spite of everything she had lived her life to the full. It was not the easiest life, she reflected, but she had tried her best.

And in the end, she decided, she had triumphed. The love she carried inside her was enough to help her over any obstacle and her heart filled with immense pride and joy. She had come full circle.

There, in front of Chumpa, were her family.

And they were all the wealth she had ever wanted.

THE END